C000291651

ECHOES
OF A Life

a novel

ROBIN BYRON

Matador
9 Priory Business Park,
Wistow Road, Kibworth Beauchamp,
Leicestershire. LE8 0RX
Tel: 0116 279 2299
Email: books@troubador.co.uk
Web: www.troubador.co.uk/matador
Twitter: @matadorbooks

ISBN 978 1800463 615

British Library Cataloguing in Publication Data.
A catalogue record for this book is available from the British Library.

Printed and bound in Great Britain by 4edge Limited
Typeset in 11pt Adobe Garamond Pro by Troubador Publishing Ltd, Leicester, UK

Matador is an imprint of Troubador Publishing Ltd

To the memory of Richard

Part I

In my heart
There is a vigil, and these eyes but close
To look within;

From 'Manfred', by Lord Byron

1

An old woman hobbled along the path to the small lily pond at the end of her garden. Releasing the arm of her companion, she lowered herself onto the stone bench and gazed at the reflection of the leaves in the water. It was mirror calm and warm for late October and the acers which she had always loved so much were now approaching their full glorious red. On the trellis the bees were feasting on the ivy and to her delight she saw a pair of red admirals savouring the autumn sun.

She watched as her companion walked to the other side of the pond and began cutting the last of the roses for the house. She had made her decision now – but how to tell her – her Anna, who had become such an important part of her life? She felt numb; her mind didn't seem to be functioning at all. She stared down at the water. Sometimes, in her imagination, this little pond merged with that dangerous water from her childhood; foolish, of course, but memories can be so treacherous.

Now back with her cuttings, Anna stood beside the bench. 'You are very quiet today, Marianne?' She looked up into Anna's broad face with those distinctive grey-blue eyes and she had some sense of the struggle which the next few weeks would bring. 'Let's go back,' she said, and disregarding the pain in her hips, she clutched Anna's arm and marched back to the house, determined to continue with the process she had started.

First, she called her oldest friend, Dorrie, and asked her to come around that evening. Then she sat down to write to her sister. *My Dearest Claire*, she wrote, *we are perhaps the last generation who will write letters to each other...* But further words eluded her. She moved to her armchair and sat staring out of the window. From her seat, she could see the sun shining through the leaves of the Liquidambar. She marvelled at the way the colours erupted through the branches: green to a creamy beige, then different shades of pink and at the top a majestic imperial purple. There was a popular name for it, what was it? She couldn't remember.

Tipping back her chair, she closed her eyes, hoping – though not expecting – to sleep. She tried to view the past with equanimity, but she knew there remained inside her that sense of her own culpability which she had never been able to dislodge. Even the catastrophes, when they are random, can be borne. The agony may seem overwhelming, but there is a purity about it – a pain which can be endured and finally conquered. It was those other events, times tainted with personal fault, which were hardest to live with. As the past became ever more mixed with the present, it was those episodes which loomed largest in her mind.

4

Rhubarb and custard – it suddenly came to her – that's what they called the Liquidambar. Like the TV cartoon Izzy used to watch – except they had spelled that Roobarb. With that thought she fell asleep.

2

Moscow, Autumn 1973

Afterwards she thought it must have been the music. Don McLean's haunting tribute to her former idol was coming from the other side of the dance floor as she entered the room. She couldn't help stopping to listen; only when the mysterious lyrics had faded out did she move across to a table laden with drinks where she accepted a glass of sparkling wine from a waiter whilst looking around the smoky room in case she might see someone she knew. A faint smile appeared on her face when the music went back a decade to an early Ray Charles number, but it was when the DJ put on Bobby Darin's 'Dream Lover' that a little shiver went down her spine; she couldn't hear that song without thinking of him – without tasting the nicotine on his tongue and feeling the press of his body against her. It had been Betsy who had played it non-stop all that summer vacation, but it was Daniel who materialised genie-like before her when she heard those familiar harmonies.

It's like a virus, the music that you craved in those early teenage years. It lives inside you, part of your flesh, dormant for months or years but ready to break out in nerve tingling sweet-and-sour ecstasy when you least expect it. It doesn't matter how much your tastes may have changed, it's always there, a visceral element that's inescapably part of you.

First there was Elvis. Everyone was desperate for those thrilling new sounds – but she was not quite ready. To be mad for Elvis was like saying you wanted sex; that was a step too far for a twelve-year-old, embarrassed to acknowledge her feelings in the face of strong parental disapproval. Then, just before her thirteenth birthday, 'That'll Be the Day' topped the charts and a few weeks later she had seen him with The Crickets singing 'Peggy Sue' on *The Ed Sullivan Show*. For the next fourteen months Buddy became her deity and who could object to such a clean-cut musical god? Then, as if to teach her an early lesson in mortality, her god crashed in flames and she did not need any reminder of how she had felt, how she had hugged Betsy and wept all the way to school, on that icy February morning when she heard the news.

For months after his death she had mourned him, endlessly playing his hits on the little crimson turntable in her bedroom. Of course, there were other stars, but nobody could take the place of Buddy for her, at least nobody until she set eyes on Daniel.

Ever since Betsy Morgan had become her best friend in Junior High, Marianne had known that Betsy had an elder brother away at college. She had seen his photographs in silver frames scattered around Betsy's home but it wasn't until a day in early June when Daniel was home for the summer vacation that she encountered him for the first time as he brushed past her on the staircase, without eye contact or acknowledgement, until his mother had called up from the hall below: 'Danny, say hello to Marianne – Marianne is Betsy's special friend.'

Danny – how she hated that version of his name. To most of his friends and all of his family he was Danny, but to her he had been mostly Dan – though now always Daniel in her memory. Daniel had turned and looked up at her with a cool silent appraisal which lasted for several seconds. She blushed under the intensity of his gaze, trying nevertheless to retain eye contact until eventually he manoeuvred his face into a small ironic smile. 'Pleased to meet you, Marianne,' he said, before heading down through the hall and out of the front door.

Apart from the novel but flattering experience of a clothes-stripping stare from a twenty-one-year-old college boy she paid little attention to the brief encounter. It wasn't until the following day when he had agreed to give Betsy and her a lift into town and she saw him wearing his thick-rimmed Buddy Holly glasses that she was able to study him more closely. His dark hair was creamed and quaffed, like all the boys in those days; what fascinated her were his lips – what she later learned to think of as Mick Jagger lips – set beneath a surprisingly small and well-proportioned nose.

And here he was again, walking towards her across the room, with his dark-framed glasses, lips parted in that same ironic smile. Only of course it wasn't him – it was a stranger who was now standing beside her, saying something which she couldn't seem to hear. Catching only the word '… lost', she held out her hand:

'Hello, I'm Marianne Davenport.'

'Larry. Larry Anderson. Cultural attaché. Are you enjoying the party?'

'Yes… well, actually I've only just arrived. I don't know anyone here.'

'Well, as one of the hosts I must look after you. Is this your first time at an embassy party?'

'First and last, I expect. Why have I been invited?'

'We like to rope in as many as we can of our citizens who find themselves here in Moscow. You're at the university, aren't you?'

'How did you know?'

'I remember from the guest list. Actually, I was partly responsible for drawing up the list. I remember thinking your name sounded French.'

'My mother grew up in France – that's the Marianne; Davenport is my husband's name. So why didn't you invite my husband?'

'Oh dear. That was a blunder. I don't think we had you down as married.'

'I didn't know you had me down at all, but married I certainly am, and to an Englishman, so perhaps that disqualifies him from getting an invitation.'

'Of course not – not as your spouse – although as you can see we do have quite a crowd this evening.'

Larry talked to her about life in Moscow and his work at the embassy but all the time she couldn't stop thinking of Daniel. Larry had such an old-fashioned look about him, he could easily have been Daniel a dozen years older. The same generous lips and questioning smile. While most men were now wearing their hair fashionably long, and some were sprouting lavish horseshoe moustaches, Larry was more short-back-and-sides, and although there was no quiff as such, his hair tended to a natural curl at the front which lifted it off his forehead. Then there were the glasses. No thin gold frames for him, but authentic, thick Buddy Holly rims which seemed a perfect match for his unfashionably narrow tie. It was as if the 1960s had passed him by and left no trace on his cosmetic or sartorial choices.

No, it wasn't only the music; the look was so like Daniel that goose bumps broke out down Marianne's arms and she felt disorientated and unable to concentrate on what he was telling her. And what had happened to the music now? The couples on the dance floor had moved together, the music had gone slow. Oh God, she remembered it: 'Smoke Gets in Your Eyes'.

'Who chose the music?' she asked, interrupting the flow of his conversation.

'Don't you like it? I can ask him to play something more up to date…'

'No, no – I do like it, it's just – some of these numbers I haven't heard for years…'

'It's the music of our teens – at least mine – perhaps you are too young.'

'Hardly.'

'Those wild, reckless days…'

'In the fifties? Come on. Anyway, you don't look as if you were ever wild or reckless.'

'Don't I? You've rumbled me already. But we can invent, can't we? Once we are over thirty we can invent for ourselves a tempestuous and irresponsible youth…'

Tempestuous, she thought, yes that's a good way to describe my early teens, even if I strove to contain my own inner tempest. When my parents agreed to my going on holiday with Betsy's family, they would never have conceived any danger to their fourteen-year-old daughter from a young man who would shortly be starting his senior year at college.

Sitting alone at a small table while Larry went to get her another drink and the music throbbed around her, Marianne let her mind drift back. She is squeezed into the family Dodge between Betsy and her brother Daniel as they drive to the house in Ogunquit, which Betsy's family rent every year for their summer vacation. A grey clapboard house with white shutters, it is just possible to glimpse the ocean through the large trees which provide a screen of privacy. From the house a rough track leads down to the coastal path which continues around the rocky shoreline to a small cove.

It starts that first evening. She and Betsy wander into Daniel's room to listen to the music he is playing. Daniel is remarkably tolerant of his younger sister and her friend, greeting their arrival with a weary smile while he continues to lie on his bed reading. After a while Betsy ambles over and grabs the book he is holding: '*Tropic of Cancer* – what's this about? "Not to be imported into Great Britain or the USA",' she reads.

'Hey, don't be so goddamn stupid. Give it back. That's a valuable book.'

'How come you're reading it if it can't be imported into the US?'

'Because I am borrowing it from a friend who bought it in Paris.'

'Why can't it be sold here?' says Betsy, opening the book and peering at the text. Daniel just smiles as he grabs the book and puts it under his pillow. 'Can I read it after you?' she says, changing her tune.

'Absolutely not.'

'In which case, I will tell Mom and Dad you're reading an illegal book…'

'I wouldn't recommend it if you know what's good for you.' The brother-sister banter carries on for a while as Marianne looks on, fascinated – the dynamics of Betsy's relationship with her elder brother are quite outside Marianne's experience, which is limited to bossing her five-year-old sister Claire.

'Why don't you come and dance?' asks Betsy, trying unsuccessfully to drag Daniel off his bed. 'OK, if you won't, Marianne and I will practise our rock 'n' roll.'

Marianne and Betsy go through some of their regular dance routines, while Daniel watches; his book remaining under his pillow. As she gyrates around the room with Betsy, Marianne feels more and more self-conscious under Daniel's intense gaze. It somehow doesn't surprise her when Daniel eventually gets off his bed, takes her hand and says: 'Let me dance with Marianne now.' Marianne is aware that she is probably a better dancer than Betsy, being both slimmer and having a better ear for the music, but she senses now that this isn't just about dancing. There is an urgency, almost a violence, about the way Daniel is throwing her around which both alarms and excites her. Knowing her passion for Buddy Holly he has chosen 'Oh Boy' and then 'Rave On', with the volume turned up full, until the door of the bedroom is flung open and Mrs Morgan strides in:

'Really, this is too much noise. What's going on in here?'

'Sorry, Mom,' says Daniel, turning down the volume. 'The girls wanted to practise their rock 'n' roll.'

'Well, enough of that, I think. A little quiet music, and then you girls back to your room please.' His mother leaves and Daniel smiles at Marianne, takes a new single out of its sleeve and puts it on the record player. He then bows formally to her with a look that is all of a sudden more serious and less ironic, takes her hand and pulls her towards him as the deep tones of Elvis singing 'Love Me Tender' fill the room; he holds her tight to his body, pressing her hard against his chest, as they move together in time to the slow rhythm of the music.

All these memories returned to Marianne in a series of brief pulsating flashes – the feeling of Daniel's hand caressing her hair, the sense of something happening to his body which she is loath to acknowledge or identify, the awareness of Betsy's eyes boring into her back with shock and disapproval and then the strained tone in which Betsy says, 'Marianne, Mom wanted us to go back to our room,' when the record finally comes to an end.

Marianne realised with a start that Larry had returned and was talking to her – indeed he seemed to be giving her an invitation. She tried to concentrate.

'… dinner a week Friday – a few Moscow neophytes you might like to meet – I'd appreciate it if you and your husband could come.'

'Um… thank you. I mean I'll have to check with my husband, with Edward, if we're…'

'Yes, of course. Anyhow, I'll mail you an invitation, but in case you haven't received it in a few days, give me a call. Here's my card.'

As Marianne left the party, glancing back at the surprisingly run-down converted apartment building, with its yellow stucco walls, which comprised the US embassy in Moscow, she still felt a sense of dislocation. A twenty-eight-year-old married mother is not supposed suddenly to go weak at the knees at the memory of a first adolescent love. Surely these early fumblings should be moments of acute embarrassment to be locked away for ever, or, at the very least, looked back on with amused indulgence from the comforting security that hindsight provides. But that's not how it was with Daniel. Perhaps it was the lack of consummation – the fact that their relationship had been forbidden; that their respective parents, assisted by the powers of the state, had erected an impenetrable barrier – yes, Marianne thought to herself wryly, it really was an iron curtain which had been brought down between them after that holiday in Maine.

Descending now down the long escalator into the *Krasnopresnenskaya* metro station, Marianne was brought back to the present by the *Alice in Wonderland* feeling which going down into the Moscow underground always aroused in her. Despite several visits to Moscow as a tourist, and the three months which she had now spent living in Moscow with Edward, she still could not get used to the sheer ostentation compared to the grimness and drab conformity of so much of 1970s Moscow. Huge rectangular pillars of red granite and white marble rose from the polished stone floor, creating graceful arches supporting domed ceilings; it was as if some team of architects had been briefed to convert the vaults of a medieval cathedral into a casino or five-star hotel.

Down in this subterranean fantasy land Marianne let her thoughts return to Daniel. Nothing more is said between her and Betsy that night after her long clinch, although Marianne receives some curious looks from her best friend. The following day Daniel behaves quite normally until late in the afternoon when, to the whole family's surprise, he starts a campaign to persuade Betsy that she owes a courtesy visit to Martha, a girl with whom she has spent time on previous vacations in the absence of any other friends of her own age. Betsy's mother comes down on Daniel's side: 'I think Danny is right,' she says. 'Just because you have Marianne staying with you doesn't mean you can completely ignore Martha.'

Grumpily, and with a long death stare at Marianne, Betsy allows herself to be driven off by Daniel to visit Martha. Having dropped her off, he returns to the house where Marianne has positioned herself – as she later acknowledges – so that Daniel will notice her as soon as he comes through the door.

Smiling when he sees her, with a look which is surprisingly diffident, he proposes a walk to the beach and they set off side by side in silence – if it could be called silence in Marianne's case, given the thunderous noise her heart makes as it pounds through her ears. It's a moist and breezy afternoon and she can taste the salt spray on the wind which is blowing her hair in damp strands across her face. Once they are out of sight of the house it seems natural, inevitable even, when he pulls her towards him and kisses her. It's not the first time she has been kissed by a boy but there is a difference this time: there's a confidence about Daniel – an assurance which allows her a freedom of response she has not experienced before. He takes her hand and they walk on towards the cove; several times he stops and kisses her again. Will he speak to her? It seems not – and she is too nervous to say anything herself.

In the days following their cliff walk, Daniel becomes more talkative and she becomes more confident of her status in his eyes – albeit a status not to be acknowledged or referred to in front of the rest of his family.

'My Marylou…' he calls her.

'Who's Marylou?' she asks.

15

'Just a character in a book I'm reading – a sixteen-year-old girl. But I guess that's kind of unfair. You're really no way like her.'

'What's the book about?'

'It's just a couple of guys travelling around the country and it's what I'm going to do when I've finished college. Me and Randy, we're just going to drive around for a year – to the west coast, maybe down to Mexico.'

'What about your dad's business? Aren't you supposed to be starting there as soon as you've finished college?'

'That's his theory. But it's not what I'm planning...'

Marianne divulges some of her secrets; she tells him that she was born in France during the last year of the war and that she doesn't know who her biological father was because her mother won't talk about it, but she thinks he might have been German. She tells him about the bad dream which she still sometimes has which is hardly a dream at all, more a sensation, a sudden waking with her heart pounding – a glimpse of a mysterious face before it disappears – and a sense that something terrible has happened. He kisses her and tells her that when she can sleep with him she won't have bad dreams anymore.

The closer that Marianne gets to Daniel that summer the more outraged Betsy becomes. 'I thought you were my friend,' she says.

'Of course I'm your friend – we're best friends, aren't we?'

'How can we be best friends now when you're behaving like a goddamn little slut with my brother?'

'What?'

'Sniffing round Danny like some underage tramp.'

'Come on? What's your problem? Just coz Dan likes me...'

'Can't you see how ridiculous you're being? Danny's twenty-one – you're not even fifteen – what does he want with a girl like you?'

What indeed does he want with me, Marianne wonders, since Daniel repeatedly tells her how much he respects her, how she is too young to go all the way and he will wait at least until she is sixteen? She knows, though, that she will do anything he asks and when he does ask for something she doesn't hesitate to comply.

'You have to do this for me,' he says, taking her hand and putting it down his pants. Timidly at first, she touches him, then puts her fingers around him, feeling him bone hard but not knowing what to do next; she looks up into his muddy-green eyes which seem to be focused somewhere out to sea. He holds her wrist and moves himself against her. A few seconds later she knows something has happened when he gives a groan and she feels her hand wet and slippery against his flesh.

In the remaining weeks of their vacation, Marianne spends as much time as she can with Daniel. Sometimes it is in his room, Daniel bribing Betsy – or is it threatening, Marianne is never quite sure – to keep her out of the way. Daniel lies on his bed smoking while they listen to music. Marianne sits close to him, but on the floor – nothing too physical can take place in the house in case they are interrupted. More often though, they escape to the cliffs where a grassy ledge hidden behind some bushes provides a degree of privacy. Between bouts of kissing and heavy petting, Daniel reads Marianne passages from novels or poems which he thinks she will like and, fascinated by her ability to speak fluent French, he makes her read extracts from a French novel left over at their holiday house by some previous occupant, even though he can understand barely a word. Sometimes she teaches him phrases in French and laughs at his clumsy pronunciation; then he laughs at himself and blows smoke in her face until she grabs his cigarette and throws it down the cliff.

As each day passes she feels his deepening attachment to her. He tells her that he loves her and, believing it to be true, she loves him back with all the fierce certainty that a million years of evolution have programmed into the first flowering of adolescent passion. And so together they spend those few short weeks, reading about the past and talking of the future, pledging their enduring love and existing only for each other in the fantasy of their imagined world, in their bubble of erotic adventure, in their kingdom by the sea.

The train doors were opening and Marianne was jolted back to the present. As she emerged onto the platform she was confronted by a giant poster: a majestic soldier in a greatcoat, carrying under one arm a small child, was slashing with his enormous sword at the Hydra-like beast of the Soviet enemies: in giant letters of the Cyrillic script, the poster screamed 'DON'T FORGET THE LESSONS OF HISTORY' as the sword severed the serpent heads of 'revanchism, espionage and anticommunism'. Ah yes, she thought, that's what he was sent to fight, communism – the cancer of world-wide communism – keeping the world safe for democracy. He was twenty-six when he was drafted into the army and he was twenty-eight – the same age as I am now – when his luck ran out in some blood-filled ditch of the Vietnam slaughterhouse.

3

'You had a letter?' said Edward, as he poured coffee into two red-and-white-striped mugs and passed one across to Marianne.

'Yes, it was that invitation I told you about. From this guy Larry, at the embassy. It's some sort of dinner he's holding.'

'I suppose it will be a hundred per cent Americans?'

'Not quite, as long as you come with me,' she said, blowing him a kiss. 'And anyway, us Americans are not so bad, are we?'

'Hmm... and by the way, I counted eleven cockroaches in the kitchen this morning.'

'Oh dear. Is that a record?'

'Probably not. Anyway, I'm off now. Is Izzy still asleep?'

'Yes, don't wake her. A bad night, if you remember – and hey, give me a kiss – I know I got you into this and it's hard for you but you'll look back on it as a worthwhile experience in years to come.'

I doubt whether he will, thought Marianne, as she watched the door of the apartment close behind her husband. For her, these three years in Moscow would be an important stage in her academic career, enabling her to complete her PhD and improve her chances of a good job back in England. She also enjoyed the few English classes which she taught. For Edward, having spent nearly two years in high-powered medical research, this was a career siding: teaching anatomy to foreign English-speaking medical students and helping in the general surgical wards. Sometimes she felt guilty for dragging him to Moscow. Not for the first time in their five years of marriage, Marianne was conscious that she should be careful not to exploit Edward's good nature. His gentle demeanour and English politeness would always tend to mask genuine unhappiness.

She could still hear the muffled sound of Procol Harum's 'Whiter Shade of Pale' coming through the thin wall of her temporary lodgings in London where she stayed when she first arrived in England. It was 1967, and her fellow graduates from Cornell were heading west to Haight Ashbury for the summer of love, whereas she headed east to England to study French and Russian literature at Cambridge.

Life in Cambridge was an idyllic bubble away from the constant drumbeat of conscription and the Vietnam war and she went a little mad, smoking dope, drinking too much, forgetting to take her pill and ending up pregnant before the end of her first year.

The father was Edward, a graduate of Pembroke College and at that time a junior registrar at Addenbrooke's Hospital. Edward wanted to marry her and she agreed. They went over to her parents' home in Vermont and were married in August; Isabelle was born the following January. An unplanned pregnancy was something of an embarrassment to a woman who prided herself on being in full control of her life, but Marianne was still at an age when she didn't doubt her past decisions or that her life was on the right course. Izzy might have been an accident, but it was an accident for which she felt doubly blessed.

Putting her mug into the sink, Marianne went into the bedroom where Izzy was still asleep in her cot at the foot of their bed. Marianne would have much preferred her daughter to have slept in a separate room but that was an impossibility in Moscow. As it was, they were lucky with their apartment: two good-sized rooms with a kitchen, bathroom and efficient central heating. However, at four and a half, Izzy was no longer a baby and their sex life had not been improved by this arrangement. They tended now – if they were both in the mood, which seemed less and less often – to make love on the living room sofa or on the floor, before going into the bedroom. Recently Edward had developed a taste for her kneeling on the rug, which wasn't her favourite position, but at least it seemed to get him fired up and he hadn't been in the best frame of mind since their arrival in Moscow.

Marianne sat at the end of the bed and watched her daughter. Her breathing now was quiet and steady; her darkening yellow curls spread across the pillow, her hair colour slowly changing towards Marianne's own blonde-brown. From the side, her profile showed her little upturned nose and the distinctive curve of her eyebrows.

For some time now Edward had been talking about enlarging their family and expressing concern about the age

21

gap which would exist between Izzy and any future child, but Marianne did not feel ready. She knew that the tiredness and nausea which had marked the early stages of her pregnancy would play havoc with her work and she was determined to complete her doctorate before starting another pregnancy. The age gap would already be too great to provide a companion for Izzy.

Marianne held her daughter's hand as they walked past the policeman in the guard box at the front of their apartment block and made their way towards the metro station. Autumn is the best season in Moscow, Marianne had been assured, and she acknowledged that sentiment now as she breathed in the freshness of the air after the stifling heat of the summer. The sun felt warm on her face despite the coolness of the air; watermelons were still on sale in the fruit stands but accompanied now by crates of Hungarian apples.

'Can we go past the magic castle?' asked Izzy, skipping along beside her mother.

'I'm not sure that we will have time, darling,' said Marianne, smiling to herself as she remembered Izzy's name for St Basil's Cathedral. 'We are going to buy you some new clothes today because you are growing out of everything and you start at kindergarten next week.'

'Don't want to go.'

'I'm sure you will enjoy it. There will be lots of other children to play with. And think about it. If you don't go to kindergarten, I won't be able to do my own work. Do you remember I told you the Russian words for kindergarten?'

'No.'

'Yes, you do, think.'

'Oh... sad, you said it's sad.'

'Not just sad,' laughed Marianne, '*detsky sad*, and today we're going to a shop called *Detsky Mir*, which means "Children's World".' It was an article of faith for Marianne that Isabelle would pick up fluent Russian while they were in Moscow. Then, with Marianne's help, she would be able to keep it all her life. Later Marianne would introduce her to French and send her to stay with her cousins in France.

Emerging from the metro at Dzerzhinsky Square, Marianne and Izzy were met by the large and imposing statue of Felix Dzerzhinsky, known as Iron Felix, founder of the Soviet secret police. And behind the statue loomed the massive Lubyanka building, headquarters of the KGB. There was a certain irony, Marianne thought, that the Children's World should be almost next door to the sinister Lubyanka. Moving towards the front of *Detsky Mir*, Marianne's heart sank at the sight of the crowds thronging the entrance. Everyone had said that this was the place where you had to go for children's clothes or toys but it seemed that the whole of Moscow was there as well.

'So, a hard day's shopping,' said Edward, when she was back in the flat that evening.

'Whatever you were doing today, I guarantee it was better than going to that place.'

'I wouldn't be so sure,' said Edward. 'My day was quite distressing.'

There was something about Edward's tone which suggested to Marianne that he had more to say. She stopped stirring the goulash and turned to look at him. 'How come?'

'I had to assist at an appendectomy for a twelve-year-old boy. Simple, you might think – except when it's done under local anaesthetic which doesn't last long enough and the boy is writhing in agony.'

'Appendix out under a local?'

'Yes. The thing is, no one thought this to be particularly strange.'

'How horrible.'

'Yes, it's obscene. A country which builds nuclear missiles and sends people into space…'

'Are they short of the right drugs?'

'Probably – also short of trained anaesthetists.'

'My poor honey,' said Marianne walking over to her husband and giving him a long hug. 'Despite being a doctor, you've never been good with pain.'

'That's true. Neither my own nor others. But I think doctors should be sensitive to pain. Managing pain is as important as curing the sick.'

Marianne felt unusually animated as she and Edward prepared to leave the flat to attend their dinner invitation with Larry. Perhaps, she thought, it's because we don't often get to go out now or perhaps it's the prospect of dinner at the *Aragvi*. Edward was less cheerful. He was upset because one of the nurses was leaving the hospital. 'You know, we are the ones who screw up their system,' he said. 'Yevgenia only made seventy roubles a month. Now she has doubled that working as a nanny for some foreign family like us.'

Indeed, thought Marianne, as she watched their babysitter Lyudmila smiling and laughing as she and Izzy played some incomprehensible game together. Marianne didn't mind that Lyudmila spoke very little English, jabbering away to Izzy in

Russian, and it seemed that Izzy didn't mind too much either. 'Don't worry,' she had been assured soon after arriving in Moscow, 'all Russians love children,' and that had certainly been her experience to date.

It took Marianne and Edward longer to get to the restaurant than they had expected and all the other guests had arrived before them. Marianne had tried to cheer Edward up, explaining that the *Aragvi* was a famous Georgian restaurant – perhaps the best known in the whole of Moscow – which had been popular for decades with the Soviet elite and especially with Stalin's favourite henchman Beria.

As introductions were being made at the table Marianne tried to concentrate. She noted she was being seated to the right of Larry. On the other side was Hank, a large, baby-faced Texan with cropped blond hair. Opposite was Hank's wife, Cynthia, a sharp, angular woman who gave Marianne a 'don't mess with my husband' look. Next to Cynthia, she was surprised to find a good-looking Russian man, a theatre director, Andrei – was that his name? – contradicting what she had been told, that Soviet citizens weren't supposed to mix with embassy people. Further down was his attractive wife Galina and at Edward's end of the table another American couple, Barbara and some man whose name she didn't quite catch.

'So, have they fixed you up with some decent accommodation?' asked Baby-face.

'Not too bad, apart from the cockroaches.'

'Ah well, hunting cockroaches is a national sport in Moscow – isn't that so, Larry?'

'True,' said Larry, 'though actually it's often the newer apartments with central heating that have the most

25

cockroaches – they come up the pipe tunnels.' As conversation flowed back and forth Marianne was pleasantly surprised that there didn't seem to be any subjects off-limits. From further down the table she could hear discussion about the events of 1968 in Czechoslovakia; Galina was saying, '… unfortunate, I agree, but remember our people died to save them in the war, so they have to make the same sacrifices as we do.' Opposite her, Andrei seemed to raise his elegant eyebrows a little and Marianne leant forward and said to him in Russian:

'I sense that perhaps you don't entirely agree?'

'Ah, my dear, I never dare to disagree with my wife. And may I say that your Russian is excellent but I think it would be rude for us not to speak English when not all of our company can speak Russian as well as you.' Then, continuing in English, he said, 'Larry tells me you are at the university, finishing your doctorate in Russian literature.'

'Yes.'

'May I ask on what subject?'

'It's to do with Lermontov's use of the Byronic Hero.'

'Goodness! Quite the intellectual then,' said sharp-faced Cynthia joining in the conversation. 'And I hear you have a four-year-old daughter to take care of as well.'

'Yes, but I have just started her at the local kindergarten so that will be a big help.'

'You mean a Russian kindergarten?'

'Yes.'

'That's incredibly brave. Does she understand any Russian?'

'Not much yet, but I'm sure she will in time.'

'Well, I'd rather my children stick with the language they know. I think that's better for their development. And I've heard some alarming stories about the kindergartens here:

how they smack the children and sometimes lock them in the closet if they misbehave.'

'Well, it's true they are strict, but they seem kind enough and I'm sure Izzy will tell me if anything like that happens to her.'

On their arrival at the table Marianne had noticed that there was already an elaborate spread of food. Plates of cold herring and fried trout with pomegranate, interspersed with small dishes of red caviar; a meat dish which Marianne recognised as cold chicken with walnuts and garlic was immediately in front of her and she noted several plates of crushed French beans further down the table. A waiter handed around hot flat bread which he held out in a damask napkin.

'Quite a banquet you've got for us,' she said, turning to Larry.

'This is just the beginning,' he said. 'There are lots more dishes to come. You know there is a tradition in Georgia that when you are entertaining guests there should be as much food on the table at the end of the meal as there was at the beginning.'

'That seems incredibly wasteful.'

'True – and we won't be quite that extravagant tonight, so enjoy what's on the table but leave some room for what's to come.' Sure enough, the cold dishes were gradually replaced with hot ones. '*Khachapuri* – that's like a cheese pie,' said Larry. '*Khinkali* – dumplings, very popular in Georgia, and that's a Georgian *Solyanka*, a kind of meat stew. These are fried eggplant – try some.'

'Ah, yes. Aubergine,' said Marianne, smiling at Larry.

Despite his encouragement that Marianne should sample all the dishes that appeared on the table, Larry appeared to eat sparingly whilst keeping up a steady dialogue with her. She learnt that he was thirty-six and had been in Moscow for two and a half years. He had been married but the marriage had broken down before he had left America and he was now divorced. They spoke of Russian culture and history: he seemed well informed even though he had no academic background in Russian and had only started to learn the language in a six-month crash course in Washington.

Marianne found Larry an easy conversationalist. He didn't flirt or boast but spoke quietly, sometimes earnestly, but with a lacing of irony which she found refreshing – for all that it was surprisingly un-American. She managed to forget the startling similarity to Daniel which had so unsettled her at the embassy party; or perhaps it was precisely that similarity, that sense of the familiar, which gave her the feeling that she had known him for years already. They spoke of the increasingly harsh tone which the authorities were using against Solzhenitsyn and the continuing newspaper campaign against him and Andrei Sakharov.

'There was a remarkable article only a few days ago, I don't know whether you saw it. Lydia Chukovskaya – she wrote a piece called "The People's Wrath" in support of Sakharov.'

'Oh dear, I'm so wrapped up in the nineteenth century that I'm a bit out of touch with the current scene. What will happen – will they go after her now?'

'Perhaps, although she's always lived on the edge. Ultimately her father's status as a major Russian poet may protect her.'

'Delicious food, I'll give you that,' said Edward as they left the restaurant later that evening.

'It certainly was. And how was the company at your end?'

'Not that exciting. The Russian woman was quite sparky – although very orthodox in her views. The American couple were a bit predictable, with all the usual moans about living in Moscow. You seemed to be getting on well with Larry?'

'Yes, it's curious...' Marianne paused for a moment before continuing. 'He says he wants to meet me for a coffee tomorrow.'

'Are you serious? He's trying to get off with you even though he knows you're married. That's outrageous.'

'No, I really don't think so. He wasn't at all flirtatious. Said he has a meeting with a Professor Belozersky at the university and wanted me to join them. It sounds innocuous. Do you mind?'

'No, I don't mind. But don't forget that this isn't London or New York. You have to have some care who you are seen to be talking to.'

Marianne put an arm around Edward. 'My very wise and understanding hubby. I promise I will be alert for anything untoward and if he makes a pass at me I'll give him one of those slaps they do in the movies...'

'Be serious, Marianne. I'm not sure I care for this Larry friend of yours.'

4

Marianne did not feel any great need to be wary as she approached the university for her meeting with Larry. She felt stimulated after the previous night's dinner, and not for the first time she felt a spring in her step approaching the massive edifice which loomed before her. It was not fashionable to admire the new Moscow University building on Sparrow Hills, tarnished as it was in the minds of many by its Stalinist origins and the *gulag* labour used in its construction, but Marianne could not conceal from herself a sense of awe as she approached the grandiose structure; its central tower, the tallest building in Europe, flanked on either side by its massive gothic wings.

Once she had arrived at the cafeteria and armed herself with a coffee – the usual milky and metallic substance she was training herself to drink – Marianne was introduced to Professor Belozersky. The professor promptly made a few polite enquiries as to Marianne's well-being, and then excused himself, leaving her alone with Larry.

'So what was that all about? And why did your professor leave so quickly?'

'Vasilli? He was just sharing a few thoughts with me. But he would naturally be circumspect with someone he didn't know.'

'What sort of thoughts?'

'Well, he's Jewish, or at any rate part Jewish, so that may give you some idea.'

'Is there really much anti-semitism in the Soviet Union?'

'Well, you know, it's subtle and difficult to characterise. Jews flourish within the universities, in the film and television industries, in medicine and law. In fact, they say that Jews have three times more university graduates than other nationalities in the Soviet Union.'

'You talk about nationalities, but Jewishness is not a nationality, is it?'

'In the Soviet Union most definitely it is. Don't forget there are a great many nationalities which make up the Soviet Union and a Soviet Citizen's internal passport will have a box for nationality. If you are Jewish then it will say "nationality: Jewish".'

'So it does matter then?'

'Well, there are definite restrictions on how far Jews can advance in the Party and in the uppermost reaches of the professions. But there is also the question of emigration and Israel. After the Six Day War the Soviet Union became aligned firmly with the Arab states and Israel and Zionism became dirty words.'

'They do allow emigration now, though?'

'Up to a point, but once a request to leave has been made then a whole programme of harassment begins. Pensions are

31

cut off, people get fired from their jobs and sometimes attacked by "outraged citizens" for being anti-Soviet. If in the end their application to leave is turned down, then their future can be very bleak.'

'I see,' said Marianne. 'But anyway, why did you ask to meet me here today?'

'I'll tell you. I want you to give me a little assistance. It's my job to keep abreast of current Soviet culture; with ideas and opinions which may be circulating, particularly among what we might call the intelligentsia. That's why I have a coffee with Vasilli from time to time and that's why I would like to do the same with you. What's the gossip in the university about political matters? Do you hear cynicism about the Soviet bureaucracy? Jokes about politicians? Hostility or admiration for the West? I would like you to keep your eyes open for any interesting *samizdats* – you know, self-published news sheets, essays, literary works and similar stuff which may be circulating informally around the university.'

Marianne sat in silence contemplating what she had heard. Although she had suspected some ulterior motive in Larry's desire to meet her – and of course she had no reason to suspect he might make advances to her nor indeed, she was sure, any wish for him to do so – she nevertheless felt somehow used and not a little angered by his request. 'You want me to spy for you?'

'Well, I was coming on to the details. We'll have to get you kitted out – the miniature camera, dead letter drops, the cyanide pill…'

She stared at him, her lips pulled back in a rictus.

'Marianne, don't dramatise – it's not spying. I just want us to meet for a drink or an ice-cream every couple of weeks

– here at the university or elsewhere if you prefer – and just chat and you can tell me of any interesting conversations you may have had with Russian colleagues at the university. You know, you are young – and, if I may say so, very attractive – and you speak excellent Russian. People will talk to you if you let them.'

Marianne drained the last of her coffee, wrinkling her nose in distaste. 'I'm not sure. I don't know whether my husband would like it.' (God, why am I sheltering behind Edward, she thought – make up your own mind, girl.)

'You can tell him, of course. We wouldn't want him to get the wrong idea, would we? He may also have some interesting things to tell you from the medical world.'

'Edward's not like that. He wouldn't want to get involved. He's very English, you know, not American.'

'If you say so. Though I thought Cambridge graduates were natural spies.'

'That's not so funny.'

'No, sorry. Listen, just think about it. Same time, same place next week? You can tell me what you've decided then. If you don't want to meet again after that, fine. It's entirely up to you. We won't talk about it anymore now. Tell me how your daughter is getting on. How is she finding the kindergarten?'

When Larry left half an hour later, Marianne was not sure whether she had agreed to meet him the following week. I suppose I have plenty of time to consider it, she thought.

In the event, it was her row with Edward that persuaded Marianne to meet Larry again – although in truth it was scarcely a row, since it takes two to have a decent fight and Edward never allowed himself to descend into such vulgarity.

'My God, what a nerve these people have,' Edward said, when she told him of Larry's request. 'They pick on an innocent young woman like you and try to ensnare them into their web of deceit...'

'Hang on, Ed, that's a bit extreme. He's a cultural attaché; he needs to get out and meet people and find out what's being talked about in academic circles.'

'But surely you're not thinking of going along with this, are you?'

'Well, I haven't made up my mind. I wouldn't go out of my way to do anything particular – and anyway, I doubt I'd have much to tell him – but I don't see that meeting him occasionally for a coffee or ice-cream, as he put it, would do any harm.'

'That's just a start, Marianne, don't you see?'

'I don't agree. I don't think it's any more than that.'

'Marianne, don't you remember the undertaking that we both had to sign before we came to Moscow about not getting involved in any political activity...'

'But this isn't political activity.'

'It is, Marianne. It's highly political. And anyway, I didn't take to this Larry, despite – or perhaps because of – being wined and dined at an expensive restaurant.'

'That's what embassy people...'

'... I think he's smarmy and untrustworthy.'

'So that's your real problem, is it? That I actually get to talk to another man from time to time – rather than spending all my time locked away in the library...'

'Marianne...'

'… while you spend the day with all these Russian nurses you admire so much…'

'… this is unworthy of you.'

'Well, I shall make up my own mind and I don't need any lectures from you about who I'm allowed to meet.'

5

'*Detsky bad. Detsky bad-bad-bad,*' shouted Izzy, her blue eyes flashing as Marianne struggled to get her daughter's arms into her overcoat. This was a routine which had become quite familiar to Marianne as Izzy played games with the Russian name for kindergarten. At first she seemed to have got it into her head that *detsky sad* meant she was going to a place where she was sure to be sad. Now it was often *detsky bad* or even *detsky mad* – a variation Izzy had been particularly pleased with.

'Come on, darling, it's not so terrible. What happened to *detsky glad*?' asked Marianne. 'You'll get to play with Yelena and Irina – they're your friends, aren't they?'

'Sometimes… but yesterday Irina was mean to me and… and… Yelena…'

Getting her young daughter used to the idea of going to kindergarten every day had been no easier than Marianne had expected but she tried to keep the battles away from the kindergarten itself. The first morning that she had delivered her, Izzy had kicked and screamed and created a scene which would not have seemed unusual at an English or American nursery but was watched in stunned silence by both teachers and children in the Moscow kindergarten.

Now that Izzy had been at the kindergarten for nearly two months her resistance was little more than token and having dropped her off without further fuss, Marianne made her way to the park for what had now become a twice-weekly meeting with Larry. She no longer mentioned these meetings to Edward and he no longer interrogated her on whether she was still seeing him. Indeed, they barely seemed to have any conversation now, his hours at the hospital extending late into the evening when he would come home and go straight to bed. Did he assume she had stopped meeting Larry? She didn't know and preferred not to think about it.

The freshness of autumn had now given way to the chill of early winter with the first snows expected any day. It was damp, depressing weather, which Muscovites particularly disliked; no matter how low the temperature might drop they looked forward to the real winter when the air would become clear and the cold somehow more bearable. It was too chilly to linger in the park that day and Larry guided her to a nearby café.

Marianne suffered a bout of coughing as she entered the thick smoky atmosphere where the stench of Russian tobacco, mixed with damp wool and animal fur, combined to overwhelm the more agreeable smell of ground coffee beans. Larry ordered coffees for them both and lit a cigarette – one of the half dozen which he permitted himself to smoke in a day.

To begin with, Marianne's meetings with Larry had been dominated by the Yom Kippur War which had broken out between Israel and some of the Arab states a few days after their first meeting at the university. Russia, Larry told her, almost certainly had advance knowledge of the attack. She had made no special effort to pick up any gossip and when they were not discussing the war, Larry had seemed content to chat about life in Moscow or the things that they both missed from their respective homes. Marianne had lived in England for six years before moving to Moscow, had married an Englishman and fully expected to spend the rest of her life in England, but she was always happy to reminisce about her childhood or college life in America, or to tell Larry stories about her time at Cambridge.

In recent weeks, however, she had become conscious that she was making more effort to please him. She had sought out a research assistant who worked for a prominent Jewish physics professor who was believed to be contemplating applying for permission to emigrate to Israel. She told Larry about her conversation which, whilst guarded, hinted that his decision to apply was now imminent.

Larry's glasses had steamed up as he entered the café and he had kept them off as he now looked intently at Marianne across the narrow table.

She studied his face. 'Never tempted to grow a moustache?'

'Can you see me with a big biker's moustache?'

'No, I can't. I like your face as it is. And I brought you a present,' she said, passing a copy of *Pravda* across the table. Larry wouldn't look at it now but inside was a *samizdat* containing a strongly worded essay on human rights. As Marianne passed the paper across the table her knuckles brushed against his and he took her hand briefly and gave it a squeeze. It was a trifling gesture, but it was the first time he had made any such deliberate physical contact and all of a sudden it seemed to change the whole context of their meeting.

'You look a bit different today,' she said.

'You think so?' he said, holding her with a steady gaze for several seconds. 'Perhaps it's you who are different. On the other hand, of course, it may be the microwaves.'

'Microwaves?'

Larry nodded.

'You've got a microwave oven?'

'And every night I heat up my meagre supper...' He looked at her with those serious grey-green eyes which were only betrayed by the smallest hint of creasing at the corners. She waited for him to explain.

Larry leant forward and lowered his voice. 'It's a curious story and I really shouldn't be telling you, but earlier this year we – that is, the embassy staff – discovered what Kissinger and his associates had been keeping from us – that for years the Soviets have been bombarding the embassy with microwaves.'

'Seriously? Are people getting sick…?'

'You may well ask. Officially not, we have been assured they are not harmful – but as you can imagine people are not entirely reassured.'

'I don't wonder. How do you feel about it?'

'Occupational hazard, I guess. Apparently, it started in the early sixties and no one's died yet. They've been secretly monitoring our blood – can you believe it? Without telling us anything. Listen, keep all this to yourself – not even Edward, promise?'

'Of course.'

'Otherwise I will lose my job and you might end up in the *Gulags*.'

It was becoming addictive, she confessed to herself as she left the café and headed towards the university; this amateur sleuthing, finding titbits for Larry and hearing secrets about goings-on at the embassy. Or was it something to do with Larry himself? There had been a difference in him today. She felt she had glimpsed a more serious person within. Already she was looking forward to their next meeting and she was planning in her mind how to engineer the introductions which he had suggested.

As the weeks passed, Marianne became aware that Larry was occupying more and more of her time, to the detriment of her academic work – but she didn't care. She was transported into a different world; no longer researching what Lermontov was getting up to a hundred and fifty years earlier, her life was now focused on the present. She hung around the bars and cafeterias, listening to gossip and allowing men to chat her up – while keeping clear of any entanglements. She went in search of new *samizdats* which might interest Larry and spent hours tracking down rumours about a young lecturer in the foreign languages school who was believed to be the author of some of the dissident material which was circulating around the university. It was an existence utterly different from anything she had experienced in the past – an existence with which she was becoming increasingly intoxicated.

Then there was Larry himself; she had barely looked at another man since her marriage to Edward – but that look he had of Daniel, and the aura of danger which hovered around him… Of course, it was all fanciful, she told herself sternly; how could she think of deceiving Edward, the father of her beloved Izzy and the rock around which she had built her life?

Larry told her that meeting him too often in public could become awkward for her. Embassy staff had to assume they might be followed or watched. It was getting too cold now to meet outside and he had given her a name, the Minsk hotel, which was not on the Intourist A or B list but convenient for the centre of the city. 'I use it sometimes for meetings,' he had said. 'It's a safe place.'

It was a neutral request – nothing more had been said. No nods, no winks; a place to talk in confidence and she knew she could play it safe, be cool and detached. She also sensed it was an invitation she could accept if she wanted – that she was hovering on the brink of an adulterous relationship with unknowable consequences. She comforted herself that there was still plenty of time to decide. Yet when she looked into his eyes she could see desire in the liquid pools behind those thick-rimmed glasses and she suspected she knew which way she would jump.

The December snow was everywhere now and in two weeks she and Edward would be flying back to Vermont with Izzy to stay with her parents for Christmas. What she was contemplating did not affect Edward. Her love for him was steady and sure, she knew that – and she didn't doubt his love for her. Sometimes she teased him about the nurses at the hospital but she doubted that Edward would transgress. No, this was altogether separate from Edward. She had entered a parallel universe; she hadn't intended it, at least she didn't think that she had – although at that first moment she had seen him at the embassy party it was as if a seed had been planted somewhere inside her, small at first but growing steadily over the subsequent months; it seemed to her a matter of unfinished business.

Most days she would pick Izzy up at one o'clock from kindergarten but today she had told them that Izzy would stay for the after-lunch nap and then play in the snow with the other children. The teachers had built a small slide out of ice in the yard behind the school and Izzy had been gratifyingly excited about staying for the afternoon.

As she tramped along the pavement towards the Minsk hotel, wrapped in her warmest clothes, Marianne didn't think about Izzy or about Edward, she thought only about herself. She observed herself with curiosity, with an objective critique, as if she could determine the precise cause of this strange conduct, as if she had to explain to the impartial observer why this woman was heading to a hotel with every expectation of having a sexual encounter with a man who was not her husband. What was the reason for this atavistic behaviour? Was it rebellion against motherhood and domesticity or an attempt to recover a lost moment from the past?

Clearly, this could not be her, but this stranger – this previously unknown woman – had feelings she could no longer suppress. She had to know him completely, how he would look, how he would feel. She had sensed a lean and muscular body; she needed to bite his lips, taste the nicotine on his tongue. She wanted to feel his hands slipping under her blouse, peeling off her clothes and caressing her skin. She wanted to feel his skin against hers, the press of his body on her and in her; it was something she had to do – a consummation delayed for half a lifetime. She would not be denied.

As she made her way up to room 212, Marianne began to think she might have slipped into a private sexual fantasy and completely imagined their mutual intent. Larry seemed calm and matter of fact as he opened the door for her and inside the room they stood staring at each other for several seconds. He said nothing, but she felt his eyes asking her a question and with the slightest of smiles and a tiny movement of her head she answered his question in the affirmative. As she did so, he came towards her, took her head in his hands and kissed her.

Later, with her body still throbbing and burning hot in the overheated hotel bedroom she watched Larry slumber. Feeling the urge to talk, she said, 'So this is where you bring your girls?'

'Girls? No… come on, Marianne… no. I use the hotel just as a place to talk confidentially to people I need to keep in touch with.'

'Really?'

'Really, Marianne. I've never been here with a woman before.'

Did she believe him? It didn't matter. He was single. She was the adulterer. She could hardly cast stones.

'You know,' said Larry, 'I would never guess you were American if I didn't know.'

'It comes with being a linguist. After a year or so in England I'd picked up the accent and regular English vocabulary.'

'So now you grill your tomarrtoes and walk on the pavements…?'

'I do. And what's more, I know my arse from my fanny,' she said, giving him a sharp bite on the shoulder.

'Ouch! That hurt. So, am I really like this guy you fancied when you were a kid?' he said.

'A bit. But I was little more than a child and we didn't make love – at least not full sex – so I can't compare you in every detail,' she said, laughing and reaching down to caress him between his legs.

'Hey, easy… but, I mean, it was real love, was it, with this guy?'

Marianne was silent for a moment; how to explain? Then she said:

'"*But our love it was stronger by far than the love*
Of those who were older than we –
Of many far wiser than we –"'

'Where does that come from?'

'It's a poem by Edgar Allan Poe – *Annabel Lee*. Daniel sent it to me in one of his last letters. Ironic, really. The poem tells of the death of the beautiful Annabel Lee, but it was his death that followed soon after.'

'So you kept writing to each other for all those years?'

'Not exactly; for five years I neither saw him nor heard from him. Then, when I was twenty and at college I got a letter from him. He had been drafted and was about to be sent to Vietnam. I think he was suddenly lonely and wanted someone to write to. Also, he said he had to make peace with himself and with me.'

'Meaning what?'

'For allowing himself to be bullied. You know, my parents made a huge fuss when they found out what was going on. They wanted to have me examined to see if I was still a virgin, which I categorically refused to consent to – can you imagine the humiliation?'

'So what happened?'

'Well, the police interviewed Daniel and cautioned him and threatened to arrest him if he tried to continue our relationship. Really, though, there was no need for the moral panic of my parents or the threatening behaviour of the authorities. I was in no danger of losing my virginity. He was too scared to fuck me, and I was too innocent to give him any encouragement.'

'Did you try to stay in touch?'

'I wrote to him at college but I never heard back. I later found out that my parents had intercepted his letters. He also tried to send letters via his sister Betsy but she was still furious with me over the whole business and never passed the letters on.'

'That's so sad...'

'Yes, we disappeared from each other's lives. I became a diligent student and then, when I was at college, we started this correspondence which lasted for over a year. It was like another love affair. I mean, I was about twenty by then and I had had other boyfriends, but during all that time we corresponded he was the only man in my life and for a time it really seemed that perhaps we had been meant for each other.'

'That was pretty harsh of your parents not to let you see him at all.'

'Perhaps, but don't forget this was the 1950s – pre-pill days, when a pregnancy for a young teenager would be a disaster for the whole family. Most importantly though there was the age difference. I was not yet fifteen and he was twenty-one. Also, my mom had a certain amount of Catholic baggage from her early life in France.'

'I forgot that your mother was French.'

'Yes, I was born in France at the end of the war, you know, Marianne – symbol of France. That's why my mother chose the name. When I started college, my parents went to live in France with my little sister Claire. They stayed nearly ten years before heading back to Vermont.'

'You don't look that French. Fair skin, blue eyes.'

'I get that from my father.'

'How did you end up in America?'

'My mother went with my father to America when I was a baby – he was a doctor in the US army. He wasn't my biological father, but that's unimportant...'

'Who was your real father – the one who gave you your blue eyes?'

'A product of the war, was all my mother would say. German, I've always assumed – a case of *collaboration horizontale.*'

'So you grew up speaking French.'

'Yes.'

'And the Russian?'

'The Russian was learned. I had to choose a second foreign language and so I chose Russian.'

'Why?'

'So I could become a spy.'

'Well, obviously...'

'My early training...'

'Such forethought.'

'It was the literature: *Anna Karenina* first – I read it in the back of a car all the way to Florida with my parents one winter. Then it was *Crime and Punishment*, I was right inside Raskolnikov – there seemed to be something so dark but at the same time so profound in the Russian hero, or antihero, which appealed to me as a seventeen-year-old, so I decided that I had to learn the language. I was a pretty studious girl in those days.'

'Aren't you still?'

'Sometimes. When I'm not distracted by other things.'

6

The legendary Russian winter, destroyer of invading armies and prop for a thousand movie-makers, was finally coming to an end and in its place came the season of mud. For some days now the ice had been cracking in the Moscow River and everywhere the melting snow made small rivers of mud and slush. In the meantime, Marianne's parallel universe had not yet imploded. She continued to meet Larry regularly at the Minsk hotel; hurrying along the slippery pavements, splashing in the slushy puddles, hot with excitement.

That evening, though, it was different: she was going to his apartment for the first time. She had pestered him to know why they always had to go to the hotel, the small stuffy room which never seemed all that clean. 'Or is it that you've got a girlfriend you are hiding from me?' she said.

'Sure, a gorgeous, long-legged Russian girl, but I'll make

sure she's out when you come... The thing is, Marianne, it's likely that I am being spied on – and as you are married that could be bad for both of us.'

He had finally consented to her coming that evening when the cleaners had gone home and it was too dark for the security guard to get a good look at her face. Edward was working late and she had arranged for Lyudmila to baby-sit, but as she climbed the stairs to his apartment she began to wonder if it had been a good idea after all; she felt nervous. Back in their hotel room there was no hesitation; they would be stripping the clothes off each other almost before the door was closed behind them. Now, she slid past him as he opened the door and started to walk around the apartment in her overcoat.

'You can check the drawers if you like, you won't find any women's knickers.'

'Hey, come here. I know – it's just, well, it feels different being here. But thank you for letting me come.'

'It's a pretty standard Moscow apartment.'

'I know – but at least there is something of you here...' she said, looking at the soft brown leather sofa, the extensive bookcases and the huge number of LPs stacked against the wall. 'You must get a generous shipping allowance to have all this stuff brought over?'

'There are some advantages in being looked after by Uncle Sam.'

'Tell me about these photographs,' she said, looking at a large framed montage of family snaps.

Despite having wanted to see where Larry lived, Marianne didn't find it easy to relax. He told her about the photos, his brother, sisters, parents, friends – and, of course, his ex-wife.

They sat on the sofa while she drank a glass of wine and he had a whisky and they chatted about some of the curiosities of Moscow life, and the people at the university she had been trying to contact for him, but when she finally slipped into his bed, she turned her back to him, unable to look him in the face.

They lay there in silence; his body close against hers, his breath warm against her neck. Slowly, he started to caress her, whispering things in her ear. But she couldn't respond. She could feel his arousal against her thighs and not wanting to disappoint him she turned to kiss him. He responded energetically and moved to go down on her but she took his head and brought it back up.

'Slowly tonight, it's just… it feels different here.'

'Sure, let's take our time.'

Larry was a skilful and considerate lover, but despite trying his best he couldn't make it work for her that evening – and she couldn't make it work for herself. Part of her was watching from a distance: how do I fit into his life – or he mine? Is he using me – and am I risking too much? She resolved not to come to his apartment again until she had figured out these issues – though she knew there was only one answer.

Back in her own bed later that night, with Edward lying beside her, she tried to sleep, but when she shut her eyes it wasn't Edward she saw, nor was it Larry – it was that face looking at her with pleading eyes. That round face with its smudged freckles: sometimes a face without the head, sometimes a whole head – but never a body; the disembodied face hovered, faded, then reappeared with its look of infinite regret. Familiar, yet impossible to fathom, the image and its accompanying nausea had become part of her life; triggered by guilt or anxiety, it was a ghost she longed to be rid of if only she could discover how.

Marianne never returned to Larry's flat, but in the anonymity of the Minsk Hotel her old appetites soon returned and in the following weeks their lovemaking became more energetic, more varied, frantic even. Meanwhile she hadn't stopped her ferreting for Larry and she still felt the adrenalin kick in whenever she made contact with one of the targets he had given her. He was particularly interested in a scientist by the name of Aleshkovsky. She was forbidden from seeking direct contact with him – almost certainly unachievable anyway since he worked in the highly secret scientific research wing of the university; but Larry seldom missed an opportunity to ask her whether his name had cropped up in connection with possible emigration to Israel.

Exhilarating though it was, she was beginning to get nervous. A couple of times she thought she was being watched and since the beginning of March she had convinced herself that she was being followed. She remembered some of the tricks she had read about in spy novels and started to apply them in the metro – leaving a train just before the doors closed or getting on a train at the last second. I'm being stupid, she told herself. I have no training for this – and anyway, if I start behaving like a spy I'm more likely to be taken for one. Time to bring the curtain down on Larry and these games.

Edward was flying back to England for ten days over the western Easter and taking Izzy with him to spend time with his mother. Marianne had a couple of classes still to teach and was anyway behind with her research so had decided not to go with him. She told herself that this would give her one last fling with Larry and then she would end it before Edward returned.

'So, you are going to be all alone for ten days?' said Larry, as Marianne began to get dressed after a lunchtime assignation in their familiar hotel room.

'That's true.'

'I have an idea. Have you ever been down to Georgia? I have to spend a week down there and this would be a great opportunity. It will be real spring down there. We could go together – or separately, perhaps – if we don't want to be seen to travel together.'

Marianne knew instantly that this was a suggestion she was not going to be able to resist. 'Georgia – well, I can't say I'm not tempted. I have been thinking how I must see the Caucasus. I mean, they were so important to Lermontov.'

'Lermontov, of course, I forgot your research; then you must obviously come – we'll explore together.'

As Larry was due to spend the whole week in the capital Tbilisi and Marianne could not spare the time, it was agreed that she would fly down with Larry for the weekend and then come back on her own. Cautiously they made separate bookings on the same flight, deciding not to acknowledge each other at the airport and sitting some way apart on the plane. Marianne had obtained a window seat but was disappointed that her view of the high Caucasus was almost entirely obscured by cloud. However, as they cleared the mountains and came down towards Tbilisi she was able to glimpse the city straddling the S-bend of the Mtkvari River, set in a broad valley and protected by the high fortress of Narikala.

When Marianne had finally shaken off the obligatory Intourist guide who had shepherded her to the hotel, and

Larry had arrived in her room, she threw her arms around him in a hug of childlike enthusiasm. 'It's so romantic – I mean, to be in Georgia. I've always wanted to come here.'

'It's good to see you so happy,' he said, bending his head to kiss her, 'but strangely I've never thought of Georgia as being especially romantic. I've always associated it with Stalin and Beria and that whole gang of murderous thugs.'

'Oh, no, you shouldn't think like that at all. It's a place of love and poetry. Pushkin raved about Georgia, said he was literally reborn here. Let's go out for a walk. I've got a map; we should go down to the old town.'

Together Marianne and Larry made their way down to the river, past the Metekhi church on its rocky promontory and across the bridge towards the old town. It was not only the warmth in the air which enchanted Marianne but the happy blend of Asia and Europe which was so refreshing after the drabness of much of Soviet Moscow. Walking up to Lermontov Street, a natural magnet for Marianne, she admired the elegant nineteenth-century houses with their exquisite fretwork balconies. Further up they came to a square where she paused and consulted her map, then turned to Larry: 'Hey, this is the house I was telling you about. It was originally a house reserved for Russian officers and it's where Lermontov stayed when he was in Tbilisi.' Together they admired the massive overhanging balconies that seemed to defy gravity and allow the elegant lacy arches to float above the street.

Only one thought troubled Marianne as she and Larry retired to a café and ordered slices of cheese pie and a bottle of Saperavi, a local Georgian wine. I should be doing this with Edward. My universe with Larry was confined to Moscow and the Minsk hotel. It was a closely guarded citadel which was entirely separate from the rest of my life. But this is different. This is travel, a cultural exploration that I should be making with Edward; this is my work, my thesis, my real life. I shall enjoy this weekend but as soon as we are back in Moscow I must bring this affair to an end. Having made this firm vow to herself, Marianne felt able to relax and gobble up every delicious sensation the weekend had to offer, both the intimate parts in their hotel bedroom and their exploration of Tbilisi. In quiet moments, Larry read briefing papers on the suppression of Georgian nationalism and the survival of the Orthodox Church, while Marianne read guidebooks and accounts of Lermontov's visits to the Caucasus whilst planning in her mind the trip she and Edward would make later in the summer.

It was with a mixture of sadness and relief that she sat back in her seat while the plane lifted off from Tbilisi en route back to Moscow. It had been fun, satisfying and necessary to her life, but now it was over. She would meet Larry at the university and explain why it had to end. As the plane rose higher into the sky and turned north towards the Caucasus she felt a sense of cleansing; the same sense she had had on the few occasions when she had made her confession as a young teenager, still half believing in the power of the priest to absolve her from sin. No priest was necessary now for Marianne to consign the past few months with Larry into the laundry basket of her experiences, where in time it would be washed, dried and ironed by her memory into a comfortable shape – a shape she could live with and remould around herself in a harmless and agreeable way. Thus cleansed, Marianne could now resume her happy and fulfilling life immersed in the world of Russian literature and, more particularly, as Edward's wife and Izzy's mother.

Izzy – this was the longest separation she had ever had from her daughter. Of course, it was right that she should spend time with her grandmother and it was good for Edward to spend time with his daughter, but she knew that she would be counting the days now until their return.

The plane was now passing over the Caucasus but the majestic snowy peaks which Marianne knew to be there were once again covered by cloud. Now they seemed to have hit a patch of turbulence. The seatbelt sign went on, the meal service was suspended and the plane made a series of stomach-churning jolts – a few seconds during which Marianne could sense the plane being forced up and then the inevitable, sickening drop. After a particularly heavy thud, one of the overhead lockers flew open and a bag fell into the aisle, scattering its contents. An air hostess rushed to help gather up the bag and re-stow it in the locker, smiling reassuringly to Marianne as she did so. Marianne was not unduly perturbed; she was used to flying and had experienced bad weather before. She was disappointed, however, when the captain announced that the weather was bad all the way to Moscow and they would not be able to resume the food and drink service. She tried to read but the bouncing and lurching of the plane became too distracting so she sat with her eyes shut and tried to sleep.

Her efforts were not successful; with her eyes closed the illusion of security which flying creates – the banality of rows of passengers snoozing, the lucky ones drinking; some trying to read – disappeared and was replaced by the image of her body in a small metal tube being tossed around five miles up in the sky. Suddenly she felt small and vulnerable and wished she had Edward with her. Now they were approaching Moscow airport. The flight was nearly over. She began to feel more relaxed. In ten minutes, I'll be on the ground, she thought. But first the plane must land and why couldn't they stay level? Why was the plane tipping left and right as if engaged in some crazy gymnastic exercise: arms outstretched, now up left, up right, keep the arms in a straight line…

'Seems like we have a strong crosswind,' the man in the adjoining seat said. Curiously, they were the first and only words she heard him utter. And then it happened. She saw it from her window. The wing – her wing, the wing she had been watching all flight – hit the runway. The noise was strangely muted, unless it was so loud as to temporarily deafen her, but there was no escaping the sickening and disorientating somersault, an explosion of pain, screaming, followed by darkness and a brief moment of silence. Then more pain… prayers… the smell of burning… followed by more screaming; more and more screaming.

Now all I need to do is die. And as quickly as possible. To end the pain and not to burn. Please, don't let me burn. I'll just die now. But how to do it?

She hadn't thought of it like that before. Dying was something that happened to you. People said 'John died' as if John had done something, but really it was death that did it to John. 'Death took him' – a funny expression, but surely that's how it is. Death kills you. John is the victim. Yesterday, John died. *Hier, Jean est décédé. Aujourd'hui, Marianne est morte.* I like it better in French; it seems like less to do. Isn't that why we personify death – the grim reaper, the angel of death? It comes along and ends your life. But perhaps I've got that wrong. Perhaps there's more to it than that. Perhaps I need to do something which I haven't done yet. It's the last thing you do, everyone has to do it, the dying thing, but I'm not sure how.

7

Cambridge, Spring 2031

Marianne lay on the floor, a sharp pain in her wrist and the side of her face on the cold tiles. For a while she didn't try to move, waiting to recover her breath and cursing her increasing decrepitude. It wasn't the first time she had fallen visiting the bathroom in the early morning, and she knew it might not be the last.

She experimented with a small movement of her wrist; painful, but not broken, she thought. Although her face had hit the tiled floor, and she would have a nasty bruise on her cheek, the damage could have been a lot worse. Slowly, she raised herself to her knees, crawled to the edge of the bath and using her uninjured arm she got to her feet, hobbled back to her bedroom and sat on the edge of the bed.

She looked at the clock. In less than an hour Anna would be there. Marianne would normally get up and dress herself, making a conscious effort not to become over-dependent on Anna. That morning, feeling fragile after her fall, she decided to await Anna's arrival and enjoy her assistance for the routine of bathing and dressing.

Anna had been with Marianne for three years, and if it was a cliché, it was nevertheless true that now Marianne couldn't imagine life without her. She hadn't known what she was looking for when she had seen a posting which caught her eye: *I'm a 22-year-old woman from Latvia, living in Cambridge and looking for work as a carer...* 'It wasn't the right way to go about it, as Callum was at pains to tell her. She should have gone through a reputable agency, taken up references and so on, but Anna had become far more to her now than she could possibly have imagined when she replied to the advertisement. She got back under the duvet and shut her eyes.

By the time she was having her breakfast, her wrist bandaged and Anna fussing over her, Marianne began to feel better.

'You must look after yourself,' said Anna.

'Bumps and bruises have to be suffered in old age – like being a child again.'

'But the kids – they recover more quickly. You must rest today.'

'Well, I won't be able to type, but I do need to get on.'

'Maybe I could help?'

'That's kind. But I'll probably just spend the day reading. I'm still trying to work out who's who.'

'So exciting – about your family history.'

'It is, though it's hard work trying to make sense of it.'

A month earlier, her sister Claire had been sorting

through some old trunks and boxes which had belonged to their mother, and which for years had lain untouched in her attic, when she had found a pile of wartime notebooks. Claire had taken one look, then bundled them up and sent them to Marianne.

Marianne's curiosity had been aroused immediately. Her mother had died without ever disclosing any more about her wartime experiences. Most of all there was the question of Marianne's biological father. The diaries were difficult to read. Spidery writing combined with frequent use of codes and shorthand meant deciphering them was a laborious business, but bringing all her research experience to bear, Marianne had started the process of preparing a typescript and simultaneously an English translation. She had looked ahead to the last volume to see if she could find a clue about her father, but so far without success.

'I will go to the shops now,' said Anna. 'Don't forget Callum and Helen come for lunch tomorrow.'

'I haven't forgotten.'

'Maybe Leah as well?'

'I don't think so.'

Marianne's son, Callum, had come back from Australia the previous year. Initially this was due to a bad bout of pneumonia which Marianne had suffered but they had subsequently decided to stay 'for a few years' – as Callum had put it. Marianne was in no doubt that Callum was the driving force behind this plan and his wife, Helen, was far from enthusiastic about leaving her beloved Australia. It also meant that whilst their daughter Leah had come with them and was now at school in London, their elder daughter, now at Melbourne University, had stayed in Australia.

At first, Marianne had been thrilled to have Callum in the same country, and finally she was getting to know at least one of her grandchildren; but more recently she had sensed that it was causing strains in their marriage. Nothing had been said to her, but she had little doubt that Helen would whisk Callum back to Australia the moment she breathed her last.

Marianne was still feeling shaken from her morning fall, so she took one of the notebooks from her desk and sat down in her armchair, wondering what she might discover, but her eyes gradually lost focus as her mind went back to when she was first told about her father.

'*Il faut que tu saches que Papa n'est pas ton vrai père.*' 'You need to know that Papa isn't your real father.' Maman always speaks to her in French. What does she mean?

'You will understand it when you are older.'

'Why is Papa not my father?'

'Papa is your father, absolutely he's your father – it's just that… he's not what people call your natural father. You might hear someone say that one day. It's not important – don't ever worry about it – but I felt you ought to know.'

But she doesn't know. What isn't real about him? She feels herself wanting to cry, but knowing that her mother would tell her off, she runs outside to her den behind the garden shed where, under a roof made from an old tarpaulin, she has stowed the stained pink blanket her mother had thrown out and her second-best doll, Sally. Curling up in a foetal position and clasping Sally to her chest, she asks her why her father isn't real, but Sally has no answer. So, she cries for what she doesn't understand, for her father who isn't a natural father and for herself who by rights ought to have a real father like other children.

Later, she begins to wonder if she has misunderstood her mother. There doesn't seem anything unreal about Papa, and anyway perhaps it doesn't matter if Papa isn't a real father, so long as he looks like a real father and behaves like a real father. She decides it was wrong to have cried and so she whispers half a Hail Mary to show God that she is sorry.

Callum and Helen were due to arrive at around twelve thirty. Marianne decided she needed to take a walk in the garden before they came. She put on her coat and scarf and with Anna taking her arm she hobbled out into the bright but chilly March morning. A sharp wind pulled at Marianne's scarf: straight from the Urals, they had told her, when she first came to live in Cambridge. She looked towards the end of the garden where the forsythia swayed and danced as if it wanted to escape the wind's whip while the daffodils bowed in unison, acknowledging a superior force. Yellow – the colour of spring, of sunshine; an optimistic colour, so why don't I like it? she thought. Maybe it's because I associate it with this freezing weather. Maybe I resent the relentless optimism of spring: yellow for cold – and cowards.

Callum and Helen arrived in a cheerful mood; Callum embraced his mother and then, unusually for him, kissed Anna on both cheeks. Even Helen seemed less brittle than usual. They were alarmed to see Marianne's bruised face and bandaged wrist.

'Why don't you carpet the bathroom, Mum?' said Callum. 'That way at least you won't be falling on hard tiles.'

'I don't think that's the answer.'

'You need one of those portable toilets by your bed,' said Helen.

Marianne sighed. 'A commode – yes, you're probably right, but I intend to resist that for the time being. Anna and I have decided that I need a rail to hold onto along the bathroom wall, and that's what we are going to do.'

While Anna laid the table for lunch Marianne observed her son. Streaks of grey were becoming more prominent now in his thick dark hair but he was still a good-looking man. A high, smooth forehead with sculpted eyebrows and an inconspicuous nose – a handsome face, no longer too fleshy as it had been in his youth, betrayed only by a slight weakness of the chin and a trace of anxiety which always seemed to hover around his eyes. There was a lot of Edward in Callum, a genuine altruism – not a cultivated show of do-goodery but an instinctive desire to do his best for others, to put his own interests second. An admirable quality, she thought, but it had made him a pushover for a determined woman like Helen.

Marianne suspected that Helen's good humour was not unconnected to their plan to return to Australia for three weeks over Easter; a plan which involved Marianne having Leah to stay for two of those weeks. The trip to Australia was ostensibly to see their other daughter – though the logic of this escaped Marianne. 'Why don't you just fly the girl over?' she said. 'It would be cheaper than both of you going back, and I'd get a chance to see her.'

'We can't do that – she has important hockey matches,' said Helen. 'Anyway, there are things we need to do back home.'

Marianne noticed a small flicker of irritation pass across Callum's face.

'I'm thinking of inviting my great-nephew Jake here for Easter,' said Marianne, changing the subject. 'Some younger company for Leah.'

'Jake? You mean Julie's Jake,' said Helen. 'But he must be well into his twenties now.'

'Twenty-three or twenty-four, I think. I know he's working as a journalist.'

'But, Marianne, I mean, Leah's only sixteen – I'm not sure that's really… well, you know – I mean, they're not really in the same age bracket.'

'I won't let him run off with her,' said Marianne, laughing. 'Anyway, it's just an idea – he's probably got something else planned.'

'I think it would be a good idea for Leah to get to know her cousin,' said Callum. 'She might also like to learn what a career in journalism is like.'

Helen shot Callum a look of frustration but said nothing.

After lunch Helen helped Anna wash up while Callum went through to the sitting room with Marianne. It was a comfortable room with floor-to-ceiling bookcases either side of the fireplace. On one wall hung two landscapes by Nita Spilhaus, a South African impressionist artist, which her grandfather had acquired in Cape Town in the nineteen thirties – all dappled sunlight pattering through exotic foliage – which Marianne liked to imagine gave the room an air of permanent summer. In the bay window sat the partners' desk which she had picked up cheaply on account of its excessive size.

Marianne sat down in her chair close to the wood-burning stove. 'Work going OK?' she said.

'It's fine, but, you know – I enjoy designing individual houses and that work barely exists in England. Out-of-town shopping centres are less satisfying.'

'And money?'

'OK, but, well, just the same situation back in Melbourne – I was hoping I could keep things ticking over when I'm not there, but now I'm not so sure. And you? Money-wise, I mean? Anna must be costing a fair bit.'

'I'm managing.'

Walking across to the desk by the window, Callum picked up one of the old notebooks. 'So these are your mother's wartime diaries you were telling me about.'

'Yes.'

Callum peered inside. 'I wouldn't be able to make any sense of this even if I could read French.'

'It's not easy.'

'But you can read it?'

'It's like any manuscript – if you spend time on it you learn to read the writing and work out the private shorthand all writers use.'

'Well, you always were a scholar, Mum. Anything sensational?'

Marianne hesitated for a moment. 'Not yet. I'm looking at the first book – my mother is only fourteen; it's 1940 and they are fleeing from the invading Germans. If I ever complete the translation, you'll be able to read a typescript in English.'

Callum did not seem especially interested in this prospect. He came and sat beside her and took her hand. 'So everything OK, Mum? I mean, apart from the fall.'

'Everything is fine, darling.'

'And Anna?'

'Wonderful as ever.'

'I do hope you'll be alright with Leah. I think she'll behave. You know, she's rather in awe of you. She'll also have a lot of homework to do.'

'I'll keep her at it.'

'And do invite Jake for a day or two if he'll come. I gather he is much better now.'

8

Jake had just completed a six-mile run when Marianne's call came through. He had taken up running after the death of his twin sister, Fran. At first it had simply helped neutralise his anger and pain. Now he had to keep running; it had become a drug – one which came with its own thresholds of pain but without which his moods would swing between a brittle and sometimes alarming temper, and debilitating depression.

He did not have anything planned for the Easter weekend. Most of his friends seemed to be deserting London and his parents were away. Currently without a girlfriend, he had contemplated seeing if any of his old university mates were free to hang out with him. A call from his great-aunt was the last thing he had expected and at first he prevaricated. What the hell was he supposed to do, entertaining that wretched Australian girl? He was inclined to think that Marianne had gone senile and thought he was still a teenager but talking to her, she seemed sane enough; she also told him about some old family diaries which might interest him – as a historian, she said, a reference to his undergraduate degree.

Whilst neither the prospect of looking after his sixteen-year-old cousin, nor studying some ancient diaries, seemed particularly alluring, Jake paused before rejecting the invitation. When Fran had died it was Marianne – Auntie Manne as he had always known her – who had been with him in the house, who had tried to comfort him, sitting up most of the night, telling him about the sadness in her own life which he had barely understood. It was seven years since Fran's death, and there was something he badly needed to say to Marianne, something he had never quite had the courage to say before. This might be his opportunity; he agreed to go.

The morning Jake was due to arrive, Marianne sat at her desk puzzling over a passage in her mother's old notebooks while Anna busied herself with tidying the house. She sensed a tension in Anna and she suspected it was to do with her boyfriend.

'How is Stefans?'

'He's OK.'

'Just OK?'

'Well, you know, he's a bit… how you say it – grumpy.'

'Is it his job?'

'I don't know… Anyway, it doesn't matter. I must get everything ready for your visitors.'

Marianne sipped her tea. 'Is Stefans talking again about going back to Latvia?' she asked.

Anna looked uncomfortable. 'No, no, not at all.'

Marianne raised her eyebrows.

'Well, you know… I mean he doesn't enjoy his job and sometimes he say that things are much better now in Latvia, he could start his own restaurant if he goes back to Riga – but of course we are not going to…'

'Anna, you know, I've told you before…'

'Please, Marianne, don't say anything. I am not leaving you.'

'Anna, I want you to stay, of course – but I'm eighty-six now. At my age…'

'Marianne – don't think bad things. Now I am going to make beds for Leah and for Mr Jake.'

Jake had been a child when he last visited Marianne at her home near Cambridge and as he parked his car in the driveway he saw an attractive nineteenth-century red-brick house. To the right of the front door the façade projected forward under a steeply pitched roof, suggesting a generous attic space. At the far corner the architect had allowed himself a signature flourish – familiar in that age, although an immense extravagance by the standard of modern buildings – creating a small round tower under a multi-sided roof so steep it was hard to imagine that the slates could stay in place.

Jake walked towards the front door, wondering who owned the rather scruffy-looking hatchback in the driveway. As there was no sign of a doorbell he rapped twice on the lion's head brass doorknocker. The door was opened by a blonde girl in her late twenties with large grey-blue eyes and a welcoming smile. She put a finger to her lips. 'You arrive early. Marianne is having a sleep. Come into the kitchen.'

The girl introduced herself as Anna, Marianne's carer, and chatted to Jake as she busied herself in the kitchen. 'So good for Marianne to have visitors – especially young one like you. And Leah is coming this evening – you will be collecting her from the station, I think?'

'Will I?' said Jake. 'I mean, I can – of course. What time does she get in?'

'About six, I think. We check with Marianne when she's awake.'

Jake had barely had time to greet his Auntie Manne and enjoy an obligatory cup of tea before he was back in his car and heading to the station to pick up his cousin Leah – a girl he had not seen since she was a child of ten. He identified her immediately. She had been pretty when a ten-year-old and the same prettiness was present now as he watched a slim, tanned teenager in tight jeans, with streaked blonde hair and a rucksack on her back, wheeling a suitcase out of the station building.

Jake approached her. 'Hey! I'm your cousin Jake – remember? Sent to pick you up.' He kissed her on the cheek and took her case.

'Sweet – Gran said someone would be here.'

'Good ski trip?' Jake enquired as they made their way to his car.

'Awesome. There were, like, so many lifts – so many different trails – way better than skiing in Oz.'

When Anna had left for the evening, and Leah was upstairs showering, Jake decided that the moment had come to make his confession to Marianne before he lost his nerve.

Sitting down in a chair beside her, he said: 'Auntie Manne – Marianne…' Suddenly the familiar diminutive by which she had always been known to him seemed childish and not fitting for what he was about to say. 'You were not to blame, you know. Not at all.'

Marianne studied his anxious gaze. Those large brown eyes like his mother, and that purposeful chin. A good-looking young man.

'I mean, about Fran.'

'Well, I should have been more on my guard. Your sister was always inclined to be reckless.'

'No. I mean, perhaps she was, but in fact it was my fault.'

'Nonsense, Jake, you mustn't feel that. Death always makes the survivors feel guilty.'

'But I should feel guilty, you see…'

'Hey, Gran,' said Leah, coming into the room with hair streaked wet against her face, 'what's the Wi-Fi password?'

Jake got up and walked to the other side of the room, trying not to show his irritation.

The next morning Jake sat with Marianne having breakfast. Anna sat at the table with them; as yet there was no sign of Leah. Marianne talked to Jake about the diaries. She explained how her mother's family had been living near Reims in eastern France and – like millions of other families – had taken to the road to flee when the German army burst through the Ardennes in May 1940.

'The famous exodus,' said Jake.

'Yes – well, the beginning, at least. They go to Paris and when Paris is threatened they take to the road again.'

'It must be an important historical document,' he said.

Marianne shrugged. 'I don't think there is any shortage of material on the subject.'

They talked about wartime France and Marianne was impressed by his knowledge. After breakfast, they looked at the notebooks together. Jake read a few sentences. His French is very good, she thought. Pity I can't get him to help me on this.

'What exactly are you doing with them?'

'I'm making a typescript in French – doing notes on the acronyms and abbreviations – and at the same time preparing an English translation.'

'Sounds a massive job.'

'Yes, there's a lot to do, and I'm probably too old to be starting a project like this, but…' She broke off. Then she said, 'I think you ought to take Leah into Cambridge this morning. I don't think she has seen the city or the colleges.'

'Sure. I can do that.'

'I'll wake Leah. You'll need to get going. Easter Saturday, the place will be heaving.'

It was nearly twelve o'clock by the time Marianne had shooed Jake and Leah out of the house. She poured a cup of coffee and took it to her desk in the sitting room. Jake has grown into himself, she thought. For years in thrall to his headstrong twin sister, he seems a confident young man now. His interest in the diaries had given him a definite boost in her estimation.

As for Leah – well, she couldn't help sounding Australian, although Marianne had observed that her accent was far less noticeable after a term at school in London. Also, unlike her mother, she seemed enthusiastic about all she had seen and done since coming to England. She was either a great actress or she was genuinely excited about visiting Cambridge with Jake.

'Milton was at Cambridge, wasn't he?' she had said. 'And Newton – which college was he? And Rupert Brooke was at King's – I remember 'cos we're studying him. And we have to go on a punt! Can we go on a punt, Jake? I've seen so many pictures – under that bridge… Oh my God – this is so cool.' Yes, the girl had promise.

Easter Sunday tomorrow, she thought. Easter has never been quite the same to me after that escapade to Georgia. Perhaps that's why I have always felt something ominous about spring. That reckless optimism, that certainty I had everything nicely balanced, a carefully constructed tower of hubris – before it all crashed in flames.

9

Moscow, Spring 1974

Strange, incoherent thoughts. The same scene, the same sensations. Unable to move. Pain. Fear. It's my punishment, she thought. I will burn to death because I have done wrong. Come on, admit it to yourself, a little voice was saying. You have sinned. And you thought you had got rid of that funny old word. By the time you were fourteen you had disposed of sin; thrown it in the garbage bin of childhood terrors, no more demons, no more devils with pitchforks. So what's it doing dancing around in my head now? How did it sneak back in?

The light was shining in Marianne's eyes and now she knew she was awake. A nurse was standing over her, saying something. Her heart seemed to be racing. She tried to concentrate on staying awake. The nurse was gone now but she was still awake – there seemed to be numerous tubes coming from her body. I must clear my mind, she thought. She heard a woman's voice say, 'You were on the plane too?' She turned her head and saw a figure lying on a bed not far away. She answered with a small grunt. 'Don't talk if it hurts, dear,' said the woman. 'There are a lot of us here – I mean, who were on the plane. Where are you from?'

England, she replied, though no word came out; then she thought, I used to say America, curious that. Then she fell asleep again.

The next time Marianne woke up she was immediately alert to her surroundings. A curtain had been drawn around her bed and there was a man sitting beside her. It was Larry. No, she thought, that's wrong, wrong man. Where's Edward? Where's Izzy? Of course, they are back in England – but I need them here.

Larry was talking to her. He was telling her that she had made it. Thank God, he was saying, thank God you made it. He had telephoned the embassy when he heard the news. At first it had been chaotic but they had found out eventually that she had survived. He had got the next available flight to Moscow. Larry said a lot of good things to her and she listened. He told her he felt guilty – that if he hadn't persuaded her to go down to Georgia... She asked for a drink and he put the feeding cup to her lips. Then she said, 'It's over, Larry.' He stopped, looking surprised.

'Don't think about that now, Marianne. You need to concentrate on getting better. You know you have had major abdominal surgery.'

She didn't know but she allowed her mind to bypass this information. She said, 'I mean it, Larry. It's over for us. I want Edward.'

'Yes, of course, and he is on his way from London. That's

75

one of the things I came to tell you. We managed to track him down and tell him that you had been on the plane. He is already on his way here. His flight gets in at six this evening. I've arranged for an embassy car to pick him up and bring him here. After all, you're still a US citizen.'

'And Izzy?'

'Ah – I don't know whether she is with him.'

'I do hope she is.'

Larry promised to try to get her moved to a more private space. He told her about the crash. One of the wings had touched the ground on landing.

'I know,' she said. 'I saw it.'

'You saw it?'

'Yes, it was on my side.'

'Oh, anyway, there seem to have been about a dozen fatalities but most of the passengers survived. The ground crews managed to extinguish the fire. Fortunately, there was no explosion.'

'Yes,' she said. 'Yes, fortunately.'

Larry said his goodbyes, kissed her on the forehead, and left. Soon afterwards she was moved to what she later discovered was the part of the hospital reserved for foreigners. She found herself in a cubicle separated from the corridor by a large glass panel and half walls each side, with glass partitions to adjoining rooms. At the back of the room was a lavatory, bath and basin. Soon after she had been moved from a trolley to the bed a young male doctor appeared together with a nurse. The doctor peered into her eyes and asked her how she felt. He then started to tell her about the surgery. Some of the medical terminology was beyond her knowledge of Russian but she detected an apologetic tone. It seemed that some metal – perhaps some of the fuselage – had sliced across her upper leg and lower abdomen. By a miracle it hadn't severed her femoral artery. Her pelvis was fractured. There was reference to surgical repair of her bladder and some other tricky procedures. Gradually it dawned on her what he was saying: she would never again give birth to a child.

The nurse squeezed her hand. 'You have a daughter, I think? Your American friend said so.'

'Yes.'

'That's a mercy.'

'Yes.'

At first there was just numbness, a matter-of-fact acceptance. So, this was it. There had to be consequences. She was alive but something inside her was dead. Then she thought of Edward and a whole new sensation swept over her – shame for herself and misery for him. What of their plan to have at least one more child and perhaps two? And his unspoken desire for a son. How to tell him that her stupid frolic had deprived him of the chance of being a father again? That is, assuming he stays with me, she thought.

The afternoon passed in alternating phases of fearful sleep and miserable awakening. There were no tears, but self-pity was having to compete with a latent anger at what had happened to her. I've been in an accident, she told herself. This has nothing to do with Larry. You can't expect a plane to crash. I need to clear my head of all this guilt. But the guilt wouldn't let her go.

She was asleep when she first heard the sound and it didn't seem quite real. Then she heard it again. The high notes of a child, and suddenly it seemed to her that no voice had ever before sounded so sweet. 'Mummy,' Izzy cried, 'Mummy.'

And that was enough; huge sobs began to shake Marianne. Painful sobs, if she could have felt the pain. Izzy pressed her face to Marianne's cheeks. 'Why are you crying, Mummy?'

The arrival of her husband and daughter provided the most perfect balm for Marianne's distress. From Edward, there was nothing but love and sympathy. No mention was made of why she had been flying back from Georgia and Marianne never mentioned the consequences of her injuries. These conversations would have to take place, but that was for later. Mostly Edward held her hand and smiled at her, blinking away his own tears while Izzy gabbled on about their time in Cheltenham and Cambridge. How they had spent Easter with Granny and how she loved Granny's two cats and how Granddad had arranged an Easter-egg hunt and how they had to rush to the airport to return to Moscow. 'And... and... Mummy,' she said, 'our plane didn't crash.'

That night, drugged with pain killers and the powerful narcotic of her family's overwhelming love, she fell into a dreamless sleep.

Edward was with her again by noon the next day. This time he was alone and the anxiety in his eyes and slight frown hovering across his forehead told Marianne that he knew the worst about her condition. 'The doctors said that they told you.'

'Yes.'

'I mean, that you won't be able to have more children.'

'Yes, they told me.'

'Oh God, Marianne, I'm so desperately sorry – can you bear it? Thank heaven we have Izzy.' Edward spent the next hour at her bedside trying to comfort her, and although it may well have been that his pain was greater than hers, he never gave the slightest sign of anger or resentment. Marianne felt humble at his selflessness; I am unworthy of his love, she thought. The subject of her trip was raised only obliquely: 'You know, Aeroflot don't have a very good safety record.'

'Don't they? Well, I wish to God I'd never taken the trip.'

'You never mentioned that you were planning to fly down to Georgia.'

'I wasn't. At least, not then. But I was having a coffee with Larry on one of his visits to the university and he said he was going down there for a week and I rather foolishly said how much I wanted to visit the Caucasus. As a result, he offered to arrange a short trip for me… I'm sorry, Ed, I know you don't like the guy, but it was kind of him and no one could expect the plane to crash.'

Edward frowned and shook his head, but said, 'Well, I must say he was very efficient in tracking me down and telling me about the accident and sending a car to the airport. Even so…'

'I know, and I've decided I won't go on meeting him. You were right. I mustn't get involved in politics. But when I'm better, I'd like for us to go down to Georgia together. I think perhaps by train this time – it was really fascinating, and I would love it if we could go together and see the Caucasus properly…'

Edward squeezed her hand: 'Yes, that does sound like fun.'

Three days after his first visit, Larry came again to the hospital. 'So they've moved you into the foreigners' wing,' he said.

'Yes.'

'Not much privacy, though, with the toilet and bathtub in the middle of the room.'

'Well, that's not my greatest concern.'

Then he told her. He was being expelled from the Soviet

79

Union. His diplomatic status had been revoked and he had to be on a plane out the next morning.

'So I came to say goodbye.'

'I'm sorry, Larry, and look… thank you for everything… I'm sorry if…'

'Don't try to explain, Marianne. We have always understood each other. I have never had any illusions that you would leave Edward. Whatever happens in the future, I will never forget you.'

'What will happen to you now?'

'Oh, don't worry about me. It goes with the territory. Cultural attachés usually get expelled after a couple of years. We tend to mix too much with people the authorities regard as undesirable. But I should warn you, it is possible that they may try to ask you some questions. Don't worry if they do; you've done nothing wrong. It's just routine.'

Marianne was relieved that Larry hadn't stayed long at the hospital and she was also comforted that his departure from Moscow would remove any temptation that she might have had to see him in the future – not that she could imagine ever having sex again with anyone. Needless-to-say, Edward felt entirely vindicated. 'I knew he was a bloody spy,' he said.

'That's not how he sees it.'

'I doubt if you know the whole picture.'

'Probably not. Anyway, now there's no risk of my bumping into him again.'

'Well, just make sure his replacement doesn't try to contact you and carry on where he left off.'

'I can assure you, that won't happen,' said Marianne, noting to herself that this was at least one question she could answer with complete honesty.

Marianne received visits every day from Edward and most days he brought Izzy with him. She also received a surprise visit from her sister Claire, now a nineteen-year-old, studying in Paris. With her long, untidy and presumably unwashed hair, and a coat which looked as if it had been retrieved from the trenches of the first world war, she was every inch the Sorbonne student, anxious to light up her Gitanes in the corridor whenever the opportunity arose.

'Got an emergency visa,' she said, speaking in French. 'Maman insisted I come. I can only stay forty-eight hours.'

'I'd prefer to speak in English,' said Marianne.

'Forgotten your French?'

'Not at all, but...'

'This way we won't be so easily understood,' said Claire, looking around and continuing to speak in French.

Marianne shrugged. 'It was good of you to come.'

'I want to know what's going on. What were you doing in Georgia and who is the mysterious man you were with?'

Marianne had never been particularly close to Claire. The age gap of nearly ten years meant that she had always thought of Claire as a child. Part of her would have loved to have confided in her sister but she didn't know her well enough and wasn't sure she could trust her to keep her mouth shut. More importantly, however, she wanted to put the whole Larry episode behind her and wipe it from her memory. She therefore laughed off her sister's suggestion of an affair, explaining he was just an acquaintance from the embassy – and a very dull one at that.

In the meantime, Marianne tried her best to be stoical. She longed to be able to telephone her mother but although there was a payphone in the hallway, to which she was wheeled on a couple of occasions to speak to Edward, it was impossible to make international calls so all she could do was rely on Edward or Claire to relay messages. She realised that she would have ugly scarring across her lower stomach and the top of her left thigh and this was not going to look pretty in a bikini. The Russian doctors had decided that she didn't need surgery for the pelvic fracture, but they had fixed a metal frame on the outside of her body which made sleeping difficult; Edward told her she should get a second opinion as soon as she was well enough to fly to England.

The dominant topic, to which Edward reverted again and again – which had evoked sympathy even from her sister, and on which her parents had sent her a long and emotional letter – was one where Marianne recognised that she did not feel as distressed as perhaps she ought, or indeed as much as Edward or her parents expected. She covered up her feeling, but with a growing discomfort that she did not deserve this outpouring of sympathy. No more agonising about when to have more children; it was simply one less problem to figure out. It was a guilty secret now for Marianne to look at Izzy and know that she was content with this one child; a child who would never have to share her mother's love with another sibling, who would not only be her most beloved daughter but also her best friend and life-long companion.

When the serious question came – the one she might have expected Edward to have asked immediately – it took her completely by surprise. So relaxed and confident had she become – so certain that she had finessed the issue with an explanation that, whilst not entirely truthful, was not a direct lie – that at first she seemed unable to understand what he was asking.

'I have to know the truth, Marianne. Was it an affair?'

She looked at him blankly, as if the words had no meaning for her.

He stared back at her – a look of anxiety – perhaps even fear – on his normally composed features. 'Where you in a sexual relationship with Larry?' he asked, enunciating each word clearly, like a barrister addressing a witness who was feigning stupidity.

'Oh God, no. No, absolutely not. I mean, I may have been foolish, perhaps he was a spy, but an affair – no, never.' The words came out in a rush – an unpremeditated babble of denial.

Edward closed his eyes and gradually his expression relaxed. 'Thank God,' he said. 'Thank God for that. I am sorry if I doubted you, but it's been gnawing away at me.'

'I am the one who should apologise. I shouldn't have got mixed up with him – and given you cause to worry.'

Edward leant across the bed and kissed her on the forehead. 'I never really doubted you, my darling – but I had to be sure.'

Marianne spent a wretched night. I should have confessed, she told herself a hundred times. He would have forgiven me, I'm sure. We could start again on an honest basis. When sleep did come, it was inhabited by the familiar face she had learned to associate with feelings of guilt. She resolved to tell Edward the next day but when the morning came she began to doubt herself. Would he really be so forgiving? Especially as she had lied to him about it the previous day. She knew Edward as an exceptionally kind and generous man, always calm and patient, even when provoked. But this would be uncharted territory; she worried that his manifest goodness and decency might make it harder for him to accept her transgression.

Larry's gone now, she reasoned, and what's done is done. Nothing would be gained now by a confession. Best to keep quiet.

As the time approached for Marianne to leave hospital, it was agreed that they would fly back to England to allow her to recuperate there and have further medical checks. Meanwhile, her mother would fly over from Vermont to be with her and help look after Isabelle. The day before their planned departure she was waiting for Edward to arrive and pick her up from the hospital. She expected him to arrive at around eleven and when he had not turned up by twelve she hobbled into the hallway on her crutches to make a telephone call. To her surprise she was confronted by a man in uniform she had not previously noticed.

'You must return to your room,' said the man, speaking in such heavily accented Russian that at first she didn't understand him.

'I'm sorry,' she said, 'but I need to telephone my husband.'

'Please return to your room and the situation will be explained to you,' said the uniformed man, blocking her path to the telephone. Marianne reluctantly obeyed and returned to sit on her bed, worrying what might have happened to Edward. A few minutes later a younger man of about thirty-five, dressed in a typical, badly fitting Russian suit, arrived in her room.

'Ah, Mrs Davenport, are you ready to leave?' he said to her in surprisingly good English.

'I am, but I am waiting for my husband.'

'I'm afraid he won't be coming this morning. You must accompany us and everything will be explained.'

Marianne looked from one to the other. 'I'm sorry,' she said, 'but who exactly are you?' The man did not reply, but at that moment she saw one of the doctors passing her room and called out, 'Dr Kuznetzova, please. I don't understand. I was waiting for my husband to arrive and these men have come in...' The doctor looked at the men and then at Marianne.

'They are policemen,' she said in an expressionless voice. 'You must go with them.'

10

It wasn't the Lubyanka, Marianne acknowledged with relief, nor was it exactly a cell. In appearance, it was more like a hostel room at some remote truckers' stop with an iron frame single bed, a small table with upright chair and a narrow wardrobe. In one corner, a doorless cubicle housed a shower and lavatory; on the other side of the cubicle a small sink hung from the wall. The floor was covered with green lino on which lay a forlorn strip of brown carpet. A small window was obscured by frosted glass and did not seem designed to be opened.

As Marianne lay on the bed her initial feeling was one of anger towards Larry; they might ask you some questions, he had said, almost as a throw-away line – and now she had been arrested, at least she supposed that is what had happened to her, although no one had actually used those words. Shut in this dingy room, she had no idea what would happen next and no news about Edward. What if they had arrested him and there was no one to collect Izzy from kindergarten? Thanks a lot, she thought with some bitterness; you, the professional diplomat – or spy, as Edward would have it – are happily back in America while I'm here in the hands of the KGB. She tried to reassure herself that she had done nothing wrong, but was that strictly true? And what was right and wrong here anyway? Increasingly she came to realise how naïve and foolish she had been. Edward had been right; this wasn't London or New York. She should have been a lot more careful. All the same, she thought, this is not the nineteen thirties. Stalin has been dead for twenty years. Surely nothing too bad can happen to me?

For the rest of that day no one came to her room other than the same stout woman with swept-back grey hair and what appeared to be a badly repaired broken nose who had originally told her to 'make herself comfortable' and who now brought her a meal on a tray. Marianne bombarded her with questions but she merely answered, in an accent which Marianne placed as coming from somewhere east of the Urals, 'I have no information'.

Depressed at the thought of the long night ahead of her, Marianne remembered that she had with her some sleeping pills and pain killers prescribed by the hospital, which she had persuaded her crooked-nosed jailor to allow her to keep. Taking two of each she got into bed, shut her eyes and tried to will herself to sleep. Before the pills eventually did their work, she had a vague recollection of reading somewhere that the KGB always conducted their interrogations at night. Oh well, she thought, they won't get much out of me now.

Waking the next morning she felt groggy and nauseous and realised that she was extremely hungry; the now cold and congealed evening meal, lying untouched on the floor, reminded her that she had eaten nothing since the previous morning. She was pathetically grateful when at last her jailor brought in her breakfast: strong black tea with bread, butter and a bowl of yoghurt.

She didn't have long to contemplate what might have happened to her husband or daughter before the crooked-nosed woman appeared again. 'Follow me, please,' she said, setting off down a succession of corridors while Marianne hobbled after her as fast as her crutches would allow. Entering a brightly lit office, she was greeted by a uniformed man of about forty, slim, with blond hair and dark circles under his eyes who rose from his seat when she came in.

'Mrs Davenport, will you sit down,' the man said in English, 'I am sorry that we could not talk yesterday but I was rather busy. May I express my sympathy about your unfortunate accident? Are you comfortable in that seat?' Marianne ignored his expression of sympathy and launched herself into a series of questions.

'Please tell me what's going on. Why am I here? Where is my husband? What has happened to my daughter? Am I under arrest? What am I supposed…' The man held up both his hands to halt her flow of questions.

'Please, first things first. Let me introduce myself. I am Lieutenant Colonel Petroff of the Committee for State Security; as for your husband and daughter, they were escorted to the airport yesterday and will now be back in England.'

'Why?'

'Why? Oh dear, Mrs Davenport, I think you must know

the answer to that question.' Marianne said nothing, though she felt a huge surge of relief that Edward and Izzy were safe – assuming, of course, that she was being told the truth. 'Let me give you a start then,' the colonel continued, 'it seems you were an associate of the American spy Larry Anderson, who operated under diplomatic cover and who has now been expelled from the Soviet Union.'

'I knew Mr Anderson but I didn't think that he was a spy.'

'Indeed. It seems though that you were meeting him on a regular basis?'

'Yes. I met him at an embassy party soon after I arrived here. He gave me useful tips about living in Moscow. He was quite often at the university and I would have a coffee with him.'

The colonel looked at her quizzically. 'And?'

'Well, we talked about life in Moscow and reminisced about America.'

The colonel made a show of examining some papers in front of him. 'It seems that on several occasions you were seen to pass a newspaper to Anderson which he took away with him. Why would that have been?'

'I don't know. I don't remember. Perhaps there was something in it he was interested in.'

'In the newspaper – or would that be within the newspaper? Please take care what you say, Mrs Davenport. Lying to an officer of the State Security is a serious offence in this country.'

Marianne thought quickly. I have no reason to protect Larry so why not own up...

'I sometimes gave him *samizdats* which were circulating around the university.'

'Wrapped in a copy of *Pravda* or *Isvestia*?'

'Yes.'

'Why?'

Marianne shrugged.

'Come, come, Mrs Davenport. You did so because you knew that these are illegal documents produced by enemies of our state.'

'I knew that they were not approved of.'

'Not approved of – is that how you would describe it? This was an illegal activity in breach of the undertaking you gave when you entered this country.'

'I didn't think of it like that.'

'But you admit handing him illegal publications?'

'Well, I handed him these papers occasionally – but he could have got them from other people. There are plenty around.'

'But in fact, he got them from you.'

'Sometimes.'

'And sometimes from other agents. Would that be the case?'

'I was not an agent.'

'No? You were just a friend then?'

'Yes.'

'Nothing more?'

'No.'

The questions continued all morning; Marianne was repeatedly asked about her conversations with Larry: who did he ask her to meet; what issues was he concerned about? She tried to give answers that she thought would satisfy the colonel. She explained in general terms his interest in Jewish members of the university who might be thinking of applying to emigrate, but she tried as far as possible to avoid mentioning names. Why am I behaving like this? she wondered. I don't have any obligation to these people. Why am I behaving as if I really was an agent who didn't want to betray her contacts? It nevertheless seemed instinctive to try to avoid getting others into trouble if she could prevent it.

The colonel was unfailingly polite, if frequently sarcastic when he thought her answers inadequate. When he announced that the interview was over she asked, 'So what happens now? When can I leave?'

'We need to evaluate what you have told us. Answering correctly and telling the truth will speed up the process. Have you been telling the truth, Mrs Davenport?'

'Yes, certainly.'

'Good,' he said, smiling at Marianne in a way she found rather disturbing. 'You will be escorted back to your room now.'

Later that day, as Marianne lay on her bed pondering the interview, she thought that she had perhaps made a foolish mistake. Why had she not told them that Larry had been her lover? Didn't that explain her meetings in a way which was less prejudicial to her own position? After all, a love affair is just that. It explains everything. Also, they probably already knew. If they had been watching him they must have been aware of their many meetings at the Minsk Hotel. She hadn't told them, she supposed, out of an instinct for denial and secrecy which an adulterous affair gives rise to; and the fact that she had lied about it to her husband. Perhaps she was also trying to avoid giving them any information that they could then use against her. God, what a sink hole I have got myself into, she thought. She felt disgusted with herself. She resolved that when she was summoned for her next interview she would admit to her relationship with Larry.

Unfortunately, the opportunity for a pre-emptive confession did not arise. The next day she was confronted by a different man; a short stubby figure with thick black hair who immediately addressed her in Russian. 'I am afraid I don't speak English like our esteemed colonel, but I understand you speak excellent Russian. Is that so, Mrs Davenport?'

'I can speak Russian, yes,' Marianne replied. The man stared at her, saying nothing for a few seconds. Marianne opened her mouth to speak but she was cut short.

'Clearly you are a woman of many talents. Tell me, do you let all your friends fuck you?'

'I am sorry, I…'

'I am reading from the transcript of your evidence yesterday,' the man continued. He then proceeded to read in slow, halting English:

'Colonel Petroff: "You were just friends?"

'Davenport: "Yes."

'Colonel Petroff: "Nothing more?"

'Davenport: "No."'

Continuing in Russian, he said, 'You lied yesterday, and the Colonel is very disappointed with you. That's why I am here today. He does not want to waste his time when you are lying to us.'

Marianne tried to explain. 'I am very sorry. It's true that Larry Anderson and I were lovers. It's just become an instinct to be secretive about it.' Then, with a flash of what seemed like inspiration, she said: 'Perhaps you are married yourself – perhaps you have been unfaithful to your wife and have instinctively lied about it…' The man's fist came down on the table with a violence that she had not expected, causing his cup and saucer to fly into the air and crash on the floor.

Standing up, he came around to Marianne and put his face close to hers.

'Don't try to be smart with me, you sleazy bitch,' and as he spoke he slapped her hard across the cheek and then, as her face turned in response to the blow, he flicked the back of his hand up into her face where it made a hollow clunk as it collided with her nose. Marianne recoiled in pain.

'You hit me,' she said in a small voice which might have belonged to an eight-year-old girl, expressing surprise that a well-known playground bully had suddenly turned on her.

'Don't make me laugh,' the man said. 'If I'd hit you, you would be on the floor with your face in a pool of blood. We are trying to be nice to Americans now – inviting them to our country even when they regularly betray our trust. But don't push me – otherwise that fine nose of yours will never look the same again.'

Marianne was shaken by this sudden eruption of anger. She tried to blink away the tears as she wiped a small trickle of blood from her upper lip. The questions now began again, covering the same ground only this time the interrogator was a lot more aggressive.

'You lied to us yesterday,' he said, 'so today we have to start again. We have now established that the spy Anderson was running you as an agent and fucking you as well. In my considerable experience this adds a whole new dynamic; agents in this type of relationship strive particularly hard to please their spymasters.'

The following day she was confronted by the same interrogator, on account of whose short stature and dark hair she had christened 'Blackberry', Stalin's nickname for the 'bloody dwarf' Yezhov, a notorious torturer and Beria's predecessor as head of the NKVD. 'Blackberry' repeatedly asked her about people she had never heard of, and when for the third or fourth time she had denied any knowledge of the individuals mentioned, he said: 'Mrs Davenport, while you may be spared more robust interrogation methods, non-cooperation will only lead to a longer sentence. Your pretty little daughter may be quite grown up before you see her again.' Sentence, she thought, that's the first time anyone has mentioned a prison sentence, and gradually, what little confidence she had left began to turn to genuine fear. Until then she had assumed that after two or three days they would simply let her go, but perhaps she was wrong. Technically she was probably guilty of offences under Soviet law. What sort of sentence might she get?

As the interview came to an end Marianne asked, 'I would like to see someone from my embassy.'

'They know you are here,' replied her interrogator without looking up from the desk.

As if to confirm her worst fears, the next day she was not summoned for questioning. Nor the day after, nor the day after that. As the days passed Marianne's anxiety turned into serious depression. Time, like a watched pot, refused to perform its required function. Each day stretched like an eternity; she tried to sleep but fear had crept into her consciousness and kept her wakeful. And then there were the noises. Coming from the air-brick below the window. A man crying – then a scream, and another voice raised in anger. Every night she was kept awake by a noise like an electric drill. She became obsessed with the sounds seeping into her room and even when there was silence she listened intently, expecting at any moment to hear another scream and imagining what horrors might be unfolding below her.

Without word from the embassy, or any news of Edward and Izzy, Marianne was lonely and scared. Wrapped up in my world of literature, I have tried to pretend to myself that this is just like any other country, she thought. The truth is they can keep me here indefinitely. I am completely at their mercy. Who knows where I could end up next – at the mercy of thugs and torturers? She felt nauseous at the thought of what might be in store for her.

In addition to all her other anxieties, Marianne was worried about her own health. She had expected to be flying home for a check-up in an English hospital. She was still suffering from pain in her pelvis and so she decided to ask to see a doctor. Her jailor with the crooked nose had nodded in a noncommittal way but somewhat to her surprise, the next morning she came into her room followed by a young blonde woman in a white coat. Introducing herself as Doctor Sorokina, she took Marianne's temperature, examined her, and discussed her symptoms in a sympathetic way. 'Everything seems to be healing satisfactorily,' she said. Marianne asked if she could have more pain killers and sleeping pills. 'I am afraid I am not permitted to give you any,' the doctor said.

After ten days of seeing no one except her jailor and the doctor, Marianne was finally led back on her crutches to the office where the blond colonel was working at his desk. He greeted her courteously and enquired after her health. 'I understand that you have seen a doctor?' he said.

'Yes.'

'Do you have any complaints about the way you have been treated here?'

Marianne considered the question. 'No. Although the other questioner hit me in the face and threatened me.'

'Did he indeed. I suppose that would never happen in America.' Looking across the desk, he studied her. 'No harm done, I think. But we do get frustrated, especially when our time is wasted by lies.'

'I am sorry about that – it was somehow instinctive…' As she spoke the colonel was examining a brown folder which he had opened and which he was looking at intently. Marianne paid no attention; she was just happy that someone was talking to her and that it was the blond colonel and not the thuggish 'Blackberry'. The colonel then took out a large A4-sized photograph and stared at it.

Afterwards, when Marianne would replay to herself that moment when he flung the photograph across the desk to her, that half second when her brain was trying to process the information, she would have to admit that she had still not understood what was happening. It was as if someone had launched a bucket of ice-cold water at her head and yet, despite every appearance to the contrary, despite the imminence of her icy drenching, she had continued to believe that the contents must be aimed at someone else.

'Good quality, I think you will agree.'

Marianne looked in horror at the picture.

'What about this one?' he said, throwing down another photograph. 'Amazing flexibility. And this one? Quite the deep-throat specialist. How will your husband feel about that?'

Marianne had never felt so humiliated in her life. She felt a hot flush of shame rising up from her neck and spreading across her face and into the roots of her hair.

'I don't think he would like to see these pictures, would he?' said the colonel. 'Although I have enjoyed looking at them myself. As did my colleagues. In fact, they've been greatly admired.' Marianne could think of nothing to say. She looked away from the photographs. 'Come come, Mrs Davenport, you mustn't be shy about this. My colleague was wondering if you could perform some of these tricks with him? But yes, I do understand, the esteemed doctor, your husband, wouldn't like it. It's all in the detail you see. A husband can accept that his wife has been unfaithful. Perhaps it's not so bad, he may think, and anyway, it's over now – but that's because he hasn't seen it; the reality hasn't been imprinted on his retina, not the detail. What they actually did together, how she felt about it. Look at this one. I think this is my favourite.' The colonel threw another photograph across the table to Marianne. 'That smile on your face – pure ecstasy. He'd find that difficult to forget, wouldn't he?'

Crushed and mortified, Marianne cursed herself for not seeing it coming and she cursed Larry yet again for allowing this to happen to her. So much for his confidence in the security at the hotel. It was almost as if she'd been the victim of an American honey trap – except that was absurd. Anyway, she had nothing useful to offer the authorities in either country and she couldn't see what blackmailing her was likely to achieve.

'What do you want from me?' she said.

'You've already been very helpful to us,' said the colonel, smiling. 'But we'll need your continuing cooperation.'

Two days after she had been shown the photographs she received a surprise visit from a young woman from the US embassy. 'Thank God,' said Marianne, 'please tell me you are going to get me out of here?' The woman looked at her then looked around the room and made a gesture towards her ear. Yes, of course, thought Marianne, the room is certain to be bugged. The woman introduced herself as Mary Fitzgerald.

She told Marianne that the embassy had been advised of her arrest soon after her departure from the hospital but they had not been permitted to visit her. Then she took out a notebook. 'OK physically?' she wrote, then pushed the notebook and pencil over to Marianne.

'Yes, OK – but what now?' wrote Marianne, handing the notebook back to Fitzgerald, so they could continue their written exchange.

'More questions – then probably a confession to sign.'

'Should I sign?'

'Difficult. You have to judge: are they making you the innocent dupe or something more sinister?'

'If I sign, what then?'

'Either they let you go or put you on trial.'

'If I'm tried?'

'You will be convicted.'

'And…?'

'A prison sentence – measured in years. Ten is usual, maybe only five.' No doubt Mary Fitzgerald noticed how pale Marianne had gone because she took the notebook back and added: 'Likely you are not important enough to put on trial so good chance they will let you go.'

'The other thing is,' said Marianne, taking back the notebook and pausing for thought. 'They have some photographs,' she wrote, '… of Larry and I…'

Fitzgerald nodded. 'I can guess,' she wrote. 'Anderson should have known better. His bosses are not pleased.'

'What will they do with the photographs?'

'Keep them, and… who knows…?'

The days after Fitzgerald's visit were the most distressing of all for Marianne. Hour after hour of exhausting interrogations by 'Blackberry' which, as far as she could see, were going nowhere and all the time she thought about the possibility (or was it even a probability?) of a long prison sentence. In addition to the photographs, they had tapes of her conversations with Larry at the Minsk Hotel. Who were these individuals you spoke of, they demanded to know? Who was Solomon? Who was Abraham? Who was David? She had to acknowledge that they were code names for members of the Jewish community, but she tried to maintain that she couldn't remember exactly who they referred to. In the evenings, she would vomit up her meal and then lie awake nauseous but hungry. The thought that it might be years before she saw Izzy again was making her physically ill. The pain in her pelvis was getting worse and although she had asked to see the doctor again nothing had happened.

Finally, after another ten days had passed, she was given a confession to sign. It was uncomfortable reading but perhaps not as bad as it could have been. The emphasis was on how she had been seduced by the spy Anderson who was a CIA agent with links to Mossad (this was a new one to her) and how he had tricked her into assisting him in fermenting trouble amongst Russian Jews and persuading promising scientists to steal state secrets and then defect to Israel. There were some references to individual names and also much about the betrayal of the hospitality that had been shown to her in Moscow, and her deep regret and shame that she had allowed herself to be used and exploited by the enemies of the Soviet people. She expressed her gratitude for the good treatment which she had received and was thankful that she had been given the opportunity to express her remorse and explain the treacherous conduct of the spy Anderson.

Well, it looks like I'm the dupe, she thought, and Larry's safe enough now so I can't see it matters much what I say about him. She signed. Two days later she was escorted back to her flat, where she packed as much of her remaining clothing as she could take before she was driven to the airport.

'We will be expecting your continued cooperation,' was the last thing the colonel had said to her before wishing her good luck with her research into Russian literature. 'I hope we meet again some day, Mrs Davenport.'

11

Cambridge, 1986

Marianne sat at her desk watching the light fade through the tulip tree at the end of their garden while a sharp East Anglian wind blew yellow leaves across the grass. It was twelve years now since she had been expelled from the Soviet Union and five years since she and Edward had achieved their ambition of returning to Cambridge after what they now felt to have been exile from their natural home. Edward had finally obtained the consultant's position at Addenbrooke's which he had craved, and she had followed him back to the city which had been her first love when she had arrived in England nearly twenty years earlier.

Turning her gaze back to the screen of her word processor she thought again about her novel... filling the hiatus in her academic career and making use of all that knowledge of Russian history and literature, she had told herself. Initially worried that it might lower her standing among her academic peers, Marianne had started cautiously, then with increasing enthusiasm before hitting the buffers of self-doubt. What hubris, she thought, to imagine that I – French-born, American-bred, and now wed to England and an Englishman – how can I inhabit the Russian psyche, that place of such profound contradictions that even the greatest Russian authors are baffled by their own mysteries?

'Writing from a background of impressive scholarship,' Marianne doodled onto her screen, 'Davenport weaves a complex story of love and betrayal…' Then again: 'Davenport's impressive first novel converts her profound knowledge of early-nineteenth-century Russia into a story of suffering and survival, a redemptive tale of love and endurance…'

Hearing the front door slam, Marianne deleted the text on her screen and went downstairs to greet her husband, only to find that it was Izzy slipping past her to the kitchen.

'Hello, darling, I wasn't sure you were coming back for supper… As soon as Dad's back I'll start cooking – it won't take long…'

'No time,' said her daughter, pouring milk into a bowl of cereal and beginning to munch at speed.

'Does this mean you are going out again?'

'Uh huh.'

'You need more than cereal, particularly…' Deciding not to continue in that vein, she added, 'Why don't you let me make you an omelette or some cheese on toast – or I could make some pasta quickly…' Izzy shook her head. As she finished her bowl and stood up, Marianne said, 'You know, darling, we really need to have a talk…'

'Not now, Mum,' she replied, tearing past Marianne and up the stairs. Marianne sighed. What was it she had told herself all those years ago when she had learnt that she could never have another child? Izzy will be my cherished daughter and also my best friend. What a conceit that was. Maybe it would happen one day, but the last couple of years had not been easy and now this – a week ago – casually dropped into the conversation: 'No thanks, Dad. Pregnancy seems to have turned me off coffee.' Since then Izzy had avoided any discussion of the subject. At first she and Edward had wondered whether she was joking, but Marianne's close observation of Izzy's queasy look in the morning and unusual tiredness convinced her that it must be true.

'You just missed Izzy,' she said to Edward when he arrived home half an hour later.

'That's a shame. She's gone out for the evening, I suppose? Has she said anything?'

'No. I tried, but she wouldn't talk.'

'Do you get any feeling as to whether she'll want to have it?'

'No idea. I need to pin her down.'

'Are you going to try to steer her?'

Am I? Marianne wondered. She's seventeen and a half. It's now the beginning of November. The baby must be due around June. If she's lucky she might just get through her A-levels – if not, it would be a disaster. One way or another a baby at this age will seriously interfere with her life. And then there is the father. Either Andy – about whose unsuitability as a father she and Edward were in complete agreement – or some other unidentified boy. Marianne shook her head. 'I just don't know.'

'If she wants a termination, she should get on with it quickly,' said Edward. 'That way there's much less trauma – physical as well as psychological.'

'You think that's the right choice?'

'Yes.'

'You may be right, but I don't feel it's our place to encourage her to have an abortion. Anyway, if we lean one way she's highly likely to do the opposite.'

'Well, we must encourage her to make a decision. And soon. Then we can plan.'

After they had eaten, Edward turned on the television while Marianne glanced at the day's newspaper. Her attention was caught by a lengthy piece about Russia and Gorbachev's new policy of *perestroika*. Marianne had been a compulsive reader of articles on the politics of the Soviet Union ever since she had left the country a dozen years earlier. She longed to return for a visit but did not dare – even if she had been able to obtain a visa, which did not seem likely. She was encouraged by what she read about the attitude of the new regime. At least now, she thought, those terrible photographs must have been forgotten.

The photographs had not been without their consequences. Six months after she had returned from Moscow, a middle-aged man had turned up at their south London flat. Introducing himself as a diplomat from the Soviet embassy he asked her, in his strongly accented English, whether she had now settled back into her life in England after her 'interesting time' in Moscow, and enquired as to the progress of her studies in Russian literature. After the pleasantries were over Marianne said, 'So, what exactly have you come here for?'

'Mrs Davenport,' the man said, 'we would be greatly honoured if you would write an article for publication about your time in Moscow.'

'What sort of article?'

'We have taken the liberty of preparing a draft,' he replied, handing her several pages of typescript. Marianne started to read. The tone was not dissimilar to the 'confession' she had signed in Moscow, although it avoided any suggestion of a sexual liaison. It told the story of how she had been 'tricked' into helping Larry Anderson, a CIA spy, to gather material and how she had been persuaded to go to Georgia with him on 'a spying mission' and had been severely injured in an air crash. The article was part autobiographical thriller, part *mea culpa* for her involvement in espionage, but most of all an attack on her American spy master and his 'CIA bosses'. The whole concoction was laced through with such lavish praise for life in the Soviet Union that she couldn't help laughing.

'No respectable journal would publish this – and even if they did, no reader would believe it. It's completely over the top.' Sensing that he didn't understand her, she added in Russian, 'It's too obvious. Crude propaganda – no one would believe it.'

The man bowed his head. 'I understand. You do not have to follow the wording precisely. Please submit to us a re-draft.'

'What if I don't want to do this?' Marianne said, though she knew perfectly well what it was all about.

The man shrugged. 'There might be consequences. Moscow has led me to believe that you will cooperate.'

For the next few weeks Marianne agonised over whether to do what they wanted. Several times she had come close to telling Edward that she was being blackmailed but she pulled back at the last moment, remembering how she had lied to his face only six months earlier and how relieved he had been to hear her denial. As the colonel had said, it's one thing to suspect a past indiscretion – it's another to see the gory evidence.

She didn't feel any great compunction about being critical of Larry and his associates who had landed her in such an invidious position, but at the same time she did not want to be too offensive. Could there be some repercussions when she travelled to America, she wondered. Some adverse consequences to her parents?

In the end the whole process had become increasingly farcical. Drafts went back and forth between her and the Soviet embassy until eventually a text was agreed and, following instructions from the embassy, she duly submitted the article to the *New Statesman*, who promptly rejected it. Eventually the article was accepted by a small left-leaning journal in America where it lingered and died in the obscurity it doubtless deserved.

The photographs, however, remained with the KGB.

While Marianne no longer feared the ploys of Soviet propagandists, there were other consequences of her time in Russia which were less easy to forget. Her fractured pelvis had not healed well and she still walked with a noticeable limp – her war wound, as she called it; she knew now she would always walk with a limp and suffer recurring bouts of sciatica. Yet aside from the physical scars, her year in Moscow was now a well-ordered memory. In the security of her present life it seemed like a curious aberration; a time when she had lived dangerously – a high-octane existence bringing with it an intensity which would never be repeated. She had come close to catastrophe and nearly destroyed her marriage, but there was still some part of her which couldn't quite wish for that year to be wiped from her past.

Perhaps that's how soldiers feel, returning from a war, she thought, as she set off from her meeting at St John's

College towards the University Library the other side of the river. The sun had emerged suddenly after a heavy shower and was now reflecting off the wet road into Marianne's eyes as she trudged down Trinity Street. Deciding to cut through the college, she turned into Great Court, marvelling, as she always did, how to walk through Great Gate was almost to enter another dimension; a space unreasonably large but at the same time enclosed and private – almost intimate – enhanced by the perfect positioning of the fountain with its slim ionic columns now glistening wet in the low November sun. Crossing Trinity Bridge, Marianne glanced back at the Wren Library, imagining Byron sitting in his silent marble contemplation.

'Don't go there – I won't let you think like that,' said Dorrie the following morning when she and Marianne sat over their morning coffee discussing the welfare of Marianne's daughter. 'You're falling into that terrible cliché of "what did I do wrong?"; you haven't done anything wrong. You have been an exemplary mother. No one could have been more loving and supportive than you.'

'Perhaps too much?'

'That's ridiculous. Be positive. Izzy is a clever girl; whatever else she's done, she hasn't neglected her studies.'

Although several years younger than Marianne, Dorrie had become her closest friend. Having toyed with pursuing an academic career, Dorrie now taught English and drama at a secondary school in the city. Marianne would never forget her first sighting of Dorrie one warm afternoon in early summer as – with her flowing red hair and bare freckled arms – she tore about the stage, transporting Izzy's class of twelve-year-olds into the mysteries of Wonderland. Marianne respected her unsentimental approach to life.

'Have you talked to her yet?' Dorrie asked.

'Not yet.'

'Why ever not?'

'I've tried but there hasn't really been a good moment...'

'Don't be so feeble, Marianne. Kids respond to straight talking.'

'And you've had so many children.'

'I may not have had children, but I see them every day. You are forgetting that teenagers are my life now. I had to spend half of yesterday trying to get some year ten girl in my English class to stop snivelling over a failed love affair. We've had our share of pregnancies too.'

'OK, granted; you probably do know more about it than I do – except it's different when it's your own child... Anyway, you're right, of course. I must force the issue. I do worry that this will screw up her studies.'

'Not necessarily...'

'Fine, but...'

'I know; you'd love her to get into the university here but that was never likely to happen – partly because she is unlikely to get the grades but mainly because she doesn't want it. It's all too close to home for her.'

'Edward is furious with her for getting pregnant – though he hasn't said anything to her.'

'He has a point. There's no excuse for a girl of her age and intelligence.'

'I did, and I was a lot older than her. Our family are highly fertile – miss the pill for a couple of days and that's it.'

Dorrie smiled. 'I suppose if that wasn't the case you might not have had Izzy… Anyway, how's the novel going?'

'Badly. What am I doing, peeping about under the feet of the giants of Russian literature?'

'You mustn't…'

'It's OK, I haven't given up – but every time I try to work out what my characters might think or do, there's Bezukhov, or Levin, or Pushkin's Tatyana, answering for me.'

'You'll get there,' said Dorrie, rising from the table and giving Marianne a long hug. 'Keep at it – and speak to that daughter of yours!'

That night, as Marianne drifted into sleep, she found herself back in South America. It was the holiday she had taken with Edward to celebrate their return to Cambridge before he started at Addenbrooke's. Izzy is with them – how old is she? Perhaps ten or eleven. Those last years of innocence before the teenage battles begin. They are visiting the multiple waterfalls at Iguazu and paddling a canoe at the bottom of one of the falls. A rainbow arches over their heads – an almost tangible roof of colour which seems to Marianne a sign of divine approbation: your lives are in my protection. Izzy's blue eyes sparkle with wonder and Marianne feels a happiness which is painful in its intensity.

Edward smiles at her across the boat – the noise of the water is too loud for conversation – and she wonders again how she ended up with a man so kind and gentle: no virtue exhibitionist, but a truly good man. How weak it sounds to be labelled good; history swallows good men without trace. But to be good is surely the summation of all virtues; who would you rather have as a husband, she thinks, some artistic genius like Picasso – or a Burns or Byron? Surely not – Edward is a good man and I am a fortunate woman.

The following morning, being a Saturday, Marianne resolved to have a serious talk to her daughter. She listened periodically outside Izzy's door; when she heard noises suggesting that Izzy was awake, she went in and sat on the edge of her bed. 'How are you feeling, darling?' she asked.

'What's this all about?'

'I want to know if you've thought about it – I mean, what you're going to do?'

Izzy rolled her eyes and looked askance at her mother but said nothing.

Marianne sighed. 'About the fact that you are pregnant.'

'I didn't know I had to do anything. It just happens, doesn't it? You know, the baby grows inside you – then it comes out.'

'So does this mean that you've decided to have the child?'

'Oh, I see, you've come to tell me to have an abortion, is that it?'

'I haven't come to tell you anything. I just want you to know that I'll help you in whatever choice you make.'

'You'd prefer that I get rid of it, wouldn't you? I've rather spoilt your and Dad's idea of a perfect daughter.'

'Izzy, don't play games. It's your decision, of course, and you must think through the consequences carefully. But if you've decided to have the child, Dad and I will give you all the support we can.'

'Yeah, well, I'm not going to kill it if that's what you want to know.'

Marianne paused to consider this statement and compose her thoughts. 'That's fine, darling – I'm glad,' and she leant across to give Izzy a kiss on the forehead. 'I think that's brave but I think it's a good decision. You're going to have to be much more careful, though, with your health – cut out the alcohol and smoking, all kinds of smoking. What does Andy think? I mean, Andy is the father, I suppose?'

'You suppose? Do you think I shag every boy I meet?'

'Izzy, just tell me how Andy feels about becoming a father?'

'Actually, Andy's cool about it.'

'Well, that's good. Now come downstairs and have some breakfast, and we'll talk about a few practical things.'

Two hours later, when Edward returned to the house, he looked enquiringly at Marianne.

'She's going to have it,' Marianne said.

'Is she…' and for a few seconds Edward was silent, looking past Marianne, up the stairs, as if searching for inspiration. Then a smile spread slowly across his face. 'Do you know, I'm pleased. I didn't think I would be, but I am. Just think, Marianne, us as grandparents, a small baby in the house – it's really rather wonderful.'

Marianne threw her arms around his neck. 'I'm so pleased you think like that, Ed, because I do too.'

Marianne looked across to a photograph of Izzy, taken in Moscow during that winter – her blonde curls just showing under the little fur hat, her vivid blue eyes shining out – she could easily have passed for a Russian girl – that little girl now soon to become a mother herself. Marianne felt a great swelling of optimism and hope for the future. Tears began to prick her eyes. 'We'll make it work, Ed,' she said. 'With Izzy. Together, we'll make it all work.'

12

Marianne began to hang decorations on the tree.

'You look as if you are actually enjoying the whole palaver of Christmas,' said Dorrie, watching from the comfort of an armchair.

'That's because I am. This will be the first Christmas we've spent here in five years.'

It had become a routine for her and her sister Claire to go with their families to visit their parents in Vermont, but this year, with Edward's father unwell, they were staying in Cambridge and her parents were coming over to visit them. Her mother was especially looking forward to seeing Callum again – now an eighteen-month-old toddler.

Marianne also had much in her own life to give her satisfaction. She had been thrilled to find a publisher for the novel over which she had struggled for so long, and most of the reviews had been complimentary; equally important in terms of her academic career, she had just been awarded a research fellowship at recently established Robinson College to work on the dissemination of the Russian romantic poets into Europe through English and French translations. It was a project she had long wanted to embark on; the next few years promised to be busy.

'I'm just popping up to check on Callum. Help yourself to another drink if you want.'

'Thanks, but I must be going in a minute,' said Dorrie, draining the last of her whisky.

Marianne went upstairs and put her nose into the spare room to check that Callum was still asleep. She gazed at his chubby face. She didn't see much resemblance to Izzy, but then Callum was also different in temperament; far easier and more placid than Izzy had been at the same age – her daughter was fortunate. The birth of Callum, and the year Izzy had spent at home while Marianne helped her look after her child, had ended the stand-off between mother and daughter. Izzy seemed to have grown out of her need to fight with her parents and now appeared genuinely grateful for their support. Finally, her child had become the friend she always imagined.

'Are you getting Izzy home for the weekend?' asked Dorrie, getting up from her armchair when Marianne returned to the living room.

'I certainly hope so. She's gone to London to join Andy at a gig this evening, but she should be here tomorrow – perhaps even tonight.'

Now that Izzy had started her degree at Leeds it had been decided that during term time Marianne and Edward would look after Callum from Monday to Friday and Izzy would be back home on Friday night; at least, that was the theory, though sometimes it was not till Saturday that she would make it home to be with Callum. They had bought her a car, which Andy was also insured to drive, on condition that he never again took Izzy on the back of his motorbike, but she wasn't too keen on either of them driving the car late at night after a concert somewhere the other side of London.

'Andy still on the scene then?' said Dorrie.

'Yes, he's stuck around – I have to acknowledge that much in his favour, though part of me is inclined to think that Izzy would be better off without him.'

Andy didn't seem to have a job or any visible means of support – living, Marianne suspected, partly off Izzy and partly by scrounging occasional handouts from his mother in Glasgow. In term time he mostly hung around Izzy in her hall at Leeds; when in Cambridge he seemed to doss down at a squat somewhere off Mill Road. They didn't object to him staying with Izzy in their house but often he preferred not to – or Izzy discouraged him, they were never quite sure which. Possibly he found their home too restrictive for his drinking and smoking habits.

'I really must go now,' said Dorrie, giving Marianne a long hug. 'It's really all turned out pretty well hasn't it? The great baby drama.'

'I suppose it has,' said Marianne, laughing. 'Have a fantastic Christmas and see you in the New Year.'

'I will – and give my love to Ed and your beautiful daughter.'

Returning to the tree, Marianne was thinking about her parents arriving on Sunday, when she heard the front door slam and a few seconds later Edward came into the room.

'You've just missed Dorrie.'

'Oh, that's a shame,' he said, kissing Marianne and standing back to admire her decorations. 'I like it. But, I wonder, don't you think perhaps there are too many of those silver baubles – particularly on the window side?'

'I don't think so,' said Marianne, trying to keep the irritation out of her voice.

'What news of Izzy?' he said, walking back to the kitchen and pouring Marianne and himself a glass of wine.

'I don't expect her home till tomorrow. She said that if she can get away in time she might try to get back tonight, but I doubt she will.'

'Doesn't she have to go back to Leeds anyway?'

'Apparently – for a couple of days to finish some work.'

'Why doesn't she go straight back to Leeds then?'

'Ed, it's the weekend. It's supposed to be her time with Callum. Also, I need her here. I can't get anything done if I'm looking after Callum all day.'

'Well, it's a freezing night, not ideal for driving – I presume she's got the car?'

'That's a point – I suppose she might have taken the train.'

'Well, if she comes by train I hope she'll get a taxi and not hang around at the station for a bus. If she's not too late I don't mind picking her up.'

Conversation that evening centred on the arrangements for Christmas and the still unresolved issue of whether Claire and her family would come to Cambridge for Christmas Day or whether they would all go down to London to the rather grand house Claire's husband Peter had bought in Holland Park. They heard nothing from Izzy that evening and shortly before midnight they went to bed.

Marianne dreamed she was in Vermont. They were all skating on the pond: her parents, Claire and her family, Edward, Izzy, and Larry was there too – or was it Daniel? Whoever it was, he was pulling Callum round and round on a little plastic sledge and for some reason he seemed to think that he was Callum's father. Izzy skated behind Callum, lithe and graceful in her black woollen tights and red skirt, her fur hat pulled down over her ears, gazing with maternal pride at her tiny son. There was music playing, and now Izzy was doing pirouettes, faster and faster, but the music was too loud; sharp, high notes like bells – bells which turned into shrill ringing, dragging Marianne back into consciousness. She picked up the phone.

'Hello... What... who are you? Yes... say that again. Yes, I'm Marianne Davenport... Oh God... Oh no...'

'Who is it, Marianne?'

'... the police,' she whispered, turning to Edward. 'Yes,' she said back into the telephone. 'Yes, I understand – yes, the hospital... Yes, we'll come at once...' Putting back the receiver, she said, 'Oh, Ed, I can't bear it – there's been an accident...'

It was impossible later for Marianne to reconstruct the events of that night or the following days. Time ceased to be linear. It bulged; it contracted; it sprung forward at terrifying speed only to stall in a paralysing moment of agony from which she seemed unable to escape. Terrible fear, small shafts of hope, but mostly a crushing pain – a pain in her chest so all-consuming that it seemed impossible that she would be able to draw her next breath. There was also anger – a deep rage that this worthless boy had broken his promise not to take her on his bike and had destroyed their precious daughter.

On the fourth day – the nurse told her this; she had no idea how much time had elapsed – Marianne sat with Edward at Izzy's bedside with a form and a pen in her hand. She looked at her daughter, then again at the form.

The eyes were the hardest part. She knew them too well. Until she had suckled Izzy as an infant she hadn't believed it was possible for any human being to have such pure blue eyes: huge, round irises of the deepest sapphire which seemed to leave no room for the surrounding white. As she got older the blue became lighter with flecks of green and grey. Sometimes, if she was in a rage, Marianne would see flashes of yellow, like tiny nuggets of gold. But when she was happy her eyes seemed to bombard you with a beam of brilliant blue particles; it was an effervescence which few could resist.

The heart was easy. She was not sentimental about the heart. I could say that Izzy had a big heart, she thought, and it would be true; I could say she was generous hearted and that would also be true; I could even say that part of me was lodged in her heart, but what use are metaphors now? She ticked the box for heart just like she ticked the box for liver and kidneys and all those vital bits of our anatomy which we know are there but never see. Those parts were easy, but she couldn't do it for the eyes.

Edward reached out and put his hand on her arm. Marianne gave a small shake of her head. Gently he took the form from her, studied it, then ticked the box for eyes, signed it and handed it back to her.

Marianne took the pen from him and for a few moments she stared at Izzy's profile. Her small delicate nose, so perfectly proportioned, and her eyebrows with that distinctive curl which formed a slight upward tick at the outer extremity. The accident which destroyed her brain had left her face untouched, but the tape over her eyes and her slack mouth with the ugly ventilation tube marred the illusion of a natural sleep. Eventually she forced herself to look down at the form and make a scribble under Edward's firm signature. A half-hearted, deniable, apology for a signature was all she would permit herself before she dropped the form on the chair and hurried from the room.

On the way home in the car Edward said, 'It's just the corneas they need.'

'It said eyes,' she replied.

'Yes, but the only part of the eye they use is the cornea.'

'Old people donate their corneas,' she said. 'They must have enough of them.'

'They like to match up ages so they need corneas from young people as well.'

'What do they do with the rest of the eye then?'

'Well, they're valuable for research.'

'Spoken like a true doctor.'

Edward was silent but she couldn't resist continuing her assault. 'Can't you think like a father for once? They'll get every other bit of her; I just didn't want them to take her eyes. Couldn't you have just signed the form as it was?'

Marianne knew she was lashing out at him in her agony but she couldn't help herself.

'We didn't have to tick every box,' she said. 'It's not all or nothing. The form makes it clear that you can choose.'

'You're being illogical, Marianne. It makes no sense to be selective.'

118

'Why do I have to have sense? At this one moment in my life don't I have the right not to have any sense? To be senseless – to be foolish, even. To be a grieving mother?'

They continued their half-hearted quarrel – or at least Marianne's attempt at a quarrel and Edward's measured responses – but all the time she was hating herself for attacking him. *If anyone is to be reproached it should be me. Isabelle was the product of my upbringing. Still, her rebellious spirit has left one legacy,* she thought, *and I intend to cling on to him with every ounce of my strength.*

'How has he been?' she asked her mother when they got back from the hospital.

'No problem. He's been perfect. And sound asleep now.'

Marianne went to Izzy's room and looked in the cot where Callum lay. She didn't want to wake him but she couldn't help herself; she had to hold him. She picked him up and clutched him tightly, burying her face in his neck. Being such an easy child, he didn't wake up but merely murmured to himself and clung to her hair with one hand.

'You look exhausted, *ma chérie,*' said her mother, giving Marianne a long hug. 'I've cooked some pasta. Come and sit down and eat. Papa and I have already eaten so it's all for you and Ed.'

'Thank you, Maman – and thank you for being here. I don't know what we would have done without you.'

Marianne and Edward sat down at the table. At first there seemed to be nothing left for them to say, but Marianne wanted to turn their thoughts to something positive and that could only be their plans for Callum's future.

'We will adopt him, won't we?' she said.

'I hope we can, but it might depend on Andy.'

'But he's not going to live, is he?'

'I don't think so, but you never know. His injuries weren't as severe as Izzy's.'

The thought that Andy could live but Izzy die filled her with silent fury. That boy who had broken his solemn promise to them and thereby killed their only child. That useless layabout – what right has he to take Callum away from us?

Edward seemed to read her mind. 'It would be better for Callum to grow up knowing one of his parents.'

'Why?'

Edward didn't respond but simply raised his eyebrows at her.

'You know that Bill is not my real father – God, I hate that expression. No one could be more real. But he's not my biological father.'

'I know, and if Andy dies so be it – but if he pulls through?'

'What's wrong with us? We've spent more time with Callum in his short life even than Izzy – let alone Andy.'

'You can't deny the right of a parent.'

'We are young enough to be his natural parents. What can Andy offer this child? He has no job, no prospects…'

'It's not just about material things.'

'Maybe, but how could he look after Callum? Or are you thinking about his mother? My God, is that what you're thinking? He'd want to take Callum up to Glasgow for his mother to look after? We can't let that happen, Edward. Please tell me we won't let them take Callum away.'

'Calm down, Marianne. Andy is in a coma and is unlikely to survive. We'll continue to look after Callum and see what happens.'

Possession is nine tenths of the law, she was thinking, but somehow it didn't seem right to say it in relation to a child.

Still, the longer Andy stays in a coma the better. Better still that he should never wake up.

'So what is the prognosis for Andy then?' she asked. 'What condition will he be in if he does wake up?'

'Hard to tell. The longer he is in a coma the worse the outlook. He might wake eventually to full consciousness, or he might technically wake up but remain in an unresponsive vegetative state.'

'What happens to him then – I mean, if he is in what you call a vegetative state?'

'Well, they just continue to look after him.'

'For ever?'

'Pretty much. What else can they do?'

'Is that so different from Izzy then?'

Edward sighed, and reaching across the table, took Marianne's hand. 'Darling, I've explained before. It's completely different. Izzy's brain stem has died. None of her most basic bodily functions work anymore. If they were to turn off the ventilator, then sooner or later her heart would stop. Andy can breathe on his own. Even though he's unconscious, his reflexes still function.'

After a pause while Marianne stared at her plate, Edward went on. 'You are right in one sense, however; if Andy stays in a long-term coma or wakes up in only a vegetative state then it would probably be better for all concerned – and especially for him – that he should die.'

Marianne had heard all this before but she kept on needing to hear it again. Brain death is so hard to come to terms with. She could sit with Izzy and hold her soft warm hand, feel her pulse and hear the beep of her heart monitor. Every now and then there would even be a small twitch of movement. She talked to her all the time even though she had been told a dozen times there was no possibility that she could be heard.

The previous day Marianne had taken Callum to say goodbye to his mother. She recognised that this was her own conceit and Edward had been strongly opposed.

'Izzy cannot be aware of what you are doing and Callum will either be indifferent or possibly you will succeed in upsetting him,' he said. 'Either way, nothing will be gained.'

Marianne had been determined to go ahead, notwithstanding Edward's objections. Part of the reason – which she would never have admitted to Edward – was a lingering fantasy that somehow the doctors had got it all wrong and the presence of Callum nestling against his mother, or perhaps crying for her attention, would trigger a response in some deep recess of her brain which was still alive. She chose a different argument in her response to Edward.

'Just because we can't remember anything that happens at that age doesn't make it meaningless; it doesn't mean the child has no emotional response.'

'Of course he will recognise his mother, but I don't know what you mean by emotional response. He can't understand illness or death.'

'He will be pleased to see her.'

'I'm not sure he will. He won't understand what's going on. He'll be disappointed that she won't wake up for him. Don't forget, she has tape over her eyes and a tube coming out of her mouth.'

'Well, I'm doing it anyway,' she said. 'If he cries and is upset, then somewhere that experience will lodge in his subconscious and that would be a perfectly proper response to the death of his mother.'

122

In the event, Callum hadn't cried, although Marianne had rather hoped he would. He climbed over Izzy, tried to take the tube out of her mouth, poked her around the face a bit and then got bored. I don't suppose he'll have even the most residual memory of seeing her, she thought, but it was important to me, and perhaps that's justification enough.

That night, as Marianne lay beside Edward, she sensed a tension between them. They both seemed to know that despite their disagreement there was nothing more to be said. In time, she could feel that he was drifting into sleep, but she remained resolutely awake. She felt she had been awake the whole night, floundering in misery and self-hatred, but she realised she must have slept for a while when she awoke from a dream in which Izzy's ice-blue eyes were fixed on her. 'You always said you loved me but now you have come to kill me,' said the Izzy of her dream. Marianne's heart was beating violently with the thought that she might be betraying her daughter in her hour of greatest need. She turned to see that Edward was already awake. He smiled at her.

'Did you get some sleep?' he said.

'A little. Ed… we are due at the hospital this morning to give them the final go ahead…'

'Yes.'

'… to switch off Izzy's life support and take her organs?'

'That's right.'

'I know we've talked about this many times already, but I want to ask you this once more – and I shall never ask you a more important question.'

'Ask then.'

'Please don't answer immediately. Think about it as if for the very first time. Is there any chance – even a one per cent

123

chance, even the tiniest chance that you can't even quantify – that if Izzy was kept alive, that perhaps there might be some change in her condition or perhaps a breakthrough in medical science, some new development that would restore her brain and allow her to resume her life?'

'Marianne...'

'I said don't answer immediately.'

'Alright...'

Marianne lay in silence for several minutes while Edward got up and went to the bathroom. She didn't doubt what his answer would be but she felt that she owed it to Izzy to make this one last plea.

'The first thing to understand,' said Edward, coming back into the room, 'is that Izzy is already dead. Although we use the expression "life support", what we really mean is that her tissue and organs are being temporarily kept in a viable state by artificial means. No one is going to end her life by switching off the ventilator and disconnecting the feeding tube, or indeed by removing her organs.'

Coming around to Marianne's side of the bed, Edward sat down and held her hands in both of his. 'Brain death is a very conservative diagnosis, Marianne, there is no such thing as being almost brain dead. Like pregnancy, it's either yes or no. Every possible test has been carried out to confirm the diagnosis. But to answer your question directly: without a sufficient blood supply, the cells in the brain begin to break down – soon there won't even be the remnants of a brain to restore. Also, without an active brain, it's not possible to preserve the body's organs artificially for very long. Everything will soon begin to decay.'

She put her arms around Edward's neck and pulled him

down towards her, holding him tightly to her chest. 'Thank you. I love you, Ed – and I'm sorry to go on...'

'I wouldn't expect anything else.'

'Do you mind if I spend some time alone with Izzy this morning?'

'Of course.'

'Can you come back for me at lunchtime? I'm going to need you then.'

'I'll come back whenever you want.'

So Marianne went alone to the little side ward in the hospital where Izzy, or whatever was left of her, was being kept in that state which Edward insisted was death, but which to her non-medical mother still looked cruelly like a form of life and she said all the things that she couldn't say in front of Edward. She begged for Izzy's forgiveness where she thought she had failed her, and forgave her for the occasions she had disappointed them. She rejoiced with her in all that she had crammed into her short life; she was happy that she had known love and sexual fulfilment; she praised her courage in keeping her child and gave thanks for the satisfaction that motherhood had brought her. She congratulated her on the early stages of academic success and thanked her for the love and happiness she had given to her parents. Above all, she promised she would do everything in her power to ensure the security and happiness of Callum.

She wished there had been some part of her that still believed in the possibility she could be with Izzy again in an afterlife, but if she had ever believed in that fairytale, such time had long since passed.

When she had exhausted everything she had to say, she let her tears flow until she was choking with heavy sobs, like a steam train slowly gathering speed out of the station. This time she didn't hold back; she lay on the bed beside Izzy and howled in anguish at the death of her beloved daughter; a long series of tortured, animal howls came from deep inside her until the noise she was making brought two nurses into the room. Gently they prised her from the bed and sat her in an armchair and wiped her face with a warm cloth while one of them called Edward and told him she was ready to go home.

13

When she thought about it afterwards, Marianne would acknowledge the curiosity she had felt when she first saw the hand-written envelope with its Russian stamps. Curiosity, but not alarm. She didn't recognise the handwriting as belonging to either of her academic correspondents. Who was the mysterious Russian letter writer, she wondered? Perhaps a fan of her novel – but that would normally come via her publishers. Perhaps an invitation to attend a conference or give a lecture? This was certainly possible now that the old Soviet Union had come to an end.

Dropping the bills and junk mail onto the kitchen table, Marianne opened the envelope and studied the contents. Her first reaction was to laugh – but it was a laugh with a distinctly hysterical edge. I am being blackmailed, she thought. Good old-fashioned blackmail for money. Twenty thousand pounds or the photos go to her husband, her parents and anyone else the blackmailer thought 'would be interested to see them'. Inside the envelope, folded in a square, was a colour photocopy of one of the pictures Colonel Petroff had shown her nearly twenty years earlier.

A good thing Edward's at work, she thought, as she studied the picture carefully for the first time. Although wincing at its pornographic nature and at the long-forgotten images of Larry, she couldn't help a frisson of self-regard – I was pretty fit in those days, she thought – and Larry wasn't so bad either. Then she carefully burned the picture in the sink and washed the ashes down the drain. The letter itself she concealed in her study.

Marianne had watched with growing satisfaction the implosion of the old Soviet Union and the collapse of communism. With every new development, she had felt further removed from any lingering anxiety that the past still had power to harm her. Now, with a sharp constriction in the muscles of her stomach, she realised how naïve she had been. Chaos, economic collapse and wide scale corruption were what characterised Russia under its new president, Boris Yeltsin; what better environment could there be for a former KGB file keeper to make a bit of money on the side?

Marianne went to her car to drive into Cambridge. She and Edward had moved out of the city two years earlier; it was a move facilitated by Edward's inheritance from his father, but it suited Marianne to escape the constant reminders of Izzy. Their new house, a strangely shaped piece of Victorian gothic in a village a few miles from Cambridge, had appealed to her; a bit of an ugly duckling, one of her friends had called it, but to her it had already become an elegant swan.

For the rest of the day Marianne tried not to think about the letter. Holly, her child minder, would be picking Callum up from school. She had two student supervisions in the afternoon. It was absurd, she thought, to be worried about what happened all those years ago. With some degree of success, she ploughed through her day, returning to the house in time to help Callum – now nearly six – make a tower from Lego, practise his piano and his writing and then read to him before he went to sleep. As usual with Callum, the book had to involve machines – this time a submarine called Penelope.

Edward was working late at the hospital that evening – not an unusual event – so she cooked herself some supper, cleaned up the kitchen and sat down with a book and a glass of red wine. Really, I should cut out the wine, she thought, it's shocking how much weight I've put on since Izzy died. Tonight, however, I definitely need a drink. She forced herself to look down at her book, though without much expectation of being able to read. Christ, this is bad timing, she thought; just when our marriage has regained some form of equilibrium after years of tension over Callum.

It all went back to Izzy. The agony of her death had rocked their marriage; she sensed unspoken criticism from Edward even though she wasn't sure why. The loss had fired in Marianne an unspeakable grief but also a fierce determination to hold on to Izzy's child. The problem was Andy – he had started to recover. He had been moved up to Glasgow to be closer to his mother. What else could she have done? Why couldn't Edward see it her way? She shut her eyes and found herself re-living those impossible months.

Every day she is getting bulletins about Andy's improved condition and every day she fears that sooner or later he will want to take Callum away from them. Edward infuriates her with his calmness. 'We must wait,' he says, 'talk to him when he is fully recovered. See what he wants to do.'

'No,' she insists, 'we must act.' Every day the same conversation in different forms.

'I've spoken to the hospital,' Edward says. 'They say he is still quite confused and certainly not in a position to make any long-term decisions about his future or Callum's.'

'But his brain is not damaged?'

'They don't think so, but the accident caused a haemorrhage which has affected the movement of his left side.'

She decides to visit Andy herself. 'Fine,' says Edward, 'but bear in mind he was in a coma for ten days – you'll need to treat him gently.'

Marianne sits in the train as it rattles its way north towards Glasgow. My husband may be a saint, she thinks, but I am not. Why does this wretched boy deserve to be treated gently when he broke his promise and took her on the back of his bike; rode through an icy December night and killed my precious child – my beautiful Isabelle.

The pain of her loss gnaws at Marianne – a hungry rodent forever feasting on her organs. I will not take any risks with Callum, she vows. I promised it to Izzy – a death-bed promise to care for Callum always. There has hardly been a day when I haven't held him in my arms. How could I ever contemplate giving him up?

She finds Andy in a rehabilitation room at the hospital – beige walls only partially enlivened by some naïve oil paintings in strong primary colours donated by friends of the hospital. He is sitting in a wheelchair by a window. 'Hello Andy,' she says. He looks at her calmly but without emotion, then turns away. His head has been shaved and now the hair is beginning to grow back unevenly. A thick scar is visible from his right ear to the centre of his crown.

'I am glad to see you are getting better,' she says. He nods.

'You know that Izzy is dead?' She knows that he has been told but she has to say it anyway. She looks for a sign of contrition but again he simply nods. She wonders if he can speak – then it occurs to her she hasn't yet asked him a real question.

'How do you feel?' she asks. 'Are you in pain?'

He looks at her with a mixture of anger and resignation; a lopsided half smile moves across his face but his eyes are cold. 'Aam feckin' brilliant – can ye nae see?'

OK! she thinks. This is more like the Andy I know – except he tended to be a little less Glaswegian when he was in Cambridge. She expresses regret about his injuries. How bad is his paralysis? she wonders. He sits so still it's difficult to tell. She tells him about Callum – they are looking after him; he is happy and well. Then she broaches the subject of adoption. She and Edward think this would be for the best. Does he agree? She waits nervously for an answer. She has a sackload of arguments ready to deploy if necessary – including financial inducement – but it isn't necessary.

'Micht as weel. I'm nae much use tae him noo.'

'Yes, well…' She is confused by his ready agreement and not sure how to respond.

'Noo she's gone,' he adds, looking at the floor, and it suddenly occurs to Marianne that Izzy was the focal point of Andy's existence. She is not the only one who is devastated by Izzy's death.

'Yes,' she says. 'Yes, it's hard for all of us to think of life without her.'

Marianne talks on for a while, then she moves to the second part of her plan – get him to put it in writing. She knows that in the circumstances it has little value but she wants to come home with something tangible.

Andy seems indifferent, and under her slow dictation he writes: *'Dear Marianne, I agree that it will be best for Callum if he is adopted by you and Edward.'* She gets him to sign and date the note then she tucks it away in her handbag.

For reasons which she can't fully understand, Edward is furious with her. 'Don't you see how wrong it was to put pressure on him when he is still traumatised by the accident?' he says.

'I absolutely did not put any pressure on him…'

'It's worthless, what you got him to sign – probably counterproductive…'

'It's just a start, Ed – don't you understand? But it's the right start.'

But he doesn't understand. He seems wilfully obtuse in his refusal to comprehend that what she is doing is best for them all: for Callum, for her and Edward – even for Andy. Andy will be free of any responsibility for the child – free to make a fresh start, she tells Edward, but he doesn't want to listen.

Under her urging they start the adoption process; social workers visit regularly. Edward cooperates but frequently criticises her: 'We're rushing this, Marianne. Andy is getting better – he'll be a different person in a year or two.'

'Rushing! More like the proverbial tortoise, if you ask me. It could be another two years before we get the adoption through.' And all the time Marianne frets that Andy will change his mind. She has been told that he has regained almost complete movement on his left side and mentally seems fully recovered. She knows they will be talking to him. 'Are you absolutely sure?' they will say. Daily she expects to be told that Andy is coming to visit, or that he is having second thoughts.

She prepares for this eventuality – her counter-attack. No holds will be barred; she will beg, she will bribe, she will threaten – she will blame him for Izzy's death. She will raise arguments about his fitness to have anything to do with Callum – his past drug taking, his physical and mental state.

She worries that Edward's misgivings will be detected by the social workers, and so does everything possible to ensure that Edward is out when they come. 'We really must make an appointment when your husband is here next time,' they say.

She sighs. 'You know how it is – marriage to a hardworking and dedicated doctor,' and they smile in acknowledgement.

She is sure she is fighting this battle both for herself and Edward. She is determined that they won't share Callum, that it would not be in his best interest to have two fathers. No halfway house will satisfy her – only full adoption with Andy giving up all rights. And in the meantime, she continues to fight with Edward.

'I can't believe what you were saying tonight,' he declares one evening after a dinner with friends. 'All that stuff about Andy being half paralysed and brain damaged. It was never true, and certainly not now. Why do you have to fucking lie to everyone?'

Edward hardly ever swears but he has been drinking more than usual that evening. This time she is the calm one. 'It's what you have to say in these cases, Ed – explain why the birth parent is giving up the child for adoption. It's what we'll tell Callum: "Andy couldn't look after you." If I exaggerate a little it's just to make it easier to explain.'

'And to satisfy your own conscience for stealing his child.'

'God, you talk shit sometimes. I don't know why you are acting like this.'

And she doesn't. She doesn't understand Edward at all now. He always wanted a son. He loves his grandson – he will be a perfect father to Callum as he was to Izzy, but somewhere in that complicated mind of her husband he can't accept what is happening. Some kind of self-denying ordinance is at work; he wants to be a father to Callum but not at the expense of someone else – someone whom he thinks has a better claim to love and be loved by their three-year-old grandson.

Then it happens, the event that she has dreaded. Andy is coming for a visit. She remains calm. What is the thinking behind this? she asks. It seems that the Scottish social workers think Andy should see his child again before making an irrevocable decision. 'Best if your husband is here as well,' they say.

'Of course,' she says, but she deliberately agrees a date when she knows he will be in London. She doesn't know how he'll react and she doesn't want to take any risks.

When Andy arrives, he is smartly dressed and accompanied by two social workers: Yvonne, her normal Cambridge visitor, and another woman from Glasgow. He walks with a trace of a limp but otherwise seems recovered. He gives Marianne a sheepish look.

'Hello Andy,' she says, 'you are looking very well.' Her voice sounds a little too loud.

'I'm fine,' he says, and she notices that this time the Glaswegian accent is largely absent. They stand around awkwardly in the kitchen watching Callum through the window as he plays in the sandpit outside.

'I'll bring him in,' she says.

134

'It's OK, we can go out,' Andy says, and to her surprise he leads them all outside.

'Hello, Callum,' says Yvonne, squatting down beside him. 'Are you making a castle?'

'Boat,' says Callum.

'Callum, darling, this is Andy,' says Marianne. 'I don't suppose you remember him, do you?' Eighteen months ago he had been Daddy but she won't use that word now – not now Edward is Daddy. Callum looks briefly at Andy then turns back to the sand.

'How you daein', Cal?' says Andy. Callum ignores him. Marianne says she will make coffee and returns to the kitchen, watching through the window as the group outside watch Callum – standing around in a self-conscious semi-circle. They are just here to observe him, she tells herself. Yvonne had promised they would not confuse Callum by trying to re-awaken a lost connection, but when they come into the house the other woman does exactly that.

'Don't you remember your first Daddy?' she says, kneeling beside Callum and looking towards Andy. 'Come and give him a cuddle,' and she takes Callum's hand and half leads and half drags him towards Andy. Predictably, Callum struggles, falls over and starts to whimper. Marianne shoots an angry glance at the woman, picks him up, puts him on her knee and lets him nibble a biscuit. The visit seems to drag on interminably. She watches Andy out of a corner of her eye. She senses he is feeling less and less comfortable and she also notices how his eyes keep straying towards Izzy's framed photo on the dresser. Andy's silence fills the room. Marianne declines to interrupt so the two social workers make small talk and try to interest Callum in a toy car.

Andy stands up. 'I think I'd like to leave now,' he says. Muttering their acquiescence, they all rise to their feet. She is standing directly opposite him. They look at each other. She is searching for the right words but he speaks first. 'It's for the best,' he says. He looks again at Izzy's photo. 'It's what she would have wanted.' Marianne takes a step forward and hugs him. He turns away blinking, seemingly embarrassed at his own emotion. And then they are all gone. Marianne sits on the sofa and hugs Callum; she presses her face into his neck and then she is also weeping, for herself and for Isabelle – but also for Andy.

Marianne knew she needed to talk to someone and so the next day she arranged to have a lunchtime sandwich at The Eagle with her friend Dorrie. The day was warm for the end of March and she and Dorrie sat outside in the yard. Dorrie sipped her lager and gazed at Marianne with her kelly-green eyes, while Marianne gave her an abbreviated version of her affair with Larry twenty years earlier and the photos which the blackmailer now had in his possession.

'For fuck's sake Marianne – just tell him,' she said. 'I mean, that long ago...'

'It's different for you.'

'What – because I've gone off men?'

'Not just that. I mean, you've chosen a different way – no commitments... Edward is just so... so moral – I don't know how he'd react. And the pictures...'

'Explicit, are they?'

'You could say that...'

'Well, my advice is to do nothing. Blackmail is a game of bluff – if the blackmailer has to pull the trigger, then he's lost.'

'But then so have I?'

'Look, I doubt this guy has any experience of the world outside Russia. For all he knows the letter didn't arrive, or more likely your husband knows all about the affair and you are already having a laugh together about it.'

'You are probably right, but…'

'Anyway, you don't have a choice. If you pay him money, he'll only come back for more. Even if you get hold of the negatives you don't know how many prints he may have.'

Marianne looked down at the remains of her prawn sandwich. 'So I have to sit it out?'

'What else? Go to the police – there is nothing they can do; and the Russian police? They would probably want their cut of the blackmail price. My guess is that you'll get a couple more letters then he'll give up.'

Marianne contemplated Dorrie's advice as she walked back down a narrow lane towards the river and her own college. The high walls on either side seemed to speak to her sense of entrapment. Not for the first time she cursed her cowardice all those years ago in not confessing everything to Edward. In the years after their return to England, their marriage had been rock solid and Edward was such a kind and considerate man… But now things felt different. Izzy's death had damaged them both; she suspected that he looked back to the time he had tried to persuade her to have a second child – and the accident that had finally prevented it. Then there was the adoption. Even now he was inclined to criticise her for 'lying' about the extent of Andy's incapacity. God, what a shithole I have dug for myself, she thought.

And so, she waited; and as Dorrie had predicted, another letter arrived a week later which she also ignored. A month passed without any more developments until one Saturday morning Edward walked into the kitchen, holding an envelope addressed to her.

'No stamp,' he said. 'It must have been hand delivered.'

Some student wanting more time, she thought. Really, they should leave these notes for me in college. Tearing open the envelope, she watched as a folded square of paper floated to the ground.

'Something's fallen out,' Edward said, but as he bent down to pick it up, its familiar shape sent a stab of adrenalin down to her fingertips and she made a grab for it first. Holding the folded square in one hand she glanced at the letter, muttered, 'Usual student nonsense...' and retreated as casually as she could to the privacy of her upstairs study.

This letter had a more personal flavour than the previous one. The author was arranging for it to be delivered by hand. He was poor – a former servant of the state, now unemployed. She was rich – a fellow at a Cambridge college and successful novelist (hardly, she thought). He didn't like what he was doing but he had no choice. He would accept £15,000 but this was her last chance. She should write back to the Russian address immediately confirming her consent and she would then receive payment instructions.

The fact that a 'friend' of the blackmailer had been to their front door felt uncomfortably threatening and the temptation to pay up was now almost too much for her. She knew that she would be happy to pay if she could be certain that the matter would end there but – as Dorrie reminded her in several phone calls – there could be no such certainty. So once again she let time pass and gradually it seemed that she had successfully called his bluff. She congratulated herself on staying strong and thanked Dorrie for her wise advice.

It was the day before Callum's sixth birthday and she had just put him to bed after a fraught session with his reading book. So much slower with his reading than Izzy, she thought, and yet his physical coordination never ceased to impress her. He could copy a picture with surprising accuracy and already he was able to play simple tunes using all his fingers on the piano. She was in the final stages of making his birthday cake – an elaborate structure which had to be turned into a medieval castle – when Edward returned to the house.

He looked pale, and her first thought was that he must be sick. 'Are you OK?' she asked, but he barely looked at her as he went upstairs. She continued her cake construction and a few minutes later he came downstairs again carrying a small hold-all.

'I'm going out,' he said.

'Is something the matter?'

'Yes – something is the matter,' and then it happened all over again. Just as the KGB colonel had thrown the photos across the desk to her, Edward reached into his bag, took out a large brown envelope and threw it onto the floor at Marianne's feet. 'I daresay you will recognise the scenes,' he said, before marching out of the front door.

She didn't need to look inside the envelope, but she did anyway – and then she ran out into the driveway where Edward was getting into his car. 'Ed – Ed, please… Don't rush off like this. Please talk to me – I'm sorry, but I can explain.'

'Explain?' he said, opening the car window. 'What is there

to explain? Except perhaps my stupidity in trusting you all these years.'

Marianne watched as Edward accelerated out of the drive. Slowly she walked back into the house, hesitated at the bottom of the stairs and then walked up to Callum's room. Lying on his bed, she stroked his hair while her tears pooled onto the pillow beside him.

Although Edward was back in the house within twenty-four hours he refused to say anything to her and moved his things into the spare room. For days, they didn't speak, avoiding each other in the house. Edward spent long hours at work, coming back late and going straight to his room. Marianne struggled through her working days, wrestling with her predicament. Forty-eight, getting fat, my only child dead. I have my wonderful grandson but now I may lose my husband. At night it was there again: a round face, blond hair and a squat upturned nose. The bright cornflower eyes staring at her, pale and frightened, before the face began to fade, slipping from her sight like a regretful moon behind a bank of dark and threatening clouds. The worst thing was that now the face sometimes metamorphosed into Izzy and sometimes even Callum. She would wake breathless and run to check on Callum, before returning to her bed and another long and sleepless night.

She was desperate to lance the boil with Edward. There needs to be a row, she thought. He needs to swear at me and let out his anger. Then perhaps we can be reconciled. She knew, though, that Edward was almost incapable of rowing so she had to provoke it herself.

'For God's sake, say something to me,' she said, ambushing Edward in the kitchen one morning before he left for work. 'I know it was wrong, and I'm very sorry, but it was a long time ago and not everyone is as perfect as you. And perhaps you could have a little sympathy for me – for months they've been trying to blackmail me with these wretched photographs.'

Edward turned from filling the kettle and surveyed her calmly. 'It's not so much the affair – that upsets me certainly – but you lied when I asked you directly and you've been lying ever since.'

'That's a terrible cliché, Ed – it's also a crappy argument. An affair is a lie – it's one and the same thing. Successful day's research, darling? Absolutely, when I wasn't fucking Larry in the Minsk Hotel.'

'I didn't mean those kind – I mean…'

'You mean when you asked me directly…'

'Exactly.'

'It's all the same. I lied because that's what people do – to avoid your anger but also to spare you pain. Anyway, it was all over by then. But look – I did regret afterwards that I hadn't told you the truth, but my denial just spilled out, and then… well… you looked so relieved I just couldn't bring myself to tell you…'

'… no lack of opportunity.'

'Sure – best part of twenty years, but…'

'I've begun to see you as a different person these last few years – the easy way you lie about Andy and Callum – now I realise that's how you are; you find it easy to deceive people when you want your own way…'

'Is that how you really think about me – one indiscretion in twenty years and I've become a serial liar?'

'How do I know there weren't others.'

'There weren't.'

Edward shrugged. 'I'm going to London for a few days,' he said. 'I'll let you know when I'll be back.'

Marianne sat at the kitchen table. I am losing my husband, she thought. It's absurd – ridiculous, if it wasn't so tragic... how has this happened? Our perfect marriage destroyed by what? An unimportant affair so long ago it sometimes feels as if I dreamed the whole thing. And Callum; my insistence on adopting our motherless grandchild. How could we have done anything else? Surely this can't be the end?

She called Dorrie and left a message: 'Please, please I need to speak to you.'

14

Marianne watched as her sister Claire strolled across the airport concourse towards a fashionable clothes shop; slim, elegant and still with an unmistakably Gallic air, Marianne couldn't help feeling a stab of jealousy. Claire had made a big fuss the previous year about becoming forty – the sort of fuss people only make when they know that they are a showcase for their age: hey, look at me and admire; still slim and sexy with barely a wrinkle; unbelievable that I could actually be forty! Marianne, on the other hand, felt all of her fifty years and had no wish to advertise her age.

Claire also had the good fortune to be rich, having married a merchant banker who had been in the right place at the right time for the Big Bang of 1986, whilst Marianne had borrowed every penny she could to buy Edward out of his share of the house at the time of their divorce, and then had to convert part of the house to a separate flat to help pay the mortgage.

As they settled into their seats for the transatlantic flight, they talked briefly about the painful circumstances of their trip – their father's failing health – before Claire turned to the subject of Marianne's love life.

'Well?'

'Nothing doing.'

'Nothing? No sex since Edward? It must be over two years now?'

Marianne hesitated. She wasn't about to tell her sister. It was six months after she had parted from Edward. Sunday morning. Callum is staying with his father. She hasn't slept well, still in her dressing gown, she is sitting up in bed. Dorrie is visiting and has brought her a cup of coffee. Dorrie is comforting her – she leans forward, her red hair falling across her face, and kisses Marianne on the cheek. The kiss turns to a hug and then they are lying face to face on the bed. Dorrie moves closer and kisses her gently on the lips. Shocked by the sudden intimacy, Marianne doesn't know how to respond. She feels the heat from Dorrie's body and wants to pull her closer but something prevents her. Dorrie is caressing her – stroking her face, feeling her breasts through her nightie – but Marianne is frozen with indecision. Now Dorrie's hand feels cool on her bare thigh. She knows she wants to be touched but she does nothing, and says nothing. To her immense relief Dorrie doesn't stop.

Later that timeless Sunday morning – as it glides deep into the afternoon – she becomes more confident. The touch of skin on skin, the smells and tastes of another body, re-awaken her senses, dormant since Edward threw the manila envelope to her across the kitchen floor. Her anxiety about the scarring across her pelvis subsides – helped by Dorrie's jokes about her own bodily imperfections. Seldom has the proximity of another person felt so good.

'No. No men in my life at present.'

'I still can't believe that Edward left you because of that affair twenty years earlier in Russia.'

'I suppose there were some other things around the edges.'

'Like him not being so faithful himself?'

'No, no – not at all. Edward wasn't like that.'

'Are you so sure? When I stayed with him that time I visited you in Moscow, I overheard some phone calls – I mean, I didn't like to say anything with you being so badly injured – but I had my suspicions…'

'I'm sorry, Claire, you don't know what you are talking about.'

'OK, if you say so.'

England may be a green and pleasant land, thought Marianne, as she gazed out of the car window, but surely nothing can match Vermont at the end of May for its multiple shades of green, its absurdly luxuriant grass populated by the ubiquitous black and white Holstein cows, the emerald green of the beech trees and the lime green sugar maples. 'I will lift up mine eyes unto the hills.' She had always loved the opening words of that psalm. From the bedroom of her childhood home she could see the distant hills changing colour with the seasons. 'From whence cometh my help.' She had misunderstood the psalmist in those days. She didn't understand why help would come from the hills but perhaps it was because they rose up towards heaven, because they were closer to God.

Sitting in the back seat beside her sister, Marianne watched as the hills gradually disappeared and the Burlington road entered the coastal strip alongside Lake Champlain. While her mother drove them to the hospital with Aunt Edith beside her, Marianne had a sudden recollection of being taken to see her great-grandmother a few days before her death. She remembered how upset she had been to be dragged away from their mountain holiday. When she thought about it now she realised Gran-gran had never been a real person to her – just something old and smelly, sometimes in a chair with a blanket over her knees, other times propped up in bed. Usually she had seemed cross and visits had been intolerably dull. Even her dolls had been more real to Marianne than this old woman.

Visiting her beloved father now would be a wholly different experience. A fit and active man of seventy-five – a retired doctor who hardly ever sought medical advice for himself – he had begun to suffer from sore throats and indigestion. His own doctor diagnosed a virus and prescribed antibiotics. The sore throats didn't improve, he began to suffer from difficulty in swallowing, saw a specialist, had further tests, and suddenly he had oesophageal cancer; a six-centimetre tumour in the gastro-oesophageal junction.

That diagnosis had been eighteen months earlier. Marianne had flown over to visit and found him in robust spirits, but chemotherapy, an operation, followed by another bout of chemo had taken its toll. Now the only hope was deemed to be a further operation. They had been warned that despite – or perhaps because of – his medical background, he was not coping well with being a patient. She wished she was seeing him alone, or perhaps just with her mother.

'When will they operate?' said Claire, leaning forward to speak to her mother.

'Tomorrow, I think – they postponed it for a couple of days so you can see him first.'

'Does that mean they think he won't survive the operation?'

Marianne watched as her mother flinched at the bluntness of Claire's question. 'Don't be silly, of course he'll survive – the doctors wouldn't do it if they didn't think it would help him. It's just that... well, he'll be very weak for a while afterwards.'

The visit to her sick father proved even more difficult than Marianne had anticipated. Confronted simultaneously by his wife, his sister and his two daughters, the suffering man had looked acutely uncomfortable. It was not that he was displeased to see his daughters, Marianne later surmised, but to be seen in this state of vulnerability – hairless, shrivelled, eyes sunk in their sockets, his face a mask of pain and anxiety – was obviously torture to a man who had spent his life curing the sick and being the bedrock for his family.

Marianne longed to throw her arms around him and cry, but somehow the etiquette of the occasion seemed to preclude any overt show of emotion. They made stilted conversation – showed him photographs of their respective children and told him what was happening in their lives – while their mother and Aunt Edith talked as if he would soon be home and cured from this temporary indisposition.

After their visit, Marianne's mother went to do some shopping with Edith while Marianne and Claire walked from the hospital, past the imposing buildings of the university and down College Street towards the lake, remembering the time when Burlington was the biggest metropolis they had known.

'You're limping,' said Claire.

'How observant. I've limped for twenty years – since the plane crash.'

'I never realised.'

'You saw me limping in France.'

'I must have forgotten.'

Turning in to the Church Street Market Place, they stopped at a pavement café. Marianne gazed across to the mock-Georgian City Hall building, such a solid and comforting presence from her past. She watched Claire look down the pretty street as if seeing it for the first time; her body language suggesting that, while she was prepared to sit there for a coffee, this was not where she belonged; it was not London and certainly not Paris.

'Callum will be disappointed if I don't have a Ben & Jerry's,' said Marianne. 'It's the only thing he remembers about coming here before.'

'Well, it is about the only thing Burlington is famous for.'

For a while the sisters sat in silence. There was much that could have been said: their father was clearly dying, though their mother seemed to be in denial, but neither felt able to articulate their thoughts. Eventually Claire said, 'You know I can't stay very long.'

'Meaning?'

'Assuming the operation goes OK I'm going to fly back at the weekend.'

Marianne shrugged. 'If you have to.'

'What about you?'

'I think I'll stay. I think Maman needs someone.'

'How long?'

'I've subcontracted my last week of teaching for the term and then it's vacation. I'm thinking I will fly Callum over and spend the summer here. I can carry on with my writing and Maman would enjoy getting to know him better.'

'Really, I am the one who should be staying – after all, he's my father.'

'Oh, so you think he's not my father too? For Christ's sake…'

'You know what I mean…'

'I do know what you mean, but it doesn't make the slightest difference…'

'Hey, chill. I didn't mean to upset you. I think it would be good if you stayed. I would like to but it's just not possible…'

Exactly why it was not possible, Marianne was unsure, given all the resources at her sister's disposal, but she said nothing more on the subject. She knew it wouldn't work for them both to stay and she had already decided she would be the one to see her father through to the end.

They had been warned that the operation would be lengthy so they didn't arrive at the hospital till midday but it was a shock to find that the surgery was still on-going. Two hours later the surgeon came out to announce that the operation had been a success – though his ashen face didn't reflect the optimism of his words. He explained that the severity of the operation meant that the patient would be kept sedated and breathing through a ventilator until the following morning. Since it was only possible for one person to stay Marianne and Claire prepared to leave their mother and return the next day.

It was something about the expression on her mother's face which alerted Marianne.

'Are you sure you're OK to stay, Maman?'

'I'll be fine.'

Marianne looked at her sister. 'One of us could stay if you prefer?'

'Sure,' said Claire, looking far from enthusiastic.

Marianne turned back to her mother who looked away, muttering, 'I think it really should be me.'

A polite argument ensued, broken finally by Marianne's insistence that she would stay and the others could return early the next day to be there by the time he woke.

In retrospect Marianne rather wished she had not been the one to stay. She would never forget the moment her father began to regain consciousness. It was earlier than she had been led to expect – before six o'clock – and the duty nurse had just left the room, when her father started to cough. His face – pale but calm under sedation – began to turn crimson and as he opened his eyes his face took on a look of such terror that for a moment Marianne was unable to act. It was the heart monitor – now beeping at an alarming rate – that finally sent her screaming for the nurses. It seemed to take forever, while her father coughed and writhed in obvious agony, but eventually they removed the ventilator. For Marianne, it was incredibly distressing even to witness the scene; she could only imagine what it must have been like for her father.

15

It was over an hour's drive from her parents' village to the
hospital in Burlington and Marianne and her mother took it
in turns to visit. Sometimes Callum, taken out of school early
and now in Vermont with Marianne, would come too. The
visits were not getting any easier. The more Marianne tried to
comfort her father the more it felt as if he was trying to push
her away. His physical pain seemed to be getting worse and
this in turn was setting up an emotional barrier she couldn't
penetrate.

'You don't have to come every day,' he would say.

'I don't. I take it in turns with Maman.'

'Either of you.'

'We want to see you.'

'I can't imagine why…'

'Papa…'

'… such a disgusting wreck. It might be better if you came less…'

'I love you, Papa.' She reached out for his hand. 'I know I haven't been around enough since I left home but I want to be with you now. Just let me sit here – you don't have to talk.' She watched as her father turned away from her and screwed up his eyes, his pale thin lips clenched together. It's his pain, she thought, he wants to be alone to cope with his agony, but when she queried his obvious pain with the hospital she was told – not for the first time – that he was not yet 'due' his next medication.

Marianne also saw it as her role to keep up her mother's spirits. Often she would try to steer the conversation away from her father's illness and reminisce about some happier times in the past, but this was not proving easy as her mother gradually retreated into herself and became increasingly unwilling to engage in anything beyond the most mundane conversation. Marianne had imagined long intimate evenings with her mother during which she might be able to piece together some of the missing episodes in her early life. She might even – she imagined – persuade her mother to open up about her wartime experiences and Marianne's biological father. He must have been a German or else surely Maman would have been more open about it; but who cares now – who would blame her, here in America, fifty years after the end of the war? I will have another go at her tonight, she resolved.

Back in her parents' house Marianne watched as her mother prepared a dish of duck with a sweet cherry sauce for their dinner. Callum had been tired so she had fed him early and let him go to his room. She poured a glass of wine for them both and said, 'Maman, will you tell me something about my biological father? I mean, you've never even…'

Her mother's reaction had been sharper even than she had expected. 'Your father is the man lying in hospital in Burlington.'

'Of course, but…'

'You don't need to think about any other father.'

'I don't understand why you can't even tell me…'

'You were conceived during the war; that much you already know. You never knew the man and he never knew you. You don't need to concern yourself about it. Please don't ask me again.'

Marianne put down her glass and left the room in frustration. She went to Callum's bedroom, sat down on the bed and gave him a big hug. Honestly, she thought, my mother treats me like a child. So ridiculous.

'Mum, I'm trying to watch this,' said Callum, wriggling from his mother's embrace. Marianne got up. She didn't approve of television in the bedroom – still, this was only a temporary treat for him. Right, she thought, if Maman won't talk to me about my father, there is another subject on which I need an answer and I won't let her off the hook on this.

Back in the kitchen Marianne helped her mother peel and slice vegetables, then she said, 'Maman, you know all my life I've had this vision, this apparition – I wouldn't really call it a dream – it's a child's face, and it seems to be accusing me and then it fades away. It doesn't sound like much but it's not just the face which I see, but the nausea – terror, even – which invariably come with it.'

'I remember you had bad dreams, but I thought you had got over them.'

'Well, I haven't. Do you know why I see this face?'

'I always assumed it was the boy next door – you used to play with him. I think you were missing him.'

'Missing him?'

'After they moved.'

'Are you keeping something back about this, Maman?'

'What do you mean?'

'Why did they move away?'

'I don't know – perhaps after the boy drowned…'

'He drowned? Christ, you never told me that.'

'Didn't I? Well, it happened when you were quite little and then they moved to another village.'

'What was the boy's name?'

'Ryan, I think it was.'

'So why don't I remember him if he was my friend?'

'You used to play with him when you were two – you were not quite three when he died – people don't remember what they did at that age.'

'So what happened?'

'What happened? I don't remember exactly.'

'When did he drown?'

'I couldn't say, but it was soon after Christmas – about two years after we came to live in Vermont. You would have been three that January.'

'Was I involved?'

'Involved – no, why should you have been?'

'I just don't know why this face I see – if it's his face – should evoke such a feeling.' Marianne walked to the window. I will lift up mine eyes unto the hills. She watched as the evening sun decorated the distant summits with tints of pink and yellow leaving heavy shadow in the foreground, a lake of darkness across the valley. Could she see that face now if she concentrated? She wasn't sure.

'Was it because of the accident that they moved?'

'I don't know. Perhaps.'

'I remember the house and the pond – but not very well. When did we move?'

'Really, Marianne, why are you asking me all these questions? I can't remember exactly. It was when your father started to work in Burlington. Before Claire was born. I suppose you were about eight or nine.'

'So what happened exactly? How did the boy – Ryan – drown?'

'I have no idea, I don't think anyone knows – now come and sit down.'

Marianne sat at the table and helped herself from the dishes which her mother had set out. Usually they would find things to talk about while they ate but this time they chewed in silence. Her mother seemed to be lost in thought and Marianne was sure she knew more than she was letting on.

'Maman, I'm sorry but I still think there is more to this than you are telling me.'

Her mother looked up, confused, as if she had been in another place. 'More to what, *Chérie*?'

'To the drowning of Ryan – and how it relates to me.'

Her mother said nothing, but a frown came over her face and she looked away from Marianne as if she saw something on the kitchen wall behind her, something perhaps in the montage of family snaps taken at different times over the years: Marianne making a snowman in the back garden, carrying baby Claire in her arms, skiing between her father's legs.

'Look at me, Maman. I am hardly a child. I am fifty. If there is something to tell, then for God's sake let me hear it.'

'You may be fifty but you are a post-war child,' said her mother, suddenly more animated and looking intently at Marianne. 'You didn't live through what we lived through. Amnesia is a blessing. I couldn't live if I had to remember all the bad things that happened. Forgetting has been my way of survival – it's nature's way to heal us and I am convinced it's the best way.'

'We are not talking about the war…'

'This modern obsession with rummaging in the cupboard for old memories,' her mother continued, ignoring Marianne's intervention, 'dusting them down, examining them under a microscope, adding a dash of imagination – a touch of fantasy – to what is barely a memory at all, and then worrying how these best forgotten events might be affecting your life today; it's a terrible mistake. Leads to nothing but unhappiness.'

'Maman…'

'In your case, you don't actually remember so it's pointless to speculate on what may have happened.'

'If I had no memory at all then I might agree with you. But I do have something: the face and the terrible feeling which goes with it – it's been with me all my life and I need to understand. It might help…'

'The truth is I don't actually know…'

'But you know more than you've told me?'

'Yes.'

'So?'

'It won't help you, Marianne.'

'Please, Maman, just tell me.'

'Pour me another glass of wine and I'll try to tell you. The truth is I've done my best to block out the memory myself, so I can't be sure what I really do remember.'

156

Marianne refilled her mother's glass and waited.

'As I said, it was a few days after Christmas. The weather, which had been very cold, had thawed somewhat and there was wet slush on the ground.'

'In the morning?'

'Yes, the morning. You know, we regarded the garden as a safe place, so by the time you were nearly three we weren't necessarily watching you all the time.'

'Was Ryan there?'

'Please don't interrupt all the time, *Chérie* – no, Ryan was not there. Do you remember the layout of our house and the O'Connors' – later on, the Johnsons' – next door?'

'More or less. There was a pond at the bottom of the garden which somehow went through to their house as well.'

'Yes – both houses had gardens which backed onto the same pond. Naturally, with a small child in the house we had the pond securely fenced off.'

'What about their garden?'

'I'm coming to that. They had also fenced the bottom of their garden but anyway there was a wooden picket fence between the two gardens – as well as trees and shrubs – so you couldn't just walk through. When we wanted you two to play together we – or the O'Connors – would lift one of you over the fence.'

'So, what happened that morning?' said Marianne, knowing that she should let her mother tell the story in her own way, but desperate to get to the heart of it.

'I was doing something in the house – I can't remember quite what – when I heard you crying and found you at the back door, wet to the skin and shivering with cold. I was mystified as to how you had got so wet but sometimes there were big puddles when the snow was melting so I thought you might have rolled in one.'

'My God – so I might have been in the pond as well?'

'At that moment I didn't think of the pond – I knew it was safely fenced off, and my main concern was to dry you off and comfort you. Then... well... the phone rang and it was Margaret O'Connor sounding agitated and wondering whether we had Ryan. I said no, but I would come downstairs and check. I met her in the garden and we spoke over the fence. A couple of minutes later, she discovered that the ice was broken on the pond and she became hysterical, screaming Ryan's name. I climbed over the fence into their garden and ran down to where she was.'

Marianne watched, transfixed, as her mother took another sip from her wine glass. Why have I never heard this before? she thought. How can I be hearing this for the first time now?

'The wire fence at the bottom of the O'Connors' garden was quite high,' her mother continued, 'too high for her to climb over, but Margaret just launched herself at it, fought it like a mortal enemy, and somehow broke it down enough to get to the pond. She tried to walk on the ice to where the broken area was – about ten yards in – but the ice wouldn't support her weight and she was floundering up to her waist in the water, trying to break her way through the ice. I could see it was hopeless so I ran back to the house and called the police and fire service.'

'So what was I doing while this was going on?'

'I couldn't say exactly but when I got back to the house you were sitting silently at the top of the stairs holding one of your dolls. Of course, I tried to question you, how did you get so wet, did you go on the ice, did Ryan fall in, did you fall in? But you wouldn't answer. In fact, you didn't speak for the rest of the day.'

'And the police came?'

'Yes, the police came and… well, I don't know exactly how long it took, but they found little Ryan's body at the bottom of the pond – under the ice.'

'How did he get through the fence?'

'The police came to the conclusion that he must have rolled under it.'

Marianne shut her eyes. I was there, she thought. I'm sure I was there. Then it suddenly came to her, a small fragment of memory. 'I climbed the fence. I mean, the wooden fence into their garden.' She said it as a statement but her mother took it as a question.

'I don't know, but it's possible.'

'No, no, I remember now.'

'How can you?'

'That old wooden pony with wheels, I pushed it up against the fence.'

Her mother nodded.

'So you know I did. You knew about the pony?'

'Well, of course I was anxious to know whether you had been there, so I looked at the fence and I did see your horse, but if you did climb over I don't know how you got back again.'

'Easy, there was a tree nearer the pond – on the other side of the fence – it had a low branch a couple of feet off the ground.'

'I think you're now remembering from your later childhood, *Chérie*.'

Marianne shook her head. 'No, I was there. I know it. I must have been in the water with Ryan. How else could I have got so wet?' Her mother was silent and Marianne knew that this was what she believed as well. 'You never told the O'Connells, did you? That I had come in wet and crying and what you later suspected?'

Her mother shook her head.

'Did you even tell Papa?'

'I told him something but not everything.'

'You buried the whole thing.'

'In a way we both did. You never spoke about it. I thought that perhaps you had suffered some sort of trauma – normally you would jabber away but you didn't speak a word for the rest of the day. Later you seemed to have forgotten about it – nature's healing amnesia – and that's how I left it. Whatever happened – and we will never know – was best left like that: unknown and unknowable.'

'Maman, I was there – in the water with him – I know it.'

'Now there you go, Marianne. That's exactly why I never wanted to tell you, because now your imagination is taking over. You will think you remember things which actually you don't.' It was then that her mother articulated a thought which was lodged in the back of Marianne's mind but which she hadn't quite had the courage to confront. 'I don't think you could have fallen through the ice with Ryan because, if you had, I don't see how you would have got out.'

How did I get out? It was a question which haunted Marianne throughout that summer and beyond. If I was in the water – and I'm sure that I was – why didn't I drown too. In the following days Marianne tried to ask more questions but her mother had clammed up. 'I have told you everything I know – and I can see already that it was a mistake.'

Marianne tried to put the whole episode from her mind and concentrate on being strong for her mother and doing what she could for her father in the last days of his life. She also tried her best to ensure Callum had a good time, taking him camping in the mountains and on swimming trips to the lake. Her days were busy enough, as she watched the long, drawn-out trauma of the ending of her father's life; but at night, when she wasn't thinking of her father, and wondering whether there wasn't an easier way for a life to end, she would sometimes see that face again and then the same question would come back to her: how did I get out?

Part II

And the commencement of atonement is
The sense of its necessity.

16

Spring, 2033

Nearly forty years had passed since her mother's revelations about her early childhood in Vermont, and if now, in her eighties, Marianne sometimes struggled to remember familiar names, her memory of the drowning boy had expanded and intensified; what had been once merely a haunting face, had become a distinct narrative – still fragmentary and still mysterious – but with a conclusion she could not avoid. Although objections could be made as to the reliability of her memory – and she was critical enough to make these to herself – such objections did nothing to lessen the clarity of the images which continued to float into her consciousness when she least expected.

While the mystery of the dead boy continued to haunt her, a different mystery had been resolved in a more straightforward way. Her mother's diaries had finally revealed the identity of her biological father – at least by way of his nationality and a letter of the alphabet. It was this information which she had just disclosed to Callum, and to her disappointment he appeared less interested than she had expected. Still, she thought, for someone who never even knew his own father, information about his great-grandfather must seem very remote.

It was the beginning of the Easter school holidays and Callum and Helen were making another trip to Australia. Callum had driven up on his own to see Marianne and say goodbye. Without Helen beside him he had been unusually frank about some of the problems in his life. While in England he had been trying to keep his architectural practice in Melbourne ticking over. This had now reached a tipping point. One of his two associates had already left and with little new work coming in he would have to make the other one redundant. The business would have to close, with significant debts to pay off.

Callum bent down to kiss his mother on the cheek. 'Don't get up,' he said, 'I'll let myself out. And don't forget Leah will be coming on Tuesday.'

Marianne smiled. 'I'm not likely to forget. I'll ask Anna to pick her up from the station. And one of these days I would like to see my other grand-daughter again.'

'Well, I'm hoping she might come over this summer.'

Marianne wished her son a safe trip and listened to the front door close before getting up from her armchair and walking over to her desk. Opening her laptop, she logged on to her bank account and her separate mortgage account. She was also draining money faster than she could afford. Interest on the equity release scheme was ratcheting up the debt. Even with the separate flat rented out, the house was still costing her too much. Anna's salary was a luxury she could barely afford but she couldn't contemplate doing without her. Then there was the money she had loaned to Anna and her boyfriend so that he could start his own restaurant. That had not been an entirely altruistic gesture, she acknowledged to herself. Finally, there were Leah's school fees. It had been an impulsive gesture to offer to pay for private schooling for Leah – and one which she certainly couldn't afford. Still, only one more term to pay.

Despite her own difficulties, she wanted to help Callum; it seemed suddenly a matter of great urgency, and she sat staring at her screen trying to imagine a way this might be done while the light faded around her.

Back in France, she is sitting with her sister Claire on a swing sofa at *Les Trois Cheminées*, watching Callum across the lawn on the other side of the garden. He is attempting to make a drawing of the house in his careful, methodical way. He is seventeen, and whereas at that age Izzy was slim, agile, sharply opinionated, and often confrontational, Callum is the opposite. Although certainly not fat, he has a solid build and walks with a slightly rolling gait. His face has a fleshy appearance and his eyes – though technically blue – are much paler than Izzy's, with tinges of yellow and muddy green. Lacking the physical grace of his mother, he gives the impression of having a rather precise and fussy air; famously tidy to the point of obsession, he contradicts the stereotype of the messy teenager with which Marianne became familiar from years of picking up after her daughter. What worries Marianne is that – unlike Izzy, who was never short of friends, both male and female – Callum often seems almost to relish a solitary existence.

Les Trois Cheminées, so called after its three prominent chimney stacks, is Claire and Peter's farmhouse in the

Auvergne. A tranquil spot, not far from the fast-flowing Allier river. Heavy clouds are beginning to roll up the valley and a warm wind tugs at the awning over their seat. The forecast thunderstorm may well be on its way. Marianne notices that Callum has stopped drawing and is now hunched over his mobile phone.

'I'm afraid there is no signal here,' says Claire.

'He doesn't need a signal,' Marianne says. 'He'll only be playing a game.'

'I'm worried Callum's a bit on his own here. Bernard seems to think Callum is too young to bother with, but I'll speak to Juliette when she's back from her nature walk. She needs to look after him – he's a guest here after all.'

It's the Saturday at the end of their first week at the house. Juliette, a botany student, has decided to go for a walk and Callum has volunteered to go with her. Marianne is both amused and delighted that Callum has taken to following Juliette around like an obedient spaniel. Having had to cope with her daughter's boyfriends from the age of thirteen, she has watched closely for signs of Callum's interest in the opposite sex – but has detected none. She has, on the other hand, observed some traits – a dismissive, almost contemptuous attitude towards girls, which causes her some concern. Perhaps I am worrying unnecessarily, she thinks, as she sees Juliette and Callum head off together. Is it wrong of me to hope that she might seduce him this holiday? Do all mothers think like this about their sons? She doubts, however, that it is likely to happen. Juliette, a gentle and well-mannered girl of twenty, tolerates Callum. She does not look like a sexual predator.

The plan for the day involves an expedition to the historic town of Le Puy en Velay. Peter and Bernard have gone off early while Marianne and Claire have agreed to stay behind until Juliette and Callum get back from their walk; they will all then meet in Le Puy for lunch. Juliette has promised to be back by noon.

By the time it gets to 12.45 Claire has lost patience. 'I have tried to call her but it's highly unlikely they will have signal wherever they are.' She scribbles a note saying there is cheese and pâté in the fridge, leaves the key in the usual place, and together with Marianne they set off for Le Puy. 'I know what Juliette's like once she gets into plant mode; she forgets about everything else,' says Claire.

'Well, Callum certainly won't do anything to hurry her.'

'No, I don't suppose that he will.'

It is not the first time that Marianne has visited Le Puy en Velay and as they approach the town she sees again the colossal statue of the Virgin and Child high on the *Rocher Corneille*, incongruously pink in the midday sun. With his hand raised in blessing, the Christ Child seems to turn away from the other startling pinnacle of rock, where the tenth century chapel of Saint Michel d'Aiguilhe perches precariously above the town. Visiting Puy, a place steeped in religious tradition and famous as a starting point for pilgrimages to Santiago de Compostela, elicits in Marianne a surprising sense of wistfulness, almost of regret. Despite her intellectual atheism, somewhere inside her there lurks a yearning for the certainties of her Catholic upbringing – when a Hail Mary, repeated enough times, could expunge wrongdoing and confession could wash away all sins. How satisfying it must be, she thinks, to be able to walk the St James's Way and know that you could reduce your own or someone else's time in purgatory. What greater sense of purpose could there be in life?

169

'When we stop I'll call the house to see if those two are back yet,' says Claire. 'I don't suppose they'll mind being on their own.'

Marianne smiles to herself at the thought of Callum and Juliette spending the day together – though within minutes, as if delivering a sharp slap across her face as reward for her presumption, the day proves to be anything but the romantic tryst for which she has secretly been hoping.

As they drive into Puy, looking for somewhere to park, Claire's phone rings. 'Hello? Hello… Peter…? What? A snake? Are you serious? Oh Christ… yes… Langeac. OK… we'll turn around… OK… at the hospital – we'll meet you there.'

'What's happened?' asks Marianne, seized by a sudden panic for her son.

'Juliette's been bitten by a snake – poor child. She's quite allergic to stings and bites so this won't be doing her any good.'

Marianne immediately tries to suppress the shameful sense of relief that it is Juliette, not Callum, who has been bitten.

'Are they dangerous – snakes around here?' she asks.

'Can be.'

'How did they get to the hospital?'

'Apparently, Callum carried Juliette to the road and flagged down a car; thank God he was with her.'

Marianne observes Claire; she is driving fast but she does not seem unduly worried. 'Do you need me to look at the map?' she asks.

'No, I think I'm OK.'

Twenty minutes later, when they are still some way from Langeac, Claire's phone rings again. Marianne holds out her hand ready to take the phone – rather preferring Claire to keep both hands on the steering wheel – but Claire grabs the phone and presses it to her ear. 'Peter... Christ... where are you...? What? Bad? How bad...? Brioude? Alright, we'll head up there. She's going to be alright, isn't she? Asp...? Callum did... God... Oh God... We're on our way.' Putting the phone down, she turns to Marianne: 'Christ, they're taking her by ambulance to Brioude. It seems they haven't got the right anti-venom in Langeac.' This time there was real fear in Claire's voice. 'It was an asp viper – the most dangerous type of viper – and she's having a bad reaction.'

Silently, Marianne presses her hands together and says a prayer – a fervent prayer to expunge the guilt of her own relief that Callum is not in danger, and to beg that non-existent deity to save Juliette.

'How do they know what kind of snake it was?' she asks.

'Your son photographed it with his mobile. Can you believe it? Fucking genius, that boy – you underrate him.'

As the car hurtles north, Marianne shoots discreet glances at her sister. Her usually relaxed features are transposed into a rigid mask; the tendons of her neck tight as the strings of a violin, a damp patch glistening on her cheek below the sunglasses. Marianne searches for something reassuring to say.

'At least she's in an ambulance now.'

Claire nods. After a long silence she mutters again, as if to herself, 'Thank God he was with her.'

Forty-eight hours later, when Juliette is no longer in danger and the events of that day have been pieced together, there is no shortage of praise for Callum's role in the saga. 'I was trying to reach a type of rock-rose I hadn't seen before,' says Juliette to her mother, 'and I stepped backwards onto the snake. While I was like, screaming in shock, Callum took a photo of the snake.

'And Mum... Mum, he carried me – piggybacked me –

for nearly two miles to the road. And he only put me down once in all that time. They said at the hospital that if I had had to walk – which I don't think I could have done anyway – the poison would have spread around my body and I would probably be dead now. And he was so sweet, Mum. I mean, I was in total fucking agony and screaming and crying with my whole leg swelling up in a really gross way and I was beginning to feel I couldn't breathe and he just kept on telling me to stay calm. The only thing he was worried about was not speaking French. "Just in case you lose consciousness," he said, "give me the words for snakebite and hospital."'

The night before they are due to leave, Marianne is having dinner with Claire and Peter while the others have gone to town to have a drink – Juliette's first drink since she has been released from hospital.

'You know, Marianne,' Claire says to her, 'it's as if Callum had been trained for that event. He did everything right: photographed the snake, carried Juliette to the road – which was an amazing feat of strength and endurance. He flagged down the first car and persuaded the driver to take her to the hospital. Remarkable.'

'What's more,' says Peter, 'Juliette told me that she hadn't a clue how to get to the nearest road but Callum somehow seemed to know. When I asked him about it he told me that he had been looking at the big Michelin map which we have on the wall. He said that he liked maps.'

'That's true,' says Marianne, 'and he's always had an extraordinarily good sense of direction.'

'All I can say,' says Peter, 'is that you don't need to worry about that boy. Steady under fire – that's what I'd call it; a pretty useful quality in life.'

172

It is impossible for Marianne not to feel pride and gratitude that Callum has acquitted himself so well and that the snakebite saga has not turned into the tragedy it could so easily have been. He may not have had a romantic adventure, she thinks, but he has clearly grown in stature this holiday, bathed, as he has been, in the gratitude of Claire's family.

When the time comes to say goodbye, Juliette gives Callum a long hug and a kiss. 'If you decide to check out the uni at Edinburgh,' she says, 'make sure you come and see me.'

What a pity their ages are not reversed, Marianne thinks. They are really quite well suited.

'So Leah is coming to stay tomorrow – I must buy food,' shouted Anna through the open kitchen door.

'Yes, I'm going to help her revise for her A-levels.'

'She's a lucky girl – to have you help her,' said Anna, bringing a cup of coffee to Marianne's desk.

Marianne sipped her coffee and thought again about Callum and the snake saga. There had always been something dutiful, almost heroic, about Callum and yet sometimes his response disappointed her. What she had discovered in the diaries about her father – which she had found so extraordinary that she hadn't known whether to laugh or cry – had not elicited the expected response. A remarkable coincidence, he had acknowledged, though without appearing much interested.

Now that I've told Callum I can tell Anna, she thought, and she smiled as she watched Anna carry a plate into the kitchen and then come back to wipe the table. When Anna noticed she was being watched so carefully – almost, it seemed, obsessively – she smiled back, but with a look of puzzlement hovering around her eyes.

'Sometimes you look at me in strange way.'

'Do I? It's just that I'm feeling happy today. You make me happy.'

'I do? That's nice – but I don't know how.'

She had made the discovery a few weeks earlier but had kept it to herself. At first her mother's diary had seemed to confirm what she had always suspected – that her biological father had been a German soldier. Referred to only as 'V', it had seemed a brief but genuine love affair with a young soldier billeted at their house. Then she had come across the critical passages. She checked them, read them again and then sat back and laughed out loud.

'I have discovered something about my real… my natural father.'

'You mean in Second World War.'

'Yes.'

'He was German, perhaps?'

'No, not German.'

'So he was French, like your mother?'

'No, not French, Anna. Latvian.'

Anna stared at her. Perhaps unsure about what she had heard, she said, 'Your father was Latvian – like me?'

'Exactly.'

'Oh my God! You are serious? My God – Latvian. I can't believe it. Perhaps we are related?'

'That might be expecting too much.'

'I can't… that's just… just so fuckin' amazing – I'm sorry, I shouldn't say that – but show me where it say this. What was his name?'

'Sadly she never seems to name him. Only just the letter "V".'

'V – could be Vanags, or Vasiljevs or…'

'I think the V may have been his first name…'

'Oh, I see…'

Marianne showed Anna the passages where her mother had referred to conversations with V about Latvia – its perilous geography, sandwiched between Soviet Russia and Nazi Germany – and how he had been a reluctant conscript into the German army.

'That's right,' Anna said, suddenly serious, 'our history in last century was very hard.' Then, brightening, she said, 'We need to give him a name. Perhaps Valdis? Or Vilns? Or would you prefer Viktors?'

Marianne laughed. 'Yes, alright, we'll call him Viktors,' and she watched while Anna danced from one foot to another, her eyes shining wet.

'You are Latvian – it's like we are related. I can't believe it – so amazing.' Then she said, 'We must celebrate. Stefans works tonight so I will stay and cook you dinner and you can tell me what you know about Viktors and I will tell you about Latvia – and maybe we drink a little wine…'

'Alright,' said Marianne, and she found that she too had to blink away the tears.

Leah had been in the house for barely five minutes before Anna broke the news to her.

'Are you serious?' said Leah. 'Gran's real father was Latvian?'

'It's true – Marianne showed me in the old diaries.'

'Wow – that's so cool,' and she gave Anna a long hug. When Marianne confirmed the news to her, Leah said, 'You've got to write a book about all this, Gran.'

Marianne laughed. 'I suppose that's what I am trying to do – but first I have to complete the translation.'

'Dad's told me about your Russian novels – I'm planning to read them.'

'Well, you're very welcome but best wait till after your exams.'

Leah was one of those teenagers who didn't like to work alone. Marianne had identified this trait on earlier visits, so now she and Leah worked together in her sitting room, swapping from desk to armchair or sometimes sitting at opposite sides of Marianne's large partners' desk. On this occasion Leah was occupying the whole of the desk, laptop open and books spread around her. Marianne sat reading in her armchair but would occasionally look up – usually when Leah started muttering to herself, such mutterings being a precursor to a request for help.

'Oh Lear, Lear, Leah. Beat at this gate – and get my fucking mind to work.'

Marianne looked up from her papers.

'Sorry, Gran – I just don't seem able to get my brain into gear today.'

'I supposed you've had some fun with those puns.'

'Not me, but the kids in my class think it's hilarious. "Is Leah completely mad, or just a fool?" – that kind of thing.'

'Have you got a problem?'

'OK – so why does Cordelia die? It's so unnecessary.'

Marianne laughed. 'You're not the first person to think that. What's your own view?'

'Well, our English teacher says that she shows too much pride in not playing along with her father's game – but I don't agree.'

'She is quite brutal, what is it? "… according to my bond; no more nor less."'

'True…'

'Perhaps she should have humoured her old father?'

'Yeah, maybe in private she would have done – but not after her sisters spewed out all that bilge. The critics all concentrate on the father-daughter relationship, but that scene is more about siblings – she knows she loves her father more but she can't bring herself to compete…'

'Good – you're obviously thinking about it. So, would the play be better if Cordelia had lived?'

'Well, less grim – more balanced.'

'But is that the nature of tragedy?'

'I guess not – but there's that bit at the end where Albany says everyone should get their just deserts.'

'And do they?'

'No. Yeah, I know – small character flaws lead to big disasters in tragedies.'

'Maybe it's not Cordelia you should be concentrating on here, but Lear himself?'

'So her death is just part of his tragedy. The final punishment for rejecting the person who loved him most.'

'Exactly. But don't forget there is also redemption – before her death, and his own – he recognises her goodness and his own love.'

'Still, it's quite depressing.'

'Yes, it's a bleak outlook – perhaps a world where Cordelia might not want to go on living? Have a look at the existential critics. You don't have to agree with them – just be aware. Have you read *Hamlet* yet?'

'Yeah, sort of, but I need to go through it again. So much happens. I mean, *King Lear* is our set Shakespeare tragedy, but Mrs D wants us to know *Hamlet* for what she calls a comparison text.'

'Would you like to have a session on *Hamlet* tomorrow?'

'Yeah, that would be really helpful.'

'Good. On that note, I think I will go and make some tea.'

Marianne hobbled to the kitchen, thinking back to her daughter Izzy. Izzy had been bright and diligent but she hadn't ever wanted Marianne to help her with school work – at least not after the age of eleven. As Marianne filled the kettle, Leah appeared at her shoulder. 'Thanks again, Gran, for taking me to that concert last night. You know I really didn't want to go.'

'I could tell.'

'I mean, two hours of classical music – I would never have chosen that.'

'So how do you feel about it now?'

'Pleased I came – it was awesome, but I feel so ignorant about music.'

'Your parents do seem to have neglected your musical education – you know, your father was quite a good pianist as a child.'

'Dad? Wow, he never said. I shall have to ask him to play something.'

'Now I have another proposal – for this Friday. I have two tickets for *Richard II* at the Arts Theatre – would you like to come?'

'More Shakespeare? I don't know… If it was like, another tragedy, then maybe it would be relevant…'

'There's more to life than just your A-levels, you know. Anyway, it was originally described as a tragedy and you will find plenty of parallels with *Lear* if you want them.'

'Alright, yes. Sorry, I don't mean to appear ungrateful…'

'It will be a pleasure to have your company. Now if you help to carry the tea through we both need to get back to work.'

17

'Listen to this,' said Marianne, sitting at her desk and reading from a typescript in front of her. '"*K screaming at V again. He has sent him back for another stint cleaning the guns. He always picks on V. Perhaps because he is Latvian and not German. Now I won't see him again till Sunday. I hate K – I hate his smarmy politeness to us* (*obséquieuse politesse,* she writes, she really didn't like him) – *and the way he bullies his men – especially V. I hate him as much as I love V.*" Then she goes on about whether to tell V she loves him.'

'Amazing to discover this.'

'Yes, it is fascinating – I can't deny it.'

Dorrie got up and walked across to the desk. 'I always thought you looked on Anna as a kind of reincarnation of your own daughter Isabelle, and that was why you were so fond of her – but this Latvian connection adds a whole extra twist. Does she know?'

'Yes, I told her.'

'So how old was your mother?'

'I think she was seventeen – or perhaps just eighteen – when she got pregnant.'

'And who is K?'

'He is the German officer billeted on the family. He lives in the house and the men live in the stables.'

'How come your mother never told you? I mean, about who your real father was?'

'That's the great mystery. I used to think it might have been a rape, or something she felt ashamed of, but from the diaries it seems like a real love story. I feel sure there must have been some reason she wouldn't talk about it, but if so, I haven't discovered it yet.'

Dorrie poured them both some more tea and then settled back into her armchair. Marianne envied Dorrie's easy mobility. All walking was painful to her now and she often preferred to sit at her desk rather than sink into an armchair from which she would struggle to extricate herself. How old was Dorrie now? Eighty-two? Eighty-three? Unlike Marianne, she had refused to go grey, and her hairdresser had created a colour which was remarkably like the natural hair of her younger days. Much shorter now, but it still conveyed that certain spirit – that panache – which Marianne had always found so attractive. Dorrie had been her best friend now for over half a century; their brief spell as lovers had ended amicably, and rather than damage their friendship it had served to cement it.

'How much longer do you have Leah staying?'

'Callum and Helen are back next Friday.'

'Where is she now?'

'She's gone into town today. I mean, she's eighteen now. I can't keep her locked up all the time…'

The telephone had started to ring on Marianne's desk. 'This might be her now,' she said, picking up the receiver. 'Hello?'

Dorrie watched Marianne as long periods of silence were interrupted with the occasional 'yes', and 'that's true'. Clearly this wasn't Leah. The one-sided conversation seemed interminable but ended with Marianne agreeing to someone coming to visit her the following week.

'What on earth was all that about?'

Marianne sat staring across the room. She said nothing.

'Darling, whatever is it? You look as if you've seen a ghost.'

'It does feel like a ghost. But… no – it's just some researcher who's been burrowing in the old Soviet archives. Seems my name has come up – from the time I was arrested. He wants to hear my side of the story. God knows how he got hold of my number.'

'Surely you don't want to have to think about all that again?'

'I don't really…'

'Why not tell him to bugger off then?'

Marianne paused. She had gone very pale. 'I don't know – anyway, I didn't.'

'I'll call him back for you; tell him not to come…'

'No, don't do that. I've done plenty of research in my time. It's only fair if those who can still remember talk to these young guys. I don't mind.'

'I think you do mind.'

'No, honestly. I should see him.'

'Well, I won't let you see him alone. I'll be your minder.'

'It's OK – really, I'll be fine.'

'Don't be stupid – you've no idea who this so-called "researcher" is. Maybe some Russian gangster.'

'Anna will be here.'

'That's not the same.'

'Well, she's not keen on Russians, so she could be quite fierce.'

'Seriously. I think I ought to be with you.'

Marianne smiled. 'OK. You win. Eleven o'clock on Tuesday.'

'I'll be here at 10.30. Armed with my Luger. The old theatre store had some realistic props.'

Mikhail Libman was a small man of around thirty with a dark, closely cropped beard. His unusual eyes appeared to bulge from their sockets – although it may have been only that his thick-lensed spectacles made it seem so. Marianne, sitting behind her large desk, watched him intently as he sat in a chair in front of her, fiddling with a cheap biro while making some introductory remarks – in Russian, until she urged him to speak English.

'I'm far too old to do this in Russian,' she said.

'Of course. But I beg your pardon if I make mistakes with my English.'

'And I want to hear as well,' said Dorrie from the armchair in the corner of the room. Libman turned and gave Dorrie a slight bow, though his eyes expressed displeasure at her intervention. He showed Marianne a letter of introduction from some academic institute in Moscow – she barely looked at it – and explained he was researching the relationship

183

between the Soviet State and Russian Jews in the 1960s and
'70s. With her love of Russian history and literature, Marianne
was predisposed to be friendly to any Russians she met, but
there was something about the tense formality of this Mr
Libman that put her on edge.

'I think your contact at the American Embassy, Larry
Anderson, took a particular interest in Jewish emigration to
Israel?'

'That's true.'

'And you were helping him gather information about this?'

'Look, let me just tell you briefly how it was. Then you can
ask me any questions you like.'

'Of course. Please proceed.'

Marianne explained how she had first met Larry Anderson
at a US Embassy party and subsequently at a restaurant. How
he had wanted to learn about dissident material circulating
around the university; how they had become friendly, and in
due course lovers. 'As you can see, my role was really quite
trivial. Handing over the odd *Samizdat*, that kind of thing.
Then there was the air crash – did your archives mention that?'

'You and Anderson went to Georgia and you came back
on your own.'

'Yes, and after the crash I was in hospital for several weeks.
On the day I was about to leave and fly to England with my
husband and daughter, I was arrested.'

'Indeed so.'

'Well, I expect you know about my time under arrest?'

'I would like to hear it from you.'

'I was kept in prison for... I can't remember exactly, but
quite a long time.'

'Twenty-five days.'

'Was it? Well, if you say so.'

'Not a very long time.'

Marianne looked at him, surprised at the sudden change of tone. 'Have you spent much time yourself in prison, Mr Libman?'

'Not myself…'

'Well, let me tell you that twenty-five days with the KGB doesn't seem like a short time.'

Libman nodded.

'Do you want me to continue?'

'Please do.'

It was into this somewhat chilly atmosphere that Anna, unhappy at being excluded from the scene of Libman's visit, now emerged from the hall, kicking the door open without ceremony, and carrying a tray into the room. 'I bring coffee,' she announced in a loud voice. Placing the tray on a side table, she began pouring the coffee.

'Do you want sugar?' she asked in Russian, looking at Libman.

Her tactic had the desired effect. Libman looked suitably surprised. 'No, thank you,' he said. And then, after a pause, 'Are you Russian?'

'I'm from Riga.'

'Ah, I see.'

'And you?' said Anna, handing the coffee to him and studying him with a look of undisguised distaste.

'I'm from Moscow.'

Dorrie, sitting at the back of the room, caught Marianne's eye during this exchange, and smiled broadly. When everyone had received their coffee, and Marianne had thanked Anna sufficiently, Dorrie got up. 'I'll hold the door for you,' she

185

said, ushering Anna out of the room and following her into the kitchen.

Now alone with Libman, Marianne resumed her account of her time with the KGB. She explained about the two different interrogators, how the aggressive one had hit her in the face, about the endless questions and the revelation of the photographs.

'I just want to establish the conditions in which you were held,' said Libman. 'It wasn't a prison cell?'

'No.'

'More like a hotel room?'

'Perhaps – an extremely basic one.'

'Were you cold?'

'No.'

'And you had adequate food?'

'Adequate, yes.'

'You weren't dragged from your bed to be interrogated in the middle of the night?'

'No.'

'And I understand you saw a doctor in connection with your crash injuries?'

'That's true.'

'And someone from the embassy.'

'Only after I'd been there a couple of weeks.'

'And apart from getting a slap in the face, you didn't suffer any mistreatment?'

'It was a bit more than a slap.'

'But it wasn't a punch?'

'Maybe not, but what are you trying to get at?'

'It's just important for me to… to get a feel for what it was like in this… this so-called prison.'

'It was certainly a prison for me.'

While this exchange had been going on Dorrie had returned to the room. She looked as if she might be about to intervene, but Marianne gestured for her to stay quiet.

'You mentioned earlier that one of Anderson's main interests was Jewish emigration?'

'Yes.'

'Yet you haven't mentioned much about this?'

'What do you mean?'

'I mean, the subject of your interrogation?'

'Well, they asked a lot of questions about different individuals – most of whom I had never heard of.'

'But some that you had.'

'Yes.'

'In particular?'

'Mr Libman, I am trying to be as helpful as I can, but it's almost sixty years since these events took place. What exactly are you trying to discover?'

'I beg your pardon. I will come to that now. Transcripts exist of your conversations with Anderson at a hotel.'

'They still exist? In the archives? Really? Just transcripts – or other material… like tapes or photographs?'

'I didn't find any photographs.'

'And so, the transcripts…?'

'One name appears more often than any other. The name David. You were asked a lot of questions about this. Do you remember that name?' Marianne looked away towards the window; she shut her eyes. A long silence followed. Did she remember?

'So let us come back to "David",' he is saying. It's the second interrogator speaking – the small, squat one she named Blackberry. 'Every time you meet Anderson at your little love nest, he asks you about David' – now his face is close up to hers. 'It is insulting to our intelligence,' he is saying, 'insulting our intelligence – and yours – to pretend you can't remember. I'll ask you again, who is David?' She can hear Blackberry's voice, his thick Russian vowels, but not her replies. 'Let me help you,' he says. 'You made a slip once. Called him "Davydovitch" – which as you know was his patronymic. That was why you chose the code name David, wasn't it? Wasn't it?' How does she answer? Perhaps she tells him; she can't remember. But somehow the name is established because he is going on about him – about Aleshkovsky, the distinguished scientist wanting to emigrate to Israel. 'You knew that,' Blackberry is saying. 'You knew that the Americans were planning to assist their Zionist friends – to smuggle Aleshkovsky to Israel. You knew all about it, didn't you?'

Marianne looked back from the window and found Dorrie halfway across the room. 'Are you alright? We should stop this if it's upsetting for you.'

'It's OK, I'm fine.'

Dorrie looked angrily at Libman but resumed her seat.

'So, do you remember anything now?' said Libman, staring intently at Marianne with his bulging eyes.

'Yes, you are right. There was a lot of talk about David.'

'And do you remember now who David was?'

'I think his real name was Aleshkovsky.'

'Yes, it was. Leon Davydovitch Aleshkovsky. And you should remember, shouldn't you? After all, he is referred to in your confession.'

'My confession?'

'This document,' said Libman, placing several pages of typescript in front of Marianne.

'God, you've got hold of that load of nonsense,' she said, without picking up the paper.

'You may have thought of it as a load of nonsense, but it featured prominently at his trial. Would you like to read what you said?' Marianne didn't move, so Libman stepped forward to retrieve the document. Turning over several pages he began to read, "*I confirm that the person referred to as David during my conversations with the spy Anderson was the Soviet scientist Leon Aleshkovsky. The CIA and Mossad were conspiring, with Aleshkovsky's cooperation, to bring him to Israel.*"

Libman looked up from the document. 'You put your name to those two sentences.'

By now Dorrie was halfway across the room. 'You must stop this at once. You are upsetting Mrs Davenport. All this is ancient history. You of all people should know that the KGB could make up anything they liked. All those old Soviet show trials relied on fabricated evidence. I expect they wrote in those sentences after it was signed anyway.'

Libman ignored Dorrie's intervention. 'Would you like to have another look at the statement? This is a photocopy, of course, but it has your signature on each page. Is it a fabrication or a copy of the document you signed?'

Dorrie was now beside the desk. 'Really, I must protest...'

Marianne held up her hand to Dorrie. She smiled at her and for a few seconds no one spoke. Then she turned back to Libman. 'Yes. I signed it.'

'You alleged that Aleshkovsky was cooperating with the Americans and the Israelis – how could you know that?'

'I assumed...'

'Assumed? That was enough? You didn't know for sure?'

'No.'

189

'But you still signed.'

Marianne shrugged.

'A few weeks in – what was it? – something like a cheap hotel was enough for you to condemn a man you had never met. Did you ever try to find out what had happened to this man you had so casually accused? I suppose it didn't matter to you. You were just thinking of yourself. Shall I tell you what happened? He was tried for treason. Your statement was a big part of the evidence against him. Did you think…'

'Out. Out now!' Dorrie had Libman by the arm and was tugging him up. 'We are not going to listen to you anymore. Anna. Anna!' In less time than it took Marianne to rise to her feet, Anna had arrived to seize Libman's other arm.

'Ladies, please. Please let go of me. I am leaving now.' Turning back to Marianne he said, 'I understand. It was just a trivial matter to you. But it wasn't trivial to him. He got ten years. Ten years' hard labour. Still, he only served seven.'

By now Dorrie and Anna had let go of Libman and stood back while he put his papers back in his briefcase. Marianne was also standing.

'Only seven years because he died in the labour camp. So it wasn't trivial for him. And it wasn't trivial for his five-year-old daughter who never saw him again. Rosa Aleshkovsky. Now Rosa Libman. My mother.'

18

Jake was looking forward to a weekend out of London – and the early July weather looked promising; it was his mother's birthday on the Sunday and his own birthday the following day, so usually his parents would make it a family event and on this occasion they had invited not only his Grandmother Claire and Great-Aunt Marianne, but Callum and Helen as well.

There had been times in his teenage years when he had resented the arrival of the two oldie sisters – Granny Claire and Auntie Manne – and he and his sister Fran had shared many private jokes at their expense. 'Two of Pharaoh's cows have escaped,' she had once whispered to him. 'A fat one and a skinny one.' But now he was pleased that the house would be full – anything was better than the claustrophobic intimacy of their family threesome when Fran's empty chair still cast its chilly shadow over every meal.

It was nearly midnight before he arrived at his parents' house. Everyone seemed to have gone to bed except his father who was having a whisky in front of the television. Jake warmed some left-over lasagne in the microwave, poured himself a glass of red wine and sat down to chat to his father. Half an hour later he went to his room while his father locked the house.

It happened on the way to the bathroom. From the end of the dark corridor – Jake knew the house too well to need to turn on the landing light – the door of Fran's room opened, and the profile of a teenage girl emerged and stood looking at him, immobile within the deep shadows cast by the light from his bedroom. A small involuntary gurgle sounded in his throat as he stepped backwards and reached for the light switch. As the bulb slowly illuminated the landing he saw his cousin Leah standing in her pink pants and white tee-shirt watching him from the doorway of Fran's room.

'Jesus…'

'Sorry, did I give you a shock…?'

'It's just… no one told me you were here.'

'Oh – sorry. I was just going to the bathroom.'

'Of course – it's that door… and… well… talk in the morning,' and in so saying, Jake stepped back into his room, closed the door and threw himself onto the bed. Fuck, he thought, why the fuck didn't anyone tell me she was staying? Had he thought for a second…? No, of course not, it was just that… coming out of Fran's room in the dark. The room was not a shrine – far from it, others had slept there – but in his mind it would always be her room. Indeed, they all referred to it as Fran's room, though the only reminder of Fran left in it was an over-large portrait of her done shortly before her death as part of an A-level art project by a fellow pupil. Her face occupied almost a whole wall; it was a confident pose – as it had every right to be for a girl who had achieved much in her short life – but to Jake there now seemed an unmistakable sadness in her eyes – as if she had some premonition that her life would soon be cut short. It was a long time before he fell asleep.

Partly it was the smell, a hint of dampness, an indefinable whiff of decay mixed with the scent of the New Dawn roses flowering under his window; then there was the bed, the soft springiness under the starched white sheets; most of all, though, it was the sound, the distant groaning of the shore as the sea pounded the shingle beach half a mile across the fields from the front of the house. Without opening his eyes, Jake sensed the familiarity of his old bedroom and he let the memories flood back.

She is standing over him, shaking him awake. No words are spoken but he slips out of bed, puts on his trainers, pulls a hoody over his pyjama top and follows her down the back stairs, out of the side door and into the yard. He can hear nothing above his furiously beating heart as they creep across the concrete paving, over a small wall and suddenly they are running, running silently over the damp grass towards the gate in the privet hedge. The night is cloudy and alarmingly dark. He knows she will have brought a torch but she won't shine it till they are further from the house. Misjudging the line to the gate, Jake puts a foot into the corner of a flower bed and falls heavily onto the grass. In a second he is up again and following her through the gate. Closing it behind them they duck down behind the hedge and recover their breath. She smiles at him and in the darkness he can just see the silver line of the braces across her front teeth.

They are both thirteen and it's the last summer holidays before they are due to start their separate schools. Fran is the leader and Jake her follower and within a few seconds she is off again, running lightly along the fence line, through the first field, over the stile and heading across the second field towards the cliffs.

Reaching the top of the cliffs, Fran waits for him to catch up; they will need to stick close together with only the small torch to guide them down the steep descent to the beach. Trying not to fall and muddy his pyjamas, Jake slithers after Fran; they called it a path, but it was more of a natural gully in the stone and clay of the cliff face that he and Fran had always used to avoid the half-mile walk to the wooden steps.

Now they are at the bottom and without hesitation Fran is stripping off her clothes. Cautiously he removes his hoody but already he can see the outline of her naked body, silhouetted against the dark sea. He takes off his pyjamas and follows her. It is not the first time that Jake has crept across the wet stones towards the heaving black water, but familiarity has not increased his confidence. A small glow in the sky where a crescent moon struggles to shine through low clouds is the only source of light. Everywhere the roar of the sea fills the night air as the waves break and pull back on the steep shingle bank. Behind him, a pinprick of light from the small pocket torch marks the spot where they have left their clothes; ahead, only a soupy darkness. Naked and shivering, Jake feels the cold water wash over his ankles.

'Come on, Jake.' Fran's voice already sounds quite distant against the noise of the sea. Jake moves a little forward then stops, feeling an icy wave wash up his thighs. For a few seconds he remains immobile, alone in the darkness and noise; then, as the moon emerges briefly and projects a sliver of pale light onto the water he plunges forward. As he swims away from the shore he is conscious of nothing but a gripping cold; slowly, though, his body adjusts to the temperature of the water, merges with it, fluid and weightless; a disembodied presence surrendered to the infinite sea.

'Over here,' he hears her call.

'Where? I can't see you…'

'I am swimming further out. Are you coming?' How does he respond? Seemingly he says nothing.

On days following their night-time expeditions, when he had ambled down to the sea to swim with his family – as they did most afternoons in that warm spell in late July – it would seem strange to Jake that the same beach and the same sea, so serene and familiar in the afternoon sunshine, could appear so daunting on his nocturnal visits with Fran. It had started a few weeks earlier. Lying on the springy grass at the top of the cliff, warming themselves in the afternoon sun, Fran had raised the idea with Jake. Reluctant at first to agree, he had eventually given in and that night they had crept down, across the fields and onto the beach and experienced for the first time the delicious thrill of night swimming.

Now he is beginning to feel the cold. He can see no sign of Fran, but looking towards the shore he senses that a current has taken him down the beach and he can no longer see the light from their torch. Suddenly, he is feeling frightened. The darkness around him seems physically oppressive and he is swimming as fast as he can back to the shore. Once back within his depth he half swims and half wades towards where he believes the light to be. Hauling himself up the shingle bank and shivering violently he sees the pinprick of light and stumbles towards it, wincing with pain as the stones bruise his feet. Drying himself as best he can with the small towel that Fran has brought with them, he peers back towards the sea. The moon has now retreated behind heavy clouds and he can see almost nothing. He waits in the darkness for Fran to emerge.

Perhaps he should have kept closer to her but she is always so quick, always three steps ahead of him. Why is she never afraid, he wonders; is this quality true courage, or simply the absence of fear? Whatever it is, he knows that he doesn't possess it and this makes him love her all the more. Without her, the colours are dimmer, more monochrome. Her absence hurts him like the ache of a phantom limb. Is it permissible, he thinks, to feel like this about your sister?

He wonders if she is further down the beach. He waves the torch around and calls her name. He hears nothing. Holding the towel around him with one hand and the torch in the other he moves back to where the sea is breaking on the shingle bank, and waves the torch in the direction of the sea. The beam shines only a few yards and is quickly swallowed up by the night.

'Fran? Fran?' His voice sounds feeble against the noise of the sea. For a few moments he stands indecisively on the shore, peering into the darkness, and then takes a few steps down the bank and into the breaking waves. His mistake is immediately apparent. Losing his footing as the undertow pulls the shingles down the bank he stumbles and drops the torch. Immediately the light has gone. Putting his hand into the sea he feels for the torch but there is nothing but the stones moving back and forth with the dragging swell.

'Fran?' he shouts at the sea. 'Fran? Where are you? I've dropped the torch. Can you hear me, Fran? I'm over here.'

The clamour of the sea drowns his words. All he can hear is the noise of the waves. He calls again and again, but there is nothing except the wind and the waves mocking his reedy voice. A memory comes back to him. It's a holiday in Cornwall three years earlier; they are watching two children play on that treacherous flat rock that they know to avoid on an incoming tide. It's the day a ten-year-old Fran dived into the rough Cornish sea to try to save the girl who had been swept off the rock. It isn't Fran that he remembers, though, it is the body of the other girl when they finally pull her out.

Shaking now from the cold, he stumbles back up the beach and with difficulty puts on his pyjamas and hoody. He walks to the shore and again calls out for her, but the noise of the sea seems to have a physical density that his voice cannot penetrate. He sits on the stones to put on his trainers and a terrible nausea moves up to his throat. Should he run back to the house for help? But how long would it take him, and surely if Fran is in trouble any help would come too late? Should he go back into the sea? But what can he do in the dark? And anyway, Fran is a far better swimmer than he is. For a small seductive moment, he thinks that he might just return to the house and go back to sleep as if nothing had happened. Perhaps he would wake up and find that this had all been a bad dream. Perhaps he could pretend that he knew nothing of Fran's disappearance. Perhaps no one need ever know that he had been here.

How long does he sit on the beach that night in an agony of indecision? Probably no more than a few minutes elapse before he becomes aware of the spectre-like figure of his twin sister, a child who is now almost a woman, her body glistening palely in the emergent moonlight only a few yards in front of him. Entirely unconcerned at his relief, she shakes her hair over him like an overfriendly Labrador, castigates him mildly for losing the torch, rubs herself down, dresses quickly and together they make their way back to the house and the warmth and security of their respective beds.

Now fully awake, and anxious to shake off these memories, Jake dragged himself out of bed and into the shower. It always seemed like this when he was at home; Fran was everywhere around him and the pain of her loss was undiminished. The night swim on their familiar patch of coast may have ended happily enough – not so that day in the French countryside a few years later.

They hadn't known that Leah would be coming, Jake's mother explained over breakfast. She had just come back from a post-A-level jaunt to Ibiza and was at a loose end. Helen had called as they were leaving London to ask if they could bring her with them. In an echo of his Easter visit to Marianne two years earlier, it now appeared to be Jake's responsibility to entertain his cousin over the weekend. He did not relish the task. He remembered the breathless sixteen-year-old he had escorted around Cambridge that Easter. He remembered her as full of naïve school-girl enthusiasms mixed with a certain irritating precocity. He remembered her crude attempts to flirt and her tendency to sulk when he did not respond. He did not expect to enjoy her company.

Finishing her breakfast, Marianne took her mug of coffee and hobbled out onto the terrace where her sister Claire sat working through the quick crossword at the back of the paper. It was warm in the July sun, and well sheltered from the breezes which came in from the sea. She looked admiringly at Juliette's group of pots outside the kitchen. A large, almost spherical pittosporum provided a bright halo of apple green, in front of which the agastache paraded their purple spikes like an imperial guard while at their feet dense groups of blue and white lobelia clustered together in homage.

'Come for a walk around the garden with me,' said Juliette. 'At least you will appreciate all my hard work. My mother doesn't know a rose from a rhododendron.'

'Not entirely true, darling.'

'I'll happily stagger around with you,' said Marianne. 'Help me up then – don't forget I'm ten years older than your mother and carrying a few war wounds as well.' She also knew that she was carrying rather more weight than her sister; time, which either eats flesh or lards it on, had left Claire all fine bones and tiny ankles, whereas Marianne had been losing the battle of her girth for forty years.

Juliette took Marianne's arm and together they walked onto the lawn towards the border which backed onto the old stone milking shed, which formed the western boundary of the garden. Friends of the family often found it surprising that Claire's daughter Juliette was so unlike her mother. Despite growing up in London, it seemed she couldn't get away quickly enough, and now lived with her husband Tom in a group of converted agricultural buildings near the Dorset coast.

Looking across to the sea Marianne saw Jake and Leah heading out towards the cliffs – Jake helping Leah over the stile at the corner of the first field. It had been a joy to watch her grand-daughter grow into such a mature and confident eighteen-year-old. Hard to believe she's my great-grand-daughter, she thought. It almost seemed to her now that Izzy and Callum had been siblings – both her own children – as if by some miracle she had had a second child a dozen years after the accident in Russia.

'Does she remind you?' said Juliette.

'You mean Izzy?'

'Yes.'

'Sometimes. There's a look Izzy used to have – I see it with Leah. I mean, it's a different relationship with a grandchild – Leah is always on her best behaviour with me. Mother-daughter, that's…'

'Yes, quite different. Fran wasn't always easy either.'

'I remember.'

Juliette stood beside her in silence as they watched the two figures disappearing behind a clump of stubby, wind-bent trees. 'I never blamed you…'

'I know. But perhaps I should have been…'

'No, don't…' Juliette put her hand on Marianne's shoulder. 'Just now. I was watching you watching them, and you looked so happy. But now you look sad.'

'Of course – I'm both.'

'Why sad?'

'Partly about Fran, of course. For you, especially – but for all of us. And then… well, for myself, maybe the last time here for the birthday weekend – you never know – but, it's the same emotion now: happiness, sadness – they fuse together at my age. Can't be happy without being a little sad…'

'Hey, don't give up on life – you're looking so well, and

Callum says you're doing incredible stuff with those old diaries.'

'Well, I was, but I think it may all be too much for me. Of course, what would have made my life perfect,' said Marianne, smiling at her niece, 'would have been for Callum to have married you – did I ever tell you about that fantasy of mine, Julie darling?'

'You did,' said Juliette, her large brown eyes lighting up with an amused tolerance. 'Several times, in fact.'

As Jake walked across the fields with Leah, he found himself revising his opinion of her. She had grown up a lot in the two years since he had last seen her. She seemed calmer, comfortable about herself and at ease with her older relations. He learned that – encouraged by her grandmother Marianne – she had applied to Cambridge, though she rated her chances as slim. It seemed that her mother was keen for her to go to Melbourne, where her sister was now in her last year, whereas she preferred to go to an English university.

'Getting to Cambridge is the only way I can keep everyone happy,' she said. 'Even Mum will bow down before the altar of Oxbridge.'

When they reached the cliff, they sat on the grass and watched a pair of kite-surfers racing across the water; like tiny insects dragged behind giant birds of prey, their red and green wings lurching and diving in the squally wind blowing up the channel.

'That picture in my room – I suppose that's Fran?'

'Yes.'

'How long ago was it?'

'Eight years.'

'Did you think for a moment…? I mean, when you saw me last night – you looked so shocked…'

'I don't believe in ghosts.'

'Of course not, but…'

'You're right, though, it was a shock.'

'Tell me about her.'

Jake said nothing. He looked down at the beach where a couple walked hand in hand at the edge of the sea, occasionally jumping inshore when a larger wave threatened to wet their feet. The tide was out and a small strip of sand had appeared between the shingle and the sea. The girl took off her shoes and began to paddle. He couldn't talk about Fran – not to anyone. Nowadays he tried his utmost never to think about her, to keep that part of his life locked away. It was the only method which seemed to work. Leah didn't break the silence – for which he was grateful. At last he said, 'We used to climb down the cliff here to swim. I'll show you.'

The consecutive birthdays of Jake and Juliette were being celebrated on the Sunday and everyone was engaged in preparing for lunch. Only Claire and Marianne were permitted to sit and watch while the others worked. Jake's father, Tom, had taken charge of the barbecue, assisted by Helen who expressed disapproval at what she called 'all this palaver with charcoal'.

'Julie thinks the food tastes better on a proper charcoal barbecue,' said Tom.

'I guess if you had a barbie as often as we do you'd appreciate the gas ones,' said Helen.

Inside the kitchen, Juliette was cutting up mozzarella and avocados and chatting to Callum who was frying lardons for the potato salad. Meanwhile, Leah was browning pine nuts and making a green salad under Juliette's instruction, while Jake had been sent to pick parsley and chives from the herb garden. When Jake came back into the kitchen, Juliette said, 'Jake, darling, Leah is looking for some work experience now that she's finished school, do you think there is any chance that the *Chronicle* would take her?'

'Err, I don't know, really…' said Jake, shooting a quick glance at Leah.

'It doesn't matter, honestly…' said Leah, looking embarrassed.

'No, look, I'll ask. It might be possible.'

'Don't put yourself to any trouble, Jake, but if you could enquire,' said Callum. 'I could organise something at our office, but architecture isn't really her thing.'

'Sure, I'll ask tomorrow.'

'Thanks,' said Leah.

'No problem – email me your CV.'

'There's not much to it – but will do.'

'And just watch those pine nuts,' said Juliette.

When all the cold dishes had been prepared, the meat cooked and the umbrellas arranged at an angle to provide the maximum area of shade, they all sat down and drank a birthday toast to mother and son.

'Wow,' said Leah, looking across to Jake, 'twenty-six – not far off thirty then.'

Jake gave her a brief smile. 'About as far as you are from being fourteen.'

Callum then proposed a toast, wishing Leah good luck with her A-level results.

'What's done is done, Dad. But if drinking will improve the results, then, hey, fill up my glass again. What's more, we should drink to Gran – my very own professor and super-patient tutor. Without her I wouldn't even have got off the starting blocks.'

Marianne smiled. 'You worked hard, Leah, and you deserve to do well.'

Later that afternoon, after they had eaten their meal and Claire and Marianne had retired for a nap, Juliette asked after Marianne.

'She's doing well, thanks,' said Callum. 'Walking hurts her, but mentally she's as sharp as ever. Mind you, she was quite shaken up by that Russian business. Did you hear about that?'

'Mum mentioned something. Some young Russian turned up out of the blue and started accusing her of betraying his grandfather fifty years ago.'

'Yes, that's more or less it. I was furious when I heard about it. I mean, if the KGB were intent on persecuting his grandfather they can hardly have needed to rely on some naïve young English woman – as Mum describes herself at that time. So unfair to attack her at her age.'

'Was Auntie Manne really a spy?' asked Jake.

'No, she was just a young academic researching her PhD, but she got involved with some American diplomat who may have been – that's why they arrested her.'

'How come Auntie Manne never married again?'

'I suppose she never met the right person.'

'But Uncle Ed did.'

'Yes, my father married again,' said Callum.

'Men always do,' said Juliette, 'they're useless on their own. Tragic that your parents ever split.'

'Yes, I never really understood the explanations. She has always tended to blame herself.'

'That's because Marianne thinks well of everyone, but from what my mum told me Edward wasn't as saintly as she thought.'

'That sounds like Aunt Claire being bitchy because Peter played away.'

'Hmm, I can't remember exactly what she told me, but she had chapter and verse at the time.'

'I honestly don't think that's likely,' said Callum quickly.

'OK, Cal, I don't want to tarnish the memory of your father – *nil nisi bonum*, and all that.'

'How old is Gran now?' said Leah.

'Eighty-eight,' said Callum.

'Well, I'm glad to know she's well,' said Juliette, 'because when I spoke to Mum earlier this afternoon she seemed a bit worried about her – though she couldn't say why.'

'Oh, you shouldn't worry about Marianne,' said Helen, looking across the table to Callum. 'She's a real tough one – will make it to a hundred if you ask me.'

'I hope she does,' said Jake. 'I think Auntie Manne's a star.'

'A super-star,' said Leah.

Part III

and my duty
Is to dare all things for a righteous end.

19

Autumn, 2033

She looked at her alarm clock – 6.20. Turning on the bedside light, she started to move her hands to get through that first pain barrier of exercising the swollen and arthritic joints – necessary so she could get a firm grip on one of her sticks. Now peel back the duvet, manoeuvre into a sitting position and swing feet onto the floor. She sat at the edge of her bed for a few moments to settle herself and make sure she felt well balanced. Then, taking a stick in her right hand, she pushed herself up, grimacing as she did so at the sharp pains in her hips, steadied herself, took four steps to the side of the room, put her left hand on the rail which had been fixed to the wall, dropped the stick, pulled up her nightgown and sat down on the commode.

Marianne had steadfastly resisted the idea of a commode in her room until the previous year, when yet another fall had convinced her that this was a disagreeable but necessary further retreat in the constant struggle of old age between aesthetics and practicality. After emptying her bladder, she reversed the process and returned to her bed.

Normally she would turn on an audio book – she was listening to a new biography of Coleridge, one of several which had come out in anticipation of the bi-centenary of his death – but on this morning she lay back and let her mind explore the days and weeks ahead.

Anna was not due till later that morning, so Marianne took the opportunity to make her necessary phone calls. At eleven o'clock she telephoned to explain to Callum but ended up speaking to Helen instead. Helen had been calm but Marianne thought she had detected a trace of exhilaration in her tone. Well controlled, of course, but there nonetheless. When Anna returned from the shops she helped Marianne walk to the small pond at the end of the garden. Returning to the house, Marianne called Dorrie. What a trouper, she thought, she didn't hesitate for a moment.

By six o'clock, Dorrie was sitting in the armchair opposite Marianne with a whisky in her hand. Marianne sat the other side of the stove which Anna had fuelled up for the evening. She tried to explain her decision.

'Not you as well,' Dorrie said. 'I won't let you do it.'

'I've made up my mind.'

'Why, for God's sake?'

'You know I've been thinking about it for a while. We talked about it before.'

'Yes, of course, in theory. But there's no reason to do it now is there – or is there something you're not telling me?'

'No, not really.'

'What do you mean, "not really" – have you been diagnosed with some new illness?'

'No.'

'So what is it then?'

Marianne struggled to know how to start. She said at last, 'I think my time has come.'

'Bollocks. Complete bloody bollocks.'

'Dorrie, please try to understand.'

'I do understand – at least I understand now why you've been behaving so strangely over the last six months. In fact, ever since that Russian was here. You've been brewing this up inside you.'

'It's true I've been thinking it over for quite a while.'

'I don't blame you for being upset about what he said. But honestly – to blame yourself in any way is ridiculous.'

'Is it? I don't know. Anyway, it's nothing to do with the Russian. I have always believed in doing this. Particularly after my father's death.'

'I think you are wrong, dangerously wrong. What does Callum say about it? I hope he'll talk you out of it.'

'He hasn't said anything yet. They're coming to see me on Saturday. Ever since they changed the law I told him it's something I might do one day so he shouldn't be too shocked by it.'

'Well, if he's a decent son he should forbid you to do it.'

'If he tries he won't succeed.'

'This is nothing to do with Callum and Helen, is it? Are they threatening to go back to Australia – or do you think they want to go back, is that it?'

'No, not at all, it's nothing like that.'

211

'I need another drink,' said Dorrie, 'and I think you should have one too. Then you can try to convince me. Who else have you talked to?'

'Callum and Helen briefly on the telephone – otherwise you're the first. I am writing to my sister Claire. I won't discuss it with anyone else.'

Dorrie reached for the bottle of whisky and poured a generous measure into her glass. 'You too?' she said.

'I'll get myself something in a minute, but I need to keep my head clear so I can try to explain my decision to you.'

Dorrie sipped her whisky. 'Alright, explain away and I'll shut up for a while.'

Marianne took a deep breath: 'We all need to be braver; face death with realism. When the AD laws came in I welcomed them. When it's your time to go – get on with it.'

'But this isn't your time.'

'Please listen – I'm trying to explain. Our culture has such a terrible inhibition about death. I remember when my father was dying and the doctors were debating what further treatment to give him. I just remember the atmosphere. It was all so stilted – no one actually talked about death. "How are you feeling today, Papa?" Claire would say. "I'm not a good patient, I'm afraid," he would reply. Good patient, bad patient, what does any of that matter, I was screaming inside my head. Get on your knees, Claire, put your arms around him. Embrace him…'

'Honestly, Marianne…'

'… and I was no better. We were all inhibited. Pretending he wasn't dying because we didn't know how to deal with it.'

'I'm not getting this at all,' said Dorrie, putting her glass down with exaggerated force. 'You've booked into an AD clinic in order to end your life because twenty-five years ago you and your sister couldn't talk to your father about the fact that he was dying. Do you find that surprising? Surely it would have been remarkable if it had happened in any other way. Did you expect to have a profound conversation about the imminence of oblivion, or the possibilities of an afterlife; or perhaps a grand mutual weep-in? Is that what you wanted? Come on, Marianne, this is all nonsense.'

'No, no, that's not all, of course, but it's part of it. The fact that we can't ever confront death honestly. I don't want to end my life with everyone still pretending that I'm fine and it will only take one more dose of some noxious poison to transform me back into robust health. Anyway, you're right, there's a more fundamental point. It was the actual process of Papa's death which really persuaded me that I must never, ever, risk going through that myself.'

'Tell me,' said Dorrie.

Marianne sat in silence. 'Yes, I will tell you. But first I need a drink after all,' and she mixed herself a dry martini with a little more gin than usual.

'Hmm, I'm not sure about the gin; it seems to be making you depressed.'

'On the contrary, I'm not depressed. In fact, I have a strange sense of excitement.'

'Half in love with easeful death, are you?' For the first time Marianne detected a note of scorn in Dorrie's voice.

'Certainly not. This is not a romantic fantasy. I'm utterly calm and rational about what I intend to do.'

'I'm sorry. I shouldn't have said that. I promised to listen. You were going to tell me about your dad. Go on.'

And so Marianne talked about her father while Dorrie

213

listened. She tried to tell her about the pain; the sheer bloody agony which racked his body and gnawed at him from the inside.

'The strange thing is that people pitied me. How terrible, they said, to have to be with your father when he is in such distress. Terrible it certainly was, but my vicarious pain cannot be measured against the reality of his suffering. It went on and on and although I valued every moment we had left, in the end I longed for him to die.'

'But surely there was pain relief?' said Dorrie. 'This wasn't so long ago.'

'You would think so, wouldn't you? And obviously there was pain relief, morphine and so on. But it never seemed to be enough. I begged the doctors for more but there seemed to be some kind of rationing system applied which I never really understood.'

Dorrie stared at Marianne with a puzzled expression and Marianne could see that somehow she wasn't getting through to her, so she tried another tack. 'Honestly, it was like one of those terrible deaths you've read about in fiction. Remember that Tolstoy one – what was it? – oh God, I've forgotten the name.'

'You mean Ivan Illych.'

'Yes – that's the one. His weeks of suffering, how he screamed non-stop for the last three days of his life?' Marianne realised too late that she should have known better than to try a literary allusion with Dorrie, who pounced immediately.

'If I remember rightly, Illych's physical pain is only part of the problem. It's his spiritual suffering which makes his death unendurable. He feels he has led a worthless life. He has also failed to love his wife at the time when he could have done and ends up hating her. I can't believe any of that was true for your father or for you.'

'Yes of course you are right. Perhaps that wasn't the best example, but you know there was something in Papa's illness which changed him and which was one of the hardest things to bear.'

'How so?'

'My father had always been a very gentle man. I think he only ever shouted at me once in my life. But in the last two months – and this is what hurt me most – a hardness came over him. A bitterness, I suppose. I think he found it hard to accept that his life was coming to an end. And, of course, the pain as well. He had always been a strong man but when it came to his own suffering it overwhelmed him, and that, I think, made him feel inadequate, humiliated even. The man whose hand I held at the end wasn't the father I had loved for more than fifty years. That was what hurt most – the alienation. His agony came between us like a physical barrier, an electric fence which stung me when I tried to cross it. I couldn't reach him. That was my agony. It shouldn't have been like that. At the moment when he needed my love most…'

Marianne had to stop; tears were pricking the back of her eyes and she took a sip of her drink to try to hide her unexpected distress. 'I'm sorry,' she said, 'I didn't mean to get all weepy. I was just trying to explain how horrible the end of a life can be.'

'Of course I know that,' said Dorrie, pouring herself some more whisky, 'but what you are saying still doesn't make any sense. You are not in agony or distress and, unless you are keeping something from me, you don't even have a terminal illness. You know I don't approve of the way things are now,

215

but if you do get anywhere near that state – the state that your father reached – then you can go to one of your fancy AD clinics then.'

Marianne sat in silence looking at Dorrie. The whisky had flushed her cheeks and she looked like she was getting a little drunk. She continued to argue her case for an assisted death but it was clear that Dorrie was not convinced.

'Last month you told me the doctor was really pleased with your check-up.'

'Yes.'

'Heart strong and blood pressure of a fifty-year-old?'

'So he said.'

'No sign of diabetes?'

'That's not the point.'

'I think it is precisely the point. Honestly, "assisted dying", who came up with that euphemism? Two doctors, lots of safeguards and what happens? In no time, there are dozens of clinics springing up all over the country. I read that over a quarter of all deaths now qualify as "assisted dying". If you take away the accidents and sudden deaths that must mean that nearly half of us are having the mortal coil tugged away before we can shuffle it off ourselves.'

Marianne wanted to argue but somehow she didn't have the firepower to confront Dorrie, who was now in full flow. She tried to find the words. 'Sometimes it's only a couple of days before they would die anyway,' she said, 'it's better that way. Better for the patient and better for their relatives. Kinder, more digni…' she tried to stop herself but it was too late; Dorrie couldn't have asked for a better cue.

'More dignified? Oh, yes, so much more dignified. That's always been the great rallying cry, hasn't it? Do they think that the great object of life is dignity? Ha, the tragedy is I think that they really do. It starts with birth of course, dignity in giving birth means a caesarean. After all nothing could be more undignified than a vaginal delivery – the horror of it! The pain, the mess, the sheer ugliness. You know, in America now the rich have almost abandoned natural childbirth – by which I don't mean childbirth unaided by medicine or pain relief. Consigned it to the dustbin of history, to the dark ages of medicine. Nice, organised, hospital caesars, that's what they want. A triumph of dignity over nature.'

Dorrie was now on her feet, addressing the room as if transported to one of her drama classes. Marianne was beginning to enjoy the rant; it was cheering her up. She took another swig of her gin; perhaps I am getting a little light-headed myself, she thought. 'You're right, as ever,' she said. 'Dignity has never been the best argument. Dignity would mean abolishing old age completely.'

'Too right it would,' said Dorrie. 'A leaky bladder, haemorrhoids falling out of your bum. I won't even ask what indignities you have to suffer but I'm sure you've got your fair share.'

'I certainly have and I think there should be a law against them,' Marianne said, entering into the spirit of Dorrie's drama.

'Of course, it starts before birth,' said Dorrie. 'It starts with conception, with sex, we must dignify the act of sexual intercourse. What position do you think would be permitted under the national dignity act?'

Marianne looked on with amusement as her friend paced around her sitting room. 'Missionary, perhaps?'

'Oh no, I don't think so. Man with bum in the air. Not really dignified, is it? Have you noticed how the movies have dropped the missionary position again and gone back to the seventies and eighties with the woman sitting astride? Good view of her breasts and a manly chest exposed. Yes, I think that might be the only sexual position consistent with dignity.'

'So ban the *Kama Sutra*?'

'Ban it absolutely. No deviation permitted. I put it to you, Mrs Marianne Davenport,' said Dorrie, now in courtroom mode, striding around the room with her glass in one hand and pointing her finger at Marianne. 'I put it to you, that you have had undignified sex. How do you plead?'

'Well,' Marianne laughed, 'I fear I have to plead guilty, although generally I would blame my late husband. You see, Ed was very fond of the doggy position which, let's face it, is not that dignified for us girls. I have ingrained in my mind one occasion when I was well past my prime – I think it was not long before we separated – and we were doing it on the floor in some foreign hotel when I caught sight of myself in a mirror, face on the floor, boobs all over the place, with a pendulous belly wobbling with every motion. It's a snapshot I've never forgotten.'

Dorrie laughed and raised her glass. 'I salute you. I'm sure it was fun. Here's to a world of undignified sex,' and they drank together like fifth-form schoolgirls sharing an illicit bottle of wine on a weekend sleepover.

'OK,' Marianne said, 'your turn. Has your sex life ever strayed from the path of dignity?'

'Well,' said Dorrie, 'I do remember one occasion before I gave up on men. My then boyfriend – Tony was his name, I think – God, it was so long ago. Anyway, it was a Sunday morning and I had denied Tony his wishes as we had things to do and I knew that a morning fuck would mean him falling back to sleep again. I was trying to clean up the flat and Tony was pacing around with a meaningful look in his eye. One of the jobs I had to do was to try to clean out a drain just below our balcony, which had blocked with leaves, and this meant kneeling on the balcony floor and squeezing my head and shoulders through the rails and reaching down to the drain. This position obviously proved too much for Tony, who started fondling me from behind...' Dorrie poured some more whisky into her glass and smiled to herself at the recollection.

'And so...?' Marianne said. 'I want a full confession, please.'

'Of course I told him to stop,' Dorrie continued, 'but he took no notice, pulling down my tracksuit bottoms and knickers and coming into me from behind. I remember swearing at him because I was completely trapped, but he just laughed and said that if I didn't want to do it in bed I should be ready for other opportunities. It wouldn't have been so bad if at that moment the woman from the floor below hadn't come out onto her balcony and looked up to see my head bobbing back and forth in time to Tony's thrusts from behind. I don't remember if she said anything; I think she just stared at me in amazement...'

'And?'

'So, she was just staring up at me and I thought I needed to offer some plausible explanation so I mumbled, "Just trying, umm... trying to, umm... to... clear the leaves... from... umm... the drain," as I lurched back and forth while Tony moved steadily towards his climax.'

20

It happened very rarely, but Marianne was still asleep when Anna arrived on Saturday morning. Her head was thick and for a second she was back in her mother's story in wartime France.

'Marianne, Marianne, are you OK?' Marianne opened her eyes and saw Anna standing over her.

'What time is it?'

'It's nine thirty. I left you for an extra hour but now I worry.'

'I'm fine. I went to bed rather late last night.'

Over breakfast Anna quizzed her again about the diaries. 'So, Marianne, you are going back to your work, that is good.'

'Well, I am trying, but I don't really have the energy now.'

'Well, you must tell the story – and I want to hear more about your Latvian father, my cousin Viktors!'

'No more about him, I'm afraid. How is Stefans?'

'He's OK.'

'Any chance of a new job?'

'I don't know. He put all his hopes into that restaurant as well as most of our savings – and of course the money you give us. Oh, Marianne, I am so guilty about that.'

'Don't be silly, Anna, I told you, that was an investment that I willingly made and not all investments work out. If the restaurant had been a success, I would have made a good return on my money.'

'He's very upset about it.'

'Is there any chance of him trying to start again?'

'No, certainly not here – at the moment, anyway.'

'Well, we must find him a job in another restaurant.'

'Yes... Anyway, Callum and Helen are coming to see you today, I almost forgot. I must go to the shops to get some food for them.'

'No, there's no need for that. They're taking me to the Red Lion for lunch.'

'Oh lovely, Marianne. You will enjoy seeing them.'

By eleven thirty she was beginning to feel tired, or perhaps more likely, was still feeling tired after her late night and so she settled into her special tip-back chair – another surrender to practicality over aesthetics – and told Anna that she was going to have a nap and that she should wake her at twelve fifteen so she would be ready for when they arrived.

She shut her eyes but, unusually, sleep proved to be elusive. She kept wondering how it was going to be with Callum and Helen. She knew from personal experience that the etiquette of AD is never easy. If you visit a terminally ill patient, there are various possible responses. Cheerful optimism and denial is the one friends and relations find easiest. Commiserations and anger may well be justified if the approaching end is clearly premature. With the gradual approach of death for the elderly, at least a postponement can be hoped for: 'I'm sure you'll still be with us for Christmas, darling.' But with a voluntary death it's hard to find the right response. Marianne was anxious to make it as easy as possible for Callum and Helen; that way it would also be easier for her.

In the event, she should not have worried too much. When Callum and Helen arrived, and after the usual greetings, Helen discreetly left the room with Anna, and Callum sat down next to Marianne and took her hand. 'Mum, there's no need for you to do this, you know.'

'I think it's time.'

'Is there some special reason? Have you been falling again?'

'I did fall, but it's not that.'

'So, you are OK now?'

'You will understand when you get to my age.'

'You're not so old, Mum, you could live to be a hundred.'

'I don't want to live to a hundred.'

'Is there a problem with Anna?'

'No, Anna is as wonderful as ever.'

'But you haven't told her about your decision?'

'No.'

'Doesn't that mean you're not quite sure whether you want to do this?'

'No, I will tell her in time. I want to get through the stage two process first and then I will tell her.'

'She'll be very unhappy about it.'

'Perhaps not as unhappy as you imagine.'

'I think you should take time to think about this a bit more.'

'I have had plenty of time to think about it and I have made my decision.'

'I don't feel comfortable about it, Mum.'

'Well, we have talked about it several times and you always said you would support me when the time came.'

'Yes, I know, but I wasn't expecting it suddenly like this – out of the blue…'

'It may be out of the blue to you but to me it's been a decision I've been thinking about for a long time.'

Callum got up and went to the window. Marianne studied his profile. She had to admit it wasn't a strong face: that weakness of the chin and slightly anxious look. A desire to please those around him. His heart was in the right place but it was not difficult to see where the path of least resistance would lead on this occasion.

'So how are you surviving London?' Marianne asked. 'It's been nearly three years now. Not hankering for the sunshine?'

'No, London is fine, although the job hasn't turned out quite as I expected, as you know. But it's a really exciting change living in London after nearly twenty years in Australia.'

'Well, I'm glad you're managing alright, darling.'

'Mum, this is nothing to do with Helen and I, is it? You know we have no plans to go back to Australia.'

'No, darling, absolutely nothing to do with you and Helen. When you get to my age you will understand there comes a time when you don't want to go on anymore.'

'I know a lot of people do it nowadays but I'm not sure why you need to do it now.'

'Well, you wouldn't want me to die like my poor father, would you?'

'That was different, Mum. He had cancer. I wish AD had been around for him and of course I think it is sensible that AD is now available. It's just… well… when it comes to your own mother…'

'Well, technically I am your grandmother and at your age you're lucky to have a grandmother still alive.'

'Well, you're the only mother I have ever known so that's completely irrelevant – I don't know why you even mention it.' There was a strong tone of resentment in Callum's voice and for a while neither spoke. Marianne was not sure why she had suddenly mentioned that she was not his biological mother. Was she trying to loosen the bond between them? It was not a subject Callum ever liked to discuss but suddenly Marianne felt the need to ask him some questions.

'Callum, darling, has it bothered you in your life that I wasn't your real mother?'

'Mum, you know I always think of you as my real mother.'

'I know, but tell me truthfully. You've never seemed very curious about your actual mother.'

'I don't know about that. You've told me about her often enough.'

'Have I?'

'Of course you have, but she just comes across as a rebellious teenager so I always found it hard to see her in the role of a mother.'

'You don't have any recollection of her, do you?'

'Mum, I was only eighteen months old when she died; no one remembers anything at that age.'

'No, I suppose not. Isabelle was a good mother to you in her way. She loved you desperately. It's probably difficult for you to understand but she was quite brave to have you.'

'You mean not to have me aborted?'

'Most girls would have done so at her age. It wasn't such an obvious choice for a girl of her background to go through with having a baby at seventeen.'

'So would you have let her? I mean, abort the baby?'

'If she had wanted to she would have gone ahead and done it. That's the sort of person she was. We might never have known about it. She wouldn't even have told Andy – although she might have just casually mentioned it to us afterwards – she was capable of doing that.'

'Mum, why are we talking about this?'

'I need to know. Deep down you must have sometimes wished you had your own natural parents? Even Andy. He may have been a bit wild but if it hadn't been for the accident I think he might in the end have made a good father.'

'Mum, this is fantasy. My natural parents were dead before I had a chance to ever know them. You and Dad adopted me. Of course, I never understood why you two split up and I would have preferred you to have lived under the same roof, but it's never mattered to me that you were grandparents. You were just Mum and Dad, and that was it.'

'I'm glad, darling. Now, you're supposed to be taking me out to lunch. You'd better go and get Helen, otherwise we will be too late for our table.'

'Alright, fine, but we need to talk more about your decision after lunch.'

And so, in time-honoured fashion, it was tacitly agreed that they would have lunch without discussing the subject which was the whole purpose of the lunch – lest the lunch should thereby be spoiled.

When the three of them had settled themselves into a quiet corner table at the Red Lion, Callum went to the bar to place their orders and, despite his protests, Helen insisted on going with him to 'help'. Marianne watched from her corner while an intense whispered conversation took place at the bar, Helen's face a few inches from Callum's right ear. Ah, the debriefing, she thought. Looks like Callum is getting the third degree. Not for the first time Marianne wondered if she would have liked Helen more if they had lived in England. Had she always blamed her for taking Callum away?

When Helen returned to the table they both sat for a few moments in an uncomfortable silence.

'What news of Emma?' Marianne asked.

'Working hard for her end-of-year exams,' Helen responded brightly, appearing relieved that Marianne had broken the silence and not raised any more difficult subjects. 'She's still playing a lot of hockey.'

'I've given them our orders,' said Callum, returning to the table.

'You must miss Emma?' Marianne said, then instantly regretted the remark as soon as she had uttered it.

'Yes, of course, but we plan to go back to Oz for Christmas and...'

Helen had suddenly spotted, as Marianne had a moment earlier, that the conversation was drifting perilously close to the forbidden subject. By Christmas I shall be dead, thought Marianne – or at least I will be if things go according to my plan – so Christmas was not a proper subject for discussion. Callum had also spotted the danger and dived to the rescue.

'Well, we haven't made any definite plans yet... Now,

Mum, how is Anna looking after you? Are you getting enough decent food?'

'Yes, I've already told you, Anna is looking after me as well as ever.'

As they waited for their lunch to arrive, Callum kept the conversation reassuringly general. Dangerous subjects were circumvented: climatic differences between England and Australia, Callum's job in London, political issues in England and America – these were all safe subjects, but not the immediate future. Not for Marianne, nor for Callum and Helen.

'Ah, this is ours, I think,' said Callum, as a waitress brought over their lunch, allowing the conversation to be diverted to their choice of food.

'Ta,' said Helen as the waitress put down her caesar salad. Marianne was having the fish pie while Callum had a steak and ale pie with chips, causing Helen to comment, 'Chips as well, Cal?', eyeing his plate with disapproval.

Throughout the meal Marianne felt a curious detachment. She was both sitting in her corner seat and at the same time surveying the scene as if from above. Dorrie had mocked her when she said she had a strange kind of excitement, an intensity of feeling which she had not experienced before, but it was a fact that since her decision on Wednesday she had felt both part of the life she was leading but also separate from it, as if already viewing the life of another person.

Callum was asking her whether she wanted dessert but suddenly she had an urgent need to get back to the house and for Callum and Helen to be gone.

'No thank you, darling,' she said, 'I feel a bit tired now. I think we might go back.'

'Yes, of course. I'll just pay the bill,' and once again Callum got up and went to the bar, leaving Helen and Marianne alone. Marianne was about to launch into another bland conversation to cover an awkward silence when, to her amazement, Helen plunged into the forbidden subject.

'Are you still planning to go to the clinic on Tuesday?'

'Yes, I am.'

'Would you like me to take you? It's just that I know Cal would want to take you himself, but he has an important meeting on Tuesday.'

'Well,' Marianne said, hesitating; she had been wondering how she would get to the clinic. Normally Anna would take her anywhere she wanted to go but she hadn't told Anna yet.

'Well, if it's not too much trouble?'

'No, of course not. I've already discussed it with Cal.'

Have you indeed, thought Marianne. So, despite all Callum's expressed unhappiness about my decision, their expectation has been that I will go through with it, not that they will persuade me otherwise.

'Ready to go now,' said Callum returning to the table and taking Marianne's arm. As he helped her to her feet and they made their way out to the car park she wondered what further arguments might be in store when they got home. But back in the house, the second phase of their conversation which Callum had promised was over almost before it had begun. Helen had taken herself to the upstairs bathroom.

'So, Mum,' Callum began, 'are you sure you don't want to just forget about all this…? I mean, the AD clinic.'

'No, darling, I'm going to the stage two appointment on Tuesday.'

'Well, perhaps they will talk you out of it.'

'Perhaps they will,' she said (but if he really thinks that he doesn't know how these things work).

'Well, if you are determined to go, Helen has said that she will take you. I would come myself but I have a rather difficult day on Tuesday.'

'That's alright, Helen has already said she would take me.'

'Has she? OK then. What time should she get here?'

'The appointment is at eleven, so if she's here by ten thirty that would be fine.'

'OK, Mum, but remember what I said, won't you?'

'I will, darling. I will.'

21

Marianne sat in the Iris reception room waiting to be seen while Helen read – or pretended to read – a magazine. Every now and then Helen looked up and gave Marianne an encouraging smile, rather as if she was an anxious child before a visit to the dentist. There appeared to be some sort of glitch before Marianne could be seen and this gave her an opportunity to read some of the clinic's literature. Apparently, the Iris was the fifth clinic to be opened in England by the Dutch de Zeeou Group, now popularly known as the Daisy Chain. There was also literature explaining the environmental, cremation and burial services on offer; another arm (and a highly profitable one she had read) of the de Zeeou Group.

Eventually Marianne was called in to meet the support nurse. Helen was not allowed to accompany her during this interview. Marianne was pleasantly surprised by the attitude of the nurse. She introduced herself as Nikhita Singh; aged about fifty, with small brown, slightly hooded eyes and noticeably crooked teeth, she seemed friendly but respectful.

'I have read through your stage one notes, Mrs Davenport, and you seemed very confident that AD would be the right solution for you when the time came.'

'Yes, I have always believed in AD.'

'Yes indeed, and I understand why from your previous interviews. Now I am going to have to ask you a number of questions and you must give me an honest and truthful answer. Never say what you think I might expect or want to hear. Only your own view, is that clear?'

'Absolutely.'

'Right, here is the question sheet so you can follow what I'm asking.'

And so the process started. Marianne had an idea what to expect, from her friend Millicent who had gone through AD a few years earlier. She had explained that it's all about getting the right score. Most of the questions are about evaluating certain aspects of your life, both physical and mental. The scoring system seeks to achieve a measure of uniformity, so:

'On a scale of one to ten, Mrs Davenport, with ten being the most happy, and zero being the least happy, how would you describe your state of mind?' Of course, the questions were in many ways absurd but Marianne knew that you have to play along with the system and exaggerate a little. She opted for a two. They moved on to physical suffering.

'What aspects of your physical life cause you distress and suffering, Mrs Davenport?'

'Well, there's my hands and my hips,' she said. 'I broke my pelvis in my twenties and it didn't heal well.'

'Ah yes,' said the nurse, studying her notes.

'You will see that I had hip problems quite early in life and had replacement hips about twenty years ago. Apparently my bones have now degenerated so that it's not considered possible to have further surgery. So sooner or later I'm likely to end up in a wheelchair.'

'Yes, I understand. So, on a scale of one to ten, with ten being the most severe, how would you evaluate the pain you suffer from your hips?'

How to answer this question? How can anyone know what level ten pain could amount to? Have I had my fingernails ripped out? Have I been broken on the rack in a medieval torture chamber? I haven't even come anywhere near the pain suffered by my poor father at the end of his life. I suspect that my pain would barely register against the full capacity for human beings to suffer.

'Maybe five?' The nurse noted it down. Marianne knew that it didn't really matter what she said. Her case for AD was mental – I have a reasonably held belief, based on my physical condition, that it is no longer tolerable to go on living. Once it became settled practice that the interpretation of a serious physiological condition meant any condition which wasn't trivial then it all turned on of the reasonableness of your belief. When you were into your eighties or nineties there was seldom any argument about it.

'Yes, and your hands?' said the nurse. 'You mentioned about the pain in your hands?'

'Yes. You see, although my hips and hands are both troubling on their own, the combination is particularly difficult. I need two sticks to walk now and it's very difficult trying to hold the sticks, especially first thing in the morning, or using the commode at night.'

'So how would you score that?' Marianne opted for a four then said perhaps four and a half. Were halves allowed? It seemed they were. The nurse noted it down.

Gradually they worked through Marianne's bodily ailments. Her headaches, her sometimes painful eyes, constipation, haemorrhoids and occasional incontinence. By now Marianne was feeling acutely uncomfortable at having to talk up such common ailments of old age.

They had been going for over an hour and the nurse saw that Marianne was beginning to flag. She offered her a cup of tea or coffee and a short break. Marianne opted for tea. The nurse suggested she might like to go back and have her tea in the reception with her daughter-in-law. Marianne declined and spent a few minutes leafing through a brochure describing the legal implications of AD: the law did not permit discrimination against those who opted for an assisted death, the de Zeeou Group was pleased to inform readers, and life insurers were obliged to pay provided the policy was taken out at least three years before death.

Another article explained that euthanasia was still illegal in Britain; hence no doctor could administer a fatal dose. Patients had to self-administer the necessary drugs, but the de Zeeou clinics provided for that process to be easy, pain free and to take place in a secure environment under medical supervision.

When they resumed, Marianne realised that the topic had changed. So far it seemed that they had been concentrating on the reasonableness or otherwise of her view that life was no longer tolerable. Now they had to concentrate on ensuring that she was not being swayed by 'inappropriate' criteria. This could range from domestic circumstances, financial considerations, all the way to undue influence.

'So I take it, Mrs Davenport, from our previous discussion, that you live alone but have a carer who comes in every day.'

'Yes.'

'Can you describe the arrangement for me?'

Marianne described how Anna looked after her.

'She seems very helpful, your Anna. Would you describe it as a good relationship?' How to describe her relationship with Anna? Good wouldn't even get close. She loved Anna. She knew that she loved her too much. Too much for her own good and possibly Anna's as well.

'Yes,' she replied. 'Yes, it's a good relationship.'

The questions moved on to money. Shortage of money, as Marianne knew, is a big no-no as far as the clinics are concerned. There had been a lot of bad publicity a few years earlier when some researchers suggested that anxiety about money was the second biggest factor involved in people's decisions to go for AD. That didn't seem a particularly strange conclusion to Marianne, since health and money are the two overriding concerns of old age. Nevertheless, the research spawned a big political debate about pension levels and the cost of care with articles in the press suggesting that AD clinics were profiteering from the financial anxieties of the elderly. As a result, the clinics tried hard to show that shortage of money was not a factor in choosing AD.

Marianne disliked this part of the enquiry even more than the discussion about her health and domestic circumstances. She had always guarded the privacy of her financial affairs. 'I own my own house. I have a pension from the university and my state pension. No particular money problems,' she lied. The nurse seemed pleased with her answers.

The final section dealt with the attitude of her relations. To some extent this had already been dealt with at stage one. Callum had come with her on that occasion. He had told them that he certainly would not encourage it but he would respect his mother's decision to choose AD if the situation ever arose. Similar questions were now asked of Marianne.

'Mrs Davenport, please tell me which one of the following statements most accurately describes the attitude of your son to your decision to seek AD: strongly supports, supports, is neutral, opposes or strongly opposes?'

For the first time Marianne gave an answer which seemed to trouble the nurse: 'I would say the second.'

The nurse frowned. 'Your son is supportive of your decision?'

'Yes, I think so,' Marianne said, but she hadn't quite realised that this answer would set off an alarm bell; except in cases of extreme suffering or a severe degenerative disease, the AD clinics preferred relations to be neutral or mildly opposed. This suggested that the decision was that of the patient alone, entered into without persuasion or interference.

'So has your son played any part in persuading you to choose AD?' the nurse asked anxiously.

'No, no, not at all. He regards it as my decision and supports whatever decision I wish to make.'

'I wonder, therefore, if neutral isn't really the correct answer?' she asked.

Neutral? Marianne wondered how a son could be neutral about his mother's death. He may support the decision because he respects and loves his mother or even because he doesn't. Or he may oppose it for the same reasons. But to be neutral as to whether his mother lives or dies? And with one of those sudden flashes of memory which are a feature of old age, Marianne remembered a discussion in her literature class seventy or more years ago when they were reading *Sons and Lovers*. Paul grinds up the morphine and puts it in his mother's milk to hasten her death *'yet he loved her more than his own life'*. She had never forgotten those words. Neutral? That would hardly be possible.

'So on reflection, what shall I put down?' asked the nurse. Marianne looked down at the form and tried to focus on the question – oh, what the hell.

'Yes, you're right, neutral is better,' she said; the nurse smiled and ringed three on her form.

'And your daughter-in-law? Would the answer be the same for her?' Marianne was startled by the question. Helen? Why is she asking me about Helen? And for half a second a little devil inside her suggested, 'strongly supports'. She suppressed it immediately. Totally unfair. Helen had never expressed any view and had deliberately kept out of any conversation on the subject.

'I am sure her attitude is the same as my son's,' she said.

'Excellent,' said the nurse. 'Now we are all done.'

When she returned to reception, Marianne noticed Helen was looking both bored and anxious. 'Is everything alright?' she asked.

'It's fine but there are a lot of forms to go through.'

Helen looked relieved. 'So what happens now?' she asked.

'I have to see the two doctors who must approve my decision.'

236

'Oh, I see,' said Helen. 'There was someone else who wanted to talk to both of us together when you were finished with the nurse. I'll see if I can find her.'

In the meantime Marianne had slumped back into the armchair and shut her eyes. A few minutes later Helen arrived back with another woman; not, it appeared, a doctor or nurse but some other functionary of the clinic.

'Mrs Davenport, good morning. If you wouldn't mind just stepping in here for a minute,' the woman said, indicating a small room off the reception. This time Helen was allowed to accompany Marianne; she helped her to her feet and they moved into the room and took a seat around a conference table. 'In a few minutes,' the woman said, 'you will be going to see the doctors but, assuming that all goes to plan...' (plan... my God, what is she talking about?) 'we need to make arrangements for your final appointment.' Well, she's got that one right, I suppose, thought Marianne. It will be final.

'There are a few things we need to note down,' and the woman got out another standardised questionnaire. 'I see you have paid the deposit. The rest of the fee is payable three days before the final appointment. Will you be paying that yourself or will your family pay?'

'I will pay it myself.'

'If it would be easier...?' said Helen.

'I'll pay it.'

'Fine, if there are any problems please don't hesitate to telephone. Now, how many will be in attendance?'

'Two.'

'Would you like some food prepared?'

My God, is this some kind of last supper? she wondered. 'No, no food. Perhaps a drink,' Marianne said, surprising herself.

'A drink?'

'You know, a gin or whisky if someone feels the need.' The woman looked up wondering if Marianne was serious.

'Yes, I see, yes, I think that's possible. We'll organise a trolley.' Marianne smiled at the thought. Perhaps one trolley for the lethal stuff and one for the not quite so lethal booze. 'Now, music,' said the woman. 'Any particular requests?' This was becoming too much for Marianne. Music to die to. A complete sense of unreality gripped her. She looked at Helen who seemed thoroughly ill at ease. She felt that she was planning a party or social event. She had no sense that it was her own death they were discussing. The woman tried to be encouraging. 'Some of our patients like to have a particular piece of music playing. A favourite classical piece, perhaps, or maybe a hymn?' So, Mahler's Fifth, she thought, or perhaps I should die to Jerusalem. She remained silent. 'Never mind,' the woman said. 'We have every type of music available and you can choose something at the time. You will find that our suites are very well appointed. There is a large screen on which you can chose to see a familiar film or just some restful scenes if you prefer.'

Fortunately for Marianne's composure, the telephone rang. The woman answered it. 'Ah,' she said, 'the doctors are ready for you now. I think we've covered everything we need. We have to go over to the lifts and up to the second floor. Will you walk or would you prefer a wheelchair?' Marianne opted for the wheelchair. The woman with the clipboard disappeared and a male orderly arrived and wheeled her to the lift and up to the waiting doctors who had to approve her decision to end her life.

This was the critical interview. The doctors introduced themselves; friendly but serious. There was an older one, tall with grey hair and half-moon glasses over a prominent nose, who greeted Marianne with a firm handshake. The second doctor was younger and dark skinned. He didn't look quite so committed to the process.

'Mrs Davenport,' the elder doctor began, 'we have examined your answers to Mrs Singh, the nurse you have just seen, but we need to be certain that you have a firm and settled intention to end your life with our assistance at this clinic. Do you understand?'

'Yes, I understand.'

'And is it your firm intention to end your life when you return to the clinic at the time of your next appointment?'

'Yes, it is.'

'We see that you went through stage one about two years ago. Why have you chosen to ask for an assisted death now?'

'Well, I am two years older now. More pain, less mobility, things getting worse. It's not a decent life anymore.'

'So you find your life intolerable?'

'Yes, I do.'

'Is this entirely your own decision?'

'Yes.'

'Has anyone else sought to persuade you to seek an assisted death?'

'No, they have not.' More questions followed on a similar theme. The consultant's report on her hips, her back and her arthritic hands were commented on. Marianne felt exhausted and in a slight daze, but eventually it seemed she had said the right things as their questions came to an end.

'Well, Mrs Davenport,' said the senior doctor, 'we are satisfied that you qualify for the right to choose an assisted death and are of sound mind and have made this decision of your own free will. We would ask you please to sign this form. You should have already received a copy of it to study in advance.'

'Yes, I have.'

'Very well. Please sign the form, but please note what it says here in bold. You are, of course, absolutely free to change your mind at any time. Just ring the clinic or ask someone to call on your behalf. Do you understand?'

'Yes,' Marianne said, as she signed the form. She noted that the doctors didn't mention the small print about the cancellation charges which would apply – but of course that would be far too grubby.

'Thank you, Mrs Davenport. You will be asked to sign a final consent form next time. Do you have any questions?'

'No.'

'Fine.' The doctors stood up. 'Just remember that if you have any questions you want to raise or any concerns please telephone your nurse, Mrs Singh, and she will be able to help you.'

'Thank you,' Marianne said, and waited for the orderly to come and take her back down in the lift. Back at reception she was met by the same woman.

'Everything alright?'

Marianne mumbled an assent.

'Good. We just need to fix a date then. As you know there has to be a gap of three weeks after stage two,' she said, looking down at her electronic diary. 'That would take us to Wednesday 23rd or Thursday 24th?'

Marianne shrugged and looked at Helen.

'Actually, I think Thursday…' Helen began.

'Thursday, then,' said Marianne.

'Excellent. I'll put you in the diary for Thursday 24th November. If you're here about ten o'clock that would be perfect.'

22

Jake was crossing Clapham Common for the fourth time on Sunday morning when he felt his phone vibrate in his pocket. The marathon season was now over but he was determined to keep fit over the winter months. He had completed London in three and a half hours that spring and shaved nearly ten minutes off that time at the Berlin Marathon in September. Breaking the three-hour barrier now seemed a realistic objective.

The call was from Leah. There was something she urgently wanted to discuss with him – and not about work, she emphasised. Leah had now been at the *Chronicle* for nearly two months as an intern and Jake saw her almost every day. Having secured her the position, she had become his responsibility, and they were currently working together on a story about electoral corruption in the use of postal votes. He was surprised – but not displeased – that she wanted to see him on a Sunday and agreed to meet her in St James's Park.

It was early afternoon when Jake emerged from Westminster tube station and began walking up towards the park. A weak sun shone through the London Plane trees which now seemed to have finally succumbed to the approaching winter and were shedding a blizzard of yellow and brown leaves. He spotted her immediately, sitting on a bench near the bridge, her head bent over her mobile phone. He kissed her on the cheek and sat down beside her.

'Well?' he said.

'What do you know about assisted dying?'

'AD? Well, it's been legal now for ten or fifteen years. It's getting to become quite common, I believe. Why?'

'Dad told me that Gran is thinking of having an assisted death.'

'Auntie Manne, really? You mean sometime in the future – or, like, soon?'

'I got the impression quite soon. Dad was very vague – but I felt I was being softened up. I asked Mum and she confirmed it – in fact, she was keen to tell me it was all for the best. But the thing is, she doesn't seem to have any particular illness. I mean, don't you have to be terminal or something? Mum says we must respect her decision when the time comes, but it just seems so fucking wrong. I mean, how can they even think about it with someone as brilliant as Gran?'

Jake was silent for a while, trying to formulate his response and absentmindedly tearing small strips off a fallen leaf. He watched while some fat ducks waddled past, lured by a woman throwing bread into the water.

'Jeez, Jake – are you getting this at all?' said Leah. 'This is my family we're talking about,' and she reached out suddenly and flicked the remains of the leaf out of Jake's hand.

'I'm sorry,' said Jake, resting his hand lightly on Leah's for a few seconds. 'My family too – and yes, it is surprising, and sad, but...'

'Sad? Is that all you can say? It's fucking criminal. You don't understand. I love Gran – she's, like, so inspirational. It's Gran who really motivated me to work hard these last two years – and to apply to Cambridge. She's just... talked to me about so many things. And I have been reading her novels set in Russia – I'm on the third one. God, they're just brilliant...'

'Yes, I've read them – they are very good. But look, maybe this is all a bit premature. Maybe she is just thinking about it for the future – or maybe there is something we don't know about. I'll talk to Mum – or Claire, she knows everything.'

'No – you mustn't talk to them. Dad said he wasn't sure he should have told me and I absolutely wasn't to say anything to anyone.'

'OK. But I'll make discreet soundings and I may hear something. And you try to find out more from your parents.'

'OK, sorry for getting cross. I just wanted to tell you 'cos, you know, I'm away for most of next week. God, I still can't believe it...'

'Let's walk for a bit,' said Jake.

They set off on a slow amble around the central lake, talking about Marianne and the merits of assisted dying.

'Do you believe in anything?' Leah asked.

'Believe? Are we talking religious belief?'

'If you like.'

'No, I can't say I do. I suppose most people get their religion from their parents. My parents are pretty much atheists; they tend to regard all religions as a bit like a nasty virus – something they hoped their children wouldn't catch.'

'I was interested in Buddhism for a time.'

'Not now?

'No. It appealed to me when I felt I was suffering – teenage angst, I guess. You know, the Buddhist concept of *dukkha*. You have to accept suffering in life; part of the Karmic Cycle.'

'Did you meditate?'

'I tried. I liked the idea of trying to separate mind and body – to disregard all the bodily senses, to let your mind drift apart. For a time, I got interested in suicide from a Buddhist perspective.'

'Buddhism doesn't encourage suicide, does it?'

'Not exactly, but it doesn't condemn it like Christianity. It's regarded as, like, a negative thought – and so against the path of enlightenment. But since the whole point of Buddhism is not to be attached to life, it seems to me that suicide might seem quite logical.'

'To me the whole idea of Nirvana is pretty close to being dead,' said Jake, kicking out at a pigeon in his path. 'You know, having no desires, no aversions. Freedom from suffering, freedom from individual existence.'

'Right.'

'It's the antithesis of the life of feeling, the life force which we tend to value: *the great object of life is sensation – to feel that we exist – even though in pain…*'

'Who said that?'

'I can't remember – one of the Romantics, I think.'

'I like it – pain is then, like, intensifying life, it can be an upper, not just to be endured.'

'Sometimes, yes.'

As they crossed the bridge for the second time, a shaft of sun light emerged from a bank of cloud over Buckingham Palace, shimmering on the water and lighting up the roofs of Whitehall. 'I love this park,' said Leah. 'I feel I'm in the heart of London – the centre of my world now.'

'Australia…?'

'I'm in no hurry to go back.'

As they turned and walked beside the lake, past Horse Guards Parade, there was a sudden gust of wind and a shower of leaves began to fall around them, dancing and jerking in the breeze. Jake held out his hand to catch a dark red leaf but just as it appeared certain to fall into his hand it made a sudden swerve and his fist closed on air.

'Missed it,' said Leah, laughing.

'OK, quit laughing, it's not so easy.'

Leah focused on a leaf spinning in the low autumn sunlight, flashing its orange wings like a summer butterfly. 'Shit,' she said, as at the last minute it spun out of her reach. While she spoke, as if to compensate for her previous miss, a large lazy leaf, shaped like a child's fan, wafted gently into her arms.

'Look,' she said, holding up the perfect, butter-yellow specimen. 'I got one. What is it?'

'It's a Ginkgo – Chinese.'

'How come you know about trees and stuff?'

'My mum…'

'Of course, Aunt Julie. It's exquisite – reminds me of a scallop shell, a golden scallop.'

'Yes, and now you will have good luck.'

'I already have,' she said, touching Jake on the arm.

Before he realised what he was doing, Jake found himself moving his head down towards Leah, while at the same time she looked up into his face, her lips slightly parted. In that split second he realised he was about to kiss her – he badly wanted to kiss her; he could smell her hair and felt the scent of her breath on his face – but a warning bell had rung somewhere inside him – she's your little cousin, just out of school – and he turned to brush his lips against her cheek.

To hide their mutual confusion, he squeezed her hand and said, 'You'll be back by Saturday won't you? Shall we go for a meal, or maybe take in a movie…?'

For a moment Leah looked irritated and disappointed, then she shrugged and said, 'Sure, if you like.'

'Any preferences?'

'Why don't you surprise me.'

Back in his flat Jake went straight to his laptop. Closing some personal writing, he clicked on 'Assisted Dying'. He realised he knew almost nothing about the topic. He began by looking at the original legislation. Lots of safeguards, two independent doctors, a review of the patient's physical and mental state, a sound mind, '*a voluntary, clear, settled and informed wish*', a cooling-off period between the expressed intention and the assisted death itself. It seemed, as far as Jake could understand it, that the original proposal of an assisted death for those with a terminal illness had been rejected as discriminating against those with chronic long-term conditions, and the final formula talked about '*intolerable physical or mental suffering brought about by a medically serious somatic condition*'.

So, Jake thought, no AD if you lose your mind but if your 'serious' physical condition causes unbearable mental suffering, that would be enough.

In so far as Jake had ever thought about the issue before, it had always seemed eminently sensible. After all, it was more than seventy years since suicide itself had ceased to be a crime. It was surely necessary that assisted suicide, or assisted dying as it was now called, should also cease to be a crime. Looking back to social commentators, writing before the law had been changed, Jake noted with approval the prescience of the fantasy writer Terry Pratchett, who had written in 2011: '*The truth is that assisted dying in the UK will happen sooner or later, because it is how the world works: eventually the unthinkable is the everyday, quite often for the best.*'

The low hum of conversation around the open-plan office reverberated in Jake's head that Monday morning as he tried to finish a short piece on homing pigeons. Wakefield Council had ordered a Mr Ted Burrows to get rid of his pigeons. He had tried to get rid of them, Mr Burrows explained to the magistrates, but they had merely done what they were trained to do, which was always to return to the same place. Pressing the send button and rubbing his eyes, Jake got up to stretch his legs. What a load of crap, he thought, as he walked slowly to the coffee machine and pushed espresso twice. Passing a colleague on his way back to his desk he said, 'Hi, George – do you know if we've ever done anything on AD?'

George looked up, surprised. 'What have you heard?'

'Heard? Nothing – what do you mean?'

George looked around. 'I need a coffee.'

Jake followed him back to the coffee machine.

'So what's your interest in AD?' George asked.

'One of my rellies. Rumoured to be contemplating an assisted death – that's all.'

'OK, I thought you might have picked up some gossip somewhere – Charlie is terrified we may be scooped but he's got some deep throat at one of these AD clinics. Thinks it all smells a bit. We're planning an exposé – but I don't know too much about it. If you're interested, you should talk to Mills.'

Bringing his coffee back to his desk, Jake put his head into a small glass office where Mills was working. 'George tells me that you're doing an investigation into AD?'

'Correct – but keep it to yourself.'

'What's the story?'

Mills shrugged. 'As you probably know, the NHS won't touch AD, nor will private sector hospitals, so it's all in the hands of the specialist AD clinics. What we've found is stuff like heavy commercial pressure from management to maximise "throughput"; staff bonuses linked to secret targets; evidence from one clinic that has never turned away a single applicant; and aggressive marketing to NHS trusts. There's also this,' she said, handing him a sheet of paper with a passage highlighted.

Jake began to read. 'Shit, I see what you mean. The clinics are paying commission back to the NHS hospitals and GPs. That's shocking.'

'Is it?'

Jake turned and saw that Charlie had come into the room. 'More interested in our research than your own,' Charlie added, 'or are you flirting with Mills?'

'No chance,' said Mills. 'He's only got eyes for his young cousin…'

'Hey, that's not…'

'Come over here,' said Charlie as he walked to his own screen.

'What is it?'

'Just read,' and he pointed to his screen. '*DEATH PATHWAY. TRUSTS PAID MILLIONS.*' Jake read on: '*The majority of hospitals in England are being given financial rewards for placing terminally ill patients on a "pathway" to death, it can be disclosed. Almost two thirds of NHS trusts using the Liverpool Care Pathway have received pay-outs totalling millions of pounds for reaching targets related to its use…*' Jake looked at the date – November 2012.

'Twenty-one years ago,' said Charlie. 'You can find a lot of articles around that time on a similar theme.'

'Yes, but surely that was completely different?' said Jake. 'I mean, the Liverpool Pathway… wasn't that considered good clinical practice for those who were shortly about to die in any event? It wasn't medically assisted suicide.'

'Theoretically that's true, but if you read the contemporary material you will see that there was an element of hastening the end, denial of water and so on, and this was linked to specific financial incentives to NHS hospital trusts.'

'So, you don't think there is a problem?' asked Jake.

'Oh yes, there are abuses in the way that AD operates today and we are going to expose them. But there are also deficiencies in the present law – it doesn't work for dementia sufferers – which is why some patients are rushing to the clinics at the first hint of Alzheimer's. All I'm saying is that managing death has never been easy. Now I suggest you get on with your own work. I'm expecting that investigation of yours to be wrapped up in the next week.'

23

Marianne heard a door close and she knew it must be Dorrie using the front-door key she had given her. Dorrie greeted her warmly but with a quizzical look.

'Well? Tell me how it went,' she said, sitting across the kitchen table and measuring a small amount of milk into her tea.

'It was entirely predictable,' Marianne replied.

'Well, what you may have been able to predict is not within the range of my more limited powers, so you're just going to have to tell me.'

Marianne shrugged. 'OK, I'll tell you – but after that I don't want to talk about it anymore today.'

'OK, fine.'

So Marianne told Dorrie how it had gone at the clinic. Rather to her surprise, she found it a relief to have someone she could share the experience with and to have a laugh about the absurdities of the process. She tried to inject a little irony into the description and she thought she might have succeeded because Dorrie acknowledged the humorous side.

'Hard to know whether to laugh or cry; but seriously, Marianne, you're not going to go on with this, are you?'

'Yes, I am.'

'But why now? That's what I don't understand.'

Marianne sighed. 'I don't know whether you remember how things were in England before the law was changed, when people went off to that awful blue chalet in Switzerland?'

'I remember.'

'Well, what was most tragic about those cases was the fact that the patients were going off far too early, but they didn't dare leave it any longer in case they found it was too late and were no longer able to travel.'

'And so…?'

'AD is still only possible if you are deemed to be of sound mind. If I had a stroke tomorrow which left me mentally disabled, then even if I still had the wit to ask for an assisted death the chances are that it would be refused.'

'Maybe, but I had the impression they were fairly flexible on that now. I've known some friends who were pretty gaga but they were still accepted for AD.'

'If they were, then the law was being broken; it's not a risk I am prepared to take.'

Dorrie got up from the kitchen table and went over to the window. It was almost dark and the East Anglian wind was blowing small streaks of rain onto the glass panes. She pulled down the blind and turned back towards Marianne. 'Morally – doesn't it trouble you…?'

'In what way?'

'It's curious – I've never been religious but to me there is something fundamentally wrong with ending your life early, unless you really are *in extremis*. But you had a Catholic upbringing – and I know that some traces still remain. Yet committing suicide doesn't seem to bother you?'

Marianne thought about the question. What was left of her Catholicism was largely emotional: a sense of the transcendent when she entered an ancient cathedral; a well-developed capacity to feel guilt; and in the past – but less now – an instinctive prayer in a moment of crisis. Yet somewhere inside her there remained a need for absolution. Not the kind a priest could give, but something she had to achieve for herself; the only sacrifice she had left to make, a means to atone finally for what she had done wrong in her life.

'Seems now I look only for utility,' she said, 'and here I am confident the balance favours what I'm doing.'

Dorrie sat down at the table and poured herself some more tea. 'The Hindus have a concept called *Prayopavesa* – where an old person is permitted to starve themselves to death when they have no desire or ambition left, and no responsibilities remaining in life – is that how you see yourself?'

Marianne pondered for a moment. She still had ambitions but it was too late now to fulfil them; as for responsibilities, hers all lay the other way. 'Well, I don't fancy starving myself,' she said. 'I prefer to get on with it. Anyway, we weren't going to talk about it anymore.'

'That's fine, but only if you promise me another opportunity to try to dissuade you.'

Marianne duly made her promise to Dorrie; she was relieved to put the whole subject to one side and talk about something else.

'It's good to see you've got those old wartime diaries of your mother out; that was the big project you were working on.'

'It has been, but it's all too much for me now.' Marianne gazed at her desk with its pile of notebooks and her pages of typescript, and wondered again what she would do with all the material. It was to have been her last project, only it had come to her too late. She had started with enthusiasm – it made her feel her life had a purpose again – and she had expected to complete the project within a year; but bouts of ill health, combined with a certain slothfulness that seemed to have overtaken her in the last year, meant that it remained unfinished. Now she must type up her remaining notes and leave the material in a state where someone could take over the task. It seemed that person would have to be Claire, though she doubted Claire would have the interest or energy to do much with it.

'No more surprises – like your father?'

Marianne shook her head.

'Has it bothered you much in life – about who your real father was?'

'Not at all. My mother told me when I was very young – before I was old enough to understand. I just shut the knowledge away in a little box inside me. When I was older – well, I had always known, so it didn't seem so important. My father wanted the world to think he was my natural parent and that was fine with me – I didn't want any ghost coming between me and my papa. Personally, I've never set too much store on the whole blood thing – the idea that you don't know who you are unless you know your natural parents.'

Marianne continued her explanations to Dorrie, repeating

253

the answers she had spent a lifetime giving. But as they talked, she sensed a growing tension in Dorrie – a suppression of what she wanted to say but had agreed not to. Finally, when Dorrie got up to leave she looked Marianne in the eye. 'You've got to stop this nonsense. I am going to speak to Callum.'

Marianne sighed. 'I don't think that's necessary.'

'Well I am sure that it is necessary. Indeed, it's vital. There's nothing wrong with you, Marianne. Snap out of it. Sometimes a child has to stop a parent doing something stupid, just as parents do for their children, and there is something stubborn and – dare I say it? – almost childish in your desire to end your life prematurely.'

'Prematurely – at nearly ninety…?'

'Age isn't the test; it can't be. Legally, age is irrelevant. You are eighty-eight…'

'Eighty-nine in January…'

'… and fundamentally you are quite healthy. Stacks of people are living to a hundred now and you have more to live for than most.'

Marianne said nothing, only shaking her head.

'Stupid and selfish – that's the only way I can describe it.'

'Selfish? It's the complete…'

'… I shall speak to Callum – and I shall be waiting your call to say that you've come to your senses.'

'Callum understands…'

'If he thinks he understands, he's badly mistaken.'

'He has promised…'

'Wake up, Marianne! Wake up and see how wrong this is. Stupid, selfish and wrong… I'll let myself out,' she added, as she stomped from the room.

Marianne moved from the kitchen to the living room and

slumped into her chair. She hated quarrelling with Dorrie. But how could it be otherwise? She wrapped herself in her cashmere blanket, dimmed the light and tried to force herself to sleep.

The air is damp and misty, the sky heavy with yellow clouds and the light more like dusk than mid-morning. She stares over the top of the white picket fence to where the small boy is trying to repair a snowman, now dissolving fast in the morning drizzle. She finds Pony and pushes the toy horse up against the fence. Holding onto the wooden struts, she stands on Pony's back and puts her stomach onto the pointed fence top; it's not comfortable but her winter jacket cushions the pain and she brings up her legs and rolls forward, landing sideways onto the soggy ground. Getting up, she walks over to where the boy is digging slush with a plastic spade from around what is left of the snowman, as if trying to rescue a sandcastle with wet sand from the remorseless approach of the tide.

For a few minutes she tries to help him with her bare hands, then, getting bored, she starts to wander down towards the pond at the bottom of the garden. A few seconds later the boy runs past her and they are both now staring out at the ice through the high wire fencing. She is still peering through the wire when she sees that the boy has moved to where a bush is growing up against the fence and is on his knees scrabbling at the bottom of the wire. Now she is beside him and they are both digging like chipmunks, scraping away the last of the snow and exposing a strip of wire which doesn't quite reach the ground.

When they are both under the fence they stand together looking at the frozen surface of the pond. A thin layer of melting snow covers the ice which has trapped various twigs and small branches, fallen from the overhanging trees. 'I can slide,' says the boy, as he steps out onto the ice. Groaning and creaking noises come from the surface but the ice holds. The boy pushes off and slides a couple of feet; smiling, he turns back towards her as if seeking her approval. Cautiously, she tries to slide herself and then they are both sliding and laughing and clinging to each other and trying to use each other to push off as they move further towards the centre of the pond. Is it her foot, or is it his, which catches on a twig protruding from the surface of the ice? Whichever it is, they reach for each other and together they fall heavily onto the ice which breaks all around them. Both her arms go down into the icy water. She tries to stand up but there is nothing solid under her. The water grips her legs, then her stomach, now up to her shoulders as her arms flail at the broken ice, trying to find something to grip onto. Beside her the boy is also struggling, but this is not helping her. The water is gripping her around the neck, now swilling against her face and in her mouth and nose. She coughs violently; she needs to do something. She reaches out a hand to the boy's shoulder and as she does so she sees his face – surprised, frightened, the blue eyes questioning her. For a moment she hesitates – caught in the grip of his pleading eyes – then she pushes down with one hand while with the other she desperately tries to dig her nails into a rough part of the ice. The movement helps lift her body and now her knee is on something soft and yielding and as she pushes again her stomach is on the surface of the ice and one hand has found some purchase on a piece of wood. Something is clinging to her leg, pulling her back down, but with a final kick she frees herself and is out of the water and lying on the surface of the pond.

She lies there motionless for a few seconds, then she sits up and looks back at the hole in the ice. Broken pieces float on the surface. There is no sign of the boy. She knows something terrible has happened. But what should she do? 'Ryan?' she calls quietly. 'Ryan?' Then she starts to scream and her arms are thrashing but something is obstructing her. She tries to throw it off and then she is sitting up in her chair with her blanket on the floor.

Marianne lay back in the chair, breathing hard with her heart pounding in her ears. I remember everything. I have remembered for years. I started my life by drowning that poor boy. And I didn't even run for help. I pretended to myself and to the world that it hadn't happened. As if pretending could make it so.

24

The rattle of a passing train temporarily drowned their conversation as Jake and Leah walked across the Jubilee Bridge towards Charing Cross. So much water, Jake marvelled, great streams of gushing grey water flowing each side of the pillars; why was it that, when walking over a bridge, the Thames always seemed so much wider than he remembered? Was it merely the greyness of the afternoon, with sky and water competing for the same place on the artist's palette, or was it the way the river curved around to St Paul's and the City which made it seem especially wide at this point? A sharp wind was blowing down the river and Jake turned his gaze to the east where Wren's masterpiece lay like a recumbent empress surrounded by her praetorian guard of glass and steel towers.

Jake was surprised to find that he was holding Leah's hand; he did not recall making any conscious decision to do so. Yet somehow her hand had come into his, and he found himself remembering how powerfully intimate this simple act could be. A thousand nerve endings gently caressing each other, speaking in their own silent language of sensation, while the controlling minds danced a more cautious minuet with words.

'So you haven't told me yet what we are going to do,' said Leah.

'You said you wanted a surprise.'

'Yeah, but now is the time to surprise me.'

'OK – we are going to the theatre.'

'Cool, so what are we going to see?'

'It's a revival. *Arcadia*, by Tom Stoppard, have you heard of it?'

'Yeah… Stoppard… yeah, I remember, didn't he write the script for *Shakespeare in Love*? We saw it at school.'

'Yes, I think he did.'

'Yeah, I remember something else. Mrs Duckworth, our English teacher, talked about Stoppard – I think she approved of him.'

'Well, that's a relief!' said Jake.

'Hey!' said Leah, giving Jake's hand a squeeze. 'Don't mock my Mrs D – she was a brilliant teacher. What's *Arcadia* about?'

'Well, it happens in different time zones – you move back and forth from early nineteenth century to late twentieth century, with overlapping themes. To tell you the truth, the only production I've ever seen was about five years ago at university, so it's all a bit hazy, but I'm looking forward to seeing it again. I seem to remember there's lots of maths in it.'

'Maths! Is it going to be entertainment or hard work?'

'I think you'll enjoy it.'

'OK, and hey, thank you, this is a real treat for me, you know.'

Jake turned and smiled at his companion; this definitely has the feeling of a date, he thought, noticing again that Leah's familiar jeans had given way to a skirt – short, but not ostentatiously so, over which a black woollen coat had replaced the normal grey jacket, and a new emerald green scarf which looked like cashmere was wound tightly around her neck. A modest amount of makeup – which he had never seen on her before – completed the transformation.

Jake was looking forward to seeing the play again, but ten minutes into the production, as details of the plot and characters came flooding back to him, he began to wonder whether he had made a wise choice. She's never going to believe me if I tell her I couldn't remember that it featured a young teenage girl and her tutor. She's going to see all sorts of parallels which I did not intend and which I could really do without. His expectations were fulfilled as soon as the interval arrived.

'Are you trying to tell me something?' Leah asked as soon as the applause had died down and they had begun to move slowly from their seats towards the bar. 'Do you think of me as Thomasina? I'm not thirteen, you know, and I think I can just about get the meaning of "carnal embrace".'

Jake was ready with his answer. 'To be honest, Leah, I had forgotten almost everything about the play except for the bare outline. I didn't even remember the characters of Thomasina or Septimus. I wanted to see it again because it's regarded as maybe Stoppard's best play – it's clever and funny, and I thought you would enjoy it.'

Leah smiled, and Jake was relieved to feel that the moment of tension had evaporated. 'Yeah, it's really cool, and I love

Thomasina. She may be ignorant of life but she's so ferociously clever. Books, literature – that's all very well. But maths and physics – that takes real intelligence. I wish I understood that part better.'

'Don't worry about it, hardly anyone else does either. Just sit back and enjoy it and in the meantime stay here while I fight my way to the bar to get us a drink.'

Leah seemed strangely preoccupied as they walked away from the matinée performance towards the Italian bistro in Soho where Jake had booked a table. Her hands remained firmly in the pockets of her coat and Jake chose not to force a conversation but guided her through the early evening crowds towards the restaurant. Their table wasn't ready so they took a seat at the bar and Jake ordered a bottle of the Pinot Grigio. As they sipped their wine and nibbled on grissini, it wasn't long before Leah recovered her voice. 'So Thomasina dies in a fire on her seventeenth birthday – I can't bear it. All that brilliance going to waste.'

For a fleeting moment Jake thought of his twin sister and remembered why the play had affected him so much when he had first seen it. Then he laughed. 'It's a story, Leah. Her death is just a theatrical device.'

'Yeah, I know that, but you have to believe in the characters. They have to be real to you – otherwise what's the point?'

'By all means believe in the characters – but it's the ideas that make you think.'

'So who's right?' asked Leah. 'They never really tell you, these authors, do they? They love teasing you – posing questions. I mean, the creepy prof who rubbishes science. Stoppard didn't really think that science was a waste of time, did he? Or perhaps he did – I mean he was a writer, so perhaps he's just for art and poetry. The human heart and all that stuff.'

'Well, I think he's saying you need both.'

'Yeah, but I suppose the prof character…'

'You mean Bernard?'

'Yeah, Bernard, I mean, he's right in a way, isn't he? We can get on with our lives as humans always have, eating, sleeping, mating, without knowing what's happening in the universe or why.'

'Well, I suppose some aspects of science, some technologies, medicine and so on are pretty useful to us.'

'Yeah, but Stoppard's not talking about practical science; he's talking about maths, about the second law of thermodynamics – Newton, Einstein, the end of the universe.'

'So, what seems most important to you?'

'How do you mean?'

'I mean, to have a scientific understanding of the universe – as far as that's possible – or to hell with it.'

'It has to be to hell with it,' said Leah, 'because I can't get my mind around all this higher maths, these iterated algorithms – so I'm a simple romantic by default. Perhaps as I grow older I will change and morph into a mathematician or a philosopher.'

Jake laughed. 'I think you are right – human life reverses the historical pattern. In history, romanticism arrives as a reaction to classicism – a break out from the rigidity of the classical world. A "decline from thinking to feeling", the play calls it, but in life we are all born as romantics, able to feel long before we can think seriously.'

Leah frowned and nibbled on her grissini. 'I'm not so sure about that. When we are very young we have instincts – to suckle, to cling to our mothers – but that's not proper feeling. As we grow older we are constantly applying our brains to things, thinking all the time, asking questions of ourselves and others and trying to make sense of the world.' Leah paused and sipped her wine. 'You know, little kids – they ask direct questions. Is Grandpa going to die? Do cats go to heaven? They are supremely rational with a strong sense of logic but their feelings are still shallow. At six or seven we may be sad if someone close to us dies but we don't really feel it. Not deep down. Not like we do when we are older – when we know what death really means…'

Leah's torrent of words dried up and Jake was suddenly reminded that Leah was only eighteen herself. A teenager wrestling with familiar philosophical questions as well as real-life events. Marianne's demise, whenever and however it came about, would likely be her first experience of death. He was relieved, therefore, when the arrival of a waiter to show them to their seats blew away the spectre of Auntie Manne, draining the last dregs of her hemlock, which for a moment had floated down between them.

It was Leah, however, who returned to the subject of death. 'You said you were going to tell me something more about AD?'

'Yes, as I said, I'm not supposed to know this, but the *Chronicle* is doing some investigation into AD and Mills told me a bit about it. What they're interested in is whether all these commercial clinics which have sprung up are bending the law and offering AD to people who shouldn't qualify. They've got a source at one of the clinics feeding them information.

Apparently, the clinics are paying commissions to hospitals and GPs to get patient referrals.'

As he talked, Jake sensed that while Leah appeared to be listening politely her mind was elsewhere. 'I think I'm boring you with all this,' he said.

Leah smiled. 'I am listening, but it's true, I can't get the play out of my mind. So, Thomasina and Septimus are falling in love at the end? And when she dies we are supposed to understand that Septimus goes to live in the hermitage? So in many ways he is a romantic figure, living the life of a hermit and trying to unravel the mysteries of the universe which were puzzling poor Thomasina.'

'I suppose you can see him as a romantic figure.'

'Can you see yourself in a cave then – dreaming of a lost girl?' said Leah, and for a brief moment Jake thought again of Fran and realised that it was exactly such a black pit at the edge of which his life had, for a time, been precariously balanced. He was also conscious that Leah was now flirting with him, but he saw no reason not to reciprocate.

'I suppose if the girl was as brilliant and beautiful as Thomasina, then perhaps I might.'

'Indeed, but where would you find such a girl?' said Leah. 'You know, I like the name Septimus – better than Jake, don't you think? Perhaps I shall call you Septimus – then you will be both my tutor and my pupil.'

'… quite a challenge.'

'Mind you, spending the rest of his life in a hermitage was something of a transformation for Septimus and not entirely believable – even as an act of devotion to the tragic Thomasina. From friend of Lord Byron and summer-house shagger, to a lifetime hermit – I don't think that quite stacks up in terms of character. What about you, Septimus?' she said, looking hard at Jake. 'Do you get up to that kind of thing? In the gazebo – with other people's wives?'

'Preferably not with other people's wives,' said Jake, laughing. 'And come to think of it, probably not in a gazebo either.' What he thought, though, as he looked across the table to his now grown-up cousin with her infectious smile and sparkling blue eyes, was shit – bloody brilliant, this girl. Clever, funny and highly shaggable – take her back and fuck her to bits – but I mustn't. No, I shouldn't think like that. I must be careful, so far and no further...

He had the same thought when Leah planted a discreet kiss on the edge of his lips to thank him for the dinner. He thought it again when it was clear that she was expecting to come back to his flat and not be put into a taxi or escorted to the nearest tube station; and most strongly did he think it yet again when, back in his flat and almost as soon as the door had closed behind them, he found himself in an embrace with Leah where her tongue was slipping stealthily between his lips. In his mind, it was clear to him that he must resist, but it seemed his body was intent on a different plan, as his left hand moved beneath her hair to caress her neck and his right hand clutched firmly at her bottom.

When they broke from their embrace, Leah disappeared to the bathroom and Jake rearranged his clothing and sat down on the sofa to recover his composure. Just a kiss, an after-dinner kiss – of course that's fine, can't be criticised. So perhaps a drink now, tea or coffee, then one more kiss and I'll call a taxi for her. Jake had hardly gathered his thoughts when Leah was out of the bathroom.

'Would you like a coffee or another drink?' he asked. Leah

shook her head, came towards the sofa and promptly sat on his lap, twisting her body towards him and with both arms around his neck resumed where they had left off.

The effect of her twisted body on her already short skirt was to further expose her long creamy legs, on one of which Jake rested his hand a little above her knee. As they continued to kiss and his state of arousal grew, he longed to move his hand further up her leg but he was equally determined not to do so, and thus his hand remained, clamped and immobile, on her soft warm thigh. As if she sensed his own struggle, Leah broke off from their kiss and whispered, 'It's OK, I want you to touch me,' and, taking his hand, she moved it up between her thighs until the tips of his fingers met her soft wet flesh.

The effect electrified them both. For Leah, there was a short gasp and her mouth locked back onto his. For Jake, a realisation that he was about to pass the point of no return, made him remove his hand and leap to his feet with Leah still clinging to his neck, so that they both almost toppled to the ground.

'What the fuck...'

'Leah, we mustn't.'

'What do you mean?'

'I mean, it's not really right – I'm your cousin and I'm a lot older than you...'

'You still think of me as a child, don't you?'

'No, not at all, Leah. I think you're incredibly grown up... and there's nothing I'd like more than to make love to you, but don't you see? Your mum and dad – I have some responsibility to them. They think I'm giving you work experience, looking after you, mentoring you – not seducing you...'

'Well, you're certainly not doing that – it seems I'm doing most of the heavy lifting, in case you hadn't noticed?'

'Of course I want to, but…'

'Always some "but", isn't there? Do you think I've never done it before? Christ, I've shagged boys with bigger balls than you.'

'Leah…'

'I'm leaving now,' and slipping her feet back into her shoes Leah reached for her coat and bag and made towards the door.

'Leah, wait. I'm sorry. Please…'

He watched as the door slammed behind her.

25

Marianne knew that from now on it could only get harder. She knew that Dorrie had spoken to Callum; she had also received a message herself. '*The champagne is on ice,*' Dorrie had concluded. '*Tell me that you have abandoned this terrible idea and we will celebrate together.*'

The possibility that she might change her mind was, Marianne now realised, a vital straw which friends and relatives had to cling on to. Death is just too final, too incomprehensible; even the most phlegmatic need some wriggle-room, some sense that their goodbye may not be the final word. Even Callum, who was now visiting with Leah, seemed to be sheltering behind the thought that there was still plenty of time for her to change her mind.

It was Marianne who had persuaded Callum to bring Leah with him. 'You haven't told her, have you?' she said to him when he called to say he was coming.

'No.'

'Good. It will be my goodbye to her – not the other way around.' She had no intention of inflicting an emotional scene on the poor girl – she would say nothing to her, but she wanted to see her one last time. 'Tell her I have a present for her which I meant to give her on her eighteenth birthday but, being the stupid old woman I am, I forgot.' She did indeed have a present for Leah – a necklace which had belonged to her mother: a string of antique pearls with a large central pearl surrounded by an outer ring of small diamonds.

To give himself an opportunity to see his mother alone, Callum had dropped Leah off in Cambridge to visit a school friend. He waited till Anna had gone, then said, 'So Anna doesn't know yet?'

'Not yet.'

'Good.'

'I suppose you think that means that I haven't finally decided – but you're wrong.'

'I see it as an indication you might still change your mind.'

Perhaps I should let him believe that, Marianne thought. Whatever makes it easiest for him also makes it easiest for me. She shrugged. 'I'll have to tell her eventually of course – but closer to the time will be better.'

'You know I'm really not comfortable about this.'

'I know, darling, but you did say you would support my decision when the time came.'

'That's the point – I don't see that the time has come yet.'

'Was it Dorrie who prompted you to come today?'

'Mum – I'm here for myself – but Dorrie made a very strong case that you still have a lot to live for. She's a good friend to you.'

Poor Callum, thought Marianne, as she listened to his argument. Assaulted on every side. His wife no doubt whispering in his ear that it was high time he let his mother go and if she didn't die soon there wouldn't be anything left for them to inherit; now a contrary broadside from Dorrie. Marianne felt wretched that she was putting her son in this invidious position, but she was sure that it was for the best. In a few months he would be grateful for what she was doing.

When Leah arrived on the bus, Callum took the opportunity to go into another room and make some phone calls, while Marianne talked to her about her visit to Cambridge and her life in London. Getting to know at least one of her (great) grandchildren had been a delight which Marianne had never anticipated in the last years of her life. There was something about the girl which seemed to transcend the limitations of her parents: she had managed to avoid both the stolid quality which had always marked out Callum and the aura of discontent which hovered around her mother. Maybe it's just the energy of youth, she thought, but the girl has blossomed since she's been in England.

'Any news on your Cambridge application?' she asked.

'No. But it could be, like, the next couple of weeks.'

'I'll keep my fingers crossed for you.'

'I'm not that hopeful.'

'Well, let's wait and see. And life in London?'

'Sweet as.'

Marianne raised her eyebrows.

'Sorry, Gran – that's Aussie talk. Life's good.'

'I gather you are helping Jake with his work?'

'Yeah, I'm really enjoying it.'

'And going to the theatre with him, I hear.'

'Yeah, that was… yeah, a really interesting play. *Arcadia* – it was like… well, I expect you know it…'

Marianne watched as a blush rose up from Leah's neck.

'Do I detect that there is something going on between you two?'

Leah looked uncomfortable and turned to see if her father was anywhere near. 'Would it be very wrong – I mean, if Jake and I got together, like in a relationship?'

'Why ever should it be wrong?'

'I mean with us being cousins and stuff…'

'Nonsense. You're quite distant.'

Leah looked at Marianne with gratitude. 'I know he's a bit older than I am…'

'Don't be silly, Leah – you're eighteen. Girls of your age used to marry men of forty, sometimes still do. So, do I take it that there is something going on between you?'

'Well…'

'Have you shagged…'

'Gran!'

'… if that's the right expression – or am I out of date?'

Leah turned again to look at the door.

'Don't look so shocked – even in my day we did it occasionally.'

'Well, it's early days – but don't say anything to Mum and Dad. Especially not to Mum – I know she won't approve.'

'I won't say a word. But if your mother gets difficult about it you can tell her from me that I think it's absolutely fine. I think Jake is a charming young man and would make an excellent boyfriend for you.'

'Oh, Gran,' said Leah, as she knelt to kiss Marianne. 'You're such a star.'

What irony, thought Marianne, those years when I wanted Callum to get together with Juliette and now Leah has fallen for Jake. And what if I had been allowed to go on seeing Daniel... And for a moment she was back in her own past – seventy-five years dissolving in an instant – and she was lying in their little hideaway by the cliff, reading to Daniel, reading the French novel he couldn't understand, while he tried to imitate her sounds, before he rolled on top of her, pressing her down into the grass...

'Gran?'

Marianne shook herself out of her reverie. 'Yes, I'm dreaming. Disappearing into my past – I'm afraid it's what happens when you get to my age. Now I mustn't forget the main reason I asked you to come today,' and Marianne reached for the battered green leather jewellery box beside her chair and handed it to Leah. 'I meant to give it to you for your birthday in April. It's a little old for you, perhaps, but I hope you will wear it in time.'

Leah picked up the necklace and held it up. 'Wow, Gran – it's awesome. Incredible.'

'Try it on then.'

Marianne watched as Leah put the necklace on; she had cut her hair since Marianne had last seen her and at shoulder length it suited her better. As Leah fastened the clasp and lifted her head Marianne felt a choke in her throat – she knew that this was the last time she would ever see Leah, but it wasn't just that: there was something about the girl's eyebrows, that suggestion of a curl at the outer edge, and those piercing blue eyes that brought back Izzy so strongly... She remembered when Izzy had tried on the necklace at the same age. It came over Marianne suddenly and with such violence that she couldn't help herself; tears began to roll down her cheeks.

Leah looked alarmed. 'Are you OK, Gran?'

She nodded and put out her arms as Leah knelt to hug and thank her. Marianne held on to her as long as she could – perhaps longer than was quite seemly – but Leah was also clinging tightly to her. Gently Marianne pushed her away. 'You remind me so much… you're so like her – Isabelle – your real grandmother,' she said, reaching for a handkerchief to blow her nose. 'Now go and get your father off the telephone and we'll have some tea before you leave.' As Leah got to her feet, Marianne noticed that she also seemed close to tears. Perhaps she does know, she thought. I wonder if Callum told her?

Jake had spent the afternoon in his office reviewing all the material they had gathered on postal voting. He was about to leave the office when his phone buzzed with a message. Leah needed to talk to him urgently – could he stay at the office till she got there? Since the evening when Leah had stormed out of his flat, they had maintained a self-consciously formal relationship in the office, occasionally discussing Marianne but avoiding all mention of the theatre and its aftermath. Jake was not expecting to see Leah that evening. He knew she had gone to Cambridge with her father to see Marianne, and Leah knew that he had a longstanding arrangement to see a new film with Gemma, an old friend from Bristol. Jake's friendship with Gemma had developed from the university film club and a shared enthusiasm for French New Wave cinema of the 1960s, which no one else in their circle could be bothered with. Pretentious philosophical waffle, his friends thought, but Jake confessed to a weakness for those evenings of delicious melancholy and those 'lost girls with greasy hair', as some critic had memorably described a certain period of French cinema. The film they were due to see that evening – though apparently quite violent – was billed as homage to Chabrol and other film makers of the sixties and seventies.

Jake was reluctant to stand up his old college soulmate and sent a text back to Leah asking if it was important and reminding her that he was booked to go to the movies with an old friend. The message came back: 'fucking is – Gran definitely going for AD – Dad just confirmed – we've got to do something.'

Jake sat back in his chair. He realised it must be nearly six months since he had seen Marianne. He would need to visit her before it was too late. Once the initial moment of shock had passed, Jake felt a more general sadness, but also some irritation with Leah. Reluctantly he confirmed that he would wait for her and then called Gemma to explain why he had to pull out at short notice.

The large open-plan office in Covent Garden where Jake worked was half empty by the time Leah arrived. As a temporary intern she had her own pass and suddenly he realised she was standing beside him, pouring out her distress and anger in a confused and confusing torrent of words. Jake swiftly closed down his screen, took her by the arm and led her out towards the lifts. 'People are still working, Leah. Let's go somewhere we can talk.'

By the time they had found their way to the corner of a basement bar, Jake had deduced that Leah's anger was largely because she felt she had been treated like a child. 'I was not supposed to know so I couldn't, like, say anything. Then Gran gave me this incredible necklace and started to be all, like, emotional – but I couldn't say a fucking word to her, even though that might be the last time I will ever see my grandmother. I mean, Dad admitted afterwards it was her way of saying goodbye to me – can you believe it? – but no one gave me the chance to say anything…'

'I suppose it's hard for her…'

'… and Dad's so bloody calm about it – as if it's just a detail that his mum's going off to kill herself.'

'Did he give you any clue why…?'

'No, that's the point. There doesn't seem to be any reason for it. No terminal illness, just, just… well, nothing.'

Jake reached across the table and put his hand on her arm. 'I'm really sorry about this – I love her too, but I know she's your grandmother, not mine.'

'We need to do something…'

'I'll speak to my grandmother Claire – she'll know what's going on for sure.'

'We have to think of a strategy. I need you on my side.'

'I am on your side.'

'I'm glad,' she said, and gave his hand a squeeze.

Half an hour passed in discussing what they knew of Marianne's circumstances before Jake said, 'Another drink? Or do you want to come back to my place and I will cook you something?'

Leah looked at him sceptically. 'Back to your flat?'

'Yes.'

Leah paused. 'I'll come if you promise to treat me as an adult.'

'I've never… well, of course, yes – I promise.'

275

'No more talk about your so-called responsibility to my parents?'

'Fine.'

'And no more talk about age and cousins or any of that shit?'

'Not a word.'

The meal which Jake had promised did not get cooked. They were barely inside the door when they started pulling at each other's clothes. On this occasion neither held back and before long they were tottering half undressed onto Jake's bed.

Afterwards, as he lay on his back with Leah's head on his chest he realised he must have fallen asleep. He knew he had been too quick for her and now he could feel her hand exploring the contours of his stomach. Slowly she traced a finger down the slope of his chest to his flat abdomen – no six-pack but a firmness which suggested sufficient muscularity. Pausing at the neat circle of his belly button, she traced a wide arc down one leg to the extremity of her reach, coming to rest on the inside of his thigh. For a few seconds, she stroked both thighs before bringing her hand up between his legs.

Jake lay still, enjoying the attention. As his state of arousal increased, he moved Leah onto her back and started kissing her breasts. She shut her eyes as his kisses moved down her body. For a few seconds he felt her tense as his tongue probed between her legs. Although she had remained silent in their first encounter, when his tongue reached the right place she let out a small involuntary cry. 'Yes,' she whispered, 'just there.' Later she muttered, 'Don't stop,' as well as, 'Oh shit,' and, much louder, 'Fucking beautiful,' and other obscenities which would have caused Jake to smile, if smiling had been possible at that time.

Much later, when calmness had returned to both of them, Jake asked her whether anyone had done that to her before.

'Chance would be a fine thing,' she said. 'The boys expect us to do it to them, but we don't get it back.'

'Sounds a bit selfish.'

'That's why I like having an older man,' she whispered, biting his ear lobe.

Later, while Leah was taking a bath, Jake called his mother and discovered that she had heard the same news about Marianne from Claire the day before. 'It's all rather a mystery, darling,' she said. 'No one seems to know what's suddenly triggered this.' When he called Claire himself, she was brusque and to the point. 'I'm glad you've telephoned. Come over tomorrow evening. I may have a task for you. I'll expect you at seven.'

26

Jake was still trying to work out how he should respond to the news about Marianne as he made his way towards Holland Park for supper with his grandmother. As he rang the bell he remembered how intimidating he had found her house as a child. The elegance of the first-floor drawing room, with its polished wood floors and soft Persian rugs, could not have been further removed from the utilitarian living room in his parents' converted cowshed on the edge of a muddy field in Dorset. A separate dining room, with its long mahogany table and eighteenth-century Hepplewhite chairs with padded leather seats seemed impossibly grand, compared with the small pine table at the end of the kitchen where Jake and his family ate their meals.

Following his grandmother up the wide staircase into the drawing room, where long, floor-length curtains were drawn across the pair of tall sash widows, he was waved to a sofa while Claire mixed him a gin and tonic, without asking what he wanted.

'So you heard about it from Callum's girl?'

'From Leah – yes. She's an intern in our office. She took the news badly.'

'I can imagine. Of course, I've known Marianne has been thinking about this for a while, but I confess it took me by surprise when I received her letter a couple of days ago,' and Claire reached for an envelope beside her chair. 'Here, you might as well read it – it concerns you in part.'

Jake took the letter from Claire and began to read.

My dearest Claire,

We are perhaps the last generation who will ever send letters to each other and this is a hard one to write. Several times in the past we have discussed the possible advantages of AD and I think you know that it has been on my mind a lot in the last few months.

So far only Callum and Helen and one other close friend know this, but I have booked into an AD clinic and will end my life very shortly. It feels strange writing that last sentence. In the past, the very recent past, it would have been, 'I don't think I have much longer to live,' but now I already know the date of my death. There are many reasons why I have decided to do this but suffice it to say I am nearly ninety now and I feel it's the right time for me to go.

I know that I should say goodbye to you in person but I know you will understand when I say what a difficult process this is, and it is probably easier for both of us if I say goodbye to you this way. The same goes for Julie and Tom as well as for Jake. I just can't do too many face-to-face goodbyes so I will rely on you to tell them.

It may be that we will speak before the end, but I wanted to take this opportunity to mention our mother's wartime diaries which I have been slaving over these last two years. As you know, Callum can't read French and is not interested anyway, so I have made it clear to him that the notebooks, as well as the translations and notes I have made, are to go to you. What you do with it all is up to you. I think it may be of some historical as well as family interest. A year or two ago your grandson Jake expressed some slight appreciation of what I was doing and he might have an interest in helping to finish what I have started.

Darling Claire – my little sister – we were not close as children but it has been a wonderful journey getting to know you over the years. We have had some marvellous times together, particularly at Les Trois Cheminées, where you and Peter were always such generous hosts. As for the tragedy of Fran's death: I don't believe I was to blame, but if you and Julie feel that I was, then I hope you can find it in your hearts to forgive me. I could say so much more but I don't have the strength now. You know it anyway. My utmost love to you all.

Marianne

Jake contemplated the letter he had just read. His great-aunt, who had been a permanent fixture in his life, who was still alive and apparently well, would shortly be dead. Despite his sympathy for the concept of AD, the reality of Marianne's imminent but voluntary death shocked him.

'Do you know any more about why she is doing this?'

Claire sighed. 'The way I see it, Marianne has always wanted to be in control. Of herself and others. As she said, we were not close as children. I was nearly ten years younger and she was like an extra mother – extremely bossy – and I wasn't always very fond of her.'

'And then you lived apart?'

'Yes, when I was about nine and Marianne was away at college, my mother declared she was homesick for France and she and my father moved to Normandy, where they stayed for nearly ten years – which is why I grew up essentially a French girl. I saw very little of Marianne till I moved to England at the end of the seventies.'

'But there must have been something to trigger this – are you sure she hasn't got some condition she's not telling you about?'

'I really don't think so. I called Callum as soon as I got the letter, and he is pretty sure there is no mysterious illness.'

'How does he feel?'

'Torn, I think – between respecting her decision and the responsibility of a son for his elderly mother.'

'I got the impression from Leah that Helen might be something of an *agent provocateur* in this.'

'It wouldn't surprise me.'

They continued to talk as Claire led him to the kitchen where a variety of cold meats had been laid on the table. Claire went to the stove and heated some onion soup which she ladled into two bowls. Jake wondered how often Claire used that imposing dining room which used to intimidate him so much as a child.

'These diaries – do you know how far she has got?' he asked, as he swallowed a mouthful of soup.

'No – and it's one of the things I want you to find out. I want you to go and visit her as soon as possible. She doesn't want to see me – and she's probably right; it would be too painful for both of us. But she always had a soft spot for you, and with her mention of the diaries it gives you the perfect excuse.'

'Will she agree to my coming?'

'I think she will. I want you to find out if she is really serious – although I fear that she probably is.'

It seemed to Jake that his Granny Claire was taking the imminent death of her sister very calmly, but he also detected an undertone of disapproval. 'Are you against AD?' he asked.

'You know, Jake,' she said, as she ladled more soup into his bowl, 'I have had several friends who have gone down that route – not because of great suffering but because they thought it was expected of them. And I will tell you one thing – in many ways it's made the process of old age harder.'

'How do you mean?'

'Twenty years ago, apart from a few extreme cases where people travelled to Switzerland, or persuaded a friendly doctor to give them an overdose, you carried on with your life, however hard it was, until you died. You had no choice on the timing of your death.'

'But would you want to go back to the way it was before? I mean, I understood from Mum that – well, that Grandpapa...'

'Yes, right at the end he was helped; but these clinics that Marianne is talking about – most of their patients are not in extremis.'

'They have to have a serious illness...'

Claire sniffed. 'In theory – but once you are in your eighties and beyond, most people have enough ailments to satisfy the test.'

'That's the impression I am beginning to get – but there are supposed to be safeguards – I mean to ensure people are not pressured…'

Claire said nothing and Jake wondered whether she was finding the conversation uncomfortable. He was about to change the subject when she said, 'It's not about external pressures; it's about how old people start to think of themselves: am I becoming a burden; how long is it reasonable to go on living?'

'But you wouldn't think like that?'

'Not me – I'm too selfish, and I don't have any financial worries – but I know people who have done it, and I know others who are thinking about it.'

'Is it something you talk about – I mean with your friends?'

Claire didn't answer. She got up to clear the soup bowls and bring a plate of cheese to the table. Sitting back in her seat, she said, 'Believe me, Jake, while for a few it's been a blessed relief to be able to choose the timing of their death, for many it's greatly increased the anxiety of old age. Sometimes it's easier not to have a choice.'

At first Marianne was quite bewildered; to receive a telephone call from Jake was the last thing she expected, until she realised that Claire must have received her letter, and was intent on sending her grandchild as a spy – no doubt to report back on whether Marianne was serious or was playing some sort of game. She told him he couldn't come. She repeated what she had written to Claire in her letter; she was trying to create order in the last weeks of her life, and couldn't cope with seeing him.

Marianne knew she had only just held herself together with Leah. But she had achieved something. Leah would have a positive memory of her as a sentient human being and not some drooling semi-corpse in a nursing home; the memory of others being the only sliver of immortality we can hope for. As for Jake, she was fond of him, but if she wasn't going to say goodbye in person to Claire or Julie, she certainly didn't need a face-to-face session with Jake.

To her surprise, however, he had been remarkably persistent. He appeared genuinely interested in the diaries and asked a lot of questions about her mother's experiences. She had also been reminded that he spoke good French and was well educated on the history of France and the Second World War.

In the end Marianne found she was unable to say no; she agreed that he could come.

To speak to Jake was inevitably to bring back thoughts of that afternoon at *Les Trois Cheminées*, when, in her memory now, a premonition of death hung in the air. She has been asleep in her room. When she opens her eyes, she closes them again immediately. Although the shutters are fastened, a streak of sunlight lies across her bed. For perhaps half a minute she lies without moving. Then with one hand she pushes her damp hair away from her face, reaches for another pillow to put behind her, opens her eyes again and sits up.

With her familiar hobbled gait she moves to the window and opens the shutters. The brilliance of the afternoon sun forces her back into the room. In the dimness of the shuttered bedroom the walls had looked grey, but as the sun now picks out the mouldings on the opposite side to her bed, it seems that a more distinct colour has been intended. Is it a long-faded *eau de nil*? She isn't sure. She will ask Claire.

Now she is walking down the corridor to the bathroom and splashing water onto her face. Reaching for a towel she begins to frown: the image on her retina – the sun reflecting off the long gravel drive – isn't right. She returns to the window. Perhaps she simply hasn't seen it. Blinking to adjust her eyes to the brightness, she gazes out at the familiar vista. It isn't the wooded valley that has her attention however, it's the drive leading down to the gate, and the absence of the old Renault van.

Jake has been out all day, but Fran was in the house when she went upstairs. She goes to check her bedroom; a paperback lies face down on the unmade bed. Is there still a hint of warmth on the bed? She picks up the book. A thriller – but at least it's in French, she notes. Good girl. She calls from the top of the stairs. Getting no reply, she searches the house and then goes outside. Fran's bicycle is propped up against the side wall but there is no sign of the old van.

Later, when the police arrive at the front door, they almost carry Jake from the car; his red-rimmed eyes and his ghostly white complexion tell her everything. He says nothing while the gendarmes give her an outline of what has happened, and she then has the agonising task of telephoning their mother, Juliette, and trying to comfort Jake. All evening he will neither speak nor eat but she manages to get a little cognac into him. Not wanting to leave him alone, she sits at the end of his bed and talks to him; talks about his sister Fran; talks through the night about her own life and losses; talks till the light begins to creep under the shutters and she is too exhausted to continue.

Jake got out of bed and pulled on a shirt and jeans, before heading to the corner of his living room which passed for a kitchen; meanwhile Leah was pacing around the flat wearing his baggy blue sweatshirt and complaining about his refusal to take her with him on his intended visit to Marianne. 'I don't understand your objection – and I'm a closer relation than you are,' she said.

Jake put some water on to boil and looked in his cupboard; food wasn't in great abundance, so he took down a jar with a little pesto left in the bottom, to which he added some olive oil. 'It wouldn't be fair to ambush her like that,' he said.

'Tell her in advance then – I told you, she knows about us, and she approves.'

'That's not the point – she chose a way to say goodbye to you that was easiest for her and I think you have to respect that.'

'So I'm never to see her again?'

'I am not saying that. Just let me go on my own this time – I had difficulty enough in persuading her to let me come. When I've seen her we can decide what to do.'

'We need to persuade her to change her mind – there's nothing wrong with her.'

Jake put a frying pan onto the gas and sprinkled some pine nuts into the pan. 'Is that really our job? We don't know what it's like to be her age. We can't tell exactly how she feels…'

Leah sniffed and continued her trawl around the flat – examining objects and putting them down again. Picking up a pad from his desk she studied it. 'Is this a poem?'

'Don't look at that.'

'Too late – I already have. I like it.'

'You do want some pasta then?'

'Is this Fran?' she said, picking up a framed photograph of a teenage girl.

'Yes.'

'I don't see much resemblance to you.'

'I've put some pasta on for you anyway.'

'Why won't you tell me about her?'

'She was my twin sister who died in a crash.'

'I mean about her. Everyone says you were very close.'

'She was my twin.'

'Is that all you are going to say? Did you love her very much?'

'What do you think?'

'So are you going to tackle Marianne properly – make her change her mind? I want to know.'

Jake pulled out a strand of spaghetti and put it in his mouth.

'So you're not even going to try?'

'I'll see how it goes – but the best person to influence her would be your father. What are you doing?'

'Getting dressed.'

'Aren't you going to have something…?'

'I'm going home.'

'Now?

'Yes.'

'Don't you want to eat?'

'Do you remember your promise – to treat me as an adult? You're worse than my parents. A little girl who has to be kept out of adult business – that's what you think, isn't it?'

'Don't be ridiculous. And if you want to be treated as an adult you should start behaving like one.'

'Not that fucking cliché. It's what our Head used to spout all the time.'

'This is about respecting Marianne.'

'Well, I'm off.'

'Leah…'

'Tell me about it when you get back – if you think I'm old enough to know about such grown-up matters.'

27

It was, Jake had to admit, a fine example of Victorian gothic, albeit on a domestic scale. Marianne had told him once that the architect, for a long time completely forgotten, was now highly regarded and had recently been the subject of several learned articles. He stood for a while staring up at the roof line of the house, marvelling again at the extravagant flourishes and attention to detail which nearly two hundred years ago had gone into the construction of an ordinary middle-class dwelling.

As he stood looking up, the front door opened and Anna came out. 'You like the house?' she said, coming down the front step to embrace him.

'I do – I've always wondered what happens in that little tower?'

'That's where Marianne locks me if I am bad!'

Jake laughed. 'And you let your hair down for your lover to climb up – like Rapunzel. Do you know the fairy story?'

'Of course – we have same story in Latvia. But the tower is disappointing inside: so small all you can do is just stand in it – no real use.'

Jake had been told that Anna knew nothing of Marianne's decision to have an assisted death and consequently he avoided the subject. 'I've come to help Marianne with her mother's old diaries,' he said.

'That's good,' said Anna, suddenly more serious. 'I think she needs help – recently she seem a bit… well… quiet.'

'Then we must cheer her up.'

'Looking at the old books may help. You know she found out her real father was Latvian, like me.'

'Yes, Leah told me – incredible.'

'Marianne say it is fate. Such an interesting lady. She was a spy in Russia once, you know.'

'I heard the story.'

'Callum told me. She was supposed to be a teacher but she was expelled for spying. I ask her once and she laugh and say, "It's true, I was thrown out, but I was never a spy." But I'm sure she was.'

'You must have become very fond of her?'

'Of course. I do everything for her. And when I am not working sometimes we play cards or just talk together. When she needs to go somewhere I drive her. I try to be like daughter to her.'

'I think she is very lucky to have you,' said Jake.

Despite her original refusal to see Jake, Marianne had begun looking forward to his visit. Perhaps I was right and he will be the one to complete the project, she thought. She was fond of Jake; he had been so devoted to his twin sister that for a time Fran's death had completely destroyed his confidence. For a year or more she had heard reports that he was suffering from depression and Juliette and Tom had tried to get him into therapy. It seemed that he had managed to dig himself out during his university years, and when she had seen him since he had struck her as a charming and articulate young man.

On this occasion, Jake did not disappoint her. It might also be said that Jake surprised himself with his enthusiasm for her project. What had seemed like an assignment which promised to be both awkward and depressing, now seemed a fascinating piece of detective work. Instead of having to feign interest, he found his natural enthusiasm for history was provoked by what he saw of the contents of the diaries. Sitting together with Marianne, they looked at random pages and Jake began to get a sense of life with her mother's family, their relationship with the German soldiers billeted on them and, as the bombs began to fall, their understandable anxieties about being caught up in any allied landings.

'Leah told me about your real father being Latvian.'

'Yes. I was a war baby. I used to think from a German father, but actually he was Latvian – though part of the German army.'

'And he died in the war?'

'Almost certainly.'

'Did you want to publish the diaries when you finish?'

'Possibly, but to tell the truth I had another idea. The material is quite fragmentary with a lot of gaps which one longs to fill in. It could form the basis for a marvellous work of historical fiction.'

'Of course you were quite a famous novelist in your time – I loved those Russian stories.'

'Don't flatter me. Three novels to my name only; the first one attracted some favourable reviews – the two I wrote after my retirement less so. It will be up to you and Claire what you decide to do; it's too late for me to contemplate anything like that now.'

'I don't see why. I mean I saw what you wrote to Claire, but it seems like you still have plenty to live for.'

'We won't discuss it.'

'I'm sorry – I know it's really none of my business, but I've been looking into the whole subject and it would really help me to understand…'

'I'm not a test case, Jake. Try to use your imagination. I don't want a messy end. Get out while you're ahead. Now the subject is closed.'

'But it's not just me – I don't think Claire understands it either.'

'Well, perhaps she will when she reaches my age.'

'Callum told Leah in the car – after they visited you. She was quite upset.'

'Of course. I was upset to say goodbye to her. What do you expect?'

'I mean – because she didn't know she was saying goodbye.'

'I think she did know.'

'You guessed?'

'Yes.'

'But you didn't say anything?'

'No. I'm sorry, but it was easier for me that way. Tell her I'm a selfish old woman.'

'She wants to come again…'

'No, Jake – please tell her not to. You understand, I'm sure. You can explain to her.'

'But she doesn't understand why you are doing it. Just being... whatever age you are – it doesn't seem enough.'

'I can't help it if people don't understand. Now, I'm not going to discuss this with you anymore. I'm sorry, Jake, but if you persist in asking more questions I'll have to ask you to leave.'

'OK. I'm sorry...'

'Incidentally – I gather you and Leah have got together. I hope you are serious. You have some responsibility – being that much older.'

'Of course – I mean, it's only... but, yes, I am serious.'

'Good. I am naturally protective of my grand-daughter; I think she is a special girl and I hope it works out for you both.'

Once they had discussed the diaries, and his feelings for Leah, and with further discussion of AD being off limits, conversation drifted towards the past and it wasn't long before it lodged on the craggy rocks of the Auvergne and that hot night in August when she had sat on the edge of Jake's bed and tried to console his grief.

Jake remembered how Marianne had told him something of her own agony at her daughter's death, but such was his self-absorption at the time that the words had meant nothing to him. He also remembered – and this he had never forgotten – that she didn't try to minimise his pain, or tell him that he would get over it in time, or bring out any clichés about growing up and new friends. She had talked about Fran, her wonderful spirit, the way she lit up the room, her sense of humour and how lucky he was to have had such a twin sister.

'I think I understand now a little about how you must

have felt when your daughter was killed. Even worse to lose your own grown-up child…'

'There's no competition in grief, Jake.'

'No – but there is responsibility. A few years ago, I tried to tell you – I never told my parents – but it was me; I persuaded her to take the car that day. It was quite wrong of me. If I hadn't…'

'Jake, don't torture yourself. An accidental death has a million tiny precursors – if I hadn't done that, if I had said something different. I went through it all myself. If I hadn't told Izzy she had to come back to Cambridge for the weekend, she might still be alive.'

'But…'

'No buts – it's always the same. Everyone feels it. Part of the guilt of the living. It's unavoidable but you must try to overcome it or it will eat you up. I said we wouldn't talk about my decision to have an assisted death but I will tell you one thing. When I'm gone – even at my age – certain people may feel guilty. They shouldn't – but they may.'

'I understand,' said Jake.

'Do you?' she said. 'I hope so. You must tell Claire and your mother and anyone who may be interested that nothing and nobody can make any difference to my decision. It's my long-held and deeply considered wish to control the time of my death. Only I can know when the time has come and no one should gainsay me. Please remember that when I'm gone.'

Jake was only a few miles out of Marianne's village when he turned off the main road and drove down a small country lane desperately looking for somewhere quiet to stop. After half a mile, he saw a farm track and, turning down it, he drove another fifty yards before pulling up. Getting out of the car he walked to a gate and, leaning on it, gazed sightlessly across the flat Cambridgeshire field, his body casting a long, ghoulish shadow in the late afternoon sun.

In planning his visit to Marianne, Jake had been so concerned with the practicalities – would she see him; what about the diaries; should he be trying to dissuade her – that he had overlooked the obvious fact that in all probability this would be the final goodbye to his Auntie Manne who had been such a fixture in his life. He had been quite unprepared for the emotional turmoil he felt as he hugged her for the last time before turning to leave the house; now he needed to calm himself and gather his thoughts.

As he began to regain his composure, Jake felt distress turn imperceptibly to anger, though the exact object of his anger was not easy to determine. Partly it was directed at himself: had he handled the meeting well? Should he have tried harder to get her to change her mind – or at least get to the root of her decision? The other source of his anger, though he was reluctant to admit it, was Marianne herself. Couldn't she wait a bit longer till she was clearly on the way out, and not cause her relations all this stress? Christ, this AD business is so fucking cold-blooded, and he gave the gate a hefty kick.

There was another source to Jake's frustration – usually well buried but capable of coming to the surface when the subject of this sister's death was mentioned. He wanted to explain to her how it had happened, and how he felt about it now. He needed the absolution that perhaps only she who had been there could give him – but she wouldn't listen. Twice he had tried to talk to her and twice she had dismissed it as the cliché of survivor's guilt. Why the fuck couldn't she listen properly? he thought, and he kicked the gate for a second time.

28

During a tedious drive back from Cambridge, Jake spoke briefly to Leah and arranged to meet her at his flat. When in London, and to try to improve his mood, he went for a run round Clapham Common and had just arrived back and turned on the bath when Leah rang the bell. He let her in, kissed her, then went back to the bathroom while she stood at the door listening to the description of his meeting with Marianne. He knew she would be disappointed with what he told her.

'Why are you being so feeble about this?' she said, taking off her jacket and throwing it onto the bedroom floor. 'Are you happy with what she is doing?'

'No, of course not – but it's not so easy. I did try, but after all it's her life. If she really wants…'

'Unless there's something she's not saying, I don't see that she qualifies. I've looked at the rules…'

'What are you suggesting – we call the police?'

'Of course not.'

'Then I don't see there is much we can do. If she's determined and the clinic accepts her…'

'But you told me, the clinics almost never turn people away – that's the whole fucking point. I thought that's why the *Chronicle* are doing this investigation…'

Jake took off the last of his clothing and lowered himself gingerly into the hot water. The old bath in his flat might have lost some enamel but it was long, and putting his feet each side of the taps at the far end, he lowered his shoulders and head below the water and stayed under for several seconds. Sitting up again, he pushed his hair back and said, 'Let's separate these two things, Leah. Maybe there are abuses in the way AD works and perhaps Charlie and Mills will uncover them. Marianne's decision to end her life when she is nearly ninety is nothing to do with that – it's just a coincidence. It may or may not be strictly within the law but it happens every day and I don't think it's our role to try to stop her.'

'That's all your aunt is to you then – an unfortunate coincidence?'

Jake sighed. 'You're picking out words. Look, I'm as upset about her decision as you are. For what it's worth I think she's wrong. Her life is still worth living – no question – and I don't agree with what she is doing, but the only person who has any chance of making her change her mind is your father.'

'I've tried. Dad says she might still change her mind, but if she doesn't we have to respect her decision.'

'Well then…'

'Why don't you speak to Dad – to him I'm just a child. He might listen more to you.'

'Fine. I will if you want me to.'

'Promise?'

'Of course.'

'Tomorrow?'

'If you want.'

'Sweet. Thank you – sorry for going on at you. It's just that no one is arguing against her. Dad should be on his knees pleading with her not to do it. That's what I would do. Can I get into your bath? I'm shit cold.'

'Sure.'

Leah stripped off quickly and stepped into the opposite end of the bath from Jake, sinking slowly into the hot water and causing it to rise perilously close to the rim. Wrapping a towel over the taps, she lay back and stretched out her legs between Jake's, letting her feet rest either side of his chest. 'I got really cold feet coming here,' she said.

Jake took one of her feet and began rubbing soap into it. 'Better now?'

'Mmm, good as, you can do that all day if you like.'

After a few minutes Leah said, 'I haven't done this since I used to bath with Emma. Did you bath with Fran?'

'Of course, when we were young. I mean, being twins it was logical for our mother to bath us together.'

'So, like, for how long did you go on bathing together?'

'Probably till we were about eight or nine.'

'What made you stop?'

'Well, you get to a certain age…'

'Yeah, but I just wondered, which one of you didn't want to go on…'

'Actually, I think it was our mother. She just said, "I think you're getting a bit old to bath together," and that was it.'

'I've always wondered what it would be like to have a brother. I mean, did you fancy your sister?'

'Come on...'

'No, I mean, seriously – I know you're not supposed to, and it's, like, forbidden and all that, but when you hit puberty and there's this cute girl living with you...'

'You just don't allow yourself to think like that.'

'But if you did allow yourself – I mean, what you say suggests you actually did find her attractive, or is there some mechanism which makes a sibling repellent...?'

'Leah!'

'OK, sorry, forget it. I'm getting out. Let's hurry to this pub of yours in case they run out of food. I'm starving.'

Fortunately, the pub had not run out of food when they arrived and the small bistro-style restaurant was busy with Saturday night diners. Jake cursed himself for not making a booking, but to his relief a table came free almost immediately and they took their seats and studied the menus.

As the meal progressed, Leah resumed her enquiries about Jake's twin sister. 'So, tell me more about Fran,' she said. 'Like, when you were kids.'

'Well, as I've said, we were twins with no other siblings, so we did a lot together.'

'What sort of things?'

'Pretty much everything kids do. Play games, watch TV and movies, sometimes we would go swimming together, either at home or if we were on holiday.'

'... and fight?'

'Actually, not much.'

When Leah said nothing, Jake sipped from the glass of Côte du Rhone the waiter had just delivered and continued:

'I think it was her courage that was her most striking feature; not just physical bravery, although she had plenty of that, but her readiness to say whatever she wanted regardless of the audience.'

'Like what?'

'I remember once at school; we were about eleven and were in the same class for maths. The teacher – a large, overweight man with a foul temper who was a natural bully – was picking on a boy who was hopeless at maths, mocking his answers until the boy was almost in tears. The rest of the class was largely complicit in what was happening. The boy was slightly odd-looking and far from popular. Then Fran stood up and said, "Excuse me, sir, I think you are being unfair to Simon. You know he finds maths very difficult. You need to explain the concept again rather than make fun of him for not following what you said."'

'What happened?'

'Well, it's hard to convey what an electrifying effect this had on the whole class. The teacher went a deep shade of purple and responded in a sarcastic way about not needing her help to run the class. But he stopped bullying the boy.'

Leah looked at him but said nothing.

'Sometimes she would do this kind of thing at home,' Jake continued. 'Challenging our parents when she thought they were being illogical or hypocritical, as all parents are sometimes – and I must say, I found these occasions quite uncomfortable myself. I know that her directness would sometimes hurt them, but that's the way she was.'

'Sounds like a precocious brat to me.'

Jake flinched. He knew he was overprotective of Fran's memory, but any criticism was always painful. It was one of the reasons he hated talking about her and he was irritated now that he had been drawn into this conversation. No one, he felt, had really understood her like he had. He remained silent, looking past Leah towards the entrance of the restaurant.

'No,' he said finally. 'That's quite wrong.'

'I'm sorry, I shouldn't have said that. I apologise.'

'OK, but perhaps I've given you the wrong idea; she was actually very down to earth, clever without being brilliant, amusing and generous, but most of all she was fun to be with.'

'What about when you were older, in your teens – did she have boyfriends?'

Jake hesitated. It was a question he had generally avoided thinking about as he didn't know the answer. 'Well, at thirteen we went away to separate schools so I didn't see much of her during the term time, but we still got on very well in the holidays.'

'Was she at a co-ed school?'

'Yes, it was a boarding school, but co-ed.'

'So she must have had boyfriends?'

'Why does it interest you whether she had boyfriends? Maybe she did, but I don't think anyone serious. She never brought any boys home.'

'I guess she didn't need to.'

'Sorry?'

'Forget it.'

Leah suddenly seemed aware that her persistent questioning about Fran had spoilt the atmosphere between them. Jake became taciturn, drinking more than usual. She tried to repair it with talk of Australia and amusing stories about her own childhood, but as the meal limped to its conclusion she was unable to re-kindle their usual warmth and sparkle.

Later that evening, as they got into bed together, Leah returned to the subject of Jake's twin sister. 'Tell me what happened to Fran,' she said, 'and then I promise I won't ask you any more questions about her.' Jake said nothing. He had wanted to tell Marianne earlier but she hadn't been inclined to listen. Now here was someone who wanted to know. Suddenly it seemed to Jake that Leah was the perfect recipient for his long-awaited confession.

There were two versions of the story. One was the version he had told to everyone who had ever asked; the version his parents believed, the version he would have liked to have believed himself if he could have rid himself of the other version, *la vérité vraie*, as he thought of it – using the French phrase to wrap the concept up in his mind and keep it hidden, even from himself.

He shut his eyes. For nearly ten years he had fought to supress the memories; now he relaxed his grip on the safety valve and up they came from the depths, like so many giant bubbles of gas bursting through a murky pond.

The sun is hot on his back as he lies on the grass watching his fishing line – nothing has bitten all day. He gazes down at the river washing past, tugging at a branch caught between two rocks. For a hundred metres below where he lies, the river cascades through rapids before flattening out again and rushing along a narrow valley. Opposite him, the river has bent around a sheer rock face where a deep natural pool has been formed, perfect for swimming. But he is bored with swimming. And he is bored with fishing. Without Fran, there is no fun. She is back at the house, unwilling that morning to cycle down to the river with him.

If they had the kayak, he thinks, they could shoot the rapids together as they have done in the past. He decides to call her. She answers, but she is not impressed by his suggestion. She wants to finish her book. He presses her. 'Come, and bring the kayak,' he urges. 'It's already on the roof.'

'There's only Auntie Manne here, stupid,' she replies, 'and she doesn't drive in France, remember?'

'You could drive.'

'What, the old van? Are you crazy?'

'Why not?'

'Ah – let me see: haven't passed my test, no licence, no insurance, only had three lessons in my life – and they were in an automatic – and the shitty old van has gears, if you remember. We're in France, where, in case you hadn't noticed, they drive on the other side of the road. Auntie Manne would probably stop me anyway and Granny would be furious if she found out. So, no real reasons, I guess.'

'You've driven a car with gears – remember?'

'Yes, a couple of times on the beach in Wales.'

But he doesn't give up. He keeps on at her. 'You could easily do it,' he tells her. 'Auntie Manne is usually having her snooze at this time. It's a quiet little road – hardly any traffic – just the main road to cross over, which we do on our bicycles every day, then you are in the lane leading down to the river.'

'I'm trying to finish my book,' she says again, 'and, frankly, I'd rather do that than come down to the river to entertain you.'

Why doesn't he just give up? Let it go? Treat it as the joke it should always have been? But he doesn't. To his everlasting shame he plays his trump card. 'You're scared to do it, aren't you? I'd drive it if I was at the house. It's not such a big deal. I'll drive it back if you like.'

She says nothing. He continues his assault. Plays on her pride. The girl who is never afraid, who is defined by her fearlessness; who cannot resist a challenge.

She listens to him in silence. Then suddenly, switching into French and using that voice she sometimes uses which makes it hard to judge whether she is being serious or ironic, she says, '*Mais oui, pourquoi pas?*' and immediately hangs up.

He believes she will come and he is happy; she was just being lazy, wanting to read her book. Such is his confidence in his twin sister that he foresees no danger in the enterprise. There is almost nothing that she cannot accomplish successfully. He waits impatiently, then decides he will cycle up the lane and perhaps meet her halfway. Maybe he will drive the van down the last part of the lane himself. He arrives at the crossroads and waits. The traffic is passing at speed, coming around the tight corner in the way it always does, which means you have to be quick and decisive when crossing – but they have done it many times before. Then he sees her: the blue Renault van with the kayak on its roof arriving at the crossroads. He gives her a wave which she acknowledges with a brief smile and a few fingers raised from the steering wheel. She waits for a lapse in the traffic.

Now the picture becomes jerky; a gap appears in the traffic, the Renault leaps forward at the same time as a white truck appears from around the corner. It shouldn't matter. Fran will be well across by the time the truck reaches her. But to his horror he sees that the Renault is stationary in the middle of the main road. His brain calculates the distance and angles. There is room for the truck to go behind her. All will be well. But it isn't. At the last minute, the truck swings across the road as if to pass in front of Fran, and at exactly that moment the Renault leaps forward for the second time.

There is noise, far too much noise, and he hears a scream he recognises – his own voice. He tries to move into the road but is forced to retreat as another car narrowly misses the tangled wreck of the Renault wedged underneath the overturned truck. Soon other cars have stopped and he is kneeling, looking into the space where Fran should be. What is left of her body is folded in on itself at impossible angles. Bone protrudes from where an arm should be, raw and bloody.

Later, he is there when they cut her out and lay her mangled body onto a stretcher. An airbag has protected her face: except for a trickle of dried blood from her nose, it appears undamaged. Her mouth is half open and the expression is one of mild surprise. Tubes are put into her body. An oxygen mask over her face. By some extraordinary miracle it seems she is still alive. A germ of hope begins to take hold but it is soon snuffed out. Someone tells him she is dead.

Lying on his back and gazing at the ceiling, but seeing only the memories parading before him, Jake told his story to Leah; without embellishment but unsparing of himself. 'And you see,' he said, 'within the family, Marianne was blamed because she had been asked by Claire to "keep an eye on the twins", which was ridiculous given our age – and hers. Several times I have tried to tell her this – tell her that it was all my fault – but she just won't listen.

'The point, though,' and now Jake raised his voice. 'The point is that I asked Fran to come. I summoned her; I provoked her into doing a foolish and illegal act, and what's worse, I never told anyone – not my parents, not the French police, though they could have seen from her phone that I had called her a few minutes earlier – but then no one asked. You see, it was so much in her character to do something reckless that no one thought to blame me. And all the time I said nothing. I didn't even tell anyone I had seen the crash. I said I had arrived after it had happened. I've lived with this ever since. I've known that if I hadn't used those words – made that foolish suggestion, urged her to do it – she would still be alive today. By my own stupidity and selfishness, I killed the person I loved best in the world.'

For a while they both lay there in silence, Leah seeming unsure how to respond to the weight of his confession. Then she said, 'It was an accident, Jake – you can't go on blaming yourself.'

Jake sat up, pushing back the duvet. 'Oh, but I can, Leah,' he almost shouted, 'and I do. Don't you see? We are not talking wings of a butterfly here – this is direct cause and effect. She died because of me – because on a fine August afternoon in rural France, her stupid brother, in a moment of *ennui*, without much thought, asked his sister – urged her, dared her even, a girl who had never been afraid of anything in her life – dared her to drive down to the river; to drive a car she had never driven before in a foreign country when she barely knew the rudiments of how to drive at all – he sent her on this frolic to her death, to her final and everlasting oblivion. Because he was bored.'

Dammed up and contained for years, the sluice gate had now opened and the words poured from Jake as if he had been practising this speech for half a lifetime. Perhaps sensing the depth of his pain, Leah moved closer to him, nestling her head on his shoulder and running a hand down his chest. 'I don't blame you and nor would she. You have to let her go. It's nearly ten years. She's gone, Jake – you've got me now.'

Whether it was Leah's touch – or her words – or something inside him which triggered the response, Jake couldn't afterwards be sure, but without warning he turned towards Leah and rolled on top of her.

'Jake?' she said.

He said nothing – pushing her legs apart with his knees.

'Hang on…'

Ignoring her incipient protest, and without words or preliminaries he shoved at her clumsily and hard, entered her, and thrust forcefully until he reached his climax.

After he had rolled away, they both lay still for several minutes, before Leah whispered, 'I feel as if I've just been raped.'

Jake said nothing. He was too confused by his own actions to know how to respond.

'Jeez, Jake,' she said, now sitting up in bed. 'What the shit was all that about? Were you fucking me or your beloved sister? What's with all this aggression? I don't get it.'

Jake put his arms out and pulled her close to him. She allowed herself to be drawn towards him, though her body remained tense. Hugging her tightly, and pressing her face into his neck, he whispered, 'I'm sorry. Christ, Leah, I'm so sorry.'

Part IV

'tis not so difficult to die.

29

It started in the way it always did, wriggling under the wire, sliding on the ice, the freezing water, the struggling boy, but this time she is the one being pulled down; there is water in her mouth, in her throat, she tries to cough but there is no air to breathe, only icy water in her windpipe and paralysis in her chest. With all her strength, she fights to get to the surface, she fights to get to the air, but it's impossible, something is clinging to her legs, pulling her down.

Slowly at first, but with ever increasing speed, she is falling; no longer in the water she is plunging through the air – only there is still no air to breathe – her lungs are screaming but she cannot take a breath. She is hurtling down through a deep crevasse; the walls press closer and closer but never quite touch her body. On and on she falls into the dark abyss and she knows what is going to happen; she will reach the bottom and her body will shatter like an egg dropped from a great height – and what was once the perfect form of life will be no more than a dark stain on the earth floor, and then the world will come to an end. In one moment of terrifying finality it will all be as if it had never been. Unimaginable oblivion.

Marianne woke with her nightdress soaked in sweat, conscious that something strange and alarming had happened. Fear, which she thought she had skilfully circumvented, had found her out. Such a dream would have been nothing, except that being awake failed to calm or reassure her. For years now, even before she had ever visited the clinic, Marianne had contemplated her death with relative equanimity. Indeed, she had practised dying. She had lain in bed with her eyes shut ready to flick the switch; she had reviewed her eighty-odd years, marked her conduct, felt gratitude for the good things, sadness at the losses, guilt and shame where she thought she had behaved badly and then slipped into an imagined death with scarcely a moment of regret. Reviewing her 'death' with the benefit of hindsight it had seemed easy, welcome even, a friendly companion ready to be called upon whenever she should demand it; or, should it conspire to take her by surprise, she was prepared to go quietly. There would be no rage – and above all, no fear.

And yet she was afraid. And more than afraid; she was in a black hole of lethargy and depression which she had not felt since Izzy's death nearly fifty years earlier. She spent all morning in bed; she was unable to contemplate food; she was surly to Anna and refused to speak to Dorrie on the telephone. She was hating the world, and most of all hating herself.

Suddenly, she realised, nothing had meaning anymore. I am trapped in a cul-de-sac of solipsism; Callum, the girls,

Anna and Dorrie – when I die, they die too. The world that I have known, that I have tried to understand, occasionally hated for its cruelty but more often loved for its magnificence, will end with me. None of it will matter anymore. My own existence is the only reality. My non-existence, which I have contemplated with equanimity for so long, now seems impossible to comprehend.

Anna came into Marianne's bedroom. 'I will go now,' she said, 'but Dorrie coming to visit you this afternoon.'

Marianne said nothing.

'Did you hear what I said? Dorrie will come to visit you.'

Marianne kept her face turned away from Anna.

'I know you're not well today, Marianne, but please say something.'

'I told you, I don't want to see her.'

'But, Marianne, she worries about you. She is a good friend. You must see her.'

'I'm really very tired today, Anna.'

'Is this something to do with the test you have at the hospital? Did they give you some new drug?'

'No, no new drugs.'

'And your tests are OK?'

'Yes.'

'Maybe you have tired yourself out with all this work on the old books?'

'Maybe.'

'Anyway, Dorrie say she is worried about you and is coming to visit. She has her own key so she will be able to let herself in.'

Marianne didn't reply.

'OK, you are not well today, I think. Say hello to Dorrie

for me,' she added, closing the door behind her. Marianne kept her eyes closed.

Jake woke late on Sunday morning. Leah was lying with her back to him, seeming to hug the far side of the bed; still apparently asleep. He slipped out of bed and went into the bathroom. He tried to focus on the events of the night before but they had a dreamlike quality – dissolving into mist when he tried to interrogate his conduct. Finally he had told someone – though not his parents, as it should have been, nor even Marianne. He stepped into the shower and let the water cascade onto his face. Although the telling had been cathartic, his subsequent behaviour was impossible to explain.

Back in the bedroom he stared at the bed. Was there perhaps some movement? 'I'll make some coffee,' he said, as if to himself.

While he was in the next room he sensed rather than saw Leah disappear into the bathroom. It was a long time before she emerged.

'Would you like me to cook some eggs?'

She didn't answer but carried on dressing without looking at him.

He walked over, intending to embrace her until he sensed her body stiffening.

'I'm really sorry about last night...'

She nodded without looking at him.

'I think I'll just go home now,' she said when she had finished dressing.

'Please, Leah. Have some coffee and let's talk.'

She stared at him with eyes which didn't want to see; a blank stare, stripped of any emotion, naked as glass. The look terrified him.

Her voice came out close to a whisper: 'I don't know who I'd be talking to.'

'Leah…'

'No doubt we'll see each other at the office tomorrow.'

She ignored the first knock on the door, and the second. After the second, Dorrie entered her room.

'Anna tells me you're not your usual self?' she said.

'I'm tired.'

'Just tired? Or is it something more?' Dorrie brought a chair up to Marianne's bed. 'Anyway, I take this as a good sign. If you're feeling depressed about your recent visit to the clinic and your idiotic plan to kill yourself, then that's the best news I've heard for a long time. Humans are designed to resist death up to the end. Anything else is unnatural.'

'Is it?' Marianne said. 'Is it natural to resist when every part of me aches?'

'*Cogito, ergo sum*, Marianne – have you forgotten that? Your brain is still there and that's all that matters at your age.'

'I remembered that boy again last night. But this time I was the one who drowned. Then it all turned into a terrible falling dream.'

'We've talked about this before. It's not a memory, just your overactive imagination. Your mother's instinct was right – she should never have told you.'

'I had the memory before she told me. Just not all the detail. More importantly, I had the feeling – that sick dread that something terrible had happened – and now I know for certain that it did.'

'Even if what you remember was true, it's like Siamese twins; sometimes one has to die so the other can live.'

'But I was a sentient being. I was three years old. Even if I couldn't help myself in struggling to get out, I could have run to his mother – they might have been able to save him. You know, I've read about it – children have been rescued from under the ice after thirty minutes or more; the cold protects their brain…'

'I am not going to listen to any more of this. I am going to make some tea and I'll make some for you.'

When Dorrie came back into the room Marianne had turned on her side and lay with her face to the wall. 'I've brought you some tea,' she said. Marianne gave no response. Dorrie started to talk to her. She told her some gossip from the village. Marianne didn't respond, so Dorrie talked to her about some things that were going on in her own life. After a while she said, 'Now it's your turn to talk to me.'

'Memories,' Marianne mumbled into her pillow without turning around.

'No more about the drowned boy, please.'

'It's the way the mind controls them. I'm not thinking of the boy. I'm thinking about the confession I signed in Russia. Somewhere inside me I think I've always known that there was something in that document that I shouldn't have put my name to. That it wasn't entirely harmless. But I supressed it. Blocked it so successfully that you could say I had forgotten. But at a deeper level I think it's always been there, waiting to be rediscovered – to be released.'

Dorrie sighed. 'Let's forget memories. Let's talk about the present. How was your visit from Callum and Leah?'

'Fine.'

'And?'

'Just a trot around the same circuit – no change.'

'You told Leah?'

'No, but Callum has told her.'

'What about Claire? Did you write to her?'

'Yes, and I had a surprise visit from her grandchild, Jake – sent to spy on me by Claire. And guess what,' she said, turning to face Dorrie. 'I think he's sleeping with Leah.'

'Cousins?'

'So what.'

'You don't mind? She's quite young.'

'Eighteen for God's sake – I was in love at fourteen – but there was no pill in those days. No, I think it's wonderful. You know what a terrible old romantic I am. It brought back memories of Daniel.'

'I remember about your Daniel. "*I was a child and she was a child*" – how does it go? You quoted that Poe verse.'

'I don't remember exactly, but yes – he quoted it in a letter to me before he died. Sometimes I still feel like a teenager.'

Dorrie got up and walked to the window. Autumn was now well advanced; the trees almost bare against the grey sky. She gazed down towards the small pond at the bottom of Marianne's garden where the water was barely visible through the covering of leaves. 'To ourselves, we're always young,' she said. 'That's the irony of old age. All our self-discovery – our self-awareness – happens when we are young. By the time we have become fully formed adults we know where we belong – to the tribe of the young. We never desert that tribe – it's who we are. Our friends get older; children – our own or other people's – get rapidly older. Others see us getting older and it's true we begin to suffer creeping decrepitude – but to ourselves we will always be young, because that's how we first defined ourselves – different, and forever different, from the old.'

Dorrie stayed on and talked for another hour. Although Marianne still felt low, she knew that she had been distracted for a time from her self-absorption and she felt grateful to Dorrie for her loyalty and friendship. She turned on an audio book in the hope of distracting herself but, as the evening turned towards night, her fear and distress returned.

30

Monday lunchtime found Jake and Leah in the basement bar close to their office, engaged in an intense conversation about what had happened on Saturday night.

He tried to explain the emotion that had overwhelmed him when telling her about Fran, repeatedly apologising for his rough behaviour. He told her how much it meant to him to have confided in her and how close he felt to her now. For her part, Leah was prepared – once enough protests had been registered – to give some limited indication of forgiveness, acknowledging that she may have acquiesced but that she certainly didn't expect him to treat her like that again.

'We are having dinner with my parents tonight.' The abrupt change of tone seemed to indicate that Leah regarded the previous subject as closed.

'Tonight?'

'You promised, remember? I want you to tackle Dad about Marianne.'

As their tube train rattled its way towards Victoria, Jake had a sense that this was far more like a joint endeavour by two work colleagues, rather than a girl taking her boyfriend to meet her parents. He tried to lighten the atmosphere by taking Leah's hand but she batted him away. 'Just remember what I told you. Concentrate your fire on my father. Mum will be more difficult – and bear in mind she has been trying to grill me about you but I have refused to say anything. She knows now that I've spent nights with you and she definitely doesn't approve.'

As Jake walked down Victoria Street with Leah, past the byzantine edifice of Westminster Cathedral, with its crazy domes and striped brick tower, he wondered how best to open the discussion. Whilst he was supposed to tackle the highly delicate question of Marianne, he was conscious that it was his relationship with Leah which was likely to be of more immediate concern to her parents.

Arriving at their flat, the door was opened by a blonde woman in her late forties or early fifties with a narrow face and multiple small creases around her eyes and lips.

'Hello, Helen,' he said.

'Come in,' she said, turning back into the hallway and not giving Jake a chance to kiss her on the cheek, as he had been intending.

The atmosphere was noticeably chilly as Jake and Leah followed Helen into the living room, but Callum seemed intent on being friendly. Getting up to shake his hand, he offered Jake a drink, and enquired after his mother. Jake made the customary joke that she had not succumbed to any more snake bites despite spending all her available hours out of doors. In the meantime, he noticed that Helen and Leah had left the room, no doubt for a mother-daughter face-off.

Jake explained about Marianne's letter to Claire and his trip to Cambridge to look at the French diaries. 'The thing is,' he said, 'your mother wants Claire to have the diaries and perhaps for me to finish the work of translating them that she has started. But, I mean, Claire wanted to be sure that was OK with you. I mean, in case you had any interest in them yourself?'

'That's thoughtful of you,' said Callum, 'but Claire knows I don't read French so there's nothing much I could do with them. Claire is welcome to have them.'

'OK, thanks. I just didn't want to step on anyone's toes. And, well, the other thing is, I was quite shocked that she has apparently decided to have an assisted death – I mean, very soon, judging from the letter she wrote to Claire.'

'I realise it might come as a surprise to you, but then you wouldn't have seen much of her recently. She's been planning it for years.'

'I can understand it in principle, of course. But she seemed very well – and mentally alert.'

Callum was silent for a moment and Jake saw a mask coming across his face while his body language showed an element of discomfort. 'It's what she wants,' he said.

'I think it's such a relief for old people,' said Helen, coming back into the room and joining in the conversation. 'Being able to go when they want to, such a blessing.'

'You are obviously a supporter of assisted dying,' said Jake, who noticed Leah hovering in the doorway.

'Oh yes, absolutely. Quite a few of my friends' parents or

grandparents have gone that way; it's so much more dignified for them.'

'You don't think sometimes they feel pressured into doing it?' said Jake.

'Definitely not in my mother's case,' said Callum sharply.

'I don't mean that anyone actually puts pressure on them – but they might feel, you know, that it's somehow expected of them?'

'Nothing could make Callum's mother do what she didn't want to do,' said Helen. 'No, if you ask me, it's one of the best changes to the law that's been made in my lifetime. It's saved so much suffering.'

'Leah has told us about your interest in this,' said Callum, 'but you wouldn't have had much personal experience at your age. We've seen quite a lot of it and old people really know when they want to die.'

'I'm sure that's often the case,' said Jake. 'It's just... I mean, she still seems to have a lot to live for.'

'I hope you didn't say anything to disturb her,' said Helen. 'It's a difficult time; it's vital we let her make up her own mind and that no one tries to influence her. I'm not sure it was such a good idea for you to visit her.'

'I didn't disturb her – naturally she didn't want to speak to me about her plans, but I just wanted to know what you thought about it and whether you supported her.'

'It's not a question of whether we support her...' began Callum.

'I suppose what I'm saying is... shouldn't you be trying to dissuade her?'

'I really don't see it's any of your business,' said Helen. 'I mean, it's not as if you are direct family.'

'Well, I'm direct family – as you call it,' said Leah, emerging into the room, 'and I think it stinks.'

'Leah! Really, I don't think we should be having this conversation,' said Helen. 'And if you are…'

'Letting Gran go off and kill herself…'

'I know you're upset about this, Leah,' said Callum, interrupting his daughter. 'It's quite understandable. It's upsetting for all of us.'

'Neither of you seem very upset,' said Leah.

'Leah, honestly…'

Callum held up his hand to silence his wife and daughter. 'Leah, we'll talk about this again later – and Jake, I'm sure you mean well, but I think it's really a matter for my mother and, to some extent, for us. I don't think you should get involved.'

'No, of course. I'm not involved and I don't want to be,' said Jake. 'I simply wanted to know…'

'I'll just say this to both of you,' said Callum. 'I don't want my mother to die yet, and I am trying to persuade her to change her mind. But several years ago I promised her I would support her if, one day, she wanted to choose an assisted death. If she remains determined, then I will honour that promise. Now let's go and eat and talk about something else.'

While conversation at dinner limped and meandered around topics designed not to cause upset or embarrassment to anyone, Jake contemplated their earlier exchanges. Not surprising that they should be a little hostile, he thought; it is, after all, none of my business. Marianne is the sort of person well able to make up her own mind and it can't be an easy situation for Callum. All the same, what Leah had said about not being very upset…

Jake was shaken from his contemplation when a situation arose after dinner – no doubt carefully engineered – which he had hoped to avoid; as he loaded plates into the dishwasher he heard the door close and he found himself alone in the kitchen with Helen.

'So what's going on between you and Leah?' she said, standing with her back to the door.

Jake had no objection to being honest with Helen, but was unsure what, if anything, Leah had said to her mother. He was also in some doubt how to describe the current state of their relationship.

'Shouldn't you ask Leah that?' he said.

Helen ignored his comment. 'I am extremely upset and disappointed with you. Leah has just finished school – we thought you were looking after her. We trusted you. You were giving her some work experience.'

'She's eighteen, you know, and...'

'Yes, and you are twenty-six and her cousin. You are a close relation and you have exploited a position of trust in a really shocking way. Do you remember, Jake, when we were over here the year after your sister died? You took Emma and Leah out for a hamburger. Two little girls aged twelve and ten. You were like an uncle to them. And that's how it should have remained.'

'People grow up...'

'I think it's a disgrace and you should stop seeing her. I don't want her going to your office anymore either.'

Jake shrugged. 'Of course, if she doesn't want to.'

'I'm asking you to show adult responsibility – I don't intend to let this go...'

Fortunately for Jake, he was rescued by Leah's return to

the kitchen and the subject was not alluded to again. After a decent interval, he took his leave and Leah came down to the street with him.

'Was Mum giving you the third degree?'

'Afraid so.'

'I came as soon as I realised you were alone with her.'

'Thanks.'

'I'll walk to the station with you.'

As they walked up the road and back across the Cathedral piazza neither spoke, but Leah took his hand. When they reached the station, she gave him a chaste kiss. 'Thanks,' she said. 'I won't give up on this and neither must you.'

31

Marianne screwed up the piece of paper and threw it into the bin. She rubbed her cold and painful hands and called to Anna to check the thermostat. Well, the oil should last another week and then it won't be my problem anymore, she thought. No more problems – except for this letter to Callum, and, of course, there was still Anna. But first of all, Callum; she took another piece of paper and wrote, *My darling Callum*, then she stopped as the telephone rang.

It was Helen. This was an unusual event and Marianne wondered what had provoked the call; Helen didn't take long to get to the point. Was it true she had encouraged Leah to start a sexual relationship with Jake? Marianne didn't feel any need to apologise. She denied encouraging her, but yes, Leah had implied that something was going on with Jake and she saw no reason to criticise – indeed she had been delighted at the news. She then had to listen to Helen's many objections before the call came to an awkward and unresolved ending.

'Some problem?' said Anna.

'I'm in trouble with Helen. She objects to Leah's involvement with Jake.'

'Is that your fault?'

'She thinks I encouraged it.'

Anna laughed. 'I was surprised when you tell me – but I like Jake. I think he's OK for Leah. You should ask him to visit you again – I think he made you cheerful, no?'

'Jake – yes, I did enjoy his visit. Anyway, I must get on with this letter.'

'OK, I will leave you for half an hour and go to the shop; we need more coffee if Callum is coming tomorrow – just Callum, is it?'

'Yes, just Callum.'

Marianne turned her attention back to the letter, but the telephone rang again. This time it was Nikhita Singh, the nurse she had seen at the clinic, checking to see how she was coping.

'I know it can be a difficult time,' she said.

Not half, Marianne thought, as she assured her nurse that she was coping fine.

Turning back to the letter again, the right words wouldn't come. No, leaving a letter for Callum till after she was dead wasn't the right way; she realised that now. What she had to say must be said to his face.

When Callum arrived the following day, he greeted her cheerfully, chatted to Anna, and appeared to Marianne to be surprisingly relaxed; no sign of someone being buffeted in the vortex of the family's angst about her decision to end her life. Then she thought, is it because he doesn't have Helen with him? Callum sat down in a chair close to hers and held her hand.

'So what on earth was Jake doing coming to see you?' he said.

'Sent by Claire, of course.'

'Even so, I'm surprised you let him.'

'Well, I wasn't going to, but somehow he persuaded me and I'm glad he did. He's a charming boy and I think he might be interested in finishing off the diaries.'

'Yes, he mentioned that to me – which, of course, was quite unnecessary since you know I don't care about all that stuff. What he really wanted to do was to tell me I shouldn't let you go.'

'You mustn't blame Jake, or Dorrie, or anyone else. They are just doing what they think they have to.'

'You realise Jake is not exactly flavour of the month in our household?'

'So I gather.'

'I'm sorry Helen called you – but I can't believe you actually encouraged Leah.'

'I don't think it's anything to be too upset about.'

'Honestly, Mum – she's just out of school. What were you thinking? He's an older relation who was supposed to be looking after her – mentoring her. We are really quite shocked.'

'Well, I'm sorry if I did wrong. Put it down to a touch of dementia on the part of your old mum. From my perspective eighteen and twenty-five – or whatever he is – seem like pretty much the same age. But tell me about Claire?'

'Claire was pretty sensible, I must say. I've got a lot of time for Claire.'

'And she likes you. Always has. After all, you did save Julie. She told me once that I underestimated you.'

'It's nice to have been a hero once in your life – but all I did was carry Julie to the road.'

'It was a long way.'

'That's true – I could hardly move my arms the next day, they were so stiff.'

'And you photographed the snake.'

'It was just lucky I had got my new phone with a camera – it was one of the first ones. I think that's what amazed Claire. She didn't know then that mobile phones had cameras.'

'Anyway, what was Claire's pronouncement?'

'She was just anxious to know whether you were really fixed on the idea.'

'I hope you said that I was?'

'I did.'

'So she didn't urge you to talk me out of it?'

'She said I should keep trying to dissuade you because that would test your resolve.'

'Sounds reasonable.'

'She said that she wasn't really surprised. She thinks that you have a bit of an obsession about being in control. This would be your final demonstration of your power to control your own destiny.'

'My destiny – that's a bit dramatic. But maybe an element of truth in it.'

'When she told me that, I couldn't help thinking of the time when we were going to France and there was a delay at the airport and you got so impatient,' said Callum, laughing.

'Oh that.'

'You insisted that we cancel the flights and travel back into London; we then got the Eurostar to Paris, lugged all our gear into a taxi to the Gare de Lyon...'

'I've heard all this before.'

'... then another train... we would have been there a whole day earlier if we'd stuck to flying – and it cost a lot more money – but you felt empowered...'

'And I've never heard the end of it.'

'Claire was very amused.'

'She was; manically impatient, she called me – or something like that.'

As they continued to chat and laugh and reminisce, Marianne had a sense of ease talking to Callum which she hadn't felt for years. This is how it should always have been, she thought. There has been nothing missing in my love for Callum – just circumstances coming between us. And in so thinking, there welled up inside her such a tenderness for Callum and such shame at her own doubts that she felt shocked that she could have contemplated leaving that letter behind for him after she was dead.

'Callum, there's something I need to tell you,' she said.

'Yes?'

'I think that when you were growing up you always believed that Andy was actually dead.'

'Wasn't he?'

'No.'

'So what are you telling me?'

Marianne set about explaining to Callum how it had been. How, in her whirlpool of grief at Izzy's death, he had been her lifebelt and how she had vowed that she would be his protector. She told him how she had fought with Edward over his adoption and exaggerated the extent of Andy's injuries.

'I don't think I ever lied to you directly,' she said, 'but you got it firmly into your head that Andy was dead and it seemed easiest to let you go on believing that. Dad wanted to tell you, but somehow it never seemed to be the right time. I also wondered whether it would be fair on Andy.'

'So are you telling me he was absolutely fine – nothing wrong with him?'

'More or less. I mean, he nearly died in the accident, but he gradually recovered – although we didn't know his state of health after the adoption because we had no contact with him.'

'You're not telling me he is still alive now?'

'No. After Dad died I thought that I should find out what had happened to him, so I wrote to his mother but never received a reply. I then travelled to Glasgow and went to the last address we had and she was still there. She wasn't very friendly but she told me Andy had died of a stroke a couple of years earlier. She gave me the impression that this was all due to the accident; that his health had never been the same again.'

As Marianne was talking, Callum got up from his chair and started to walk around the room. 'Well, I can't pretend it's not a bit of a shock,' he said. 'So Andy – my real father – lived on till just before Dad died. So when I was around thirty.'

'Yes.'

'He can't have been more than fifty when he died?'

'I suppose so. I think perhaps he never fully recovered – as his mother suggested.'

'Why didn't you tell me? I mean, once I was grown up?'

'It didn't seem necessary. Would you have wanted to meet him?'

'I can't say now, can I? The point is, I never got the chance.'

'That's why I am telling you now. I prevented you ever knowing your real father, and I prevented Andy from ever knowing his son. You have every right to blame me for this. I am sorry to spring this on you, but it is right you should know the truth before I die.'

Marianne watched as Callum tried to digest this knowledge. Some men would have remonstrated, shouted, perhaps sworn, but this was not Callum's way. She watched as he tried to reconcile his conflicting emotions. So like Edward, she thought; he's unhappy about what he's heard but he wants to understand it from my point of view. That's both his strength and his weakness – he can always see the other point of view. On this occasion Marianne felt grateful for his considered reaction.

'I am surprised Dad never told me?'

'That wasn't his way. He disagreed with me, but he left it for me to decide.'

'But anyway, Andy gave up any right to see me – I mean, when he agreed to the adoption.'

'Yes.'

'He didn't have to consent – and you told me the adoption took ages to go through.'

'It certainly seemed like ages.'

'So I don't think you can say you deprived Andy of anything – he made his own decision.'

Marianne was silent as she watched Callum rationalising what he had heard; stacking the pieces in a logical and ordered pile.

'When you think about it, he was probably relieved. Absolved of any responsibility for the child.'

Marianne shrugged.

'And as for me, I lost nothing. I didn't want another father. No, I think you did the right thing.'

'I don't know whether you are just saying this – but thank you anyway.'

'Mum, don't be stupid – I'm not just saying it. I mean it.'

Callum sat down next to Marianne again and took her hand. 'If you've been getting yourself worked up into a great state of guilt then you shouldn't. My mother was dead. You took on the raising of your grandson when his natural father was neither willing nor able to do so. Letting me think he was dead was just for my own protection – and perhaps for his as well. You have no reason to blame yourself.'

'Thank you, darling.'

'Perhaps you could have told me when I was in my twenties – that's the only thing I would say.'

'I should have done, darling, and I'm very sorry – but there never seemed to be a right time.'

'It's something we have in common – not knowing our biological fathers. When you think about it, you know even less than I do – a Latvian soldier in the German army. You don't even know for sure that he died in the war.'

'No, I can't be certain.'

'And you said it never mattered to you and it doesn't matter to me. So we don't need to discuss it any more. Does Claire know?'

'I don't think so. I think she believed Andy had died a few years after the accident.'

Callum laughed. 'Claire would have a field day if she

knew this – more evidence of your controlling nature. You have always wanted to mould events to your will, she would say.'

After he had left, Marianne thought about Callum's visit. Perhaps Claire was right and she did underestimate him. First, he had made a decent job of persuading her that what she had done was nothing to be ashamed of – she wasn't quite convinced but it was good to hear his absolution; then he succeeded in cheering her up by being relaxed and not too serious; finally, he had made a short but powerful plea: not so much that she should change her mind but to postpone her appointment at the clinic. Live for another six months and see how it goes. Why not?

She had not succumbed to his blandishments but they had seemed heartfelt. What he doesn't know, she thought, is that I have been giving myself a few more months for the last year before I made the final decision. She had to acknowledge, however, that it was tempting and she had promised to think about it seriously. And I will, she thought. After all, what else do I have to think about?

32

The feeling was extraordinary; a kind of weightless euphoria had taken hold of her. She felt wonderfully energised but also completely calm. Her many sources of pain were still there in the background but had become irrelevant, as if they belonged to someone else. Apart from the occasional joint in her student days, she had never been one for recreational drugs. Perhaps I should have been more adventurous, she thought. I have never had a high quite like this before.

The reason for her sudden elation was that Marianne had decided to live. That is to say, she had decided to postpone for a while her final appointment with the AD clinic. She couldn't explain exactly how or why she had made this decision. Indeed, she didn't recall making the decision at all; she had just woken up in the morning knowing that the decision had been made. Perhaps it was down to Callum, perhaps it was

Dorrie or perhaps she had just lost her nerve, but now she was wallowing in a warm bath of rapture, the like of which she could never before remember.

So far she hadn't told anyone, but she had been upbeat when she spoke to Callum that morning, hinting that she might change her mind. She planned to call the clinic on Monday and let them know. In the meantime, comforting ideas floated around her head. She thought of her mother's diaries and then she thought of Jake. I could work with him. He could be my research assistant. To make sense of it all I need to look at contemporary records from wartime Normandy. It's all too much for me on my own but with his help… Yes, together we could make something of it, she thought.

Then she thought about her other grand-daughter, Emma. I would like to see her again before I die. I don't want to summon her from the other side of the world to a death-bed scene so I have an idea that I could travel out halfway and spend a few days with her and perhaps Leah could come too. I could stay in one of those luxury Asian hotels I have read about, perhaps even swim in the sea again. A warm sea which would wash away all my aches and pains. It would be expensive but there's still a bit more I could borrow on the house. Perhaps we could all spend Christmas out there, she thought, and images of herself lying in the shade of a palm tree while the girls played on the beach (had they suddenly got ten years younger?) floated before her.

Surely I'm not too old to travel, she thought. My friend Penny flew around the world last year and she's nearly as old as I am. She said that if you fly business class it's not uncomfortable and they whisk you through the airports on those electric carts. After all, if I peg out on the way, so what? It wouldn't be a bad way to go.

Thoughts of the future mingled with memories of the past. She recalled that moment of exhilaration when she realised she was being released from her Moscow detention and was no longer at risk of a lengthy prison sentence. Then another image from Moscow came to her. She is attending a conference on Pushkin – it must have been the end of the nineties, a good few years after the demise of the Soviet Union – the first time she has been back. She is chatting to another delegate in the bar after dinner. He introduces himself as Nicholai; a good-looking Russian professor perhaps ten years younger than her.

He pours her some vodka and they drink a toast to the great names of Russian literature. They talk about poetry, about their families, about the old Soviet Union and the new Russia – where his friends are trying to keep their heads above water in the wild, anarchic, mafia-dominated world of the modern Moscow. He seems well acquainted with her CV, and asks her about her time in Moscow in the seventies. Perhaps it's the vodka, but suddenly she is doing what she has never done before; she is pouring out the whole story of her arrest and expulsion from Russia – and how the photos were later used to try to blackmail her.

He listens, encouraging her narrative with appropriate expressions of sympathy. He says that he is ashamed; ashamed at the way his country has treated her – her, a lover of Russian literature. Anyone who loves Pushkin is a friend of Russia. They drink more vodka; he flirts and she reciprocates. She wonders vaguely what he wants from her but she doesn't care. She knows she is more than a little drunk but, cresting a wave of careless optimism, she allows him to come to her room. After all, it's been a long time.

The scene shifts to South America. That magical holiday when everything seemed so right with the world. The return to Cambridge achieved – the disasters in Moscow transformed into an exciting tale; no longer threatening to destroy her marriage and her career, but to be re-inhabited as part of a daring youth. True, her injury has not healed well but this does not intrude into the fantasy of her half-remembered narrative. Large butterflies flit amongst the purple flowers on the banks of the river, and as they approach the bottom of the falls she relives that moment of elation when she, Edward and Izzy seem enclosed in a circle of refracted light – an inviolable trinity.

Waking from her reverie, Marianne felt so cheerful that she clambered to her feet, walked across to Anna and gave her a long hug.

'So, Marianne – you are very happy today, I think?'

'I do feel much more cheerful today, Anna. I am sorry I have been so bad-tempered.'

'It's OK – shall I play some music?'

'Yes – anything you like.'

'You must choose.'

'OK – put on Beethoven's Pastoral. And if you'd like to make some coffee I think I might have another go at my mother's diaries.'

'Music coming – and I will make the coffee,' said Anna. 'It's good that you feel better today.'

Listening to the serene but cheerful opening movement of the symphony, Marianne began looking again at some passages from the first of her mother's diaries that she had not read for some time. The family had arrived in Paris after a harrowing journey from the other side of Rheims. It was the day her mother spent with her aunt before they continued their journey south. They go to the Sorbonne and while her aunt works, the fourteen-year-old Simone has an hour on her own and wanders down to the Seine. She stands gazing across to Notre Dame when a boy comes up and offers her a cigarette. Ah, how much easier pick-ups were when everyone smoked! She refuses but he tells her that they may all be dead in a week's time and she will never have smoked a cigarette. She relents, they talk, and he tells her that when the Germans get there she will have an easier time than him. It's a moment of innocence and suppressed sexuality. From the diary entries, the boy seems to have been Jewish but her mother hadn't picked up on this. I suppose she must have been too young, Marianne thought.

Reading the diaries again, another daydream had taken hold of her. Perhaps Jake might take a fancy to Anna. He would be about the right age. Really, Leah was a bit young for him. Then Anna could drop that difficult man of hers and if Jake and Anna were a couple – well, Jake could come and stay here and help me with this story while Anna looks after me. Or perhaps Leah will get to Cambridge and Jake will decide to follow her. He could get a job on a Cambridge paper, or maybe do another degree. He could live here with me and Leah would come and visit.

Fantasy it might all be, but that morning anything seemed possible. Marianne was so cheerful that Anna was amazed at the transformation. When it was time for lunch they opened a bottle of wine and played cards while they ate together – laughing and chiding each other as they had done in times past. Once Anna had gone, Marianne sank back into her chair and fell into an untroubled sleep.

As Jake and Leah emerged from the entrails of Clapham Junction late in the evening, a bubble of contentment seemed to surround them, protecting them from the icy east wind which blew into their faces. Jake was unashamedly upbeat. Charlie, his boss, had been very excited with the material they had produced on the abuses of the postal voting system and now the lawyers were crawling all over it. A provisional date of 1st December had been fixed for publication. This would be his story; an important step in his career as a journalist.

As a reward for all Leah's hard work, Jake had persuaded the *Chronicle* to allow her name to appear as a part of the investigative team.

'OK?' he said, taking her hand as they walked up Lavender Hill.

'Stoked… and don't let them change their minds! That will show Mum I'm doing a real job and not just hanging around you like some dopey lovesick teenager.'

'Aren't you?'

'Fuck off.'

Jake put his arm around her and kissed her cheek. He found it endearing that in moments of excitement her Australian accent always came to the fore. Since that strange evening the previous week, when she had pestered him about Fran and he had told her the story and then shocked himself as much as her with the sudden violence of his behaviour, a new calmness had come over him. The tension that had been part of Jake's life for so long seemed to have dissipated, and something solid and fulfilling was growing in the vacated space. He couldn't yet articulate what was happening but he sensed the changes somewhere within him.

He also knew that Leah was more relaxed because of what her father had told her that morning about Marianne. He felt sure, he had said, that she would change her mind. She hadn't said so exactly, but he had sensed it. At the very least she would delay any final decision.

'Are you going to help Gran with those diaries, then?'

'If she asks me.'

'No, I don't think you should wait to be asked. Especially in her state of mind. Call her up and offer to help. It might be just the incentive she needs.'

Jake thought for a moment. 'You're right. It might help. I will call her.'

As they entered Jake's flat together, relieved to be out of the wind on what was surely the coldest night of the year so far, the reassuring warmth which they expected was absent.

'Shit, it's cold in here,' said Leah, as Jake went to the kitchen and started fiddling with the boiler.

'Bloody thing seems to have seized up,' he said.

Leah looked at him. There was nothing in her facial expression which an observer would have noticed but a split second of eye contact was enough for Jake to follow her to the bedroom, shedding his coat on the way and falling onto the bed beside her.

'Hey, your hands are cold,' said Leah, laughing.

'Sorry, it's not exactly warm in here,' said Jake, pulling the duvet over them as they embraced and began undressing under the covers, exploring each other's flesh with cold hands.

'Fuck, I can't get these off…' said Leah.

'Let me help.'

'You need to pull from the bottom.'

'Shit… it would help if you didn't knee me in the balls.'

'Sorry. Let me make them better.'

And so, with occasional curses, and small cries of painful pleasure, they removed their clothes in the chill of their unheated flat and made love to each other with humour and tenderness.

Meanwhile Jake's phone buzzed repeatedly. Fortunately, both had long since mastered the art of ignoring their phones and the bleating failed to distract either of them from their more immediate concerns. It wasn't until later that Jake listened to the message.

'It's only George,' he said. 'Advance warning that Pauline in HR wants to speak to me tomorrow morning.'

'What about?'

'About you, he thinks. A warning against inappropriate conduct with an intern.'

'Screw inappropriate conduct,' she said, nestling close to Jake.

'My thoughts exactly.'

Perhaps it was too much to expect the mood to last. Marianne awoke to a fit of coughing, which sometimes happened for no apparent reason when she had been lying back in her chair. A terrible dry cough which made her feel she was going to choke. She had also drunk too much wine and now badly needed the lavatory. The room was almost dark – she had slept longer than expected – and as she fumbled for her glasses she knocked over the small table beside her chair. Cursing silently amid another spasm of coughing she pulled the lever to get her chair upright – but now her sticks were out of reach. Then she couldn't hold it any longer – her bladder let go and she felt the warm, wet spread of her urine.

It took her almost an hour to sort herself out, change her clothes and wipe down her chair; and sitting now at the kitchen table she tried but failed to revive the optimism of the morning. That small benevolent snapshot of Russia now seemed absurd; it had been the place where her life had taken the wrong turning, where she had deceived her husband and gravely injured herself – where, as she now knew, she had helped deliver a man into the hands of the KGB and to his death in a Siberian *gulag*.

What had she been thinking, imagining she could fly off around the world, spending money she didn't have? She had already taken out far more of the value of the house than she had intended – or that Callum was aware. Every month, the interest reduced the balance of her equity and ratcheted up the future interest payments. She had a responsibility to ensure that at least something went to her grandchildren – it was unfair that they should be burdened by debt that she had never had to cope with.

This, of course, was the secret she was keeping from Callum, from Dorrie – and most especially from herself: a sense of duty to those with a life still to lead. How could she think of wasting what little money she had left, when others needed it more? Why should she linger on when Callum and Helen needed to get on with their lives in Australia and Anna would be better off going back to Latvia with her boyfriend? A dozen times she had denied it to them, just as she continued to deny it to herself. Some part of her knew that such reasoning could not exist. To think it would be to risk communicating it; and to communicate even a hint that she was choosing to die now in order to liberate those closest to her, would destroy anything good which might come from her death. The easiest way to keep a secret, she knew, is never to know the secret – to forget what you might know but can't divulge – and so she wiped these thoughts from her mind before they could gain a foothold.

How hard it all was. She had made a decision; why was she now being so indecisive? Where was this woman of iron control that Callum had described? I suppose I don't have to do anything just now, she told herself. I can cancel any time – or else just not turn up. Tell them to stuff their wretched clinic with its giant TV screens and choice of five hundred overused musical scores to die to. I also rather fancy waiting to get Callum and Helen down here and telling them the good news. 'Hello, my darling son, and not quite so darling daughter-in-law. I have some wonderful news for you. I'm not going to die today. In fact, not today and not tomorrow either. Soon, maybe – who knows? – but I am just not in the mood for death quite yet, so let's all have a drink to celebrate.' It would be worth it just to see Helen's face. Now that is something to live for.

33

Marianne woke from her mid-morning nap to a message from Anna that Callum had telephoned and Jake had called for the second time. She had also had a call from Nikhita Singh. She didn't want to talk to anyone. It was now Monday 21st November: D-day minus three. She hadn't said anything more to Callum about her second thoughts – about her morning of euphoria a couple of days previously. Stupid to tell him unless she was sure – and she didn't feel sure about anything – except that her sciatica was hurting and she needed to get up and try to walk a little.

The persistent rain meant that going outside was impossible but, with Anna's help, she managed to walk up and down the hall a few times before sitting down at her desk. She took a couple of pain killers while she contemplated calling Callum. If she didn't, he would be sure to call again and she preferred to get it over with. She looked at the phone, thinking about what to say. With Anna coming in and out it was difficult to speak openly. In the event, the phone rang while she was still staring at it.

'I'm sorry, Mum,' said Callum, when she answered the call. 'I got my timing wrong. I hope I didn't disturb your sleep.' They talked for a few minutes in a coded language. Marianne told him that nothing had changed.

'But I had the impression when we last spoke that you would at least postpone it like I suggested?'

'I decided against.'

'But you haven't told Anna yet – so you can't be sure?'

'You shouldn't make that assumption. Just imagine how difficult things would be otherwise.'

'Well, anyway, I have some family news – I'm afraid Leah didn't get into Cambridge.'

Marianne thought about this information. She remembered how she had longed for Izzy to study at a Cambridge college, despite Edward's reservations. It's true, she admitted to herself, I have dreamed of Leah going to Cambridge. I couldn't help it. I barely knew the girl until two years ago, but as I got to know her and saw how bright she was I began to foster my old ambitions.

'Are you still there, Mum?'

'Yes, I'm here. I'm sorry about Leah. Is she very disappointed?'

'Less than I expected.'

When she had finished speaking to Callum, Marianne moved to her chair and lay back with her eyes shut. She had no intention of calling Jake back or of speaking to him if he called again. Nor would she call back the nurse. The fewer people she had to speak to the better. What had she been thinking, imagining that she could take over Jake's life to fulfil some fantasy of her own? Building castles in the air; more than castles, giant pyramids supported by nothing more than a little bubble, an absurd, foolish bubble of self-delusion. Putting it off would only prolong the agony. I owe it to myself and I owe it to everyone else in my life. Time to get out of the way.

Marianne dreaded saying goodbye to Dorrie. She didn't expect her to make it easy; she knew Dorrie was too honest for that.

'So this is it?' Dorrie said, after Anna had left the house.

'Yes.'

'Time to say goodbye.'

'I am afraid so.'

'Don't expect me to be all soft and sentimental with you because I won't.'

'I understand.'

'Do you? Do you really understand how angry I am with you? How absolutely bloody furious? What about me, have you thought about that? How do you think it feels for me when you just go quietly off to die? Do you think that makes me feel good? Are you thinking at all about those you are leaving behind? What value are you placing on our friendship?'

Marianne wanted to reply but she knew it was impossible to explain, so she bowed her head and remained silent.

'It's not enough – is that what you are saying? Our friendship – it's not a sufficient justification for staying alive? What about your son and grandchildren? What about Leah, who seems genuinely fond of you?'

'It's not like that…'

'And Anna – your wonderful Anna – she's going to feel just great to know that her patient has decided to commit suicide. Quite a testimonial.'

'In the long run…'

'No doubt I'm being obtuse,' Dorrie continued, 'but I still don't get why you're doing this. You can't control everything in life, you know – or at least you shouldn't be able to. Die when your body lets you – or if the pain is too much, then maybe a few days early. But for God's sake, not now.

'Have you any idea how lucky you are?' she went on. 'Sure, you've got a few aches and pains, but who hasn't? You may have to resort to a wheelchair one day, but is that really so bad? There are plenty of people who battle on with far more to put up with than you. And your brain is still functioning; apart from this lunatic decision, I haven't detected any signs of dementia. You also had a project – your mother's diaries – which seemed to be keeping you happily occupied.'

'People leave it too long. If my brain goes, it will be too late.'

'Is that really the reason?'

'Do you realise how hard it is to go through with this?' Marianne said. 'To fight off well-meaning people who want to talk you out of it. You need all your wits to get to the finishing line.'

'The finishing line, as you like to call it, will come in its own time. Just because it's possible to do this doesn't make it right. Would you have committed suicide if it wasn't for this idiotic law and these ghastly clinics? Are you sure you are being honest with yourself? Are you really so worried about losing your mind? I feel there are things you're not telling me. Some domestic problems you think you can only solve by dying.'

'Death does solve things.'

'So, the final solution then.'

'Your words, not mine.'

'I'm sorry, I take that back, but I told you I wasn't going to let you go easily.'

Nor did she. They battled on for a long time, or perhaps it should be said that Dorrie railed against Marianne's decision and Marianne mostly stayed silent. I expect everything she is saying is cogent, Marianne thought, but right or wrong, I have come too far to turn back now.

'You know,' Dorrie said, 'a few days ago I really thought you had changed your mind. You sounded so cheerful when I spoke to you on the telephone.'

'You are right. For a short time I did.'

'Did you tell the clinic?'

'No.'

'Or Callum?'

'No.'

'Why not, for God's sake?'

'I wanted to see if the feeling would last, but it didn't. It was a delusion. Everything remained as it had been. It didn't solve anything.'

'There you go again about solving things. Honestly, Marianne, if we reached for the suicide button every time we felt overwhelmed by problems in life we would die a thousand deaths before we reached adulthood.'

'You forget, I am older than you and my bodily condition will only deteriorate further. I can't reverse time. I've thought seriously about this for most of the last decade. I am certain now is the time to do it.'

'I don't think it's enough. I don't think your life is

intolerable. If they followed the letter of the law, they wouldn't let you do this.'

'Please, Dorrie,' Marianne said, summoning the last of her energy and courage, 'I have made up my mind and I will go through with this. Please let us end as friends. I know that everything you have said comes from the heart, and I am truly sorry to desert you – perhaps I am being cowardly and selfish – but I know it's my time to go.' With difficulty Marianne got to her feet, and holding on to the metal support which had been placed to help her get up, she stood there waiting for Dorrie to come to her. Dorrie shook her head but then she got to her feet and walked stiffly over to where Marianne was standing beside her chair.

'I'm still angry with you,' she said, with a distinct catch in her voice, 'but of course I give you my love, and if there is a God I ask for his blessing on you.' They embraced for a long time, both fighting back their tears, then Dorrie broke away and added, 'But, listen, it's never too late to change your mind. I'll keep my phone on all night. All you need to do is say, "I've changed my mind." Remember, that's all you have to say. No reason is needed. I'll take care of the clinic and Callum and everything else. Remember, it's never too late.'

Wonderful Dorrie, thought Marianne, she still hasn't given up on me.

Jake and Leah were both at the office on Wednesday morning when Leah received a message from her parents that they were going to Cambridge to see Marianne and would not be back until the following evening. She was immediately suspicious and tried to call them but without success.

'Jeez,' she said, 'what is it about Cambridge that is conspiring to give me bad vibes?' She badly needed time to have a proper conversation with Jake but he was heading into a meeting with Charlie and the lawyers.

'Probably just going to keep her company – get her to drop this plan once and for all,' Jake said. 'Keep trying to call them.'

When Leah finally managed to speak to her mother she had not been reassured. They would be sitting down and having a serious discussion with Gran; they would do what they could to help her; nobody wanted to say goodbye to her and yes, Dad thought she might have changed her mind. If she had, then that would be good, but they had to respect her wishes.

Leah reported this conversation to Jake but he was so preoccupied that he didn't give it as much attention as he might have done – or as Leah clearly felt it deserved. The earlier report that Marianne had changed her mind (he had subliminally manipulated the message to suit his own hope) was the version he was determined to cling on to – despite the warning signal that she had twice declined to return his calls. He wanted to say that they couldn't do anything anyway, but he knew this sentiment was not one which would be well received by Leah, so he contented himself with reassuring comments.

34

Marianne knew that however hard it was telling Dorrie, telling Anna was going to be far more painful. At least she had been honest with Dorrie. Thinking about it now, she had been cowardly and deceitful towards Anna. Pretending nothing was happening in her life; talking about Christmas when she would no longer be alive. She had written Anna a long letter saying all the things she knew it would be impossible to say to her face. She had put £1,000 in cash in the envelope and had also left her some money in her will – perhaps too much, Callum and Helen might think, given the state of her finances. When it came to the moment she knew she would have to be strong – brutal, even – or she would never get through it.

Callum and Helen arrived about four in the afternoon. Anna had made up the spare room for them – surprised that they were staying the night mid-week. She had looked suspiciously at Marianne who had pretended not to notice. Helen busied herself in the kitchen making tea. When Anna announced she was ready to leave Callum said, 'Stay and have some tea with us, Anna, there is something we need to talk about… something important we need to tell you.'

Anna sat down. She looked enquiringly from Callum to Marianne. Marianne looked at the ground. Helen came in with tea and a plate of little pink cakes she had brought with her. She poured tea for everyone and put cups in front of them. No one spoke. No one touched the tea or the cakes. Then Marianne looked up towards Anna with an anguished expression. 'Anna, you have been the most wonderful friend to me and I could never have managed without you these last few years, but…' She hated the sound of what she was saying; the words seemed trite and commonplace.

'What is this about?' said Anna, looking alarmed.

'It's time to say goodbye. I am going to the AD clinic tomorrow.'

'I don't understand?'

'Assisted dying, Anna. To end my life.'

'I know what AD is. Are they making you do this? Don't let them. How can you think of this?' she said, turning to Callum.

'It's Marianne's choice,' said Callum. 'I have tried to persuade her against it.'

'No, you can't – you can't do this! Marianne, just tell them no!'

'Callum is right, Anna. It is entirely my own choice.'

'I don't believe it. Why you say nothing to me before?'

'I should have done, Anna, but I didn't have the courage.'

'You must say no to her,' Anna said, turning again to Callum. 'She is just a bit depressed. Old people, you know, sometimes it's hard for them. Sometimes they get low. She will cheer up again. This is my fault, I let her get miserable, but I can make her better,' and, getting up, she ran around the low table and fell on her knees in front of Marianne. 'I will cheer you up. We will play some games together. Tell them we are good team. You say that to me once. We are a good team. I will move into the house – maybe you are alone too much. Yes, I will move in and keep you more cheerful. I am sorry, I should have said before. I didn't realise you feel so bad. I can live here with you. Why you never tell me? I can cheer you up. They don't understand. We are good together. I will help you. I'm sorry… I'm sorry…'

The tears, which Marianne dreaded, began to flow. Anna put her head on Marianne's lap and sobbed. Marianne stroked her hair but said nothing. She could feel the tears running down her own cheeks. There was so much she wanted to say to reassure Anna, but she knew she would choke if she tried to speak.

Eventually Helen got up and came over to Anna, taking her by the shoulder. 'Come on, Anna dear, you're upsetting Marianne.' The effect on Anna was electric. She leapt to her feet, pushing Helen backwards.

'Upsetting? I'm upsetting Marianne!' she shouted at Helen. 'She say tomorrow she will go to the clinic to die – so she is upset and I am upset, but why you are not upset? You and Callum – you just watch. She is your own mother, flesh and blood,' she yelled, turning to Callum. 'You want to take her away like a dog – how do you say it? – to be put down. Put down like a dog. And you,' she said, looking back towards Helen, 'you are even worse. This is your idea, I am sure.'

'That's not true…'

'This must be stopped. Marianne, I beg you! I will go to the police – I will rescue you. You two, you are criminals…'

'Stop it, Anna! Stop this at once.' Marianne's words, sharper and more authoritative than she expected, silenced Anna. 'I will say it again. This is my decision. I have been thinking about it for years. I have written you a letter, Anna, which says everything that I can't say now. I love you like a daughter, but it's time to say goodbye. Please don't make this harder for me than it already is. Come and kiss me and say goodbye and then you must leave.'

Like an obedient child, stunned into silence, Anna knelt again beside Marianne, kissed her and buried her head on Marianne's lap for a few seconds then, putting her hands to her face, she ran out of the room. Callum followed her, shutting the door behind him. A few moments later Marianne heard the front door slam.

It was nearly ten o'clock that evening when Jake answered Anna's call. As soon as he spoke to Anna he realised that she had been told that Marianne was going ahead.

'I'm sorry, but I didn't know who else to speak to,' she said. 'I thought of calling Leah but I didn't have her number.'

'That's OK. Actually, Leah's here with me.'

'Shit, is that Anna? What's happening?' said Leah.

'You don't sound very shocked,' said Anna.

'The thing is, Anna, I knew this might happen. Marianne wrote to my grandmother a couple of weeks ago and told her she had booked into an AD clinic. I spoke to Marianne about it when I came up to see her. Leah was told by her parents.'

'You English – sometimes you are so cold.'

'Anna, that's not fair. I was very upset to hear about it. I tried to dissuade her and afterwards I went to talk to Callum and Helen. But it's not as if I'm a son or grandson – I really can't interfere – you know, old people sometimes prefer to go this way.'

'What the fuck are you saying?' shouted Leah into Jake's other ear. 'Here, let me talk to her,' and, grabbing the phone, she demanded a blow-by-blow account from Anna. Jake was unable to hear the full conversation but it was clear that Leah was directing most of her anger towards her parents.

'So this conversation happened half an hour after they arrived? And they did nothing to try to dissuade her? Unbelievable – they've totally fucking lied to me. Tomorrow… Jesus… yes, I agree. Persuade Jake – yes, I'll pass you over to him now.'

'We've got to go there,' Leah hissed into his ear.

Jake could sense the mood of hysteria growing between Anna and Leah. He tried to reason with Anna.

'This is very distressing for all of us, Anna, but have you considered that it might be the right decision for her?'

'But it's not right for her. She is not ill – maybe just a bit depressed. And she has a good brain still. I know. I see more of her than anyone. Why does no one talk to me?'

'I don't know – I suppose they found it difficult to break the news to you.'

'You must come to her immediately. Both of you. She likes you. You could make all the difference.'

'I could try to call her again. Would that help?'

'I am trying to call Dad now,' said Leah.

'No,' said Anna. 'I have tried many times to call the

house but all calls just go to voicemail. You have to come yourself.'

'Anna, I really don't see that I can. I'm not sure it's right for me to try to intervene.'

'Not sure it's right. I don't know what that means. I'm sure it is right. You could prevent her killing herself. She could have years more life. She told me she was hoping you could help her with the old diaries. You and Leah are the only ones who can save her now.'

'Anna, if Callum supports what she is doing, I don't see what I can do.'

'Callum! He is weak man. I am sorry, but it is true. Helen pushes him around. I have seen it. I think if Marianne has you and Leah on her side she will change her mind.'

For a long time Anna sought to persuade him to intervene while he tried to explain why it was impossible. Eventually, he promised to think about it and talk it over with Leah. Really, this is so unfair, he thought. Why am I being made to feel responsible for Marianne's death. Christ, why does she have to do this – and why now?

'Neither Dad nor Mum are picking up,' said Leah. 'Shit, I can't believe they're letting this happen. We've got to go.'

'Leah, have you any idea how difficult it would be – I mean, turning up uninvited – when Marianne obviously doesn't want us around?'

'OK, fine if you won't come – but I'm going anyway. I'll take an early train.'

Jake sighed. 'I'd like to go, but tomorrow… Charlie wanted everyone in – I'm not sure exactly why. That actually includes you, Leah.'

'Tough. I'm going. I've got money for the train and taxi –

but I wish you'd come with me. You can talk to the office from the train. They just think of me as a child. It needs both of us to make a difference.'

Neither Jake nor Leah slept much that night. Jake continued to protest that it might be better not to intervene, but Leah remained adamant that she would go anyway. At five thirty in the morning Jake sensed that Leah had finally gone to sleep. Creeping out of bed, he went into the living room, made some tea and checked the news on his tablet. He read the lead story with incredulity. What the fuck! They've launched their AD exposé – Mills and Charlie – today of all days. No wonder Charlie wanted everyone in the office.

By the time Leah's alarm went off at 6.30 he had come to a decision. He sent a message to Charlie saying that his great-aunt was dying and he would have to go to Cambridge, but would stay in touch. He knew that aunts of any description didn't count for much in the scale of office excuses – but bugger it, this was a bit different. He couldn't see that the AD exposé was anything to do with him and even if they couldn't persuade Marianne to change her mind – and he gave them very little chance on that score – they could at least say goodbye.

35

Contrary to her original intention, Marianne had not drugged herself to sleep. What was it her mother used to say? You are dead a long time. Instead, she sat up late sending messages – a final farewell to Claire, other messages to her remaining friends, individual notes saying goodbye. One or two had replied immediately. Their remarks touched her deeply. The whole process was painful, but also comforting; a voluntary death should be tidy – no loose ends.

Eventually she had fallen asleep and dreamed that she was dead – but at the same time able to observe how the world was reacting. They were all there – all her close friends and relations, it was some kind of wake in her garden. There was a grave dug near the pond and beside it, on a pair of trestles, was her coffin, draped in a white lacy tablecloth and covered in drinks and canapés. They were all dressed for summer – Anna and her boyfriend Stefans, excited about the money they had got; that was nice to see. Callum and Helen, shocked how little money she had left, were complaining to Claire about the size of the mortgage; the house was already sold and they were flying back to Australia the next day. Dorrie was walking up and down with Edward, muttering imprecations that he should never have let her go. Even her parents were mysteriously there – sipping champagne on the stone seat – and who were those two teenagers kissing by the laurel bushes? It looked like Jake and, yes, Fran, but surely that couldn't be right…

She awoke to her radio alarm and the beeps for the seven o'clock news. For a while she thought she was still dreaming, as the discussion was all about assisted dying. Then she realised that the lead story was about abuses in AD clinics, and particularly the De Zeeou chain, into whose tender care she was about to place herself. How ironic, she thought, but it makes no difference to me. My case is as straightforward as it comes.

By eight o'clock Jake and Leah were settled into their seats on the train at King's Cross, armed with coffee and croissants. Jake sent a text to Anna telling her that they were on the train, and then started to check the news feeds.

The *Chronicle*'s lead story was already being picked up by the main networks. Jake skimmed the headlines quickly: *AD clinics in new scandal. The ugly truth behind how AD clinics operate. De Zeeou chain accused of bending the rules. Safeguards not followed by AD clinics. Daisy Chain pays kickbacks to NHS.*

Where did he stand on AD now? he wondered. Did he still hold to his original instinct that AD was both a basic human right and a blessing for many who were close to the end of their life? If that was his view, then why was he rushing off to try to persuade his great-aunt from taking what could be considered a perfectly rational decision to end her life a few weeks before her eighty-ninth birthday?

As Jake sat trying to reconcile his conflicting views, Leah's phone rang and he listened to her animated conversation with first her mother and then her father. It was clear that they were far from happy to be told that he and Leah were on their way to Cambridge.

'We're in the shit for even thinking of coming...' she said, when the call was over. 'You, in particular for putting me up to it – which I have to say is a gross fucking insult, as if I'm not capable of thinking for myself.' Despite her language, it seemed to Jake that Leah was remarkably calm. 'There's no point in talking to them anymore,' she said. 'We'll just turn up and see how we get on.'

Their train left on time, but after half an hour came to a halt in the middle of the countryside. Jake gazed out across the flat East Anglian field, the long straight plough furrows leading his eyes towards a group of isolated agricultural buildings, still partly shrouded in the morning mist, which for a moment reminded him of his parents' home in Dorset. He looked at his watch; the train was due in just before nine and Anna thought it unlikely that Marianne would leave for the clinic before ten, so they should have enough time even if they were delayed. In any event, Anna had told them she was going to the house and would watch the driveway from a distance. If they set out for the clinic before he and Leah got to Cambridge, she would warn them.

Christ, I hope we do get to the house on time, he thought. Imagine if she is already at the clinic. Do we burst into her room and throw ourselves at her feet and beg her not to kill herself? Surely that would be unethical, as well as unkind to her and deeply resented by Callum and Helen. The clinic may not even let us through the door.

As the minutes passed, Jake and Leah glanced at each other anxiously.

'No more news from Anna?' said Leah.

'No – she's in position, but no sign of movement.'

'Do you have a strategy for when we get there?'

'No – play it by ear, I guess. What's wrong with this fucking train?'

Jake shrugged. Then, as if to answer her question, an announcement came over the tannoy, apologising for the delay; they were being held behind another train due to a person on the line near Royston. Leah looked at him. 'Does that mean what I think it means?'

'Probably.'

'Jeez…'

'I know…'

'It's as if someone's mocking us…'

The morning was tense but also weirdly calm. They all sat at the table having breakfast, seemingly intent on pretending this was just like any other day. Helen talked about the girls while Callum looked at news stories on his tablet. Catching Marianne's eye, he turned the screen away from her so she wouldn't see what he was reading.

After breakfast, she began a serious talk with Callum. As ever, he seemed very aware of his responsibility to make sure that she was really determined to go ahead.

'Mum, I know this isn't the first time we've talked about it but I want to be sure you really know what you're doing.'

'I know you do, darling.'

'It's not too late. I can just call the clinic and we can forget all about it?'

'You could, but that's not what I want.'

'You're really sure?'

'Please, darling, if you love me, just let me go the way I want.'

'Oh, Mum…' and, kneeling by her chair, Callum put his head on Marianne's shoulder.

Although Callum wasn't usually very physical they held each other for a long time and Marianne said a silent apology for the wrong she might have done him all those years ago. I know today will be harder for him than it will be for me, she thought, and that's why I must remain strong.

It was another forty minutes before their train began to move. Forty minutes for Jake and Leah to contemplate the hideous irony of their situation and to wonder if they had any chance of getting to Marianne's house before she left for the clinic. Between regularly checking the time and exchanging texts with Anna, they sought to reassure each other that whatever happened, they were doing the right thing in coming.

A few moments before they were finally due to arrive at Cambridge, Jake received a text from Anna that Marianne, Callum and Helen were getting into the car. Fuck, he thought, that's a disaster. Exactly what I didn't want. This crazy venture might have had some remote chance of success if we had arrived at her house before she left, but now? Moments later he received another text from Anna with the address of the AD clinic, and then she was calling him. It would take Callum at least twenty minutes, maybe half an hour, to drive to the clinic. If they got straight into a taxi they could get there first. That way they could be waiting in reception when Marianne arrived.

Marianne's journey to the clinic passed in almost complete silence. No one now pretended this was just a routine drive. One or two staccato words were exchanged between Callum and Helen about directions to the clinic, cutting into an atmosphere which seemed entirely devoid of oxygen. Marianne, sitting in the front seat beside Callum, shut her eyes and tried to turn off the power to her brain, but absurd and trivial thoughts kept crowding in: had she got her reading glasses; where did she leave her purse; who would empty the commode in her bedroom now Anna was gone? Poor Anna – what a way to have to say goodbye for ever.

When they arrived at the clinic, a reception party was there to meet them; Nikhita Singh, the nurse who had been keeping in touch with her, the clipboard woman and an orderly with a wheelchair. Before she knew it, she was being settled into the wheelchair while she heard the clipboard woman say to Callum, 'We had you down for two family members present, but it seems...'

'Gran...'

Suddenly the cordon around her broke apart and there was a young woman advancing on her and clasping her around the neck. Such was Marianne's state of mind, her determination to blank out the immediate present, that she instinctively recoiled, unable to comprehend what was happening.

Several people started to speak at once.

'Leah!' said Callum.

'It's only me, Gran,' said Leah.

'This is a disgrace,' said Helen, turning towards Jake. 'How dare you come and interfere like this?'

'This is not helpful to Mrs Davenport,' said the clipboard woman.

It was Nikhita Singh who took charge. 'I am going to take Marianne up to her room. There will be plenty of time for the family to get together with her when she is settled. Perhaps if you could all stay down here for the time being,' and, with a nod to the orderly, Marianne was wheeled to the lifts followed by the nurse.

It was a relief to Marianne when the lift door closed and she was away from her family. Only now did she take in that Leah had come to say goodbye and Jake must have been there too, judging by the remarks of Helen. Oh well, she thought, I could have done without it, but it's touching all the same.

Her room felt very much like any room in a private hospital or nursing home, except perhaps for the over-large television screen at the end of the bed. She wondered what happened next. Her unspoken question was answered by the nurse. Although it was 'optional', most patients preferred to undress; this would make Marianne 'more comfortable'. She nodded her acquiescence. With the nurse's help Marianne undressed and put on a hospital gown. After a visit to the bathroom she was helped into bed and propped up with several pillows behind her back.

Downstairs, Marianne's family had been shown into a private waiting room where coffee and tea were available from a machine. After the initial flurry of exclamations, an uneasy quiet had descended on the room while they queued to make themselves a hot drink. Their silence was broken by a knock at the door and the entrance of Anna.

'So you are part of this gang as well,' said Helen.

'Gang?' said Anna.

Callum sighed. 'Come on in, Anna. Get yourself a coffee, and let's all sit down and we can talk quietly.'

It was Leah who launched the initial attack. 'Dad – you said that Gran had changed her mind.'

'I never said that. If you remember, all I said was that I got the feeling she was going to change her mind.'

'And you were trying to persuade her – but you never did. Anna told us. You just arrived, and…'

'Leah, listen to me for a minute. I know that this is particularly hard for you at your age…'

'My age – why is my age an issue…?'

'Because you're too young to understand properly…' said Helen.

'Shut up, Mum – I'm talking to Dad…'

'Don't speak to me like that.'

'Am I too young as well?' said Anna. 'I've looked after Marianne for over five years. So I have some knowledge…'

'This is a family matter. I don't know why you are here,' said Helen.

Callum raised his hands. 'Please. We are going to embarrass ourselves, squabbling like this. I'm dealing with Leah's question. Darling, I have tried on many occasions in the last few weeks to persuade Gran to change her mind. But she has remained determined and I think we have to respect that.'

'You didn't try yesterday.'

'Actually, I did, after Anna had gone – and again this morning.'

At this statement from her father Leah paused, and Jake thought it was time he joined the discussion. He had prepared a little speech in his head, on which he now embarked.

'Callum – we all know that you want to do your best for your mother. But I would like to ask you whether you think it's the right decision for her. We – that is, Leah and I – and particularly Anna, who, as she said, has looked after Marianne for the last five years, feel that she still has a lot to live for. She talked to me about these diaries she's been translating. I would like to help her with this. I realise it's the eleventh hour, but we came today because we felt that if we all told her how much we want her to go on living, then she might change her mind.'

As Jake finished speaking, Anna gave a little clap. 'Well said. We just want her to go on living while she is still well…'

'That's what we all want, dear,' said Helen, 'but we have to listen to what she wants.'

'So that's what you want, is it?' said Anna.

'What's that supposed to mean?'

'I think you prefer her to die now…'

'How dare you? You disgust me. And we all know why you want her to go on – so you can extort more money from her…'

'Never! I never ask for money…'

'Please, please,' Callum said, once again raising his arms. 'We mustn't fight amongst ourselves while Marianne is all alone upstairs. Helen, my love, I think you ought to go and keep her company, and I'll continue this conversation down here.'

Helen nodded, and with a last ferocious look at Anna she left the room. For a while no one spoke. Jake looked at Callum; a nervous flicker had got hold of one of his eyelids. He looked grey and miserable. He admired the way Callum had defused the situation and removed Helen from the scene. Poor man, Jake thought, he's under intolerable strain and we have not helped. He watched as Callum got up and went over to Leah and sat down beside her. Putting his arm around her, he pulled her head onto his shoulder. 'This is agony for all of us,' he said.

Jake felt uncomfortable. Leah should be allowed some time with her father. Glancing at Anna, he got up and moved towards the door. 'We'll leave you for a minute…'

'No, don't go.'

'You and Leah need some privacy…'

'No, come and sit down, Jake. We need to tackle this together.'

Jake returned to his seat while Callum got up and started walking slowly around the room. 'I want to try to answer your question, Jake. Do I think she is making the right decision?' He stopped to stare at an abstract water colour on the wall. A swirl of blue and mauve – chosen no doubt to complement the seat covers of the chairs. 'No, from my perspective it's the wrong decision – there is no need for her to end her life now.'

'So why don't we just…'

'Hear me out, Leah, darling. Of course I wish this wasn't happening. But it's not just a question of what I think. My mother is a highly intelligent woman. She has thought about this deeply over several years. It's impossible for any of us to know what it feels like to be in her position. It's not for me to make this decision for her. I have tried to talk her out of

368

it – but I haven't succeeded. What am I to do? Wash my hands of the whole thing? She doesn't need my consent. Would you rather she came here in a taxi to end her life alone? Believe me, this is the hardest day of my life, but I must be brave for her sake. And so must you all.'

For a while no one spoke. Then Anna said, 'You should have told me earlier. If I had known, I am sure I could have talked her out of it.'

'That was her decision.'

'So what happens now?' said Leah. 'Can I go and see her?'

'What do you want to say to her?'

'To make one last plea…'

'I don't think she would welcome that.'

'Of course we wouldn't want to distress her,' said Jake, 'but that is why we've come…'

'Look, I will go up and talk to my mother now. I'll tell her what you want to say and let her decide whether she wants you to come up.'

Marianne lay back on the bed with her eyes shut, while Helen paced around the room, tut-tutting about the arrival of Jake and Leah. 'This is just a bit of journalistic voyeurism for him,' she said. 'I wish to God I'd found something else to occupy Leah's time. This must be so upsetting for you.'

Marianne didn't have the energy or inclination to reply. Outside she could hear whispered discussion amongst the staff. Something odd is going on, she thought, and it's not just to do with Leah and Jake. She was relieved when Callum came up and sat on the side of the bed. He told her about the intended deputation downstairs.

'They want to come up and make a joint plea to you – a plea to go on living, is how they put it.'

Ah, the wonderful idealism of youth, she thought. Twenty-year-olds – full of optimism, immortal gods of the planet. The idea of death – the reality of death – offends them.

'No,' she said, 'it's too late for all that.'

'I thought that's what you'd say.'

'If they promise to behave and not to make a scene they can come and say goodbye – but I don't want them here at the end. Now can you find out what's going on. I haven't seen a doctor yet. No one's told me anything.'

Callum scuttled off to find someone to talk to, while Helen went on muttering about how intrusive Anna and Jake were and how brave and sensible she was being.

'It's Thursday today, isn't it?' Marianne said suddenly.

'Yes, why?'

'Nothing.' The last Thursday in November, she thought. Thanksgiving. How curious that I should have chosen this day without realising it. Appropriate, I suppose. After all, I have much to be thankful for. Both in my life and now, finally, at the end; I get the chance to atone – and my death now can still do some good.

Callum was now back in her room. 'Mum, I know this is really the last thing you need, but it seems there might be some delay. There's a story in the press this morning about the De Zeeou chain – which runs this clinic – suggesting that in some cases they may have been bending the law.'

'Delay?'

'Apparently, the board at the head office in Holland are in emergency session at this moment and in the meantime everything is on hold – a moratorium on all activity, they told me.'

'I see.'

'Yes, but the manager here thinks it could be lifted at any time, so he recommends just waiting for a while.'

'Well, that's what we'll have to do, I suppose.'

'Yes – Mum, I'm so sorry. This must be very upsetting for you.'

'It's certainly unexpected.'

'Do you want me to get you a coffee or anything?'

'No, they advise against it. But you and Helen go and get a coffee. I would appreciate a little time to myself.'

When Callum and Helen had left, Marianne lay propped up in bed in a state of stunned disbelief. This does seem a cruel trick, she thought, when I am ready to flick the switch. A stay of execution – except in this case I am trying to die and the clinic is forbidding it. What happens if they refuse to proceed today? Suddenly, the idea of going home terrified her. How long would the delay be? Would she ask Anna to come back? What would she tell her? Then there were all those people she had sent emails to. And Dorrie – it was agony being berated by her yesterday; she would see this as a timely intervention by fate – a message that her death was not supposed to happen yet.

But would she be right? Perhaps this is my rescue, the cavalry cresting the hill in a cloud of dust. Perhaps I am the ceremonial turkey to be saved by the president? If I go home today how will I feel about coming back? An unexpected sensation, warm and seductive, seemed to be infiltrating her body, creeping up slowly through her stomach. Was that a tiny flicker of relief that I felt when Callum told me the news? Like hearing that the dentist can't see you after all and, despite the continuing toothache, you feel relieved that you won't have to endure the extraction that day.

'No, no,' Marianne muttered to herself out loud. 'I can't allow myself these thoughts. That way lies madness. I must be strong.'

She thought of her dreary prison room in Moscow and the endless and increasingly pointless interrogation. Time distorted by unfamiliar environments. Watching the minute hand on the wall clock, it seemed barely to move. Was this how it had been when she sat with Izzy at the hospital? Time like an amorphous blob, like Dali's wall clock, melting in front of her, mocking her need for movement.

She thought of those moments after the air crash: moments of crushing pain and terror, terror at the thought of being roasted alive, the unimaginable agony, and how she had willed herself to die. She hadn't burnt, nor had she died – and for that salvation she had often given thanks – but now her time had come; this time she should have the magic box to switch off her life, only she couldn't get her hands on it.

Downstairs Callum reported Marianne's wishes. 'You've got to promise me, no begging – just goodbye.'

Anna put her head in her hands. 'So that's it then?'

'Yes.'

Leah moved around to sit next to Anna and held her hand. 'Can we go up now?' she said, looking at her father.

'Not quite yet – we have a bit of a delay at the moment. There are stories in the press this morning – things are on hold…'

Jake sighed. 'Yes, it's our paper, I'm afraid – but I had no idea that…'

'Of course not – but you can imagine how distressing it is for her.'

'I'm going,' said Anna.

'No, stay,' said Leah. 'Please stay. Maybe they won't go ahead at all now – what do you think, Jake?'

Jake shrugged. 'I've no idea.'

'I think this is fate intervening,' Leah said. 'The *Chronicle* have rescued Gran. It's like a miracle.'

'You mustn't think like that, darling,' said Callum.

'I really need to go,' said Anna. 'It's too hard for me. Yesterday, when she say goodbye, I cry all night. I can't say goodbye again.'

Jake watched as Leah hugged Anna. Both were crying now.

Up in her room, Marianne preferred not to think what would happen if she was sent home. She tried to clear her mind of all the jumble of thoughts. Callum and Helen came in and out without knowing what to do. Everyone thought they had to say something, but nothing made much sense. Was the room too hot, or perhaps too cold? A sip of water, maybe? Listen to some music? Something on the television screen would pass the time? Marianne declined. Nikhita Singh came in, looking a lot more frightened than Marianne herself. Was everything still OK? Any particular concerns? (You've got to be joking.) A decision was expected any minute, or soon, certainly within the hour, without fail by lunchtime (lunchtime – what the hell has lunch got to do with dying?). What if normal service could not be resumed? If 'procedures' were permanently suspended? No one dared ask. Just keep on waiting. Was she alright? they kept asking. Yes, yes, yes, she repeated, though she had lost any sense of what alright meant for her. Perhaps this is how all life ends, she thought, spouting nonsense to each other like

Didi and Gogo. Impossible to die because the rope's too short or the belt has broken – and Godot will surely come, only not quite yet.

When it happened, and the moratorium was lifted, time seemed to speed up alarmingly. Marianne didn't know how she felt because everything was happening so fast. The doctor came in for his last check to ensure that her mind was sound and that she still wished to end her life. She signed the final consent form.

Jake and Leah appeared in her room. Jake came forward and kissed her. 'Thank you for everything – and for being there for me in France…' he said.

'Goodbye, Jake,' she said.

Then Leah came to kiss her; half lying on the bed, she pushed her wet face against Marianne and emitted a small choking noise. '… love you, Gran.'

'I love you too, darling. Good luck with everything – you'll make a success of your life, I know.'

'Don't do this, Gran – don't kill your self. Please, please don't do it. I love you – don't do it…'

'Leah, darling, you promised…' said Helen, taking hold of Leah's arm.

'I don't want you to die, please, Gran. We can take you home…'

'Leah…'

'I love you, Gran,' Leah said again through her choking sobs. 'I love you.'

Helen slowly prised her from the bed. 'Come on, darling…'

Leah stood and turned. 'I hate you,' she said, looking at her mother. 'Both of you... Why are you letting this happen?'

Callum looked at Jake who came forward and took Leah in his arms. 'I think we should leave now,' he said.

'So, so wrong...' she said, as Jake led her from the room.

There was a moment of silence when the door closed behind them. Then Callum said, 'I'm sorry, Mum.'

'Don't be. She's a wonderful child. You should be proud of her.'

When Jake and Leah had left the room, the doctor returned and began to explain the procedure while Callum and Helen hovered in the background.

'I am now going to put an intravenous line into your arm,' he said, and putting on his gloves he applied a tourniquet to her upper arm, wiped the skin over her expanded vein, and inserted the needle. With a flick of his wrist he removed the tourniquet and put some strapping around the line, bandaging it to her arm. 'I am first going to connect this to a simple solution of saline, but when the time comes it will be connected to two separate lines.'

Ah yes, she thought, when the time comes; not so long now.

'One of the lines,' the doctor continued, 'connects to a powerful anaesthetic. When the anaesthetic reaches your brain, you will become unconscious. This takes around thirty seconds at the most from when you turn it on. A small computer-controlled machine, attached by electrodes, which I will apply to your scalp, will detect when you are unconscious and then release another drug which relaxes your body to such an extent that after about five minutes you will stop breathing. Shortly thereafter your heart will stop. Once you are asleep you will not be aware of any of this.

'Now I need to attach these monitors which will record your heartbeat and blood pressure.' He applied a clip to Marianne's finger and wrapped a cuff around her upper arm on the opposite side. She could hear a machine beeping in time to her heartbeat. The doctor muted the volume. 'When the time comes' (ah, that time again) 'the line will be connected here,' he said, pointing to a large piece of apparatus near to the bed, 'and you will turn this dial one half turn to the right.' He showed her the small hand-held device the size of a mobile phone, attached to a connecting cable. 'You understand that once you have turned the dial your death becomes inevitable and cannot be halted?'

'Yes,' she said, 'I understand.'

The doctor looked down at Marianne and smiled. 'Now you're all set. I'll leave you alone with your family for a while and they can let me know when you are ready.'

Marianne was not sure how much more time she needed with Callum and Helen, but suddenly they were alone together and all three seemed to realise that this was indeed almost the end.

'Still absolutely sure about this, Mum?' Callum said.

'Yes, darling, still sure.'

Helen came to stand by the bed. She squeezed Marianne's hand and bent forward to kiss her. 'Goodbye and God bless you, Marianne,' she said, before turning away. She seemed genuinely distressed.

Callum then began a little speech about what a wonderful mother she had been to him and she let him go on, although somehow she seemed to have lost the ability to connect the words to any meaning. When he had finished he also kissed her. She asked for a few moments alone to compose herself.

So, this is it, she thought. I wish I could say that I am filled with some profound thoughts or some unique spiritual insight but my mind is all fog and emptiness. My heart, though, seems to have become a furious engine, pulsating through my body with unnecessary and unexpected urgency. My breathing is fast and shallow.

They say the anaesthetic is like a tsunami sweeping over you, but I imagine it as a huge waterfall – like the one in Brazil that Edward and I visited with Izzy when she was quite young. I started my river journey when I came to the clinic a few weeks ago and I have been paddling my canoe slowly down stream since then. Once or twice I have been tempted to manoeuvre to the side and climb out, but every time I've been close to the bank the jungle has looked dense and unappealing; so I have just gone on paddling. At times, I have stopped paddling entirely but it makes no difference; the current just sweeps me on.

Now I am almost on top of the falls. I can hear the roar of the water as it cascades into the abyss below but the edge is hidden in the mist. I find I have Izzy in my arms. Her hands are clinging around my neck. I lie back and shut my eyes, clasping her tight to my chest. The noise is overwhelming and I feel the spray, soft and cool on my face. I sense I am on the brink and the boat is beginning to tip forward, and as it does so I open my eyes and through the mist I see huge blue butterflies circling in shafts of multi-coloured sunlight, but as we start to fall I shut my eyes again; there are no butterflies now as we plunge into the dark void.

Marianne heard the door open; they were coming back into the room.

'Mum?' Callum's voice, distant. 'Would you like more time?'

'No, come in.' A whisper.

'The doctor and nurse are here now…'

Silence.

'Just a little bit of this gel on your head, and now I will attach the pads.' The doctor's voice. She felt the cold of the electrodes on her temples. Silence again.

'Just connecting up to the pumps.'

Another pause.

'All set now.' She felt the control box in her hands. 'Whenever you feel ready, Mrs Davenport.'

'I love you, Mum.' Callum's voice, whispering.

Marianne tried to turn the dial but her hand, slippery with sweat, slid off.

Silence. The sound of whispering. The doctor's voice: '…must do it herself.'

She wiped her hand on her hospital gown.

A long silence. Someone coughed.

She tried again. A hum, a growing roar – then nothing. Nothing ever again.

36

Three months later

Two men sat at a table near the window. They appeared to be playing cards. One of the men was old, a small amount of grey hair covering an almost bald head. His face was lined and looked distorted, one side drooping down to where a dribble of saliva hung suspended from the corner of his mouth. Using one hand he carefully took a card from his pile and placed it face up in front of him.

He looked across to the younger man, one eye staring intently, the other wandering unfocused around the room. The younger man, who might have been approaching fifty, smiled and gave a slight shake of his head. Then the younger man took a card and placed it face up in front of him. The old man stared at the card, then up again at the younger man, who once again shook his head.

The process was repeated several times. Then, after the

old man had put down a card, the younger man looked up and smiled and the old man started to wave his hand around. 'SNAP,' he shouted. 'Snap, snap, snap. Whit dae say tae that, laddie? Ah won that – didn't ah?'

The younger man picked up a pile of cards and tucked them under the old man's pile. 'Good one,' he said.

They seemed to have stopped playing now and the younger man was talking, though whether to the old man or to himself wasn't clear. Fragmented sentences drifted across the room. '… miss her, you know… so much. But now I've found you, eh? Need to look after you, don't I…? Won't desert you. Promise.' The old man's face moved into a crooked smile.

Two nurses looked on indulgently from the doorway. 'It's wonderful to see. You know he come two or three times a week.'

'Does he realise who he is?'

'I don't think so, not really, but perhaps it doesn't matter. He enjoys the visits so much – calls him laddie. Asks where his laddie is. He's always so excited to see him.'

'Your paper stirred up quite a hornets' nest,' said Claire, as Jake settled himself onto a sofa in her elegant drawing room.

'Yes,' he said, 'all the old arguments are being rehearsed again. I see things in a different light now – but you can't put the clock back. Nothing much will change.'

Claire brought a drink over to Jake and sat down in her usual chair. 'I'm afraid you're probably right. AD has become too well established. And there seems to be a movement in some quarters saying that all this fuss is because the law is too restrictive.'

'Yes – some say AD on demand would simplify the issue.'

'It would be ironic if that was the outcome of the inquiry.'

'It will come eventually, I'm convinced. No "safeguards" – just a right to die.'

'Followed shortly by a duty to die.'

'You think?'

'Why not? After all, we have a duty to be healthy now – society and the state demand it. Why should the state resist if people begin to feel they have a duty to die?'

'The slippery slope?'

'Accept it – perhaps we do have such a duty, and anyway, society won't accept the burden of the old for ever.'

'You know, poor Marianne was caught up in the drama – she was kept waiting at the clinic while the bosses in Holland wondered what to do.'

'I never meant you to rush off to Cambridge and throw yourself at Marianne's feet.'

'It was Anna who persuaded us. It was a horrible business – Leah was traumatised. Anna is still in England, you know – she's got another job. She and Leah have become quite close.'

'Are you still with Leah?'

'Absolutely. She didn't get the Cambridge place that Marianne dreamed of – but she's got a place at UCL and she's very happy with that.'

'You realise she'll probably dump you once she starts there?'

Jake laughed. 'So different from your sister, Granny – not a romantic bone in your body. You may be right, but I certainly hope not. Leah is really important to me.'

'She cost you your job.'

'That was Helen's doing. A formal complaint. Sexual

exploitation of an intern. Leah was mortified – it's caused a real breach between her and her mother.'

'So what about Callum? Tell me about him finding his real father.'

'Yes, before she died, Marianne confessed to Callum that Andy had lived on after the crash that killed Isabelle – but she also said he died fifteen years ago. Callum is certain she believed that, but he decided to find out a bit more about what had happened. He discovered that Andy had lived with his mother until he was about forty; and then it seems he had a succession of strokes and ended up in a home in Glasgow. There he lived as a mentally retarded semi-invalid. His mother died about five years ago and since then he was not known to have any living relatives.'

'Quite a sad story.'

'Yes – so anyway, when Callum found him, and proved to the authorities that he was Andy's son, he managed to get him moved to a home on the edge of London where he visits him several times a week. Just sits with him, talks to him – sometimes, he said, they play simple games. Apparently, Andy doesn't understand that Callum is his son but he seems to appreciate the visits.'

'What a dutiful man.'

'Yes, really noble. Leah's been with him a few times, seeing her lost grandfather, but I think she finds it too depressing.'

'And Helen?'

'She's gone back to Australia. They are having a period of separation – to use Callum's words.'

'I'm not surprised.'

'No, but I feel sorry for Callum. Marianne may have thought she was doing him a favour but I think the manner of her death was more traumatic for him than he let on.'

'It was to do with Marianne that I got you over today. Before she died she sent me a last message – I've got a print of it here.'

Jake took the piece of paper from Claire and began to read.

My dearest Claire,

This is a final goodbye. It's midnight now and Callum and Helen have gone to bed. Tomorrow morning we go to the clinic.

Please don't feel sorry for me. I'm going to die the way I want. Callum will send you all the diaries and my notes. Try to persuade Jake to finish the project – I had thought of making a novel out of it – maybe he'd like to have a go. And tell him I hope it works out for him and Leah and I'm not sorry for encouraging her. I know I'm a foolish old woman – but I loved when I was very young and you don't forget.

Marianne

'I hope you never do what she did, Granny. Unless you really have to.'

'I doubt I would have the courage. What Marianne did may not have been necessary but I believe it was brave.'

Jake nodded; he remembered Marianne's little speech to him when he had visited her.

'Well, what do you think?' said Claire. 'You don't have to decide immediately, but I am prepared to pay you a salary for six months if you want to give it a go. Before you get another job.'

'I don't need time to think – that's an incredibly generous offer.'

'It will be for Marianne. In her memory. A tribute from her family. Now you had better go. Come back on Monday and we'll work out the details.'

'I will,' said Jake, 'and thank you again.' Kissing his grandmother goodbye, he walked down the graceful staircase, let himself out through the front door and stepped down into the darkening street.

Acknowledgements

I would like to express my gratitude to all those writers and bloggers who have written so eloquently about their thoughts and experiences as they approached their own imminent death, whether voluntary or involuntary, and have thereby given me some small insight into what it would be like to be in that position.

Aspects of the legislation imagined in this novel are taken from the Assisted Dying Bill, introduced in the House of Lords in July 2014, although I have extended it beyond those who are terminally ill. A number of countries have enacted legislation comparable to that envisaged.

I am greatly indebted to the authors of *An American Family in Moscow* (Little Brown, 1975) for descriptions of life in the USSR in the early 1970s, which inform the early chapters of this book. I have quoted the late Sir Terry Pratchett from an article he wrote for the *Sunday Times* (26-06-11); the quotation about the Liverpool Pathway is taken from the *Daily Telegraph* (01-11-12). There were many similar articles around that time.

I am indebted to Professor Innes Merabishvili of Tbilisi State University for introducing me to Georgia and the beauty of the Caucasus, where I discovered both Lermontov and the delights of Georgian cooking.

I would like to thank consultant anaesthetist Dr Eric Lawes for his advice on the end of life medical procedures described. Within my own family I would like to thank my daughter Emily who typed the first draft for me and offered advice; my daughter Sophie whose image adorns the front cover; my wife Robyn who has had to put up with all my preoccupations while writing the book and other members of my family for their ideas and encouragement.

Robin Byron read history at Cambridge and has spent most of his working life as a lawyer. Recently he has turned his attention to writing; *Echoes of a Life* is his first novel. Robin is the current Lord Byron and President of the Byron Society. He is married with four children and lives with his wife in Hampshire.